"Aren't you mad at me?"

"Because you were doing your job and planned on turning me over? You didn't know me when you planned that. But you know me now. At least, you know me well enough not to turn me over now, right? At least, not while we're still figuring out what's going on?"

"Of course."

"Then why would I be mad? What's the plan? Please tell me you have a plan because, honestly, I'm too tired to think one up at the moment."

Kade yanked her to him and planted a quick, hard kiss against her lips. When he pulled back she blinked at him, looking stunned.

"What was that for?" she asked.

"Hell if I know. I couldn't resist."

The grin that spread across Bailey's lips reached all the way to her eyes. "Told you I'm good."

By Lena Diaz

LENA DIAZ

FINAL EXIT

AN EXIT INC. THRILLER

AVONBOOKS

An Imprint of HarperCollinsPublishers

HarperCollins
PUBLISHERS
Since 1817

This is a work of fiction. Names, characters, places, and incidents are products of the author's imagination or are used fictitiously and are not to be construed as real. Any resemblance to actual events, locales, organizations, or persons, living or dead, is entirely coincidental.

First Avon Books mass market printing: February 2017

ISBN 978-0-06-234913-2

17 18 19 20 21   QGM   10 9 8 7 6 5 4 3 2 1

For George.

Chapter One

Friday, 11:55 p.m.

It was a perfect night to catch a killer.

A warm breeze blew out of the south at about six miles per hour. Rain-heavy clouds covered the half-moon, plunging the cliff where Special Agent Kade Quinn stood into darkness. He was betting on the old cliché, third time's a charm. And also betting on the numbers—that his six, shiny new special agents could take down one highly skilled, remarkably cunning, experienced assassin.

Not the kind of odds to go to Vegas over. But he had to work with what he had.

If things went as planned, Bailey Stark would soon be in custody like the dozens of other EXIT Inc. Enforcers that his team *had* managed to capture. The now-defunct company could never again fool the public into believing that all it did was offer vacation packages, so-called "EXtreme International Tours." The clandestine organization's true legacy as a corrupt front for government-sanctioned murder would end with the capture of the last few Enforcers. By the time his mission was over, every last one of the assassins who'd worked for EXIT would be functioning members of society.

And innocents like Abby would never again become the victims of killers like Bailey.

Between the nightmare of his wife's death and the near-constant ache in his ruined left leg, Kade had his own, very personal, debt with EXIT. And he planned on collecting.

He scanned the tree line. Past the red oak and Ponderosa pines, the Colorado Rockies squatted like dark sentinels watching over tonight's operation. Below him, in the middle of a wide, nearly treeless valley, was ground zero, the two-story cottage that Bailey believed would be her sanctuary.

Instead, it would become her last stand.

A quarter-mile-long driveway connected a two-lane highway to this remote property. At close to midnight and an hour's drive from Boulder, the road was essentially deserted. Kade couldn't have asked for a better place to launch an ambush. And if his intel was correct, Bailey should arrive within the next half hour.

Only a few minutes later the two-way radio on his belt crackled to life. "Big Bear to Lone Wolf. Come in."

Kade rolled his eyes and pressed the transmit button. "Kade here. What's the situation report, Nichols?"

"You're ruining my fun, boss."

He shook his head but played along. He had to pick his battles. "Lone Wolf to Big Bear. What's the sitrep?"

"Much better." A chuckle sounded through the radio. "A beat-up, dark blue Camaro just turned off the highway. One occupant. Looks to be our target. She's heading toward the cottage."

"Use the SUV to block the road behind her. If she gets spooked, I don't want her doing a one-eighty and making it to the highway."

"Affirmative. Big Bear out."

Kade clicked off the mic and belatedly wished he'd downed a handful of antacids before driving out here. Being assigned these eager, raw newbies had to be his penance for his breakdown after the accident. They were also the reason he was here in person rather than monitoring the mission remotely per the usual protocol. Tonight's target had already tricked his team and gotten away—twice. Kade was here to make sure that didn't happen again.

"Cord," he said through the two-way. "Sitrep."

"You mean you aren't going to call me Little Bear?"

"Do you want me to?" He was half-afraid of the answer.

"Hell no. I'm not in junior high."

"You guys know I can hear you, right?" Nichols chimed in.

"Sitrep," Kade growled.

"She just passed my ten o'clock," Cord announced. "Dom should have her in his sights in a few seconds."

"Already do," Dominic confirmed. "The car is pulling up to the house. We're all set."

"Radio silence in three, two, one." Kade clicked off the transmitter. They couldn't risk the sound of static or a mistimed transmission alerting their target. Or at least, that was the official reason for breaking communications. Unofficially, he needed a few moments of silence to get his impatience under control. What had happened to the bureau's standards? Big Bear, Little Bear? Hell, two of his agents—Dom and Jack—had tattoos. Since when had the FBI allowed tats? Quantico was going soft.

He looked through the binoculars. Instead of driving into the attached garage as expected, Bailey did a three-point turn and parked the Camaro pointing down the driveway. Was she suspicious? Had she purposely positioned her vehicle for a quick getaway?

His hands tightened around the binoculars. The driver's door opened. A petite woman in dark-colored shorts and a white T-shirt emerged. A pistol was holstered at her waist and her shoulder-length, curly red hair reflected like flames in the soft glow of the porch light. Even at this distance she had the kinds of curves that made men pay attention— including Kade, much to his chagrin. He had more reason than most to despise Enforcers, and yet his breath caught every time he looked at one of her photographs in the case file.

He couldn't imagine the effect she'd have on him if he ever got within a few feet of her in person. It was bad enough that his pulse quickened whenever those deep green eyes gazed back at him from her pictures. But what he hated the most was the odd feeling of kinship he felt toward her, a tug of empathy when he saw the shadows in her eyes, the same shadows he saw every time he looked in a mirror. He couldn't help wondering what had happened to harden her and make her look so lost, so sad, so incredibly . . . alone.

Usually, when those thoughts were going through

his head, a fuzzy image of Abby would pop up in his mind's eye, making him despise himself even more. How could he feel sorry for his enemy when his own *wife* had been murdered by one of Bailey's peers?

He shook his head in disgust.

Down below, the woman who'd caused him so much confusion and self-loathing over the past few months ducked into her car and pulled out a backpack, which she then slung over her shoulder. A few seconds later she was inside the house, seemingly oblivious to the danger surrounding her as the lights flickered on in the front room. Kade let out a breath of relief. She must not have spotted his agents.

Kade had decided the safest approach was for his team to ambush her after she fell asleep. They'd already disabled her security alarm, making it seem like it was working when it really wasn't. Cameras and listening devices had been set up inside and constantly relayed information back to the watch-like device on Cord's wrist. When Cord was confident that Bailey was asleep, he'd press a button on that insanely expensive piece of equipment that would send vibrations to the similar devices strapped to the other agents' wrists. Then all five of them—three from the front, two from the back, would quietly enter the home.

Their sixth team member, Nichols, was Plan B. If Bailey managed to make it to the highway, the hope was that Nichols would hold her off until the rest of the team arrived.

Kade really hoped it didn't come to Plan B.

They were counting on stealth and the element of surprise to give them the advantage. Now, all they had to do was wait. But since Kade's throbbing bum leg was acting up tonight, he'd have to do his waiting in his rental car.

He headed away from the cliff, stiffly maneuvering down the rocky slope. The thick, dark clouds weren't blocking the moon anymore, so he could easily see the luxury Cadillac Coupe parked beneath some twisted oak trees.

Earlier, he'd made sure the car wasn't visible from below. He'd also fashioned a small hole in the bushes near the front passenger window so he could see the cottage from inside the car. He'd tried to consider every possible variable. And so far things were going according to plan.

When he reached the car and opened the door, he debated breaking the seal on the bottle of Jim Beam that he'd impulsively bought on the way here. Sometimes the ache in his leg required something stronger than over-the-counter painkillers. And his previous abuse of prescription meds that had nearly destroyed his career left him with precious few ways to treat his pain. Group therapy sure as hell wasn't helping. He wasn't good at the whole mind over matter mentality.

After only a few seconds of deliberation, he reluctantly decided against the whiskey. He'd stood on that cliff too long. The pain in his leg and hip had gotten too bad for the relief that just a few shots of whiskey would bring. If he started drinking right now, he might not stop until the bottle was empty—which of course wasn't an option during a mission. *Jim* would have to wait until Kade was back at home base and there was no one around to witness his sorry state.

He settled into the luxurious driver's seat, the soft leather and change of position blessedly reducing the pain to a bearable level. Score one for a car he'd never expected to drive until he was old enough for a retirement home. But hauling himself up into a four-by-four pickup, his preferred mode of transportation prior to the accident, was impossible now without white-knuckling pain.

Using his binoculars again, he watched the operation play out below. Dominic, Alice, and Cord were crouched on the front porch. Even though Kade couldn't see the back of the house, he knew that Reese and Jack were waiting there.

Bailey didn't make them wait long. The lights downstairs flicked off. An upstairs light turned on. Twenty minutes later, Cord gave the signal. Making quick work of the locks, the team surged inside, weapons drawn. The only way that Bailey could escape now was if she had wings and could fly out one of the second-story windows.

Kade tossed the binoculars onto the passenger seat and leaned back, massaging the muscles of his left thigh, hoping to stave off the debilitating cramps that often came when the pain got this bad.

In spite of the heat, he didn't turn on the engine to run the air conditioner. Sound could travel for miles in these foothills. But even with the door propped open, the air inside the car was stifling.

Summer in Colorado wasn't for sissies.

At least it wasn't a steam bath like the summers in his hometown of Jacksonville, Florida. There the humidity made breathing feel like drawing air through a hot, wet sponge.

He closed his eyes, listening to the high-pitched

song of crickets and the low rustling of other night creatures. A bead of sweat rolled down the side of his face. He absently wiped it away. Time seemed to crawl. But a quick check of his watch revealed it had only been five minutes since the team went into the house. He settled back again, waiting for Cord's announcement over the radio that Bailey was in custody.

Another minute ticked by. Then another.

His eyes flew open. The crickets had stopped chirping. The woods had gone silent. He scanned his surroundings and curled his right hand around the butt of the Walther PPK holstered at his waist. All he heard was the light rustling of pine needles scraping against each other in the warm breeze.

Something was wrong.

He grabbed the binoculars and studied the cottage. The lights were on upstairs. That should be the signal that they'd apprehended Bailey. So why hadn't Cord transmitted an update?

A low rhythmic thump sounded from somewhere outside the car. Someone running? He dropped the binoculars and pointed his pistol through the door opening just as a flash of white streaked past and disappeared into the woods.

Bailey. Still wearing her shorts and white T-shirt. Kade swore.

How had she escaped this time?

He holstered his pistol and grabbed the door to pull himself to standing, cursing again when his bum leg threatened to crumple beneath him. When he was sure that he wasn't going to fall flat on his face, he clicked the transmitter on his belt.

"This is Lone Wolf," he spat out, "and he's seriously pissed. Get your heads out of your asses and get up here. Little Red Riding Hood just ran past me."

Knowing his team would never get here in time, Kade steeled himself against the pain and took off after his prey.

Chapter Two

A shout of frustration built in Bailey's throat. But she didn't dare let it out. Instead, she hurled herself against the thick wall of bushes blocking her way. And just like before, all it got her were some cuts and scrapes and some wicked sharp thorns embedded in her side.

Biting her lip to keep from cursing out loud and announcing her presence to anyone skulking around the woods, she plucked the lethal-looking thorns out, one by one. Black spots swam in front of her eyes. She realized she'd been holding her breath. She let it out and drew in precious oxygen until her vision cleared.

The throbbing in her side only added to her frustration. She grabbed one of the few spots in the lattice of vines and branches that didn't boast any thorns and shook them like an inmate desperately testing the bars of his cell. Except that Mother Nature was a far better jailer than man. The wall of her cage didn't move, not even a little.

She was trapped.

Every path she'd taken through these woods since escaping the gunmen who'd tried to ambush her at her house had sent her in circles. Or at least it seemed that way since she kept ending up at an impenetrable wall of bushes. If someone had purposely planted them to form a fence around the perimeter of the property that she'd only recently rented from another Enforcer, they'd done a whopper of a job. If she didn't figure a way through them, around them, or over them, soon, she'd end up like Amber and Sebastian.

Dead.

She hoped that Hawke was having better luck tonight than she was.

The FBI agents that were rounding up Enforcers weren't doing it to thank them for their service to their country. They weren't grateful that Enforcers had eliminated untold numbers of terrorists, preventing dozens of 9/11-types of tragedies. And the government certainly wasn't gathering up Enforcers to help reintegrate them into society as the seemingly benign requests sent through the EXIT Inc. network claimed. Anyone who'd followed the directives had disappeared and never been seen again.

The men and women of EXIT had given up their former lives, their careers, friends, families, all to do the dirty work that no other alphabet agency could stomach. Where other agencies stepped in after a crime occurred, Enforcers were tasked with preventing the loss of life in the first place, by taking out the bad guys before they struck. But when the leaders of EXIT succumbed to the lure of power and greed and tricked a few Enforcers into killing innocent people, Uncle Sam had decided to clean house. All Enforcers were judged guilty by association. Their beloved country, the one for which they'd sacrificed *everything*, was rounding them up like cattle.

To exterminate them.

Bailey, of all people, should have expected that the government would turn on her one day. She shook her head at her own stupidity and whirled around, running back the way she'd just come.

Think, Bailey. Think.

There had to be a way out of these woods that didn't include returning to the house to take her chances against an unknown number of assailants. Not that she'd normally run from a fight. But going up against armed men with her bare hands didn't give her the best odds of success.

How many agents were after her? She wasn't sure. After going to sleep tonight, she'd been awakened a few minutes later by a very insistent bladder reminding her that she'd downed a supersized Coke on the way to her hideout. She'd just stepped into the bathroom when she noticed a shadow in her peripheral vision that had nothing to do with furniture—especially since it was wearing full body armor and holding a pistol. Shadow number two stepped into the bedroom directly behind shadow number one.

With her gun on the nightstand behind both men, she'd forced herself to pretend that she hadn't seen anyone and had calmly closed the bathroom door.

Thanks to a hidden panel in the wall—like the panels in many of the walls of her newest hiding place—and an equally hidden set of back stairs, she'd escaped. If it weren't for the fact that she'd been lazy when getting ready for bed and had dropped all of her clothes—including her shorts with her cell phone in the pocket—onto the bathroom floor, she'd have had to make a run for it in nothing but her underwear.

Now, here she was, in shorts, T-shirt, and—thankfully—shoes, but without a gun, without her car keys, and hopelessly lost. Worse, there were at least two armed men searching for her.

Unless they thought she was still in the bathroom.

Picturing FBI agents waiting in the dark, counting the minutes and watching the light under the bathroom door had her smiling. She wondered how long they would wait, and her smile widened. Sometimes she had to take her pleasure in the little things.

She jumped over a fallen log, wincing when the movement pulled at the punctures in her side. If she survived this night, she fully intended to come back later with something deadly—like napalm or a flame thrower—to have her revenge on those nasty thorn bushes. She'd teach them to never mess with an Enforcer again.

A gap appeared between two thick trees straight ahead. Praying that she hadn't passed this way already, she sprinted for the opening. If this was the beginning of yet another circle of the lost, she really was going to scream, to hell with the consequences.

A fallen log blocked her path again, so she leaped over it. A dark shape loomed off to her right. She twisted around, automatically bringing up her hands to defend herself. A man slammed into her with the force of a battering ram, sending her crashing toward the ground.

KADE CLASPED BAILEY against him, twisting in midair to spare her the brunt of their fall. He landed on his back, Bailey's chin snapping against his chest. Blinding pain lanced through his bum leg, making him hiss with pain.

Bailey's surprised, wide-eyed gaze stared into his as she lay on top of him, his arms tightly clasped around her waist. A shout sounded in the distance, and Bailey exploded like a firecracker, twisting and shoving, trying to break Kade's hold. Clenching his teeth against the pain in his leg, he rolled on top of her, pinning her to the ground.

"Let me go." She pushed at him, squirming like an oiled snake, trying to get away.

"Stop fighting me." The awkward angle of his left leg was cutting off the circulation, starting to make it go blessedly numb. Without the fog of pain, he was able to better focus on the squirming woman in his grasp.

And damned if the breath didn't wheeze out of him as he stared into her beautiful green eyes, just like it always did.

As he'd feared, Bailey in person was far more devastating than Bailey on paper. The feel of her soft skin, the feminine scent of roses in her glorious red hair, had his heart hammering and his pulse buzzing in his ears. All of the lectures he'd given himself as he'd worked his way through the woods to try to cut her off were useless. *He* was useless, an equal mixture of lust and fury coursing through him.

What was it about this woman that made him so damned confused?

Even as he silently berated himself for wanting her, he couldn't stop himself from wanting to protect her. It was those shadows in her eyes. They had him thinking of her as a comrade in arms, someone who'd fought through some of life's harshest lessons as he had, a fellow survivor. And no matter how much he wanted to think of her as his enemy, he couldn't.

But that didn't mean he was going to let her go.

"I'm not going to hurt you," he assured her.

"I'll bet that's what you tell all the women you murder." She bucked beneath him, jarring his hip again.

He gritted his teeth and shoved her wrists against the ground, plastering the full weight of his body against hers. What he hadn't been able to accomplish himself, she'd just taken care of with one single word, *murder*. That word, uttered accusingly by an Enforcer of all people, had jolted the sympathy and even the lust straight out of him.

"Funny you should talk about murder when you're an assassin by trade. How many people have you killed while working for EXIT? Ten? Twenty? More?"

She stilled and studied him intently. "You're not wearing a flak jacket like the others. Who *are* you?"

"The man in charge of stopping you, and your peers, from hurting anyone else ever again."

Her eyes went wide, and an answering anger flashed in their depths. "You're their leader, aren't you? The one the government sent to destroy us. The Ghost."

"Ghost?" He laughed harshly, but he wasn't amused. Maybe because her moniker struck so close to the truth. Much of the past year was a dull fog of bleak, barely remembered images he struggled daily to hold on to. The accident had stolen so much from him, leaving him like the wraith she accused him of being.

"Ghost or not," he told her, "I'm about justice, not vigilantism. My men and I are set to destroy EXIT's legacy, not its people. Haven't you received the dispatches we've sent through the Enforcer network? We're trying to help you, not hurt you."

The sneer on her face told him she didn't believe anything that he'd said. She opened her mouth to respond when a shout sounded from one of his men. They were much closer now.

Kade turned his head to call out to them. Bailey bucked beneath him, jarring his leg and sending a fresh new wave of white-hot pain sizzling across his nerve endings. He sucked in a breath, shaking his head to clear the spots swimming in front of his eyes.

"Be still," he gasped through clenched teeth.

She suddenly twisted and jerked a hand free.

Wham!

Her fist cracked against his jaw, the force of the blow knocking him back several inches. Before he could recover, she slammed her kneecap against his left thigh, right where the bullet and twisted metal had torn into muscle and bone all those months ago. An explosion of heat burned through him like lava, scorching everything in its wake. He fell back in agony, clutching his leg.

Bailey scrambled out from beneath him. He made a desperate, one-handed grab for her, but she easily jerked out of his reach. He'd been such a fool. And he couldn't even blame it on alcohol, or the heavy painkillers he'd once been so dependent upon. Because tonight he was stone-cold sober.

"Bailey, wait."

She hesitated, glancing toward the woods, then eying him with suspicion. He hated showing weakness in front of her, in front of anyone, but the pain was too raw to ignore. He could barely breathe.

"Don't go. Please," he gasped, sucking in another breath. "I want to help you."

Her lips curled with contempt. "Like you helped Sebastian? And Amber? I see your kind of help every time I bury one of my friends."

She grabbed for her right hip, as if going for a gun. Then she shook her head in disgust when she realized she didn't have one.

"What are you talking about?" He squeezed his eyes shut against another wave of agony. One breath, two. He should go for *his* gun. But his whole body was shaking, his hands clutching his thigh.

Damn, he really needed a drink. Or a Vicodin. Or ten.

Finally, the burning bands around his thigh began to ease. The fog of pain cleared, leaving him weak, spent. He drew a shaky breath, another.

"Special Agent Quinn, are you all right, sir?"

Kade's eyes flew open. Cord was crouching in front of him, the camouflage grease smeared across his face wrinkling with concern.

And Bailey Stark was nowhere to be seen.

Ignoring the hand that Cord offered, Kade forced the muscles of his face to relax into a carefully blank expression and shoved himself to his feet, locking his knees to keep from falling when his hip wobbled under the stress.

He should have drawn his gun even though she wasn't armed. Hell, maybe he should just lop off his useless leg and be done with the whole thing.

"Sir?" Cord asked, waiting for orders.

"The target was just here," Kade said, his voice gritty and strained. "She's wearing the same clothing she had on when she arrived. No gun that I saw. Find her."

"But, sir, are you sure you're—"

"Go."

It only took Cord a few seconds to locate Bailey's footprints. Then he disappeared into the dark woods, giving orders through the transmitter to the rest of the team.

Kade limped to a tree and braced himself against it. He focused on steadying his breathing while he waited for Cord to transmit the sitrep. Ten minutes passed. Fifteen. When the twenty-minute mark approached without news from his team, the truth coiled in Kade's gut like a bad piece of meat. He punched the transmit button at his waist.

"Status," he demanded.

"We lost the trail," Cord replied. "We're sweeping in a grid pattern, but . . ."

"But, what?" Kade asked, already dreading the answer.

"It's not looking good, sir."

He scrubbed his forehead and slowly blew out a breath. They'd been so close. He'd had her in his arms. All it had taken was one quick kick to his thigh and he'd been as helpless as a new recruit.

"We'll keep searching, sir," Cord assured him.

"Give it another ten minutes, then call it." Kade didn't hold out much hope that it would make a difference. Bailey was probably long gone by now. "Station some men at her house, in case she doubles back. But I doubt she will. She's far more clever than

I gave her credit for. Have them search the inside of the house and figure out how she escaped. They can email me a report in the morning."

He shook his head again, disgusted with how the evening had turned out. "What about the team in Colorado Springs tasked with capturing Hawke? I haven't heard an update on their mission from Simmons yet. Have you?"

"None of them checked in with me, sir. If they do, you'll be the first to know."

"All right. I'm heading back to home base. We'll reconvene in the morning, figure out what went wrong and how to avoid the same mistakes next time."

"Yes, sir." Cord sounded dejected, embarrassed.

Kade knew exactly how he felt.

"Cord?"

"Sir?"

"From what I saw, you and the team did everything right. I'm the one who screwed up. Don't worry. We'll figure this out. We'll catch her next time."

"Thank you, sir." Cord sounded relieved. "'Night."

Kade flipped off the transmitter. As he limped through the woods to the Caddy, he reviewed everything that had happened, from the tip his boss had gleaned during an interrogation of an Enforcer at the retraining facility who personally knew Bailey, to what Bailey had said to Kade when he'd wrestled her to the ground.

I see your kind of help every time I bury one of my friends.

What had she meant by that? It didn't make sense.

There weren't any friends to bury, not if she meant Enforcers.

Kade didn't recall anyone named Sebastian or Amber, at least not on the list of Enforcers he'd been tasked with capturing. Had they been in the initial group that had voluntarily come in? Or the few the agent before him had captured, prior to Kade taking the lead? Maybe Kade knew them by their aliases, monikers they'd taken, like the one who called himself Hawke.

He wished Bailey would have given him more information, explained why she believed her friends had been killed. But she hadn't. And now he'd have to start over with trying to figure out where else she'd go to ground. Until he found her again, he'd have to focus his team's efforts on capturing other Enforcers, or performing surveillance to plan future captures.

Once he reached his car, he dug the keys out of his pocket, then hesitated. Bailey had managed to evade his men so far, and he'd assumed that she was making her way deeper into the woods to get away. But what if she wasn't? What were her alternatives?

She could circle back to her car. If she reached it before Cord assigned agents to watch the house, and she managed to get her keys, she'd still have Nichols and the Suburban blocking the exit onto the highway to deal with.

That still left one accessible and *unguarded* vehicle close by.

His.

He took a quick step back, wincing at the strain on his leg even as he grabbed his pistol and swept it out in front of him. But there was no sign of the curvy, petite, infuriating redhead, no flash of her white T-shirt. No footprints that he could make out, not that she'd probably leave prints here where the sun had baked the ground like a kiln earlier in the day.

Using the powerful LED light on his key chain, he inched forward and shined the light through the dark, tinted windows at the driver's seat, the back-seat, the floorboard. Nothing. No one was hiding inside.

He considered all of the options again and peered into the darkness toward the thick trees. If he were in Bailey's shoes, what would he do? He'd been studying her for months, trying to anticipate her actions, figuring out where she might hide. So what would she do?

After pondering all the alternatives for a full minute, he opened the driver's door and slid behind the steering wheel.

Then he opened the bottle of Jim Beam.

Chapter Three

Bailey rested on her stomach, her phone's screen the only thing visible in the dark as she typed a text to one of the few people she trusted—Hawke, an Enforcer she'd worked with on several rescue missions overseas.

On their last mission together, they'd been tasked with getting a diplomat's family to safety in a volatile situation where any public US involvement could have caused an international incident.

Disguised as a rebel, she'd been tucking one of the diplomat's toddler daughters into the vehicle that would whisk them to safety when an unfriendly had approached her from behind. All she'd heard was a rush of air before whirling around to see the man lying with his throat slit on the ground behind her, a machete still clutched in his hand. Hawke was standing over him, holding a knife that was dripping blood.

He'd earned her respect, her trust, and her loyalty. She'd returned the favor by saving his life the very next day. In some people's books that might make them even. But she still felt she owed him, and probably always would.

She typed out a text. I'm still evading pursuit. You?

I'm a bit of a mess, but hanging in there. Managed to get to a good hiding place to lick my wounds. The buggers will probably give up soon.

Dismay curled in her stomach. Wounds figuratively or literally?

No worries. I'll be okay.

She glanced around her hiding place, listening intently before texting her reply.

Too bad you're not in Boulder. We could do something relaxing, like bungee-jump off a cliff.

Too bad you're not in Colorado Springs. We could count cards and get thrown out of the Double Eagle.

She smiled. He still had his sense of humor. Maybe he really was okay.

I saw the Ghost tonight. Up close and personal.

An emoticon of a shocked face appeared on her screen. Guy or girl?

Most definitely a man, his broad, well-defined chest shown off to spectacular advantage in a tight, black T-shirt tucked into sexy black jeans that molded to his muscular thighs and tight rear end. Standing at about six foot two with short dark hair and an angular face that gave him a hard, dangerous look, his body could make a saint drool. Since Bailey wasn't a saint—not even close—she hadn't been immune to his hard body and earthy, male scent. Even though she'd hated herself for thinking of him that way.

Then she'd looked into his eyes.

They'd been dark wells of shocking desolation that could freeze a wildfire. Even now she shivered at how bleak they'd been.

Guy, she typed. The word didn't come close to describing the sense of power, of authority, that wrapped itself around him and had both fascinated and worried her at the same time.

You're lucky he didn't kill you. What happened?

Lucky? Perhaps. He'd been armed. She hadn't seen the pistol, but she'd felt the familiar hard edge of its grip digging into her hip as he'd pinned her down. Her mouth had practically salivated at the thought of grabbing his gun since she'd had to leave all of her weapons back at the house. But he'd clamped her wrists in an iron-tight hold. So why hadn't *he* gone for his weapon? Why was she still alive? Because he was in too much pain after she'd kicked him?

The flash of guilt that swept through her at that thought was surprising. After noticing him grimace and favor his leg, she'd purposely driven her knee into his thigh muscle. She shouldn't feel guilty about that. Hurting him was self-defense. Totally justified. And if she repeated that often enough, she might eventually believe it.

Her thumbs flew across the screen as she started typing again. I exploited his weakness. Will give deets later. Don't know his name. He had a team. Not sure how many. Only saw two.

There are four after me, Hawke texted.

Then there are probably a dozen after me. I'm more of a badass than you any day of the week.

An eye-roll emoticon popped up on the screen.

She grinned and continued typing. I didn't get a good look at the men after me, just an impression in the light of the bathroom doorway. But I think they both had shaggy hair. And one of them had a tat on his neck. If it weren't for the FBI lettering on their flak-jackets, I'd have thought they were common thugs. What do you make of that?

When he didn't reply, she typed, Hawke? She was just starting to sweat when another text popped up.

Sorry. Had to hold my breath there for a minute. They got pretty close.

Alarm shot through her. You need to get out of there.

Don't I know it. These guys are more persistent than a revenue officer when I'm on a Blackjack winning streak. What'd you mean about the FBI? You think they're fakes?

A thump sounded. She froze, listening carefully, trying to identify the sounds around her.

Bailey?

She typed faster. It was almost time to make her move. But she wanted to pass the important information to Hawke in case the worst happened. One of them needed to survive to warn the others.

Not sure. She gave him a description of the Ghost and mentioned his leg. Must be a recent injury, still healing. He almost passed out when I slammed my knee against his thigh. And get this. He carries a James Bond gun.

A few seconds went by. Then, James Bond gun?

Oh, come on. Really? A Walther PPK. I almost called him Craig, Daniel Craig.

Another eye-roll emoticon. Are you somewhere reasonably safe for the moment?

Not even a little bit, she texted.

Then stop wasting time and get out of there.

Look who's talking. Why don't you stop texting and get yourself to safety?

My best chance is to lie low and wait. Back to you. Are you surrounded?

Yes, and no, she replied. But my objective isn't escape at the moment. I can't risk losing this opportunity. Enforcers are an endangered species. We may not get another chance like this.

Chance like what? Bailey, what are you planning?

I'm going to bring down the Ghost.

Not by yourself, you aren't! Too dangerous. Get out of there.

She shook her head as she typed her reply. Last I checked, you weren't my boss.

A truly impressive string of curse words popped up on her screen. Maybe the cliché about sailors having a commanding knowledge of salty language was true. After all, Hawke had been a Navy SEAL once, ex-military like a lot of her peers. And then he'd answered his country's call by becoming an Enforcer, only to become hunted like an animal by the very people who'd once recruited him.

Do you have a gun? he asked.

Nope.

Tell me where you are, Bailey.

Why? It's not like you can help me any more than I can help you. You're nearly two hours away with your own enemies to worry about.

There might be others in Boulder who can help. I can give them your GPS coordinates.

She stiffened. If you're talking about those traitor Enforcers who turned against the rest of us and are now calling themselves Equalizers, they're the last people I'd trust.

Devlin Buchanan and the others aren't traitors. They figured out everything was going south way before the rest of us did and got out. They can help you, if you'll let me contact them. If I remember right, they already tried to recruit you once. They know who you are. They'll be happy to help.

Hot anger had her typing so fast her fingers cramped. No telling what would have happened to me if I'd accepted their offer at the time. From where I stand, the whole reason EXIT imploded is because Devlin put everything into motion. If it weren't for the Equalizers, we'd both be lying on a beach somewhere right now spending our big fat paychecks.

Instead of the sexy teasing she'd expected in reply, she got a rushed message.

Gotta go. Be safe.

Text me when you make it out of there.

She waited, hoping for one last message. But a full minute passed and her screen remained blank. Her fingers tightened around the phone. If anyone could get out of a tough situation, Hawke could. He would contact her later, when he was in the clear. She had to believe that. Because she'd already lost everyone else she'd ever cared about. She couldn't stomach the thought of losing Hawke, too.

Swallowing against the tightness in her throat, she put her phone away. Then she pulled the neon-green emergency release handle and climbed out of the trunk of the Ghost's car.

Chapter Four

Saturday, 2:25 a.m.

Bailey swept her wet bangs out of her eyes and ducked beside the black Cadillac Coupe in the driveway of the Ghost's single-story ranch house. Rain was falling steadily, soaking her through and through. But it kept any late-night curious neighbors away, which meant she didn't have to worry so much that someone might call the cops if they saw her skulking around.

Then again, maybe stealth wasn't necessary. The man who'd seemed so formidable back in the woods now seemed the complete opposite—careless and oblivious to everything around him.

After she'd heard him get out of the car, she'd carefully climbed out of the trunk. His back was turned to her and he was bobbing and weaving like a drunk. The smell of whiskey reached her even through the pouring rain. And when she peeked through the Caddy's window, the full bottle of whiskey that she'd seen in the console earlier was only half-full now. He must have been drinking the whole way home.

She was lucky that he hadn't wrecked the car and killed them both, or worse, some innocent passerby. She *had* zero respect for someone who'd risk other people's lives that way.

The man was so inebriated that a barking Rottweiler could have snuck up on him. It was taking all of his concentration to remain upright while he tried to fit his key in the side door's lock.

Even from twenty feet away she could hear the slur of his voice as he grumbled about the stubborn door. When the Ghost finally stumbled inside, Bailey shook her head in disgust. *This* was the man they'd labeled the Ghost because he appeared from out of nowhere, was elusive, a shadow? This was the man so many Enforcers had feared, worrying that he and one of his teams of gunmen would come after them next and make them disappear just like so many of their peers?

Pathetic.

In spite of his impressive build and brawn, he didn't have the discipline required of a true leader. He wasn't even worthy of her scorn, much less her fear. And somehow that made everything worse. That a man so inept could bring down so many Enforcers was insulting, embarrassing.

After waiting a full minute to make sure her nemesis didn't come back outside, she jogged from the car to the same side door he'd just gone through. Locked. No surprise there. Even a bumbling fool couldn't be *that* lax. But she didn't see any of the usual trappings of an alarm—no warning signs in the yard, no wires or metal plates in the nearest window casing to indicate the old house had been retrofitted with a modern security system. Maybe he assumed he didn't need one in an upper-middle-class neighborhood like this. And he'd never considered that one of the people he'd hunted would hitch a ride in his car and hunt him instead.

He was about to pay for both of those mistakes.

Since there were floodlights on this side of the house, making her feel dangerously exposed, she discarded the idea of picking the lock. Plus, going in cold was foolish. She needed to check the perimeter, get as much information as she could about her target before attempting entry.

Keeping her head down just in case there was a camera hidden somewhere, she walked the entire perimeter. A line of shrubs along the front of the house gave her excellent concealment, allowing her to peek in windows, straining to see as much as possible through the tiny cracks in the blinds. If there was a security system, it was well hidden. And she hadn't spotted any cameras, although she continued to keep her head down just in case. Not that it really mattered. The Ghost's men had been after her for weeks. They obviously knew what she looked like. But old habits died hard. And she'd been an Enforcer for a long time.

After making her way to the back of the house, she decided she'd enter through a dry-rotted set of French double doors that opened onto a six-by-six concrete patio. There wasn't even a porch light on back here to dissuade a potential burglar.

Or one determined, badass Enforcer.

Although she hadn't seen the Ghost when she'd peeked through the blinds in the various windows, she figured that he must be in the front room since it was the only one with a light on. He was probably sitting in some corner she couldn't see, nursing another bottle of whiskey.

A few minutes later, courtesy of the mushy wooden frame and the pry bar she took from the trunk, she was inside. After propping closed one of the ruined French doors behind her, she stepped into the center of the room.

The dim light from the archway at the back left corner of the room helped her catalog the contents—a couch to her left, two chairs to the right, a wall of bookshelves with knickknacks and paperweights on the wall opposite of where she stood, and little else. It didn't even look lived-in. It was probably just the place where the FBI—or whoever the Ghost's real employer was—had set him up while his men murdered Enforcers. She hefted the pry bar in her hand. Time to go hunting.

"I guarantee you won't find a flat tire in here to change."

Bailey whirled to her left at the sound of the deep, masculine voice.

"Hold it." A powerful flashlight clicked on from behind the couch, shining directly at her face.

She should have checked behind that couch, first thing. Now who was making the mistakes?

She held her empty hand up, shielding her eyes. "Turn the light away. I can't see anything."

"That's the point," he said dryly. The light didn't waver. "While I'd rather not put a hole in you, I will if I have to. Keep that in mind while you *carefully* and *slowly* toss that pry bar to the other side of the room."

She reluctantly pitched her only weapon away. It clattered across the hardwood floor and skittered into the corner.

"Lock your hands behind your neck and move toward the archway," he ordered.

"Do a girl a favor and put the gun down first, okay?"

"Sorry, fresh out of favors. Move."

She trudged forward, wondering why he wasn't slurring his words. And even though she could hear his uneven gait as his shoes echoed on the floor behind her, he wasn't staggering. That odd gait was most likely because of his wounded leg.

Which meant he'd never been drunk to begin with.

"You tricked me," she accused, as she half turned, raising her hand to shield her eyes from the light. "You knew I was in the trunk."

"It seemed a likely possibility."

Grudging admiration shot through her. He wasn't the fool she'd thought him to be. Everything had been too easy, which should have been her first warning. But she'd fallen victim to her own prejudices, assuming he was a lush because, seriously, who carried a full-size bottle of whiskey in their car, especially when on a mission?

Since she didn't smell any alcohol now, he must have poured it out next to the car as part of his plan to fool her. If she was going to make it out of this alive, she couldn't afford to underestimate him again. She'd have to rely on the only weapon she had left—her wits.

"Well played. What's next?" She half turned. "I'm Bailey Stark, but you know that already. What should I call you?"

"I don't particularly care. Turn around. Go into the front room."

She *really* missed her gun.

If she could find out his real name, it could be a

gold mine if she managed to escape. A name would be that little thread she could pull to unravel the rest of the government's secrets. She could follow him to his boss, and to the next boss, until she knew everyone pulling the strings against the Enforcers at every level of government. After all, she and the other remaining Enforcers couldn't effectively fight their enemies without knowing who they were.

"Unless you can outrun my trigger finger, I suggest you get moving," he said.

"You're a lousy host," she grumbled as she started forward again.

"You're a lousy guest. You destroyed the casing around my antique doors."

"Antique? They're a dry-rotted termite smorgasbord. I did you a favor by pointing out a major flaw in your security."

"Well, in that case, I suppose I should thank you." The mocking sound of his voice had her nails biting into her palms. A moment later he said, "You can stop now."

She was in the middle of the front room. A brown leather couch took up the spot under the street-facing windows. Beside it was a generously-sized blue chair, and next to that was a large oak desk, its scarred surface littered with papers.

Again, there wasn't much else to give it a lived-in appearance, just wall-to-wall bookshelves, covered mostly with stacks of paper. Reports maybe? Information about the teams searching for her and the others? She wouldn't mind a closer look.

"Turn around."

As she turned, her hands still locked behind her neck, she surveyed everything. The only exits were the front windows and the opening they'd just come through. That didn't seem right. The front door should have been nearby. But she didn't see it. She glanced around the room again, to the left and right of the windows.

"It's fake," he offered, drawing her attention. "The front door. That *is* what you were looking for, isn't it? I had it sealed off when I moved in."

Since the lights were on in this room, he'd set the flashlight down somewhere and she could see him perfectly. Including the gun in his hand. The Walther PPK didn't waver, but it wasn't pointed directly at her either. Instead, it was aimed slightly to her left, and his pointer finger was on the frame, not the trigger. It appeared that he wasn't planning on shooting her, not yet anyway. As long as she didn't provoke him, she just might figure a way out of this that didn't include her leaving in a body bag.

"Why would you bother to seal the front door and leave a half-rotten door in the back?"

She was stalling for time, but was genuinely curious to hear his answer. She glanced at the bookshelves for some sort of weapon. But there weren't any large, heavy books, and no paperweights here. Maybe that was why he'd forced her into the front room. It was safer for him than the back room with knickknacks that she could have used as missiles.

There weren't any paintings or decorations on the walls. But there was a small photograph taped on the wall near the archway. It was a picture of him with his arm around a blonde who was cover-model beautiful. Both of them were smiling into the camera. And the picture was taken before whatever had caused those deep scars on the Ghost's face.

The smooth, chiseled cheekbones and square jaw in the photo combined with a carefree smile contrasted sharply with the man in front of her. But it was the look of utter joy in his sparkling eyes in the photograph that provided the most startling contrast. The change in him seemed almost . . . tragic.

What happened to you?

"There's a solid steel pocket door I can slide closed behind the French doors," he said, answering the question she'd spoken earlier about security. "When I go to bed, I secure the pocket door. But since I was expecting company, I left it open."

His voice had an edge to it that hadn't been there a few minutes ago. It was the same tone he'd used when they were in the woods. She studied him more carefully, noting the tiny lines of strain around his mouth and eyes, the whiteness of his knuckles that were tightly clenching the gun.

He was in pain. Had the walk from the other room caused his injury to hurt again?

"How did you know I'd hidden in the trunk?" she asked.

She noticed that his stance was slightly crooked, as if he were favoring his left hip. She may have just found her way out. Again. But she needed to get closer to take advantage. Would he be ready for her this time? Would he make the same mistake twice?

He shrugged. "It's where I'd have hidden, if our roles were reversed."

She slowly lowered her hands. When he didn't tell her to put them back up, she shoved them into the pockets of her shorts, using the action to distract him from the fact that she'd taken a small step forward.

The fingers of her right hand bumped against her phone. She'd forgotten it was there. She suddenly wished that she'd smashed it before coming into the house. If she was captured and the Ghost got Hawke's number, he might be able to use it to draw him into a trap. Assuming that Hawke had escaped the net closing around him tonight.

"If you knew I was in the trunk, why didn't you open it? Why drive me to your house?"

She twisted around, glancing at the windows as if she'd heard something, again using her movements to cover that she'd moved closer.

"I didn't want to risk you shooting me in the face if you'd managed to get a gun before getting into my car," he answered amiably, as if they were just a couple of friends having a chat. He waved the pistol toward the couch. "Make yourself comfortable while we wait for my team."

She stiffened. "Your team?"

"The one from your house earlier. I heard a thump in the trunk on the way here and figured my theory was correct, that you were hiding inside. So I told the team to meet me here, just in case. Turns out I was right. Don't worry. You won't have to wait long. They'll be here soon."

She studied the play of light across the scars on his cheeks, which lent him a sinister cast. Or maybe it was the sudden urgency of her situation that made him seem that way. Escaping him, alone and unarmed, would be hard enough. Against an entire team, without any secret panels to slip through, would be nearly impossible. She had to get out of here. Now.

And she knew exactly how she was going to do it.

Chapter Five

Saturday, 2:45 a.m.

Bailey inched closer to the Ghost, instead of toward the couch where he'd told her to go. Hoping to distract him from that fact, she gestured with her hands toward the room at large.

"Why are you doing this?" she asked.

He frowned. "I'm the one asking the questions. But I *will* tell you this. The Enforcer program is over. You and your colleagues have to be debriefed, sent to a retraining facility to be reintegrated into society in a new capacity. Just as importantly, the government has to believe you aren't dangerous, in order for the Enforcers to be allowed to go free without the constraints of EXIT Inc. or a similar structure. What my teams are doing, what I'm doing, is giving EXIT's former agents a second chance. We're saving lives, Enforcers' lives."

His eyes narrowed as he studied her. "Earlier tonight, you mentioned burying your friends. But no one that we've captured has been killed. Someone has been spreading rumors, lies."

"Lies?" She laughed harshly. "Tell that to Sebastian and Amber. Oh, wait. You can't. Because they're both dead."

"I don't know who told you that but—"

"No one *told* me." She risked moving a step closer, then another. "I went to their funerals."

His gaze locked on hers with an intensity that was unnerving. "What are you talking about?"

If she didn't know better, she'd think he was truly shocked, that he hadn't known her friends had been killed. But he'd fooled her once already tonight, and she wasn't underestimating him again.

"Bailey, talk to me. I need to understand what you—"

She launched herself at him, focusing all of her body weight and muscle into slamming the heels of her tennis shoes against his left thigh. A guttural moan tore from his throat as his leg crumpled beneath him. He fell to the floor, his face a white mask of pain. Guilt swept through her as he clutched his leg, in obvious agony.

He killed Sebastian, Amber, maybe even Hawke by now, whether by his own hand or by giving orders to someone else. Remember that.

She dove across him for the gun that had fallen out of his hand. Just as she was about to grab the pistol, one of his hands clamped around her ankle.

"Oh no you don't." The gravelly words seemed torn from his throat, air wheezing between his clenched teeth.

She aimed a kick at his face. He jerked to the side, grabbed her other ankle and yanked her toward him. She slid across the polished wooden floor and he rolled on top of her—pinning her, just like he had in the woods. Her attempt to knee his vulnerable thigh again was met with a twist of his hips. Then he was pressing her down, crushing her into submission, both of her hands locked in his above her head. She glared up at him, making no attempt to hide her contempt.

"You're a vicious little thing," he accused. "Someone needs to teach you some manners."

She arched a mocking brow. "And I suppose that *someone* is you? Don't flatter yourself. You may have won the battle, but, yadda, yadda, yadda. I'm not defeated quite yet."

The steel bands of his fingers around her wrists tightened even more. Good grief, he was strong. Her hands were going numb. And he'd learned from his previous mistakes, positioning his body so that she couldn't knee his bad leg yet again.

"This ends here." His voice carried the sharp bite of authority. "This ends tonight."

Her hands jerked at the unexpected feel of cold steel circling her right wrist. Handcuffs. Panic surged through her. Trying to buck and twist beneath him, she desperately attempted to get free. But with him pressing her body down so tightly against the floor, her attempts seemed puny at best.

Click. The first cuff locked around her wrist. With ridiculous ease, he jerked her other hand close to the first and just like that, both wrists were cuffed together. But he'd moved a fraction sideways to do it, giving her the opening she needed.

She twisted violently and brought her hands up, swinging her clasped fists toward the side of his head.

He jerked back with surprising speed and she missed him completely. But he'd moved to avoid being hit. She took full advantage of the unexpected opening and rolled away from him. Bracing her cuffed hands on the floor, she lunged to her feet and sprinted for the archway.

"Bailey, damn it, stop!"

His command startled her and she fell against the side of the archway, hands scrabbling for purchase against the wall. Some kind of slick paper came off in her hands. Realizing what it was, she shoved it into her front pocket as she rushed through the opening into the other room. The Ghost's limping gait thumped behind her on the wood floor.

"Bailey!"

He was close, too close. She put on a frantic burst of speed, whirling around the couch, swinging her closed fists against the bookshelf. Knickknacks went flying behind her. Renewed cursing told her at least one of the projectiles had hit her intended target.

She didn't even slow down for the French doors, using her momentum to slam one of them open with her shoulder. It banged against the side of the house, glass exploding and pinging down onto the concrete porch like a bowlful of marbles spilling onto the floor. The force of the impact pulled her up short and she staggered for balance even as a blast of rain pummeled her and soaked her all over again.

"Don't move."

A man in black wearing a déjà-vu-inducing FBI flak jacket stood twenty feet away, pointing a pistol at her—one of the same men that she'd seen in her bedroom earlier tonight. She froze, then gasped in shock at the red laser light dancing across her chest, the unmistakable signature of a rifle aimed at her by some hidden sniper.

Wham! The Ghost tackled her from behind, throwing her to the ground a split second before a muffled cracking sound echoed through the yard. A gunshot. He rolled with her and immediately shoved to his feet, then cursed as his bad leg folded beneath him. He dropped to his knees, valiantly crouching in front of her, blocking anyone from getting a clear shot.

"Lower your weapons," he shouted, holding up his hands to signal both the man in front of him and the hidden sniper. "She's unarmed."

Bailey pulled her arms in against her chest behind him, trying to make herself less of a target. The Ghost had surprised her, yet again. And she could tell that he was in terrible pain. He was barely able to crouch on his knees, and yet he did. Sacrificing his own body to keep her safe, even though she was the one who'd hurt him. Twice. Why would he do that? It made no sense.

She glanced back at the house, looking for an escape route, and saw an impressive bullet hole from the sniper's rifle in the wood trim by the back doors—right where she'd been standing moments before. If the Ghost hadn't tackled her, she'd be seriously injured, or dead right now.

"Bailey," a man's almost imperceptible whisper sounded behind her. *From inside the house.*

"I'm an Equalizer. I work with Buchanan," the whisper continued. "Back up."

She stiffened in shock. Buchanan. He had to mean Devlin Buchanan, the leader of the Equalizers. Had Buchanan sent this man to help her?

Damn it, Hawke. I told you not to call them.

On the heel of that thought was the sickening fear that Hawke might have risked his own safety to make a desperate plea for hers. Had his call to Buchanan been his last action before being caught by the team that was closing in on him? Or had he managed to escape but for some reason couldn't contact her to let her know he was safe?

"Bailey," the voice whispered again. "Trust me, if you want to live, you need to get your ass inside the house. Now."

He was right about one thing—the odds of her getting out of this on her own, alive, were hovering around the "I wouldn't bet my life's savings on it" territory. But *trust* him? Someone working for Buchanan? A man who'd once been known as "*The* Enforcer" because he was in charge of *killing* other Enforcers if he deemed they'd gone rogue? How was she supposed to trust the man in the dark behind her when he worked for another man she *definitely* didn't trust?

The argument between the Ghost and the sniper had escalated. Apparently the man had finally stepped out of his hiding place and was now being berated for shooting at an unarmed woman, or something along those lines. Bailey hadn't paid much attention to what he was saying because she was so focused on the stranger in the shadows behind her.

Every instinct screamed for her not to trust Buchanan's lackey. Then again, compared to almost certain death, dealing with one of his men was starting to sound appealing. And if he could give her an update on Hawke, dealing with Equalizer-scum could be the best thing to happen to her all day.

Using the Ghost and the darkness for cover, she duckwalked backward to the open doorway. An arm clamped around her waist and yanked her inside.

Once they were away from the doorway, she whirled around, shoving at the man's arm. But he was already letting go and gesturing for her to follow him to the archway. He was dressed all in black, including a baseball cap pulled down low to conceal his features.

"That's a dead end," she whispered, as she wiped the dripping rainwater off her face with her clasped hands. "We should use the side door. It leads to the driveway."

"My van's across the street. We'll use the front."

"But—"

"It's not a dead end. I came in that way. The side door is too exposed."

"Wait." She could barely make out the frown on his face in the dimly lit room. He was tall, probably as tall as the Ghost. And almost as intimidating.

"What is it?" he whispered impatiently.

"You said you're an Equalizer?"

He nodded, his gaze flitting to the open French door. "Jace Atwell. I'm a former Navy SEAL and a bodyguard after that. Stick with me and you'll make it out of here alive."

"Have you always suffered from this lack of confidence?"

He didn't even crack a smile. The man had no sense of humor.

"I'm confident about one thing," he said. "The *only* chance you have to make it out of here alive is with me. But I'm not going to get myself killed waiting for you to make up your mind. If you want to live, follow me. If not—" he shrugged "—I gave you a chance. If you choose not to take it, that's on you."

Without waiting for her reply, he hurried into the front room.

The arguments on the back porch had stopped. Silence, in this case, couldn't be good. She took off for the front room. When she sprinted through the archway, a moment of panic slammed through her. The room was empty.

"Over here."

A harsh whisper had her turning to the right. Atwell had a backpack slung over his shoulder now and it looked heavy. What was he doing, robbing the place?

He slid a panel open, revealing the front door—a perfectly *working* front door. The Ghost had fooled her once again. The panel must have been for extra security, like the one in the back. But it hadn't done its job tonight.

"Hurry," Atwell snapped.

And just like that, she rushed to obey, as if he were a general and she his new recruit. The man did have a way of giving orders. Which had her resenting the hell out of him.

As soon as she reached the sliding panel, he killed the lights. He shoved the door open, and hurried outside, gesturing for her to crouch down and follow him. They headed away from the driveway side, running between the brick façade and the mature shrubs.

When he reached the end of the house, he pulled her up short. A single gold band winked in the moonlight on his left hand. Somehow, the knowledge that he was married made him seem more human. But only a little. She raised her brows in question.

He pointed toward a dark-colored minivan parked on the other side of the street. She hesitated for the briefest moment before nodding. Hawke trusted the Equalizers. And she trusted Hawke. She had to keep reminding herself of that.

The barest hint of a smile curved his lips, as if he knew the dilemma she was in and found it amusing.

They both peeked out through the bushes to see if they had company. Sure enough, a shadow moved off to their left, a man dressed in black with yet another flak jacket on. The white letters FBI were clearly stamped across the back.

"FBI my ass," Atwell muttered.

She shot him a surprised glance. Did he have the same suspicions about the Ghost's team that she had?

The man in the flak jacket ducked through the open front door, oblivious that they were hiding twenty feet away. How long before he met up with the others and told them the door was open?

Bailey peered around the brick wall, checking the side yard. She ducked back and held up one finger, letting Atwell know there was another gunman coming up fast.

He shoved her behind him, taking her place at the corner. Normally she wouldn't have stood for something like that, but he was armed and she wasn't, not to mention her hands were still cuffed together. And, well, she just didn't feel like challenging a brooding giant of a man tonight, especially if he was willing to risk his neck for her.

After he rushed into the side yard, she counted silently to six before he reappeared, giving her a curt nod. He'd taken care of the gunman.

"Go," he mouthed silently, pointing toward the van.

She immediately took off running. Soon, his footsteps pounded on the ground behind her. When they were almost to the van, he passed her and yanked open the sliding side door.

"Get in."

After she hopped inside, he shoved a gun between her clasped hands and threw open the driver's side sliding door. She knew the drill. He'd drive. She'd cover them both. She knelt down on the rough, carpeted floor of the van, facing the house with the pistol in her clasped fists, her finger on the trigger ready to shoot anyone who threatened them.

A large shadow emerged from the backyard. She steadied the gun dead center on the man's chest, then hesitated. She knew that silhouette, recognized the off-kilter stance as he favored his left leg.

The Ghost.

Somehow he'd managed to hobble after her and was pointing a gun toward the van. He appeared to be struggling to remain upright, no doubt because she'd hurt him. And yet he'd still risked his life to save her from a sniper's bullet. She couldn't seem to get past that.

Doesn't matter. He's the enemy. And he has a gun.

She tightened her finger on the trigger as the van's engine roared to life. The Ghost suddenly brought his free arm up, knocking a gun out of another man's hand that Bailey hadn't even noticed in the dark. He'd just saved her, and possibly Atwell as well.

The van took off, tires squealing. Bailey balanced her weight on her knees to keep from falling and steadied her gun. But the Ghost lowered his pistol to his side, aiming at the ground.

He was letting them go.

You've been searching for him for weeks. Shoot him. End this.

But she couldn't. She lowered her gun, staring at him in an odd truce of sorts as he faded from view.

"Bailey, you okay back there?"

It sounded more like a demand than a question as he pitched his baseball cap onto the passenger seat behind him. He slowed for a curve in the road and then punched the gas again.

"I'm good," she called back, even though she wasn't.

She was confused as hell. Two men she didn't trust had just saved her life. Go figure.

She pitched the pistol onto the bench seat so she could grasp the door handle. After sliding the door closed, she grabbed the pistol again, then used the back of one hand to swipe at the dribbles of water running down her cheeks. It figured that the one time it rained in the past two months would be tonight. Just her luck.

"If any of them catch up to us, I'll have to do some fancy driving. And this van doesn't exactly do fancy. You need to keep an eye out for a tail and cover us." He glanced over his shoulder and motioned toward her cuffed hands. "Is that a problem?"

She shook her head. "Not until the magazine runs out and I need to reload."

"Hopefully it won't come to that. I left them a surprise, or eight, back at the house to give us a better head start." He slowed to take a turn, then accelerated again.

Bailey turned around and leaned over the bench seat, aiming her pistol at the back window. A few minutes later, a set of headlights pulled around a curve and began racing toward them.

Chapter Six

Saturday, 3:01 a.m.

Kade stood in the driveway with his team, surveying the damage. All four of the Caddy's tires had been slashed. The SUV, parked a few feet away, had suffered the same fate. Eight flat tires. Whoever had helped Bailey escape had made sure they'd have one hell of a head start.

Nichols rubbed the back of his head. He had an impressive goose egg coming up from where the intruder had ambushed him in the side yard. But at least he hadn't been killed. He swore and dropped his hands to his sides. "How on earth did someone manage to do all that without at least one of us seeing them?"

Kade quirked a brow.

Nichols's face turned red.

The obvious reason hung in the air unspoken. *Secure the perimeter* was a basic tenet of their training. When the team had arrived, they knew Kade was supposed to be inside with the prisoner. The first thing they should have done was post someone to watch the Suburban, in case the target escaped and the team had to take off in pursuit.

But that's not what they'd done.

Instead, the entire team had performed a quick circuit around the outside of the house, decided to enter from the back, and had just gotten into position to cover each other when Bailey did her swan dive through one of the French doors. The only team member who hadn't screwed up was Reese, and that was only because he was still back at the cottage trying to figure out how Bailey had escaped the first time.

"Cord," Kade called out, looking around.

"Behind you." The agent made his way to the front. "Sir?"

"The security system's surveillance footage can be viewed on the computer in the main room." He gave him the password. "When you get a good, clear frame of our tire slasher, print copies of his picture for everyone here. We can't find him if we don't know what he looks like."

"Or she," Alice called out from the other side of Nichols.

"Or she," Kade agreed.

"Yes, sir." Cord hurried back into the house.

"Can't believe we had her within reach twice tonight and still lost her." Nichols shook his head.

"Could be worse," Alice piped up in a voice that had an unfortunate likeness to Minnie Mouse.

"Yeah? How?" Nichols asked.

"It could still be raining."

Nichols rolled his eyes and gave her a good-natured shove. She grinned and shoved him back.

Kade scrubbed the stubble on his chin and silently prayed to the FBI gods to save him from this ragtag group.

"Pack up the gear while I arrange for a replacement vehicle." He motioned toward the SUV and pulled out his cell phone.

As if relieved to have something constructive to do, the team surged forward. They began boxing up the various pieces of equipment they regularly hauled around for their missions and began stuffing them into duffel bags.

Kade leaned against the house to give his leg a much-needed rest while he made the call. And to give him a better vantage point. He wanted to keep an eye on the two members of the team that had him wondering if Bailey's getting away tonight was actually a *good* thing—Special Agent Dominic Wales and Special Agent Jack Martinelli.

They'd always been different from the others. But Kade had never had any pressing reason to figure out why, until tonight.

When they'd both tried to murder Bailey.

Jack had targeted her with his laser scope.

Dominic had been about to shoot her as she escaped in the van.

If Kade hadn't stopped them, Bailey would be dead. Why? Both men knew the team's objective on every single mission was to take the Enforcers alive, to use lethal force only if absolutely necessary to save their own lives, or the lives of others. Maybe Dominic could argue that he was worried about Kade getting shot if he hadn't acted—maybe. But what was Jack's justification?

He finished the call and put his phone away. A moment later, the house's side door opened and Cord stepped outside. The grim look on his face told Kade the answer even before he asked the question.

"No luck?"

Cord stopped next to him. "Oh sure. Plenty. I got a gazillion camera shots of the guy. But he never once looked up and his ball cap hid his features. I can't tell you what color his hair is, or even if he's white, purple, or green. He had long sleeves and the collar of his shirt was flipped up. Plus, it was raining pretty heavily at the time, which screws with the footage."

"In other words we have nothing."

"Pretty much. All we know is that some guy in black clothes helped our Enforcer escape."

"You're the best video guy on the team. If you couldn't get a good frame out of that footage, I don't expect anyone else could."

Cord nodded as if the praise was no big deal. But he seemed to be standing a little straighter, a little taller. Which reminded Kade yet again that he needed to stroke these kids' egos more often.

It was hard to remember just how tough it could be when first starting out, how fragile his own confidence had been when he was just a few months out of the academy. He might not always approve of his team's lack of decorum. But he couldn't complain about their work ethic, or their enthusiasm. They just needed more guidance.

His gaze slid to Dominic and Jack who were standing apart from the others near the SUV's bumper, deep in conversation. Now those were two newbies who never seemed to need a word of encouragement. And they seemed a bit older than he'd expect recent Quantico graduates to be. Of course, this could be a second career for them, which would explain the age. Still, they seemed too confident to just be starting out as new agents. And it was time for Kade to find out why.

He started toward them. His bum leg chose that moment to finally give out. He fell against the Caddy, barely catching himself before he could slide to the ground.

Cord grabbed his arm, his eyes wide with alarm. "You okay, boss?"

Great. Twice in one night, the same agent had seen him at his very worst. Kade shook Cord's hand off, mumbling a thank-you as he glanced around. Thankfully, the others didn't seem to have noticed his disgrace. Then again, they'd all seen him fall to his knees on the back porch earlier.

Tonight was not his finest hour.

When he started toward the SUV again, he was more deliberate and slow. It almost killed him to make that concession to his weakness. But it was better than ending up sprawled on the concrete again.

The conversation stopped as soon as he drew close to the back bumper.

Dominic's dark eyes met his and he tapped Jack's shoulder to get him to turn around.

"Something we can do for you, sir?" Dom asked.

"You can explain why you were both so trigger-happy tonight. You do remember our objective is to bring Enforcers in alive?"

They exchanged a glance with each other before Dom spoke again.

"Permission to speak freely, sir?"

"Of course."

He crossed his arms over his chest. The tail end of a serpent tattoo on his biceps peeked out from under his shirtsleeve. Why hadn't Kade noticed *that* tattoo before?

"Jack and I were just talking about how we both screwed up. Adrenaline rush, I guess. After losing our target at her hideout and then receiving your call that she'd stowed away in your car, well, I think we were both a bit too . . . anxious, excited, and wanted to turn a failed mission into a successful one. My apologies that we got carried away in the heat of the moment."

Jack nodded. "It won't happen again, sir. Lesson learned."

They'd said all the right things. If they were Nichols, or Alice or any of the others, Kade would probably give them some advice on how to handle the nerves and stress that came with a tense mission. But he'd never met two men *less* likely to cave under pressure. Anxious? These two? He wasn't buying it.

Trying a different approach, he said, "Thought about getting a tattoo when I was younger." He smiled and gestured toward the snake on Dominic's arm. "But they would have kicked my butt out of the academy for something like that. I didn't know they'd relaxed those rules."

Dom exchanged another silent glance with Jack before answering.

"Got this the day I graduated. As a celebration."

"Ah, I see."

He was about to ask another question when the replacement Suburban pulled up in front of the house with a flatbed tow truck behind it. Warning beeps sounded as the truck shifted into reverse and began backing up the driveway. Kade glanced toward the nearest houses, worried that the noise would wake his neighbors. A block full of curious onlookers was the last thing they needed right now.

"Guess we should get our gear." Dominic urged Jack forward. They circled around Kade to grab the duffel bags piled next to the house.

In a few short minutes, all of the agents were settled in the replacement Suburban. They'd be taken to the usual rendezvous point and from there would transfer into their personal vehicles and go their separate ways. The sabotaged SUV had already been loaded onto the tow truck and was on its way back to town.

Kade stood in the open doorway behind the driver, exchanging a few last words with the team.

"What about your ride?" Nichols asked. "They're not bringing you another car?"

"Believe it or not, the bureau doesn't keep any backup Cadillacs on standby." He smiled. "No worries. They're rounding up some tires to bring out. The car will be ready by the time I need it."

He noticed that Dom and Jack were sitting in the very back, quietly watching him. He was tempted to yank them out and haul them into the house for a full interrogation. But he'd already decided the direct approach wouldn't work. They'd have a canned answer ready for anything he asked. He nodded at them, then looked at each of the others in turn—Alice, Cord, Nichols.

"You all worked hard tonight. Did a damn good job regardless of the outcome. You should be proud of yourselves." His words garnered a few weak smiles. "You may not feel that way right now. But I've been pushing you relentlessly for weeks, with precious little downtime. And you've still managed to capture ninety-nine percent of the targets I gave you, with no casualties. You've done better than agents with twice your experience could have done."

Okay, that was a stretch, a big stretch. But he was getting through to them now. The dejected looks had faded and been replaced with more genuine smiles.

"I want you to take some time off. Catch up on your sleep, visit your loved ones, go see a ball game. Live a little. I don't want to see your sorry faces again until Wednesday at the lazy hour of thirteen hundred—that's one p.m. for those of you who already forgot everything you learned at Quantico." He smiled to make sure they knew he was teasing. "That's four days off, men, and woman." He nodded at Alice. "When you get back, we'll plan the last leg of this mission and head into the homestretch."

A cheer went up from everyone . . . everyone *except* the two sitting in the very back.

Kade shut the door and rapped on the roof to let the driver know he was out of the way.

As soon as the Suburban disappeared from sight, he pressed down hard on his left thigh, kneading the cramping muscles. By the time he'd hobbled into the front room, another ten minutes had passed.

He eased into his desk chair and grabbed a bottle of Ibuprofen from the top drawer. After dry-swallowing six of them, he clicked on the computer monitor. He was exhausted, the physical strain on his leg taking a toll on his nerves. But he couldn't sleep. Not until he got the answers to a few glaring questions.

Like who Amber and Sebastian were, and whether they were dead or alive.

It didn't take long to find them in the EXIT database once he connected to the mainframe files. Both were Enforcers who'd been captured before Kade was brought in to take over the mission. So why did Bailey think they were dead?

He checked his watch. It was going on four in the morning. He seriously doubted that his boss, Faegan, would be up this late. But Faegan was an early riser. Kade could expect to hear from him in a few hours at most if he left him a message.

He tapped out an email asking his boss to call him as soon as he got up. He was just about to push himself to his feet when his cell phone rang. Sure enough, the caller ID revealed it was Faegan. Kade brought him up to speed about the evening's events.

"I'd like to go to the retraining facility," Kade said. "Today, if possible. After I get a few hours' sleep."

"The retraining facility? Why?"

"Bailey Stark seems to think that her friends— Amber Braithwaite and Sebastian Lachlan—were killed after a team took them into custody. I told her that's not how we operate, that Enforcers are being evaluated and retrained so they can re-enter society without being a threat to anyone, including themselves. I think if I can speak to her friends, maybe even snap their pictures on my cell phone, that when we catch up to her again I can reassure her that they're okay and she has nothing to fear from us. It could make the difference between a potentially violent takedown and an uneventful surrender."

Silence stretched out for a good half minute before Faegan responded. "I'm afraid I can't let you do that. It's your job to use your computer and investigative skills to track down where each Enforcer is hiding and then direct your teams to capture them. It's my job to take the Enforcers from your team and induct them into the retraining facility. And when they're deemed rehabilitated, another agent sets them up with a new identity or whatever is needed to ensure their success without the structure of EXIT guiding them anymore. No 'one man' can ever be allowed to have the power that Cyprian Cardenas had as CEO of EXIT. That's the whole point behind this separation of power and duties. Which is why I can't tell you where the retraining facility is located. You *know* that."

He did know that, and had never questioned the setup before. So what was he supposed to say, that he believed Bailey's claims over those of his own boss? Yeah, that would go over well. Especially since he had no corroborating evidence to back up anything she'd said. Not to mention, she'd done everything she could to mislead him. So why *should* he believe her about what may or may not have happened to her friends? She'd probably made up the story about the funerals to throw him off, hoping to distract him. He *had* been distracted. She *had* escaped.

"Can you give me an update on Sebastian and Amber? Have they been released back into society yet?"

"I'll have to check. I've noted their names to follow up. Anything else?"

"Yeah, I've given my team some time off to get their heads straight. I've been pushing them pretty hard. As soon as my other teams check in, I'll give them some time off, too."

"You think that what happened with Stark is because they need a break?"

"They're young, inexperienced. This is their third attempt to capture the same Enforcer, without success. A break can only do them good. Besides, I need more time to track her down again anyway. Might as well give all the teams some downtime. We'll hit it hard after that, wrap this up."

"All right. Keep me posted. The longer this mission drags on, the more we risk exposure. I don't think I need to remind you about the harm it would cause if the public finds out what EXIT really did, and that the government sanctioned most of their activities. Heads would roll—including yours now that you're part of damage control. Understood?"

Kade stiffened. Had Faegan just threatened him?

"Special Agent Quinn, is that understood?"

"Understood," he bit out. "Sir, I have some concerns about the performance of two of the agents you assigned to me—Dominic and Jack. I'd like you to provide me a background report—"

"I don't have time or patience for gripes. You knew when you took this assignment that you were getting greenhorns. That's what makes these missions work. It's all on a need-to-know basis. Feed them a few lies and they think they're a trusted part of an inner circle. They know just enough to make them eager and are so intent on making a good impression that they don't rock the boat, they don't demand more information. More seasoned agents would drastically increase the risk. They'd connect the dots, learn enough to become a liability. That's not what either of us wants. Now, unless there's something else that actually requires my attention, we're done. Are we done, Special Agent Quinn?"

"Yes, sir. We're done."

The line clicked.

Kade clenched his cell phone so hard he was surprised the case didn't shatter. Cursing, he pitched it onto the desk. Once again he found himself wondering how he'd gotten to this point. Twelve years of glowing reviews, coveted assignments, awards. He'd been the envy of agents twice his age. Hell, even his best friend had been jealous. Now he was reduced to taking orders more often than he gave them. Faegan hadn't even given him a chance to explain his reservations about Dominic and Jack.

He tapped his hand on his desk. Life would be so much easier if he let this go, if he could ignore the doubts that Bailey Stark had raised. Was he overthinking? Was he too tired and in too much pain to look at this logically?

Everything had seemed fine until he'd stared into those disturbingly bleak, incredibly beautiful green eyes, and listened to her accusations about what was *really* happening to the Enforcers his team captured. *Could* she be right? That would mean a conspiracy, that his boss was keeping the truth from him.

The way Kade kept the truth from *his* teams?

Feed them a few lies and they think they're a trusted part of an inner circle. They know just enough to make them eager and are so intent on making a good impression that they don't rock the boat, they don't demand more information.

He froze. Was that what *he* was doing? God knew he was desperate to make a good impression on Faegan. This assignment was make it or break it for him, his chance to turn his career around. Or destroy it once and for all. Were Bailey's accusations really that compelling? Or were they just an echo of the doubts that he'd had all along but had chosen to ignore?

That thought shook him to the core.

Whatever the reason for his doubts, he had to figure out what was fact and what was fiction. To do that, he needed more information. And he needed to get that information without doing anything that might raise a red flag—like performing searches in the FBI's databases for things his boss wouldn't want him to look into.

Kade was well aware that the so-called checks and balances that Faegan had mentioned extended to him as well, for good reason. He was on probation. He'd been given a short leash when his boss had grudgingly agreed to let him start a new assignment. What Kade needed was the help of someone not in the FBI, someone who *used* to be in the FBI and understood how they operated. A person who was now working for another alphabet agency. He needed to call Robert Gannon—his former best friend.

If he gave himself time to mull it over, or waited until a decent hour to make the call, he'd talk himself out of it. He extracted a wrinkled, yellowed business card from his wallet—a card that he'd been given only because he was standing with several other people at an FBI, Homeland Security business function. It would have looked impolite if the issuer *hadn't* handed him a card, too. Neither of them had ever expected that he'd actually use it.

Two minutes later, he was on the phone with his *former* best friend from high school, a friend whom he hadn't spoken to socially since a woman had come between them—over five years ago.

"Did hell suddenly freeze over?" the sleepy voice rasped on the other end of the line.

"Hey, Gannon. Sorry for the obscene hour. How's Kendall these days? I haven't spoken to our former boss's boss since you two left the bureau."

A cough, then the clearing of a throat. "Has the President been assassinated?"

"Not that I know of," Kade said.

"World War three started, someone blew up the Statue of Liberty? No, wait, you called to tell me you're a bastard and grovel for my forgiveness."

"Already did that and it didn't make a difference."

"Maybe you should try again. If nothing else, it'll give me something to chuckle over, right before I tell you to kiss my ass."

Kade blew out a deep breath. "You're not going to make this easy, are you?"

"Why should I?"

Kade clenched his fist on top of the desk. "I wouldn't have called if it wasn't urgent. I need your help."

This time, Gannon did chuckle. "The great Kade Quinn needs me? You really think I care?"

"You cared enough to convince Faegan to give me another chance."

"Yeah, well. That was different. You got sympathy votes for being in a freaking coma. It won't happen again."

He stared at the far wall, bile rising in his throat at the thought of what he was about to say. "*Please.*"

The silence lasted so long that he pulled the phone back to make sure the call hadn't been dropped. "Gannon?" No answer. "Robert? You still there?"

"Stick with Gannon, Quinn. We start using first

names after all this time and my world's going to tilt on its axis. Seriously, man. What the hell are you calling me for? Aside from the early hour, it's been five years. Give me one reason not to hang up right now."

"I think Faegan's passing off mercenaries as federal agents."

This time the pause lasted a full minute. "Start talking."

TEN MINUTES LATER, Kade shoved himself out of his chair. A few curses and some leg massages after that and he was able to stiffly hobble toward the archway.

Gannon had been more accommodating than expected. Kade had flat-out told him that he couldn't reveal any details about his current mission. But that didn't bother Gannon. He respected the need for secrecy. He'd simply listened to Kade talk about the inconsistencies with Dominic and Jack, and then he'd promised to call tomorrow afternoon, Monday at the latest, with a full background report.

Kade couldn't ask for better than that.

Just before leaving the room, he glanced down to look at the picture of Abby taped to the wall by the bookshelf, as he did every night.

But the picture was gone.

Chapter Seven

Saturday, 3:05 a.m.

Bailey kept her gun tucked behind the seat back as she studied the second car to zoom up behind the minivan since they'd left the Ghost's house. The first one had quickly passed them, without incident. This one would likely end up doing the same. Apparently, eighty miles an hour on a remote back road wasn't good enough for the people who lived around here. And what the heck were they doing out and about at this time of morning anyway?

Suddenly the car whipped around them, horn honking as the young driver gave them the finger. If her hands weren't cuffed together with a gun clasped between them, Bailey would have returned the favor. The kid couldn't be more than sixteen, seventeen at most. Where were his manners? What was the world coming to?

She shook her head and plopped down in the seat just as Atwell slowed the van.

"What are you doing?" Alarm spiked through her as he slowed even more and turned down a gravel road.

"This road isn't used much so I figured it would be a good place to pull over. You want those handcuffs off, right? Austin probably has an extra key around here somewhere. 'Always be prepared' seems to be his life's motto."

Bailey clutched the gun, her finger nervously twitching against the frame. Damn it, she never should have gotten into the van.

After rounding a curve in the gravel road that left the highway far behind, Jace parked on the shoulder. Only then did he bother to glance at her in the rearview mirror, his face a study of shadows, lit only by the dashboard lights. He flipped on the overhead light. Bailey tensed.

Atwell began to riffle through a bunch of papers in the glove box.

She relaxed, but only slightly. Was he really looking for handcuff keys, or was he looking for something else? If there was going to be trouble, she'd face him on equal terms, not cowering in the backseat of a grocery getter. She squeezed between the two captain's chairs and plopped down in the passenger seat beside him. The backpack he'd had on earlier was on the floorboard. She picked it up, more than a little curious at what was inside, and set it on the floor behind her seat.

"Who's Austin?" she asked, breaking the awkward silence as he dug through what appeared to be a stack of car maintenance receipts and a jumbled mound of cheap sunglasses. "Is he some Boy Scout type on your team?"

The corner of his mouth quirked in amusement. "He's one of Devlin Buchanan's brothers. And he's about the farthest thing from a Boy Scout that I could imagine. He calls me *Ass*well if that's any indication of his personality."

She liked this Austin guy already. Not that she planned on ever meeting him. Signing up with this group of yahoos calling themselves Equalizers wasn't on her radar and was the last thing she'd do. She'd been alone too long to know how to play nice with others, even if she wanted to.

He jangled a small ring of keys in triumph. "Bingo."

She propped her hands on the armrest, the pistol still clutched between them.

"Lose the gun, Bailey. I'm not going to unlock the cuffs while you aim that thing at me."

It was aimed at the dashboard. But she doubted he'd appreciate her pointing that out. She hesitated, not wanting to relinquish her only weapon again.

"If I'd wanted to kill you," he said, and leaned slightly toward her, his eyes narrowed, "I'd have left you outside with the sniper."

He was right. He could have just let those agents kill her. Still, it took all of her willpower to set the gun in the console and let it go.

"Angle your right wrist the other way."

She repositioned her hands. "You're from the Carolinas aren't you? Or Georgia? I can't quite place the accent."

He unlocked one of the cuffs and twisted her wrist to unlock the second one.

"I used to know an Enforcer based out of Georgia, Savannah I think," she continued. "Long time ago. Ramsey Tate. Haven't heard from him in a long time. Do you know him?"

The cuff clicked open, and he finally looked at her. "I *knew* him."

She blinked, her stomach knotting at the implication. "I'm sorry," she said, and she truly was. "I liked Ramsey. He was funny, had a wicked fascination with NASCAR."

Something dark flickered in his eyes. Remembered pain? He frowned and motioned toward her shorts before removing the handcuffs. "What's that hanging out of your pocket?"

She looked down at the paper she'd accidentally grabbed off the wall while fleeing from the Ghost. She'd forgotten all about it.

He stowed the keys in the glove box and clicked it shut. "Looks like a picture."

She pulled it out, held it up. "It's the Ghost and some woman. I haven't had a chance to look at it closely yet."

She took the time to do so now, peering down at the smiling couple. Was the pretty blonde woman his girlfriend, wife?

Lucky girl.

Not the wife part, of course. Bailey wouldn't trust someone enough to be tied to them for all eternity. But girlfriend? Hell, Bailey would take a man like him for *one night* if that's all she could get. She could totally see herself enjoying the Ghost, fitting her curves to his hard planes, smoothing her hands across all those glorious muscles as they bunched beneath her fingers. The man was buff, the type of guy who'd probably had women drooling all over him before whatever had caused those scars on his face and injured his leg. Bailey didn't mind the scars. They added character. They were the mark of experience, the brand of a survivor. Everyone had scars, whether you could see them or not.

She sighed and idly ran a finger across the glossy surface, as if she could feel his skin beneath hers if she only imagined it hard enough. Sadly, there were no incredible one-night stands looming in her future, not with the Ghost. He was her enemy. The next time she saw him she'd probably have to kill him. What a waste.

"Why do you call him a ghost?"

She glanced up sharply. Atwell was studying her with open curiosity. She lowered the picture. "Hawke didn't tell you our nickname for the guy who's heading up the search for the Enforcers?"

"Who's Hawke?"

Her mouth went as dry as a desert canyon after a long, hard drought—pretty much like most of Colorado before the recent downpour.

"Hawke is one of us, an Enforcer," she said haltingly. "Isn't he the person who contacted Buchanan to tell him that I needed help? I assumed Hawke had smuggled a tracker on my phone or something, and that's how you found me."

He was already shaking his head before she finished her question.

"I've never heard of anyone named Hawke. Maybe Devlin has." He shrugged. "I was never an Enforcer so there are a lot of them I don't know. The people I work with—Devlin Buchanan, Mason Hunt, others—we call ourselves Equalizers. The distinction helps us keep the good guys and bad guys straight." He grinned.

She stiffened. "And the Enforcers are the bad guys? Is that what you're saying?"

The grin faded. "With EXIT defunct, I suppose—in theory—that should make the remaining Enforcers and Equalizers allies. Don't you? I still don't understand why you call Quinn a ghost."

Her mind was still dissecting what he'd meant by "defunct, in theory" when his question pulled her up short. "Quinn? You know his real name?"

He gestured toward the photograph still clutched in her hand. "FBI Special Agent Kade Quinn, thirty-three years old, originally from northeast Florida, currently on assignment here in Colorado. Unfortunately, that about sums up what I know about him. For now. But I'm working on that." He cocked his head, studying the picture. "The woman doesn't look familiar. May I?" He held his hand out.

Not seeing a point in arguing, she passed the picture to him.

A bright light clicked on, flashing across the glossy surface. Atwell had pulled a small LED flashlight from his pocket, much like the one she carried with her—when she had her keys, which she didn't.

"How do you know him?" she asked. "For that matter, if you don't know Hawke, why were you even in that house tonight?"

His gaze rose to hers. "Maybe the question you should be asking, is why were *you* in that house tonight?"

"What? What are you talking about?"

He handed her back the picture. "While you and the other remaining Enforcers have been playing cat and mouse, mostly mouse, we Equalizers are working to bring everything to an end, once and for all. We want everything to do with EXIT Inc. to fade into history. But someone in the government seems intent on going after everyone who ever worked for the clandestine side of EXIT. Which means we aren't safe, none of us is safe, until we figure out who's behind this . . . hunt, or whatever it is.

"We figured out weeks ago that someone was rounding up Enforcers, and that their immediate boss, at least in this area, is Quinn. But we need more information, like who else is involved, how many more 'Quinns' are out there, and who's giving them orders. We need to figure out how high this thing goes, and how to stop it."

He flicked off the LED light and pitched it into the console beside the gun. "Lucky for you, I was following Quinn tonight, gathering intel." He motioned toward the backpack in the floor. "I realized you were in trouble and stepped in to help. You can thank me anytime."

"Thank you." She shoved the picture into her pocket.

"You're welcome." He grinned.

She studied his eyes, the relaxed, friendly expression on his face, his smile. And then she glanced out the windshield. It was still dark, dawn a few hours away. And they were parked in an isolated location, with thick woods pressing in on them, no cars passing by. She'd known him for all of an hour, give or take. Did she really want to gamble her life that he didn't mean her harm?

Her gaze fell to the gun just inches away in the console. She lunged for it. The pistol was snatched away before she could even reach it. Atwell made a show of holstering the gun and snapping the safety strap over the top of it.

Bracing one arm on the back of his seat, the other on the steering wheel, he effectively caged her in with her back to the passenger door. Her whole body flashed hot and cold. Was this it? Was he going to try to kill her now?

"Go for my gun again and that's the last thing you'll ever do, Bailey. I promise you that." His lethal tone left no doubt that he meant every word. But if he was hoping to intimidate her, he was going about it all wrong. He was just pissing her off.

"I wouldn't have shot you," she said.

"You're right. You wouldn't have."

His arrogant confidence made her bristle with irritation. "I'm sorry." She forced the apology through clenched teeth. "I shouldn't have tried to take your gun."

"No. You shouldn't have. Why did you?"

She frowned, genuinely surprised at his question. "Like you wouldn't have done the same thing? You've parked us in the middle of nowhere and spouted off about Equalizers and Enforcers being on the same side *in theory*, implying that the opposite is true, that we're enemies. You somehow know my name even though we've never met. And you just happened to follow the Ghost tonight, of all nights, when I was cornered and needed help. Given all that, I think I have the right to be suspicious and proactive about my personal safety."

His eyes had widened with each sentence, probably because she'd spoken faster and faster and was practically shouting by the time she'd finished. Heat flushed her cheeks, which had already been hot with anger. Now they were positively burning. Thank goodness the light wasn't bright enough for him to notice.

"Your face is almost as red as your hair."

She grabbed the door handle.

Strong fingers encircled her wrist, yanking her hand back. And just like that, she was a prisoner, just as surely as if she were still wearing the handcuffs.

"What do you want from me?" she snapped.

"I want you to listen. I didn't have to rescue you tonight. But you're right, my being there wasn't a coincidence. I've been following Quinn and his men for weeks, scouting things out, passing information back to my team. It's called surveillance. So, yeah, I've seen you a few times—this wasn't the first night Quinn's men tried to capture you. I've taken pictures, sent them to Devlin. He knows every Enforcer who ever worked for EXIT Inc., at least while he was there. And he told me your name."

He started to turn away, then seemed to change his mind. "Oh, and the answer to your question is, no, I *wouldn't* have done the same thing. I wouldn't pull a gun on a man who'd risked his life to save mine. I'd give him the benefit of the doubt, *talk* to him, especially since we're both fighting the same enemy. If you're going to survive, you need to start being nice and making friends. Otherwise those mercenaries will catch you and you'll disappear just like everyone else seems to be doing."

She'd been on the verge of another apology. But something he'd said caught her attention. It was the second time tonight he'd said something similar, and mirrored her own concerns.

"What do you mean, mercenaries?" she asked. "You said Kade Quinn is an FBI agent. His team wears FBI flak jackets. Are you saying his men aren't FBI, that they're hired guns?"

"It wouldn't be the first time the government

hired assassins to do its dirty work." He cocked a brow.

The insult launched, and hit its target.

Because he had a point.

What was an Enforcer if not a hired gun when it came down to it?

Did that make her a mercenary? The idea put a sour taste in her mouth. Mercenaries had no loyalty to anything but money. And although working for EXIT had certainly been profitable, extremely profitable, that wasn't what had driven her over the years. Okay, to be honest, she'd become an Enforcer to save her own hide. But it hadn't taken long for her to realize the opportunity that had been given to her.

The money was great, but it wasn't about the money. What drove her was her belief that the innocent should be protected and that it didn't make sense to wait until *after* a mass murder to stop the person who was about to commit it.

Working for the government, even indirectly as she had at EXIT, had been a bitter pill to swallow for a woman who'd devoted her younger years to fighting "the man." But it had been a way to continue her fight against injustice, without ending up in a Ruby Ridge standoff or burned to a crisp like Koresh's nutty followers in Waco. Did that make her a mercenary? She'd never thought of herself that way before.

And she didn't like it.

She gave another hard tug on the wrist he was still holding. "You obviously don't hold people like me in high esteem. I'm surprised you didn't leave me with Quinn to die. Why *did* you help me?"

He studied her for a full minute. Then he sighed heavily and let her go. Her sudden freedom surprised her enough to make her hesitate, then she popped the door handle.

"Wait."

She hesitated, the door open.

"We have a common enemy," he said. "There's no reason we can't become allies and pool our resources. Devlin told me he tried to recruit you once but you turned him down. I'm giving you a second chance to join the Equalizers, to have an entire team with considerable resources at your back. Together we can plan a way to stop Quinn and whoever's calling the shots above him."

"Seems like the world's just full of second chances tonight." She tilted her chin defiantly. "Not interested. I already have a whole team at my back. They're called Enforcers."

He made a show of looking around. "Really? Because I don't see them anywhere. And I didn't see them earlier either. You know, when you almost got shot."

She hopped out of the car.

"Bailey."

"What?" she demanded, ready to slam the door shut.

His jaw worked, like he was struggling with some kind of inner demons before he replied. "At least let me drop you off somewhere. I assume you've got cars and go bags stashed all around the city, right? That's what most Enforcers do. Hell, it's what the Equalizers do, too, even though we're a team. We're all self-sufficient, like you. We plan for the worst. But this fight we're both fighting is easier, and safer, in numbers. I'll tell you all about the Equalizers and what we're doing, if you want to listen. But at least let me take you to one of those stashes so you're not stranded in the middle of the woods."

She eyed him warily, considering her options. She'd made a point of noting the Ghost's—Quinn's—street and house number as Atwell drove them out of the neighborhood. But a street name by itself was useless when she'd never heard of the street before.

Her phone had a map app that should help her find her way back to civilization. But it wasn't like she'd had a chance to charge it when she'd gone to bed. The thing was probably dead by now, or would be soon. Life was definitely dealing her some sour lemons right now. And she'd never been the type to make lemonade.

But this man could. At the very least, she could use him as her taxi. But it was difficult to trust someone when you weren't on a level playing field. Her gaze fell to the gun holstered on his hip.

"Would it make you feel more secure if I gave you a gun?" he asked.

Her gaze whipped to his. "You offering?"

In answer, he pulled a Cobra Derringer .38 special from a strap on his ankle. It was a small gun, which made it ideal for hiding. Normally Bailey wouldn't even consider carrying the Cobra. The trigger pull weight was horrendously heavy for someone her size, which made aiming difficult at best. But she wasn't about to turn up her nose at his generous offer. A gun of any kind was better than nothing.

When he held the Derringer out to her, she leaned in and snatched it out of his palm, fearing a trick. When he didn't draw his 9mm or try to grab her, she checked the Derringer. Fully loaded.

"What's your game?"

He shook his head. "You don't trust anyone, do you?"

"You make it sound tragic," she scoffed. "But if you'd lived the life I have, believe me, you'd have learned long ago that trust is precious and should rarely be given."

He cocked his head. "Care to share? I'm a good listener."

"I've never been good at sharing."

"Fair enough. I won't pry. You coming or not?"

She shoved the Derringer into the pocket of her shorts then hopped into the passenger seat.

"Where to?" he asked, as he started the engine.

"That depends." She pulled the door closed. "Where are we?"

"About twenty minutes southwest of Boulder."

"Closer to Windermere or Arapahoe?"

"Definitely Windermere."

"There's a self-storage facility a couple of side streets over from Windermere."

"I know the place."

He did a U-turn, then headed back toward the main road. Half an hour later he pulled to a stop in front of the storage unit she'd directed him to.

"Want me to wait?" he asked as she hopped out of the van.

She shook her head. "No need. I'll be fine. Atwell? I mean, Jace?"

He smiled approvingly at her use of his first name. "Bailey?"

"Thank you. I mean it. You saved my bacon. I owe you one."

He gave her a jaunty salute.

She stepped back and waited until the minivan

turned the corner out of sight. Then she jogged two aisles over to her real storage unit and entered the combination into the lock hanging on the door.

After a quick look around, she pulled the door open and hurried inside. It was a five-by-five unit with a single lightbulb illuminating it from over-head. If anyone else had seen inside, they'd probably be puzzled to see a lone wooden chair sitting in the middle and nothing else.

She picked up the chair and carried it to the back of the unit. After climbing on top of the chair, she stood and ran her fingers along one of the metal beams that supported the corrugated ceiling. The set of keys she kept duct-taped to the beam was still there. The tape made a ripping sound as she yanked the keys free.

A few minutes later she was at another storage facility a few blocks down from the first one. But this one was for boats, RVs, and a few cars—like her rather plain-looking sky-blue Buick that no self-respecting car thief would look at twice. Which was exactly why she'd bought it.

The engine, transmission, and pretty much ev-erything else mechanical had been replaced, while the exterior had suffered more than its share of dings and scrapes—courtesy of a ballpeen hammer she'd taken to it.

A pocketknife and bleach had worked wonders on the car's interior, giving it a sad, worn appear-ance. But the Buick's true beauty was the storage area she'd custom-built herself.

After sliding behind the steering wheel and lock-ing the doors, she pressed a hidden lever on the front of the passenger seat and flipped open the bottom cushion. A go bag, complete with cash, clothing, toiletries, a phone charger, and—hallelujah—decent guns and ammo.

She unloaded Jace's Cobra Derringer and dropped it into her bag, then shoved her own back-up weapon of choice into her ankle holster, a Bersa .380. Her favored primary gun, a Sig Sauer 9mm pistol, stayed in the bag for now. Once she stopped somewhere to freshen up and change into jeans, she'd be able to hide the Sig in her front pocket and wear a blouse hanging slightly over it to conceal it.

With the engine idling, and the air conditioner pumping out blessedly cool air, she plugged the charger in and connected it to her phone. As soon as the screen lit up, she called Hawke. One ring. Two. Three. Her fingers curled around the phone.

Come on, Hawke. Answer the phone.

He didn't. The call went to voice mail. She didn't bother to leave a message.

She let her hand fall to her lap. The three musketeers—that's what she'd called Hawke, Sebastian, and Amber. Where most Enforcers, including herself, tended to keep to themselves, those three were together every chance they got. And when Bailey had been assigned a mission with Hawke as a partner, he'd introduced her to them. In spite of her preference to remain a loner, they'd managed to wiggle under her defenses and draw her into their circle. And now they were gone. Just like everyone else in her life.

No, Hawke wasn't dead. She couldn't accept that. She and some Enforcers that she communicated with online had shared bits and pieces they'd each heard about the FBI's—or whoever's—hunt for Enforcers. And the picture those pieces painted was that most of the captured Enforcers weren't executed right away. They were held prisoner, perhaps interrogated, moved from place to place before disappearing altogether. So there was a chance, however small, that Hawke—if he'd indeed been captured and wasn't still on the run—had been locked up somewhere. Which meant, she still had a chance to save him. But where was he?

To find out, she'd have to follow the clues, starting with where he'd been holed up when the team had come for him—Colorado Springs. Hopefully he'd left her some bread crumbs to follow.

After putting the car in drive, she hesitated. Following bread crumbs could take a lot of time. Hawke might not have that much left. There had to be a better way, a faster way to find him. She straightened. All she had to do was go to the source, the man who'd ordered Hawke taken in the first place. He had to know where Hawke was.

She shoved the accelerator to the floor and rocketed down the road—the road that would lead her back to the Ghost.

Chapter Eight

Saturday, 11:53 a.m.

Kade had a new plan, one that didn't involve sitting around waiting for reports from his teams. Or taking orders from Faegan. Or even waiting for Gannon's feedback about Dominic and Jack.

He was going to find Bailey Stark, on his own.

And this time, he wasn't turning her over to someone else, not at first anyway. He was going to sit her down and have a real conversation. Maybe together they could figure out what, if anything, was going on. And if he determined that everything was on the up-and-up, then he'd lead his team straight to her.

He tossed his go bag into the nearly nonexistent backseat of the Mustang GT that the bureau had dropped off a little while ago, at his request, in exchange for the mistreated Caddy. Sacrificing comfort for maneuverability and horsepower would ensure he could make a fast getaway if he got into a tight spot.

Plus, it would be really cool to drive a muscle car once again. It had been a long time.

Straightening, he scanned the street in front of his

house. The only two cars parked nearby belonged to his neighbors and had been there since yesterday. As far as he could tell, he was alone. No one was watching him. Unless they were parked a good distance away and were using binoculars.

He glanced up at the sky. It was almost noon, the sun high and bright against a deep blue canvas, not a rain cloud in sight. Already he could feel a trickle of sweat between his shoulder blades. It was going to be a hot one. Maybe he should have headed out earlier, before the summer heat began to take hold. But the sleep had done him good. He'd also spent some time planning his next steps, and trying to figure out where Bailey would go to ground, what she'd do next.

Everything was packed. The computer's hard drive had been scuttled, even though some techs would come by later today to ensure that no one could pull any data from it. They'd remove all of the electronics before releasing the house to the landlord. Standard protocol. The location had been compromised. He had to establish a new base of operations and let his teams know. He wouldn't want them showing up later in the week wondering where he was. But that could wait.

The ache in his hip and thigh was, thankfully, almost nonexistent today. That was the way it went—some days were hell, others he barely felt a twinge of pain. But even though today seemed like it was going to be a good one, he was wearing the leg brace that he'd worn home from the hospital. Its hard plastic surface would protect him from any wayward kicks. Plus, he'd rigged the brace as another tool to help him, if he needed it.

It all depended on whether his plan came together as expected.

In spite of all that, he still debated removing the brace. The thing was hot and damned uncomfortable. But the black-and-blue bruises he'd noticed while showering had him worried. Blood flow was already compromised in the damaged muscle. Another whack, even accidental, might force him to go to a hospital. That wasn't something he had time for right now.

So the brace stayed on.

After one last look up and down the street, he slid behind the steering wheel of the Mustang and backed out of the driveway. Forty-five minutes later, he rented a room at a cheap motel north of the city. Then he pulled into a parking space around back. He reached for the door handle, then froze.

The muzzle of a Sig Sauer nine-millimeter pistol stared at him through the window. And the person holding it was Bailey Stark.

Let the games begin.

She motioned for him to roll down the window and he briefly considered going for the gun holstered on his right hip.

"Try anything and you're dead." Her voice was muffled through the glass, her intentions clear.

He rolled down the window.

"Hand me your gun," she said. "Butt first. Very carefully."

He did as she asked. She tucked his PPK into a leather bag that hung from a strap that went diagonally across her body from shoulder to hip.

"Other gun, too," she said, the muzzle of her pistol unwavering.

"What other gun?"

"Everyone wears a backup. And this nine-millimeter isn't just for show."

He held his hands up in a placating gesture. "All right. It's strapped to my ankle. Hang on."

He slipped his Hellcat .380 out of his ankle holster and handed it out the window.

It disappeared into her bag.

"Get out."

The parking lot was full of cars. But in this heat, at this hour, people were either relaxing at the pool or holed up inside having lunch. Bailey had planned her approach the same way he would have. She'd also stepped out of reach of the door, eliminating the possibility of him slamming it against her to knock her down. She wasn't a fool. She'd been doing this kind of work for a long time.

But so had he.

He popped open the door. Then he stood, holding his hands out from his body.

"I don't have any more weapons on me," he assured her.

"Prove it."

He went through the motions of turning his pockets inside out, lifting the legs of his jeans to show that he didn't have another gun or knife hidden anywhere. He even lifted up his shirt to show her nothing was concealed underneath it, front or back.

Then he slowly moved his hands to the top snap of his jeans.

Her gaze flew to his. "What are you doing?"

"Proving that I'm not hiding any other weapons." He flipped the snap open, moved his fingers to the zipper.

She suddenly laughed, her green eyes twinkling, her entire face transformed into an expression of delight. "Well played," she said, laughing again. "You're trying to fluster me. News flash, honey. I don't fluster."

News flash. She'd just flustered him. Serious Bailey tugged at his heart, made him want to help and protect her. This Bailey, looking so happy and carefree, and incredibly beautiful, sent his pulse rushing in his ears.

And everywhere else.

He shrugged and snapped his jeans closed while he still could. "It was worth a try."

"A for effort." Her smile faded, once again replaced by the somber, serious expression he was used to. She gestured with her Sig Sauer. "Car keys."

"You're taking my car?" He glanced around the parking lot. No sign of the beat-up Camaro she'd driven yesterday. "How did you get here? How did you follow me without me knowing?"

She batted her long lashes. "Flirty *and* chatty. It's my lucky day. Keys. Now."

He leaned through the open window and took the keys out of the ignition. His duffel bag, with a Glock 17 in the outside pocket, was in the backseat. But it was too far away for him to reach. And he sure as hell didn't want to risk her shooting him in the backside if he dove for the thing. He straightened and held the keys out to her, ready to grab her the second she got too close.

"Toss them on the ground."

Damn.

He pitched the keys about three feet away. But she didn't fall for that trick either. She made him back well out of lunging zone before she picked them up, all without looking away from him or lowering her gun.

"Get back in the car. Driver's seat."

He frowned. "What's the endgame here? What do you want?"

"I want you to do exactly what I say. Get in the car."

He slid into the driver's seat.

She kicked the door shut and then slowly walked backward, keeping her pistol trained on him. She backed around the front of the car to the passenger side. After pitching her bag into the back with his, she hopped in.

"One move toward me," she warned, "and I pull the trigger."

"It's hot in here. Give me the keys and I'll turn on the air."

She dropped the keys onto the seat next to her thigh. "Not yet. Where's Hawke?"

Ah, hell.

If she was looking for her fellow Enforcer, she wasn't going to be happy with anything he told her.

"Hawke?" He frowned as if trying to place the name.

"Strike one. When I get to three, I pull the trigger. Where is he?"

Was she bluffing? He studied her, the way her hand remained steady as it held the gun. He watched her breathe slowly in and out, her generous breasts rising and falling with each respiration. A bead of sweat slid down the side of his face. He was definitely getting overheated. And Bailey Stark was as cool as a summer salad.

She wasn't bluffing.

"You mean Hawke Jacobs, another Enforcer?"

He pretended to have just made the connection. Because, yeah, there were so many men named Hawke running around. It was easy to confuse them.

"Give the man a prize. Where is he?"

"If my team has completed their mission, he's resting comfortably at the retraining facility I mentioned to you last night."

An intake of breath was the only sign that she'd heard him, but it was enough. Whoever Hawke was to her, he mattered. She was risking everything to find him.

"Take me there," she ordered.

"I can't. I don't know where it is."

The pistol wobbled.

Kade swallowed, hard.

"You expect me to believe that?" she asked.

"It's the truth. I asked my boss about the facility last night. He wouldn't tell me where it is, for security reasons. But I asked him about your friends, Sebastian and Amber. He's going to get their status so I could let you know how they're doing if I saw you again."

Her lips curled like a feral animal. "Did you miss the part last night when I told you I went to their funerals? I saw Sebastian die. One of your men slaughtered him."

Everything about her posture, her tone, told him she was telling the truth, or at least, what she believed to be the truth. But he couldn't accept that she was right. If she was, then everything he believed was wrong.

"None of the Enforcers have been killed," he assured her, hoping he was right. He *had* to be right.

"Strike two."

"I'm not lying," he said. "It's what I believe. I would never have taken this mission if part of it was to murder people. That's not who I am."

Confusion crinkled her brow. "You really believe that, don't you? You think you're the good guy here? And that I'm the bad guy?"

He wouldn't touch those questions if his life depended on it. And he was pretty sure it did.

"We were in a house together," she said. "Sebastian and me. A team of men dressed all in black ambushed us. You know, the ones with those big white letters on the backs of their flak jackets, the ones that spell out FBI?"

Refusing to take the bait, he waited in silence.

"I escaped. I was running from the house and looked back in time to see one of the men put a gun to Sebastian's head and fire."

Careful to hide his shock, he asked, "Was it dark?"

She blinked. "Dark?"

"When you saw Sebastian get shot. Was it at night or during the day?"

"At night, of course. Your men always attack at night, don't they? To reduce the chance of there being any witnesses? And so you can catch us when we're asleep?"

"They weren't my men, Bailey. I wasn't working this mission when Sebastian and Amber were captured."

"You mean killed."

He sighed. "How far away were you when you supposedly saw Sebastian get shot?"

"Supposedly? What the—"

"Bailey, I'm just trying to figure out the disconnect here. Please. How far away were you?"

She shook her head. "I don't know. Fifty, sixty yards. I ran from the house to the tree line, then turned around, and *boom*." She frowned. "Actually, I didn't hear a gunshot. But the shooter probably had a suppressor so the neighbors wouldn't hear it."

"Our teams don't use suppressors."

"It wasn't your team, though, right?" She smirked.

He nodded, conceding the point. He couldn't speak for how things had been run before he'd taken the job. But the FBI wasn't in the business of buying silencers for their weapons.

"I saw him point the gun at Sebastian and then Sebastian fell to the ground. The gunshot probably made a sound and I was too shocked to register it. Doesn't change anything."

"He could have fallen down because he was unconscious," Kade argued. "One of the men could have used a tranquilizer gun. That's one of our tools of the trade. Or he could have Tased him."

"There was no Taser. Sebastian didn't move, at all, after he hit the ground. And tranks take a few seconds, even if they're really strong. He was out." She snapped the fingers on her left hand. "Like that."

"Okay. So instead of someone tranquilizing him right then, maybe they got him a few seconds before he ran outside. The meds took effect and he dropped to the ground, unconscious, not dead."

"Are you even listening to me? I went to his funeral. And Amber's." She swiped her left hand across her forehead. The heat was starting to affect her, too. She was getting agitated, which was the last thing he wanted when she was holding a gun on him.

He gestured toward the keys lying on the seat by

her drawn-up knee. "I can turn the air conditioner on and—"

"Not yet. I'm still waiting for you to admit that your men killed my friends."

"They weren't my—"

"They weren't your men, yeah, yeah. Whatever. I want to hear you admit that the *FBI's* men killed my friends. Say it."

It was a trap and they both knew it. If he said they didn't, she'd call strike three and he'd be dead. If he said they did, same outcome.

"Who set up the funerals?" he asked, keeping his tone calm, reasonable. "Did you see the bodies?"

Her mouth tightened into a hard line, giving him the answer that he'd expected. She and her friends wouldn't have stuck around to gather bodies for funerals. If they had, they'd have been captured, too. They'd probably held memorial services, no burial.

"What makes you so sure the men you saw were really FBI agents?"

"The letters FBI on flak jackets was a pretty big clue."

He ignored her quip. He was grasping, and he knew it. But he wasn't giving up without a fight. "Maybe Sebastian made some powerful enemies, assassinated the wrong person."

"Right," she said slowly, as if she thought he was mental. "So the FBI is sending teams after Enforcers and nicely taking them into custody while FBI-imposters are doing the exact same thing, going after Enforcers, except that they're killing the ones they catch. That's what you're saying. Does that sound remotely possible to you?"

Not even a little bit.

He sighed. That brilliant plan he'd come up with earlier today didn't seem quite so brilliant now. He had a thick file on Bailey, had read it front to back numerous times. And he'd bet his life that he knew her well enough to predict that she'd have snuck back into his driveway early this morning and would have put a tracker on his car. Or at the very least, that she'd have hung back somewhere close and tailed him to the motel.

Yay him. He'd been right about that part.

Too bad he'd been wrong about the next part, in thinking he could manipulate her and neutralize her as a threat, then talk through everything as if they weren't on opposite sides. Turns out, knowing someone on paper was nothing like knowing them in person. He didn't have a clue what she was going to do next.

"What about your other friend, Amber?" He was operating without a playbook now, not sure where to direct the conversation. But at least she was talking and not shooting. Yet. "You saw Amber die, too, or think you did?"

"No," she whispered. "She died alone."

The pain in her gaze nearly stole his breath. And just like that he was wishing he could pull her close, hold her, chase those damn shadows from her eyes.

Stupid. He was so stupid. She wouldn't want him to hold her. She'd put a bullet in him before that ever happened.

"Then how do you know that she's dead," he whispered back.

"I just do. I haven't heard from her. Neither has Hawke. And we heard rumors there was a shoot-out with FBI agents who came to capture her. So we held a memorial, a funeral."

He held out his hands in a placating gesture. "I haven't heard anything to make me believe that your friends are dead. My boss never reported any casualties from before I took over. And I assure you that my men have orders to bring Enforcers in alive, unharmed, and that we pass them off to another set of agents to take them to the retraining facility. Once they're deemed not a threat, they're set up with new lives—like a witness protection program. That's it. Period. No killing. What would be the point?"

"To protect whoever in the government worked with Cyprian Cardenas, the EXIT Inc. CEO, to establish the Enforcer program in the first place. Or maybe to protect whoever tried to cover it up when the program went off the rails and some Enforcers killed some innocent people," she said, her voice firm again. "Those kinds of revelations would be career killers, to say the least. I'm guessing this goes pretty high up, to someone with political aspirations who's afraid that one of the Enforcers will eventually leak information about what they used to do. Someone is shutting us up. The only question is who?"

For the first time since she'd pointed the gun at him, she moved her finger from the frame to the trigger. She was going to shoot him. And he couldn't do a damn thing about it.

"Tell me where Hawke is. I want an address."

He slowly shook his head, wondering if that was the last thing he'd ever do. "I don't have that information. Everything is on a need-to-know basis."

"Trust me," she gritted out. "You need to know."

He stared at the dark barrel of the gun. Was this it then? Would he die with all of these unanswered questions floating around in his mind? Not just about the Enforcers, and Faegan, but about *everything*.

A year ago he'd married a beautiful woman. Two months later she was dead and he was in a coma. *He'd freaking gotten married*, and he could barely even remember the ceremony—at a Justice of the Peace of all things. His memories of his wife were just fuzzy fragments, impressions, blurry images, like little vignettes. It was obscene to have supposedly loved someone and barely remember her. And yet, here he sat, his would-be killer pointing a loaded gun at his head, an assassin for God's sake, who was anathema to everything he believed in. And he still wanted to pull her into his arms and kiss her.

That was worse than anything else. At a time like this, his life should be flashing before his eyes. He should be devastated by grief over the loss of his wife.

But he wasn't.

Instead, his last moments on earth were spent desiring a stranger. He craved the feel of her sweat-slicked skin against his like a drunk craved his next drink. He fantasized about ripping off her clothes and sliding his tongue across every inch of her just to see the passion cloud over in her moss-green eyes. He wanted, needed, to hear his name on her tongue as he drove into her and made her come apart all around him. How could he feel all those things for *this* woman, when he should be repulsed by her on principle alone? In what world did that make sense? In what universe did *any* of this make sense?

He started to laugh.

Bailey's eyes widened, which only made him laugh more. He laughed so hard that tears rolled down his cheeks. He laughed until he got a stitch in his side and was gasping for breath. And all that time, Bailey stared at him as if he'd lost his mind.

Maybe he had.

He wiped the tears away, chuckled, drew several deep breaths. He waved at the gun. "Go ahead. Strike three and all of that. Get it over with."

"You're insane."

"Now on that we agree." He swiped the keys from her seat.

"Hey, hey," she called out.

"Hey yourself. It's a damn oven in here." He shoved the keys in the ignition and started the engine. The air conditioner emitted a blast of hot air, then turned blissfully, icy cold. He aimed one of the vents directly at his face and practically melted against the door. "Thank God."

He closed his eyes. The A/C continued to pump out cold air. A minute ticked by, maybe two.

"Just tell me one thing," Bailey said.

"What?" He didn't open his eyes.

"If your boss admitted that his men were killing people instead of 'debriefing' them at that training facility, what would you do?"

He slowly opened his eyes, the urge to laugh evaporating like the sweat on his skin.

"If someone was purposely killed, as opposed to an accident, I'd do everything in my power to halt the program, to stop whoever was behind the killing, and bring them to justice."

She slowly lowered the gun, but kept her finger on the trigger.

"And Hawke?" she asked quietly. "I was on the phone with him last night. A team was after him. I haven't been able to reach him since."

"Their last check-in was this morning. They haven't caught him yet but expect to soon. Until then, they'll maintain radio silence."

"Call them. Tell them to abort the mission."

"No. I won't disturb them in the middle of an assignment. It's too dangerous."

"You're in danger. They might as well be, too."

He considered her request, then shook his head. "No. I won't put my men in danger. If the phone rang, it could distract them, get them shot if they're in a standoff. Since I'm the only one who has the team lead's number, he keeps the ringer on, knowing I would only call in an emergency. But it's set up not to make a sound or even vibrate for a text message. I could send him a text. As soon as it's safe, he'll check his messages, and get back to me. Fair enough?"

She hesitated, then nodded. "Fair enough. As long as I get to approve your text before you send it."

He punched in the message, telling Simmons that if Hawke had gotten away and they were still pursuing him, that he should abort the mission. Then he held the phone up for Bailey to read. When she nodded again, he pressed send, then put the phone away.

She looked tired, weary. Had she slept last night? Probably not if she was watching his house all morning. Regardless of how tired she might be, the determined set of her jaw told him she was going to see this through to the end, whatever that end might be. And somewhere in that befuddled space between his ears, along with the rest of his traitorous body, he was silently cheering her on.

Yep. He'd lost his mind. No doubt about it.

Using her free hand, Bailey put on her seat belt and clicked it into place.

"Drive," she ordered.

He shifted in his seat to face the front and reached for his seat belt.

"No. No seat belt."

He couldn't help but smile. Without a seat belt, he couldn't risk the old trick of unclicking *her* belt and slamming the brakes once they were traveling at a high rate of speed. A woman as cunning as Bailey could go far in the FBI. Too bad she'd wasted her considerable talents on a life of crime.

Noting that she'd finally moved her finger off the trigger, he let out a small breath of relief. Without waiting for her next order, he backed out of the parking space and drove toward the front of the lot. "Where to?"

"I-25 South."

Soon they were on the interstate.

"Where are we going?" he asked.

"Colorado Springs. We're going to find Hawke."

Chapter Nine

Saturday, 2:51 p.m.

She should have taken a nap.

Bailey squinted against the bright afternoon sunlight slanting through the Mustang's windshield as Kade drove them down the interstate. She was having trouble keeping her eyes open because of the glare. Well, that and she hadn't slept since Thursday night, which meant she'd been up for about forty hours, give or take.

Her right wrist ached from holding the gun, even though it was propped against her thigh. Curling up on the seat for a nap sounded like heaven. But she didn't dare let down her guard.

She did, however, turn the bore of the pistol slightly to Kade's right and kept her finger off the trigger. After all, she didn't want to accidentally shoot him if the car went over a bump. And pointing it at him the whole time somehow seemed . . . rude.

Settling back against the seat, she checked to make sure he wasn't watching, then allowed herself the luxury of closing her eyes for one, glorious, restful second.

"We're in Colorado Springs," Kade announced.

Bailey jerked upright, blinking her eyes. "What?"

"We've reached the city limits."

She blinked again. They were in Colorado Springs already? She'd *just* closed her eyes. Could she have dozed off? She jerked her gun hand up, then slumped with relief to see that she was still holding her Sig Sauer 9mm.

She covered her mouth to conceal a yawn. She *really* needed some caffeine. Maybe they should go through a fast food drive-thru and grab a supersized soda. Or a Red Bull. The last caffeinated drink she'd had was shortly before dawn when she'd taken her go bag into a convenience-store bathroom to change her clothes and brush her teeth. The soda and stale muffin she'd bought on her way out weren't doing a thing for her now.

"We've reached the city limits," he said again.

"I heard you the first time," she grumbled, rubbing her bleary eyes.

"You snore, by the way."

She gasped. "I do not."

He didn't argue. "Where to now?"

She narrowed her eyes. Something wasn't right about what he'd said. And if she wasn't so darn sleepy, she'd know what it was.

"No texts about Hawke from your men yet?" she asked.

He yanked his cell phone out of its holder and held it out to her.

"You check it. I'm not about to let you distract me." She yawned again.

He put the phone away.

"What are you doing?"

"I don't text and drive. It's dangerous."

She waited for the punch line. It didn't come. "What are you, an altar boy? Give me the phone."

He handed it over. "I was raised Baptist. We didn't have altar boys."

She rolled her eyes and balanced the phone on her knee. Keeping the gun in her right hand, she worked the phone with her left. It was awkward, but not impossible. "It's locked. What's your password?"

He told her and a few seconds later the image of Kade and a blonde woman stared up at her from the phone's background. It was just like the photograph in her pocket.

"Who is she? The woman in the picture with you?"

His knuckles whitened on the steering wheel. "I want the photo back that you stole from my house."

"I didn't steal it. I . . . accidentally took it."

"Well that's a new one," he drew out in an exaggerated drawl.

"It's true. Tell me who she is and you can have it back."

"Let me guess. You're *accidentally* blackmailing me?"

"Oh, for Pete's sake." She pulled the picture out of her jeans pocket, grimacing when she saw the wrinkles in it. "I hope you have another copy. It's a bit . . . bent." She set it in the console.

He glanced down. His jaw tightened.

"I really am sorry," she said.

He gave her a curt nod.

Did that mean he forgave her?

Did it matter?

She puzzled over that, then decided it did. She didn't want to hurt him. Contrary to what he probably thought about her, hurting *anyone* was always her last resort. And, yes, she and Kade were enemies. But that was business, two professionals on opposite sides of a high-stakes war. Damaging a picture that obviously held sentimental value for him crossed into personal territory. And she deeply regretted it. She really should have been more careful.

If their roles were reversed, she'd have yelled and cursed at him. Her father used to tease her about her temper when she was a little girl, saying God gave her fiery red hair to warn those around her to beware. But Kade never seemed to lose his cool, even when he was upset. She couldn't seem to predict what he was going to do next. And that made her nervous.

She turned her attention to his phone. But there weren't any recent text messages.

"What's the next road I should take?" he asked.

She told him as she idly scrolled through his older messages. Yeah, she was being nosey. But she was the one with the gun.

There were exchanges between him and various team leads, going back for weeks. He gave his men advice, information on their targets, and without fail reminded them over and over that if things got dicey, their orders were to pull back and abort the mission. The safety of his men, *and the Enforcers they were going after*, seemed equally important to him. Once again, not what she would have expected. He was an interesting man, intriguing, in more ways than one.

Careful not to be obvious, she studied him from beneath her lashes. To say he was her type was a no-brainer—he was any woman with a heartbeat's type. Tall, broad-shouldered, narrow-waisted, with well-defined muscles that were in perfect proportion to his height, not outrageously overdeveloped like some bodybuilder's might be.

Without the scars on his face, he would have been too perfect . . . *GQ*, like a model—which wasn't her type at all. But with the scars, he appeared more dangerous, intent, and sexier than ever. He would have looked killer in a suit. But she couldn't find fault with how he filled out a pair of jeans either.

Oh good grief, what was she doing? Wasting time, that's what. Instead of lusting after Kade Quinn she should be focusing on finding Hawke, before it was too late. She looked down at the phone in her left hand, and it dawned on her that she had the power now to contact the man she'd wanted Kade to call earlier—the team lead who'd been assigned to capture Hawke. She flipped to the main screen and the last text that Kade had sent. After pressing the phone icon, she put it on speaker.

The first ring trilled.

Kade gave her a sharp look, then grabbed for the phone.

She yanked it out of his reach. "I have a gun. Or did you forget?"

"If I weren't driving it wouldn't matter," he snapped.

"Really. Suddenly you're impervious to bullets? Is there a big red S under your shirt and a cape that I don't know about?"

His glare should have made her hair catch fire.

"Simmons," a voice said through the phone.

"I'm calling on behalf of your boss, Special Agent Kade Quinn." Bailey noted the surprise on his face. He probably wondered how she knew his name. She doubted he'd be thrilled to discover that an Equalizer had given it to her. "If you're still in pursuit of Hawke, you need to abort the mission."

Silence.

"Simmons," she tried again. "Did you hear me? Abort the mission. Do not pursue Hawke any further. Give me an update on his status."

Again, silence.

"Simmons." She frowned at Kade. "Why isn't he saying anything?"

"He thinks my phone's been compromised, which it has."

She held it out toward him. "Since I've already broken your precious rule about not calling your lead during a mission, tell him it's okay to talk to me."

He swiped the phone away from her, took it off speaker mode and held it to his left ear where she couldn't grab it, all in the span of a few seconds. She was left holding her hand up in the air, minus the phone.

She dropped her hand to her lap. Pathetic. She might as well turn in her Enforcer card and become a librarian.

"It's Quinn." He said something else too low for Bailey to catch.

"Put it back on speaker," she told him.

The infuriating man ignored her. With him driving, there wasn't much she could do about it right now. Next time, she'd lock him in the trunk while *she* drove.

"He did what?" Kade asked.

The sharpness of his tone had Bailey straining to hear what Simmons was saying, but she could only hear Kade's side of the conversation.

He fired off a rapid volley of questions then rattled off an address that meant nothing to her. A few seconds later, he shoved the phone in its holder, looking disgusted as he mumbled something beneath his breath.

"Kade? What did he say about Hawke?"

He peered at one of the street signs as they passed it, then the next one, as if he was looking for something.

Bailey watched with alarm as the speedometer crept steadily to the right. If they got pulled over for speeding, she'd have to hide the gun. And then she'd lose her leverage to get Kade to take her to Hawke.

"Maybe we should pull over," she suggested. "You can tell me what Simmons said and we can come up with a strategy to—"

He punched the gas and yanked the steering wheel hard left. Bailey fell against the door, the pistol bobbling dangerously in her hands. She sucked in a sharp breath, just managing to steady the gun before he made another sharp turn, slamming her against the seat this time.

She glared at him, yanking on the shoulder harness to loosen it where it had tightened against her neck. She cursed several branches of his family tree, but the effort was wasted. He wasn't paying her any attention.

Then she noticed the scenery rushing past her window.

Rolling hills and thick stands of trees lined the wide road. The houses were few and far between, with lush landscaping and long, winding driveways.

She knew this road.

But Kade shouldn't.

"Why are we here?" She tried to keep her voice calm, flat, so he wouldn't sense her concern.

Several cars passed them going the other way, a truck, a black SUV.

Just like the one in Kade's driveway last night.

She half turned and watched the SUV disappear around a curve.

"Were those your men?"

His jaw tightened. "Yes."

"Shouldn't we be following them? To find Hawke?"

"Nope."

He slowed and turned down another road.

"This isn't where I told you to go."

"You wanted to look for Hawke at his house."

"Yes, but . . . this isn't . . . I gave you directions . . . you're going the wrong way."

"I think what you're trying to say is that you were giving me directions to his other house, the one most people know about. My team searched that place first. Then they came here."

He turned up a long winding driveway.

"I didn't think anyone else knew about this place," she said. "At least, no one but . . . me."

He glanced at her, frowning. "Who is Hawke to you anyway? Friend? Lover?"

"Who's the blonde in your picture? Girlfriend? Wife?" She didn't expect an answer.

He didn't disappoint.

He pulled the car to a stop in front of the glass-and-concrete structure that Hawke loved so much, that he'd worked so hard to ensure that no one in EXIT knew about.

Apparently, he hadn't worked hard enough.

Bailey had thought this house was safe, that no one could figure out that it belonged to Hawke. When she'd texted him last night from the trunk of the Caddy, she'd assumed that the agents had cornered him at one of his other homes. Like her, he had many properties, most of them hidden under layers of aliases and shell companies, and tended to go to whichever one was closer when he needed to lie low. But if he'd known that Kade's men were actively targeting him here in Colorado Springs last night, he would have gone to ground in the one place where he felt they'd never look.

The house right in front of her.

But he hadn't been here, had he? If he had, he wouldn't have been worried about anyone finding him. Which meant he had to be somewhere else.

"We're wasting time," she said. "Hawke isn't here."

"Bailey, this is where my men found him."

She blinked. "Then . . . he's . . ." She couldn't finish her question. She was too afraid of the answer.

"As far as I know he's still alive."

"As far . . . as far as you know? What happened? I don't understand."

"My men cornered him inside. The team gave chase and Simmons said Hawke got away."

Hope surged in her chest. Hawke had gotten away. He must not have been badly hurt as she'd feared. So where was he hiding now?

"I don't think he escaped, though," Kade continued. "He was injured during a struggle, then disappeared. But they didn't find a trail leading outside. They were still searching the house when you called Simmons."

Her brief surge of hope died a quick death. "What kind of struggle?"

"Simmons wasn't clear on the details. Someone drew a knife. I'm not sure if it was one of my men, or Hawke. The knife slipped, Hawke was cut."

She drew a sharp breath.

"He did manage to disappear, so chances are he's not hurt that badly. And you and I both know how you Enforcers love your secret wall panels. I'm betting that your friend is holed up inside somewhere waiting until he's certain that no one is looking for him. All we have to do is find him."

She stilled. "You know about the panels?"

"I didn't until you got away the last time. I directed Reese, one of my men, to search the cottage to figure out how you escaped. He gave me an update this morning. Bathroom closet, hidden staircase. Clever."

"Not clever enough."

He reached over the seat back as if to grab his go bag.

"Hey, what are you doing?" She brought up her gun.

He cocked a brow. "Make me."

"You don't think I'll shoot?"

"I'm beginning to think you're all nag, no follow-through."

She gasped at the insult, jerked the gun just a tad to the right. And pulled the trigger.

Click.

He swore and yanked the gun out of her hand. "I can't believe you just did that."

She unclipped her seat belt and dove for the Bersa .380 strapped to her ankle. The sound of metal sliding against metal, followed by a click, made her freeze. She slowly looked over her shoulder. Kade narrowed his eyes, holding a Glock 17 just inches from her face.

"You probably should have checked the side pocket of my go bag earlier," he said. "And made sure I couldn't reach it from the driver's seat. Give me your backup gun."

"What backup?"

"Everyone wears a backup," he mocked, throwing her own words back at her.

She swore a dozen colorful phrases at him. In two languages.

He arched a brow. "Potty mouth."

"Altar boy."

He held out his left hand. "Gun. Now."

She handed him the Bersa. "What's next? You call Simmons and tell him to come back and get me?"

"Get out."

He made her stand several yards back from the trunk, with no trees or bushes or even the car to duck behind. Smart man. While keeping the Glock trained on her, he ducked down and grabbed both of their go bags from the backseat.

She crossed her arms, pretending not to be worried. A quick scan of their surroundings confirmed what she already knew. The only hiding places were too far away for her to reach before he'd be on her. Or shoot her.

He popped the trunk and tossed the bags inside. She almost whimpered when he tucked her Sig Sauer and Bersa into his bag. At the last minute, he must have decided he preferred his Walther PPK, because he exchanged it for the Glock. He slammed the trunk and motioned for her to precede him up the walkway.

When they reached the front door, she muttered, "If I survive this, I'm tossing the Sig in a Dumpster. I've never had a gun misfire like that."

He stepped beside her, shaking his head. "I did tell you that you snore. Remember? Think about it."

She blinked, then groaned. *That's* what her sleepy brain couldn't piece together earlier. As soon as Kade had commented on her snoring, she should have checked the gun to see if he'd unloaded it. Even if he hadn't said anything, she should have known by the feel of the gun, by its lighter weight, that something was off. Probably the only reason he hadn't taken her Bersa while she was sleeping was because he couldn't reach it. But that hadn't mattered. He'd still gotten the draw on her and now she had no guns.

"I assume you made sure your PPK's loaded?" she griped.

"It's what professionals do."

She gasped.

His mouth quirked, as if he was trying not to smile.

Still smarting over his "professionals" comment, she snapped, "I need a gun, too."

"You want ammo with that?"

"Yes. Please," she gritted out between clenched teeth.

"Why? My men are gone. Hawke's your friend. Or *something*."

She ignored that little dig. "What if your men lied and one of them is still here?"

"They've got no reason to lie to me. And I'm not giving you a gun. You already shot me once."

"Doesn't count. It wasn't loaded."

"You didn't know it wasn't loaded. It counts. Don't expect me to forgive you any time soon."

"I didn't ask. And for your information, I turned the gun a little to the right before I pulled the trigger. The bullet wouldn't have hit you."

This time, he did smile. "I know." He threw open the front door and gestured her forward. "Ladies first."

She scowled and marched inside.

In spite of his "ladies first" quip, they entered the house together, walking side by side through the marble-tiled foyer. And even though he had the upper hand now that he was the one with a gun, he kept it down by his side, treating her as if she was his partner instead of his prisoner.

Was she his prisoner?

It was hard to tell. He stayed close, but seemed more of a protector than an agent assigned to capture her.

"Where's the kitchen?" he asked. "That's where Simmons said the fight happened."

"This way." She led him down a short hall to their left, then through the dining room. When she stepped into the kitchen, she froze. "Oh no."

He put his hands on her shoulders in a surprisingly gentle hold, as if he was trying to comfort her. And, heaven help her, she almost leaned back and let him.

There was so much blood.

"It may not be as bad as it looks," he said.

She nodded, but they both knew he was lying.

The travertine floor by the kitchen island was so smeared with blood that it was difficult to tell what color the tiles were supposed to be. Some of the blood was already drying, turning a dark, rusty color. The air reeked of the coppery scent.

And something else.

"Gunfire," they both said at the same time.

"There." She pointed to the wall on their left. Three small bullet holes were torn into the Sheetrock.

Kade holstered his pistol and ran his fingers across the holes. His mouth compressed into a hard line.

"Simmons has a lot of explaining to do." His voice shook with anger, and Bailey was again reminded of the text messages he'd sent to his team leads about not hurting any Enforcers.

Everything she thought she knew about the Ghost was being turned upside down. The man crouching on the floor now, studying the bloody footprints, wasn't some mustache-twirling villain out to kill Enforcers. If anything, he was the complete opposite. He cared, maybe too much. So what was happening to all the Enforcers?

Could Kade be right that they really were going to some retraining facility? Had she been wrong about Sebastian and Amber? Or was she wrong about the identity of the Ghost? Maybe Kade really was a good guy, and someone else was killing Enforcers.

"There's too much cross-contamination in here," Kade said. "I can't see a pattern. But if all of this is Hawke's blood, I don't think he could have made it that far. He has to be close by."

"Wouldn't the agent he fought know where Hawke went?"

"You would think so. But Simmons said the guy

got knocked to the floor. By the time he regained his footing and turned around, your guy was gone. However, since Simmons didn't mention that someone fired a gun in here, I'm not inclined to put much stock in anything that he told me."

He walked the perimeter of the room, feeling along the walls, pressing against them. He was looking for hidden panels.

Bailey mimicked his search on the opposite side of the room. But a few minutes later, neither of them had found anything that didn't belong in a typical kitchen.

"I suppose he could have made it into another room." He didn't sound convinced. He turned in a slow circle, then stopped. "The cabinets."

"None of them are big enough for Hawke to hide inside. He's not as big as you, but he's still a large man."

"Not *in* the cabinets. Behind them. Look at the top left corner on the end."

She did, and her pulse started pounding with excitement. "There's a tiny gap. This whole section must swing out like a door."

It took a good five minutes of feeling around and running their hands along the wood, but Bailey found the tiny switch—on the back of the stove. She pressed it and heard a loud click.

A whole section of cabinets popped out about an inch. Together they swung them open all the way, revealing a small, previously hidden room.

And Hawke lying in a puddle of blood.

Chapter Ten

Saturday, 5:03 p.m.

Bailey clutched the edges of her hard plastic chair, her knees bouncing up and down with nervous energy as she scanned the emergency room waiting area. There was the usual assortment of maladies typical in most ERs. Toddlers sniffling against their mothers' shoulders. An elderly man coughing into his handkerchief while his wife stroked his back and clucked her tongue in sympathy. A baseball coach looking equally worried and harassed as he tried, without success, to corral a handful of preteen boys while waiting to find out whether his star hitter's season was over, courtesy of a possible broken arm.

Kade leaned in close from his seat beside her. "Squeeze any harder and that chair is going to crack."

"I can't help it. Why haven't we heard anything about Hawke yet?"

"It's only been half an hour."

"Since we got here, yeah. But the ambulance arrived before us. And they must have done some kind of assessment and treatment along the way. The doctors should know something."

She expected him to give her platitudes, to tell her everything was going to be okay, the way most people would. But he didn't.

"He's going to die, isn't he," she whispered. "He lost so much blood. And we couldn't wake him up."

"We stopped the bleeding and called 911 right away. We gave him a fighting chance. It's in the doctors' hands now. And God's."

She looked up at him. "You believe in God?"

"I do. Is that a problem?"

She shook her head. "No. Just . . . unexpected."

"Because the big bad FBI guy is the epitome of evil?"

A smile tugged at the corners of her mouth. "Something like that."

"What about you?" he asked.

"My parents were devout Catholics."

"That doesn't answer my question. What about *you*? Do *you* believe?"

She looked away, thinking about his question. Did she believe? She had, once upon a time. When it was just the three of them. When everything was puppies and roses and weekend trips to any theme park with a roller coaster—because roller coasters made Bailey happy, and her adoring father loved nothing more than to make his little girl smile.

She'd believed in fairy tales, too, where mommies and daddies cuddled and laughed and read their daughter bedtime stories every night. She'd also believed in a world where bad guys didn't sneak up on you from the shadows, a world where mommies and daddies never died.

Until they did.

"Bailey?"

"Why did you call 911 for Hawke?" When he didn't answer, she looked up again. The expression on his face was a mixture of confusion and a dash of something else. Hurt? Censure?

"Why *wouldn't* I call 911?" he finally asked. "Hawke was hurt. He needed medical attention."

"But you risked exposure, risked the police asking all kinds of questions that I'm sure you don't want to answer. If an Enforcer tells someone about EXIT, the penalty can be extreme, maybe even death depending on the circumstances. But you're as deep into this as I am. I imagine you could, what, be fired? Lose your career? Worse? Why would you risk everything to help someone you've never met?"

"Because it was the right thing to do. I didn't have a choice." With that, he looked away, staring across the room at nothing at all.

Bailey felt his words sink deep into her soul. *Because it was the right thing to do.* Simple words, easily said. But he'd meant every single one of them. She could hear it in his tone, see it in his eyes, feel the censure in his body language because he was deeply offended that she might have expected otherwise.

He was right. She had. That's why she'd asked the question. People in her world rarely acted nobly. Trust was hard-won, and once given, often thrown away in the face of expediency.

She'd never met a man like the one sitting beside her now. He'd had so many opportunities today to cart her away to the so-called retraining facility, or to call his men to do it, since he supposedly didn't know where the facility was located. And yet, here he was, sitting with her inside the ER just because he knew she wanted to wait and hear how her friend was doing.

They could have called 911 and left before the ambulance had arrived. That would have ensured no probing questions from the police once the EMTs reached the scene and realized this wasn't a case of someone accidentally cutting themselves while cooking dinner. He could have handcuffed her and been done with his mission, on to the next Enforcer. But he hadn't. Could she really doubt him anymore?

He'd saved her from a sniper.

He'd saved her from the man in the bushes at his house who'd been about to shoot her.

He'd figured out that she'd follow him this morning and had planned to face her one-on-one. That was obvious to her now. He was too smart not to have realized she'd tail him. So he'd risked his life, letting her get the draw on him. All because she'd asked some questions the night before, raised some doubts about what was really happening to the Enforcers. And in response, he'd given her a chance to prove him wrong, to prove her right. Because he was a kind, decent man who wanted the truth.

Her shoulders slumped and she let out a deep sigh.

"You okay?" he asked.

"Peachy." She crossed her arms, all too aware that he was studying her, probably wondering what she was thinking. She couldn't exactly admit that she'd gone soft, that he'd managed to work past her defenses in less than a day. Damn it. She was better than this. How had she let this happen?

"Remember our cover story?" he asked softly.

"What we're supposed to tell the police if they showed up to ask questions?"

"Yeah, I remember."

"Good. Because they're here."

Two uniformed officers had just stepped into the waiting room behind a man in an immaculate gray suit, not a wrinkle in sight—obviously their boss.

She stiffened as gray-suit's gaze locked onto them and he headed their way. A nurse must have pointed them out. Then again, she and Kade both had blood on their clothes from applying pressure to Hawke's wounds. Figuring out that they were the ones who'd called 911 wasn't exactly an intellectual puzzle.

"Hold me," she whispered. "I'm distraught."

He immediately put his arm around her shoulders and pulled her against his side.

Damn if it didn't feel good.

Bailey wiped nonexistent tears from her eyes as the suit stopped in front of them, the two uniformed officers flanking him on either side.

"Special Agent Quinn?" gray suit asked.

"Yes, sir." Kade pulled his arm from around Bailey's shoulders. "Sorry, sweetheart. I need to get my wallet."

She sniffed and nodded, mystified by the thrill that shot through her when he'd called her sweetheart. It wasn't real. It was part of their act. Focusing on her own performance, she hunched her shoulders and wrapped her arms around her middle.

Kade rose to his feet and handed the officer his credentials.

"I'm Lieutenant Russell," he said as he handed Kade's wallet back to him. "Sorry to hear about your friend. Is he going to make it?"

"We're still waiting for an update. This is Miss Davenport." Kade waved toward Bailey.

The lieutenant held his hand out.

She stared at him blankly as if she didn't understand what he wanted.

He dropped his hand.

Kade flashed her a warning look and cleared his throat. "She's . . . distraught," he said, echoing her earlier words. "Hawke is a good friend. We were coming over to help him cook dinner and, well, you know what we found."

"Do you have any ID on you, Miss Davenport?" Russell asked.

She merely blinked, content to let Kade handle the questions, especially since her purse was in the Mustang. And even if she'd had it with her, she didn't exactly have ID that listed her name as Davenport. She tuned out their conversation and focused instead on the swinging double doors on the other side of the room, the ones where they'd taken Hawke.

The doors opened and closed many times, spilling nurses and doctors into the waiting room where they updated families and friends waiting for news about their loved ones. And then, finally, one of the nurses stopped beside Kade and the lieutenant, bringing their conversation to a halt.

Bailey rose and found herself reaching for Kade's hand before she thought about it.

He entwined his fingers with hers, squeezing them as if to lend her strength.

"Special Agent Quinn?" the nurse asked. "Miss Davenport? You're here about Mr. Hawke Jacobs?"

Kade nodded and the nurse began rattling off details about his injuries.

The lieutenant, looking none too happy at the interruption, stepped back a few feet, but not so far away that he couldn't hear everything the nurse was saying.

So much for privacy laws.

When the nurse finished, Bailey glanced from her to Kade, then back again, afraid that she'd heard her wrong. "You're saying he's . . . that he's alive? He's going to be okay?"

"I'm saying we just got him stabilized and if he remains that way we'll move him to ICU. As for his prognosis, you'll have to talk to the doctor. I'll take you on back if you want to see him."

"Not right now," the lieutenant protested. "I have a few more questions."

"They can wait," Kade said.

The lieutenant didn't look happy with Kade's clipped reply. But he didn't try to stop them again.

The nurse led them through the double doors into the chaos that was the treatment area. Machines beeped, doctors rattled off orders, nurses ran around trying to make sense of the whole thing and somehow succeeded.

Hawke was being treated in the last curtained-off area at the end of the long aisle, beside a door marked Stairs.

"Wait here," the nurse said, stopping them outside the curtain. "The doctor will be right out." She smiled and hurried off to help someone else.

Bailey was impatient to see her friend. But she wasn't a bundle of nerves like she'd been in the waiting room. Stable. Hawke was stable. That was so much better than she'd expected that she might have cried right then and there except that she wasn't sure she remembered how to cry. The last time she'd cried she was ten years old.

Kade's hand jerked in hers. She'd forgotten they were even holding hands. Her face heated as she let him go. But when she looked up, whatever she was about to say froze in the back of her throat.

Gone was the kind, gentle man she'd just started getting used to. In his place was a warrior, his body stiff, his jaw tight, his dark blue eyes blazing with an intensity that sent a chill down her spine as he stared at something over her shoulder.

"I'll be back," he said, his voice gritty, hard. And then he was gone, slipping through the exit door a few feet away.

Bailey whirled around, but the only thing behind her aside from the curtained-off treatment areas was a large monitor suspended from the ceiling listing patient names, bed numbers, and cryptic descriptions about their conditions.

The curtain slid back and a man in a white lab coat stood in the opening. "Miss Davenport?"

"Yes."

He smiled reassuringly. "You can come in for a few minutes. Mr. Jacobs is still unconscious but stable. I'll try to answer any questions that you have while we wait for an orderly to take him down to ICU, okay?"

She glanced at the door where Kade had disappeared, then forced a smile and followed the doctor to Hawke's bedside.

KADE TOOK THE stairs to the basement. Wasn't that where all hospital morgues were located? He strode down the long hall that ran the length of the building, unsurprised when he saw a sign pointing toward the morgue.

Hawke wasn't the only Enforcer that Kade had tracked to Colorado Springs. A second man was being monitored twenty-four seven by Special Agent Lamar Porter. The surveillance would give Kade the data that he needed before sending in a team to capture him. The target's name was Henry Sanchez—the same name listed on a monitor upstairs, next to the word *deceased*.

It was certainly possible that there was more than one man in this city with the name Henry Sanchez, and the other man just happened to have died today.

But Kade wasn't betting on it.

When he reached the morgue, he flashed his FBI credentials to the greasy-haired attendant sitting at a desk just inside the door, with a name tag that simply said Rob.

"Special Agent Kade Quinn. I'm in the middle of an undercover operation and believe that one of the men I've been looking for may be in your morgue right now."

Rob didn't even look at Kade's badge. Instead, he propped his feet on top of the desk and leaned back in his chair. "And that's my problem how?"

Kade really wanted to knock the man's feet down. But he couldn't afford to cause a commotion and bring attention to him or Bailey. Besides, he knew that smug look. He'd seen it a hundred times before. Rob was probably an ex-con who resented anyone to do with law enforcement. Or maybe this job was all he could get, a last resort, and he wanted to make everyone around him just as miserable as he was. Either way, Kade knew just how to deal with his type.

He pulled a couple of twenty-dollar bills from his wallet and slapped them on top of the desk. "His name is Henry Sanchez. I need a few minutes alone with the body and I also need to see his medical records."

Rob's brows rose and he picked up the twenties. "This'll get you five minutes with the corpse. But I ain't messin' with no privacy law crap. That'll get me hard time."

Kade tossed three more twenties onto the desk.

"You're kidding, right?"

Five more twenties landed on top of the others. "I'm tapped out," Kade lied. "That's all I've got."

Rob grinned and shoved his haul into his pocket as he stood. "I reckon you just bought yourself ten minutes to do whatever you want. But I can't give you longer than that. The ME got called in 'cause we're stackin' up back here. He's on his way."

"The records?"

He waved toward a stack of folders on the corner of the desk. "Sanchez is our newest resident. His file's on top. He's in drawer seven." He grabbed a cell phone and some earphones out of the top drawer. "I'll keep a lookout. If I tell you to get out, get out. Got it?"

Kade ignored him and flipped open the folder.

Rob mumbled some insults under his breath but stepped out of the morgue into the hallway.

Kade stood alone inside the bright white-tiled autopsy room. An empty stainless steel table sat in the middle. The whole place smelled like antiseptic and death.

Flipping through the file only took a minute.

Then Kade crossed to the wall of refrigerated drawers and opened number seven.

Even though he'd never seen Sanchez in person, he'd seen enough pictures of him to know this was the same man that he currently had under surveillance. But just to be sure, he pulled the sheet back a little farther. Unless the Enforcer had an identical twin, who also had a tattoo of Jessica Rabbit on his right forearm, then this was definitely him.

"Eight minutes," Rob called from the hallway.

He raked the sheet all the way down the body, bunching it up at the dead man's feet. The file stated that Sanchez had died of an allergic reaction, anaphylactic shock. He'd stumbled into the ER, his lips turning blue but then he'd lost consciousness and never woke up. The only reason the hospital even knew his name was from the driver's license in his wallet.

And the peanut-allergy medical bracelet on his wrist.

Kade knew several people with severe allergies. All of them carried EpiPens in case they accidentally ate something that caused a reaction and they were extremely careful about what they ate. Which made it even more suspicious that Sanchez could have ended up in the ER with a reaction severe enough to kill him.

It didn't take long for Kade to find what he'd hoped he wouldn't find—a small puncture wound in between two of Sanchez's toes. There could be no doubt. Someone had purposely injected Henry with peanut oil, or some derivative of it, enough to send him into a full-blown allergic reaction.

Since one person couldn't have held Sanchez down and injected him, whoever had done this had help. They must have given him the injection in a vehicle right outside the emergency room. The reaction would have been almost instantaneous, ensuring that Sanchez would use up his last breath to run inside for help. But he wouldn't be able to tell anyone that someone had purposely done this to him.

The theory made sense for someone wanting to kill Sanchez and make it look like an accident. An added plus was that the hospital would dispose of the body. And it was unlikely a hospital ME would even look for an injection in a case of anaphylactic shock. A clean, easy death.

The question, though, was why? Had the agent watching Sanchez been spotted? Was this his way of ensuring that Sanchez couldn't alert other Enforcers and get away? Kade couldn't imagine any FBI agents doing something like this, ever, under any circumstances. Something was very, very wrong here.

"Four minutes," the tech called out. "I'm not even sure you have that."

Kade covered the body and shoved the drawer shut. He didn't need four more minutes. But he did need to make a phone call.

He headed out of the morgue and pulled out his cell phone. But the hospital's concrete walls interfered with the signal, so he ducked into an empty office and used the landline on the desk.

"This is Quinn, calling on an unsecured line," he said, the moment that Special Agent Porter answered the phone.

"Understood. What can I do for you, sir?"

Porter sounded the same as he always did—professional, polite, calm, as if nothing had happened. Kade wanted to demand answers. But on an unsecured line, the best he could do was talk in generalities.

"Sitrep," he said.

"The subject is home right now."

He fisted a hand against the wall. "You sure about that?" Because Sanchez hadn't looked at home at all inside the cold storage drawer.

"Positive, sir. I'm in my van across the street. His blinds are open and I'm looking at him right now through my binoculars."

Damn. There was only one explanation for Porter to lie to him. He was in on this—whatever "this" was.

"All right. Continue surveillance for now."

"Yes, sir. Will do."

Kade headed upstairs to the ER, just in time to hear a doctor call out, "Time of death, 17:33."

Bailey stood in the middle of the aisle while a team of doctors and nurses began to file out of the curtained enclosure beside her.

"I'm sorry, Miss Davenport. We thought we had him stable. But he took a sudden turn for the worse. We did everything we could," Hawke's doctor said, before hurrying off to some other emergency.

Bailey stared up at Kade, a stricken look on her pale face.

"He can't be dead." Her words were choked out, barely above a whisper. She tried to shove him out of the way, but he grabbed her and pulled her closer to the exit door.

"Let me go." She twisted and tried to pull away from him, her nails scoring his skin.

"Bailey, damn it. Stop." He lightly shook her until she stopped struggling.

"It's a mistake." Her voice sounded raw, hollow. "It's a mistake."

Kade pulled her against his chest, wanting to comfort her. And he was relieved when she let him. Her arms went around his waist. She blew out a shuddering breath and hugged him tight.

"He was only twenty-seven," she whispered. "He likes the Denver Broncos and romantic comedies. And he hates ice cream."

Kade lightly stroked her hair, letting her work it out.

"He wasn't my boyfriend," she whispered.

He paused, then resumed stroking her hair. Knowing Hawke wasn't a romantic interest shouldn't have mattered at a time like this. It shouldn't have made him feel lighter inside. But it did.

"He was a good man," she continued, her voice sounding stronger now. "He saved my life more times than I could count on some rescue missions earlier this year."

"Rescue missions?"

She stiffened, then pushed out of his arms to meet his gaze. "You sound surprised. Why?"

The anger in her voice caught him off guard. Maybe this was how she dealt with loss, by striking out.

Hoping to avoid the storm, but not really sure how, he answered truthfully. "I'm not all that familiar with the Enforcers' missions. That was on a need-to-know basis."

"Need-to-know, huh? That's the second time you've told me that. Sounds like there are a lot of things you've turned a blind eye to without getting all the facts. Did you just assume that all Enforcers did was kill people?"

He looked around, relieved no one was close enough to hear her. "Keep your voice down."

"You act like you want the truth and yet you don't ask any questions." She poked her finger against his chest. "How many men and women have your teams captured while you looked the other way, don't ask don't tell?" She waved her hand toward the curtained area where Hawke's body now lay. "You're responsible for this, Kade. Men under your command did this. And you still think you're one of the good guys?"

He sucked in a pained breath at her words.

And suddenly Abby's terrified eyes filled his vision.

Her screams of terror from the passenger seat, turning into shouts of warning. The century-old oak tree rushing to meet them. Kade, desperately turning the wheel. Too late. Too late. Metal crunching, popping, crushing.

Killing.

The horrific images faded, only to be replaced with a more recent memory, Henry Sanchez's dark eyes staring up at him from the autopsy drawer. But instead of looking cloudy and unfocused, this time his eyes were open and staring at Kade in silent accusation.

You did this to me. This is your fault.

Kade swallowed the bile in his throat and slowly shook his head.

"No, Bailey. I haven't been one of the good guys in a long, long time."

Chapter Eleven

Saturday, 5:57 p.m.

Guilt was something that Bailey wasn't too familiar with, because she made it her life's mission to do what she believed was right, to never shrink away from doing something just because the path was difficult. But as she walked with Kade through the back hallways of the hospital to avoid running into Lieutenant Russell again, guilt crushed down on her like a boulder.

She couldn't quit picturing the bottomless well of pain that had flashed in his eyes when he'd told her that he wasn't a good man. Her use of him as her emotional punching bag was inexcusable. But she didn't know how to fix what she'd done.

Or even if she wanted to.

Maybe it was better, safer, for both of them to leave things the way they were now. All of this emotional stuff flowing between them was unsettling. She couldn't afford to let her guard down, and neither could he. This truce, or whatever it was, was temporary. As soon as they were out of the hospital she'd be looking for a way to ditch him so she could escape the government's net. And even if Kade was having a change of heart and wanted to help her avoid being caught, she was much better alone. Because alone meant she didn't have to worry about anyone else.

And if she wasn't with Kade, she couldn't hurt him anymore.

KADE STOPPED JUST short of the exit doors and pulled Bailey back against the wall. "I have a bad feeling about this. First Hawke, then Sanchez. I don't know which of my men I can trust anymore. We need to make damn sure no one's out there gunning for us before we step out those doors."

"Who's Sanchez?"

Her frown reminded him that he hadn't told her about the other murdered Enforcer yet. Wonderful. If she didn't hate him already, once she heard what had happened it would tip the scales the rest of the way.

He sighed and faced her. "Henry Sanchez is an Enforcer. I saw his name on the monitor outside of Hawke's room. He was brought in for an allergic reaction and died. That didn't feel right, so I verified the cause of death and that it was the same Sanchez I've had an agent following."

"You verified cause of death? How?"

"I went to the morgue."

Her brows rose. "I see."

He'd expected anger or condemnation. Surprisingly, he saw neither. She seemed to be thinking hard, as if trying to put the puzzle pieces together.

He glanced toward the doors that led to a parking garage.

"I must have taken a wrong turn," he said. "I don't think the lot where we left the Mustang is near the parking garage. But I can't risk going back into the main part of the hospital if Porter, and potentially others, are inside looking for me. I'll have to go outside and work my way around the building. But first I have to figure out what to do about you."

"Come again?" she asked. "What are you talking about?"

He let out an impatient breath. "Porter is coming after me, because I found out about Sanchez. But no one knows that you're here except for the police. I think you should hide down here in one of the storage rooms until it's safe to leave."

She put her hands on her hips. "If you think I'm going to cower somewhere while you're running for your life, then you're just as much of a jerk as I was when I said those hateful things to you upstairs. I didn't mean any of them, by the way. Okay, maybe I did, in the heat of the moment. But I don't now. I'm sorry, Kade. Really sorry. And I'm not letting you face this mess on your own. We do this together or not at all."

"Don't be stubborn, Bailey."

"You haven't begun to see stubborn. Trust me. You can't win this argument. You're just wasting time."

"I could tie you up."

"Promises, promises."

He choked out a laugh. "You're really something, you know that?"

She grinned. "And I'm nowhere near my best today. Imagine how awesome I would be if I'd actually had some sleep in the past forty-five hours or whatever the count is up to now."

"If we manage to get out of here without getting killed, I'll pull guard duty and you can sleep as long as you want."

"Deal."

They headed toward the doors again.

"I sure wish I had a gun," she complained.

"You and me both."

They'd left their weapons in the trunk, not wanting to risk that the hospital might have a metal detector. Or that the police might show up and catch them with any weapons inside.

He shoved open the door and they hurried outside.

They wound their way through the garage, around the outside of the hospital to the lot where they'd left their car. The strain of all the walking up and down stairs earlier, plus weaving through the garage and around the building, was starting to turn a good-leg day into a bad one. Sharp pain shot up the back of his thigh every time he took a step. And from the way Bailey kept glancing at him, her brow furrowed with worry, he must be limping. He focused on trying to walk without favoring his bad leg.

"I can see the car," she said as they hurried into the parking lot and started up an aisle. "A few aisles away, on the far side."

A few moments later, the hospital doors slid open. Kade looked back and saw a tall man in a suit step outside. In this heat, that alone made him seem suspicious. Kade often wore suit jackets when he needed to cover his gun. There was one in the back of the Mustang right now for just that purpose.

He pulled Bailey down behind an SUV a third of the way up the aisle and peered over the top.

A pale woman with blond hair stepped out through the same doors, also wearing a suit jacket over her white blouse and dress pants. She stopped to talk to the man, then they both looked toward the parking lot.

Kade ducked down beside Bailey. "There's a man and a woman in suits near the entrance and I'm pretty damn sure they're looking for us."

She eased her way to the end of the vehicle and poked her head out, then ducked back. "No question. I can smell a Fed a mile away. And those two reek."

"Gee, thanks."

She grinned. "No offense."

He rolled his eyes.

She peeked out again, then jerked back. "They're heading straight toward us. Did they see us?"

"I don't think so." A cold feeling settled in his gut. Had the agents tracked him here? He reached down to his leg brace and felt inside the top.

"What are you doing? Does your leg hurt?"

"Pretty much all the time," he muttered. "I'm fine," he said, in answer to her worried look. "But I came prepared to turn you over to one of my teams today, after I proved you were wrong about there being some kind of conspiracy to kill Enforcers. There's a GPS tracker in the top of the brace. Before I left the house in Boulder, I gave Faegan the frequency and told him I'd put the tracker on you once I found you. Then I was supposed to call him so he could send a team to pick you up."

She nodded matter-of-factly. "So whoever this Faegan is, he's tracking you without you calling him first. I think we know who's leading the conspiracy now."

He stared at her. "Aren't you mad at me?"

"Because you were doing your job and planned on turning me over? You didn't know me when you planned that. But you know me now. At least, you know me well enough not to turn me over now, right? At least, not while we're still figuring out what's going on?"

"Of course."

"Then why would I be mad? What's the plan? Please tell me you have a plan because, honestly, I'm too tired to think one up at the moment."

He yanked her to him and planted a quick, hard kiss against her lips. When he pulled back she blinked at him, looking stunned.

"What was that for?" she asked.

"Hell if I know. I couldn't resist."

The grin that spread across her lips reached all the way to her eyes. "Told you I'm good."

He laughed, then sobered. "Focus. Okay, give me a second."

He pulled the lining open on the leg brace and pulled out the tiny disc he'd put there earlier. There was a second disc, a backup, farther down. But he hadn't activated it, so he didn't bother digging it out.

"I doubt those two agents are the only ones after us." He tossed the disc under the SUV. "Come on."

He led her in between the cars to the second row of vehicles, then paused near a bumper. Behind them was another open aisle for cars to drive down. It was tempting to race across the empty space to the next row of cars, but they couldn't risk it just yet. They couldn't outrun a bullet, so not being seen was their best defense.

This time Bailey took a turn bending down to

look under the car they were behind. She looked right, then left, then straightened. The worry lines on her brow told him things had just gone from bad to worse.

"Two more agents," she whispered, "coming from the other direction."

Kade carefully raised up just enough to see for himself. One of the new agents was Porter. Soon the two pairs of agents would meet up in the middle, with only the length of two cars separating them from where Bailey and Kade were hiding.

Bailey pointed across the open space. She wanted them to run for it.

Kade shook his head. Too dangerous.

She frowned and pointed again. He followed the direction where she was pointing and realized they were closer to the Mustang than he'd realized. But it was still too far away, two aisles over plus a good distance down the line of cars. He'd never make it before an agent saw him. His damn leg would slow him down too much.

He pulled his keys out of his pocket, careful not to let them hit each other and make any noise. Then he held them out to her and motioned toward the Mustang.

She pointed at him and motioned for him to come with her.

He shook his head *no* and indicated his leg.

She pushed the keys back toward him, refusing to take them. Then she crossed her arms. The message was clear. She wasn't going anywhere without him.

He gave her his best frown.

Her shrug told him she was unimpressed.

He shook his head again then peeked over the top

of the car to locate the agents. All four had met in the middle of the aisle a few cars down and appeared to be discussing what to do next. Had he been wrong about the tracker? Maybe Faegan wasn't in on this after all. Maybe it was all Porter all along and he was the one with ties to someone higher up.

The agents he was directing might not even know the real reason they were there. Porter could have given them any number of stories to get them to go to the hospital with him. Even now they could just be following orders. None of them had met Kade before. They had no reason to suspect he was one of them.

Three of the agents turned their backs to him and Bailey while the fourth pointed diagonally across another aisle. Maybe they'd spotted someone and thought it was Kade?

"This is our best chance, while they're distracted," he whispered to Bailey. "Let's go."

They both took off, crouching low as they ran across the open space to the next row of cars. No sounds of pursuit echoed behind them so they kept going, not stopping until they reached the Mustang.

Kade's leg was throbbing so hard that the muscle was starting to spasm. He shoved the keys into Bailey's hand while gritting his teeth against the pain.

"You have to drive," he told her.

She glanced at his leg before dashing to the driver's side while Kade got in on the passenger side.

They were careful to pull the doors shut as softly as possible. But they must have made more noise than they'd realized. A shout sounded from one of the agents, and they took off running toward the Mustang.

Bailey started the engine and shoved the car into reverse, then swore and slammed the brake.

"Go, go," Kade urged.

"Can't unless you want grandma grandpa splatter all over the back of the car."

He looked over his shoulder. An elderly couple was slowly working their way behind the Mustang toward the hospital, one with a cane, the other with a walker. The front of the Mustang was blocked by another vehicle. They were trapped.

He whirled back around, facing the front. One of the agents was heading straight toward them. But he must have seen the couple, too, and at least had enough character not to involve them. His gun was out, but down by his thigh.

Kade turned again, watching the couple's painfully slow progress.

As soon as they cleared the bumper, he yelled, "Now."

Bailey punched the gas, tires squealing as she did a sharp turn, then slammed the gear into drive.

The windshield cracked as a gunshot rang out.

The couple screamed.

"Are they hurt?" Bailey yelled. She floored the accelerator and the car took off like a rocket toward the exit.

"No, just scared. Ah, hell." He shoved Bailey down into the seat and threw himself on top of her as more shots rang out, shattering the back window into thousands of little pieces that rained down inside the car.

He jerked upright, grabbing the wheel just in time to avoid hitting another car.

Bailey straightened and shoved his hand off the

steering wheel, then took a corner far too fast, the car lifting onto two wheels for a stomach-churning second before slamming back to earth.

More shots rang out, but none of them hit their mark. The Mustang screeched around the corner of the building, blocking the view of the parking lot and finally giving them some cover.

"There, turn there." Kade pointed to the turnoff that led to the main road.

"Got it." Bailey drove like a NASCAR driver on steroids, shifting gears and taking turns so fast that Kade was certain the car was going to roll. But through it all she maintained control, more or less.

Five minutes later they were barreling down the interstate. Kade pulled his cell phone out.

"What are you doing?"

Bailey's voice was tight with alarm, which frustrated Kade to no end. Would she ever really trust him? Then again, Hawke was dead. She'd just found out that Sanchez, another Enforcer, was dead. And four agents, one of whom had been working for him for weeks, had just tried to kill them.

Yeah, maybe expecting her to trust him was stupid after all. He didn't even trust himself. He hadn't trusted himself in a long time.

"Maybe those agents found us because of Sanchez," he said. "In fact, I'm betting they probably did and Porter's our bad apple. But I'm not taking any chances. This is a company-issued phone."

He slammed the phone against the gearshift over and over until it was a mangled mess and the computer components were hanging out in pieces. He rolled down the window and tossed the ruined phone like a Frisbee onto the highway. A semi traveling behind them finished the job of reducing it to roadkill.

"Remind me not to ever let you borrow my phone," she teased. "Anyone following us?" She wove around a slow-moving car before accelerating again.

Kade watched the road behind them for a minute. "I don't think so. But they don't have to be tracking us to know we would have headed to the highway. It was the fastest way to put some distance between us and the hospital."

He motioned toward her pocket. "If you can trust me with your phone, in spite of my destructive tendencies, I'll use your maps app to plot an alternate course."

"Don't bother." She downshifted, then squealed around another car amidst a flurry of honking horns, barely making the next exit without rolling the car. "I know where we are. I've got this."

It took a full minute before he could breathe normally again and force his fingers to uncurl from the armrest.

"I hope you're right," he finally said. "Because to me it just seems like you're going to get us killed."

She smiled and pressed the gas pedal all the way to the floor. "If I do, we'll die happy. This is fun."

Kade stared at her incredulously. Who knew she was Thelma and Louise all rolled up into one person? Hopefully there wasn't a cliff nearby for her to drive off.

Chapter Twelve

Bailey punched the security code into the keypad, then hopped back into the Mustang. As soon as the garage door was high enough to clear the roof of the car, she zipped inside. By the time Kade had even opened his car door, she'd already gotten out and pressed the button on the wall to close the garage.

Was he limping worse than before? He was definitely moving slower. She was about to ask him about his leg when he looked toward the driver's side.

"You're hell on a paint job," he said.

She leaned over, wincing when she saw the damage. "I guess I scraped it worse than I realized."

"Scraped?" He laughed. "We're lucky that guardrail held. You took that last turn way too fast."

"I've driven 'Stangs before. I knew what I could get away with. What matters is that we're alive and no one knows where we are."

"I have to admit, I'm impressed." He waved his hand to encompass the single-car garage, brightly lit by buzzing fluorescents overhead. "I never realized you had a home in Colorado Springs. How did you manage to hide it from me? I found all the other properties you own."

She quirked a brow. "The house in Florida?"

"Naples. Lovely Victorian. Could use a new paint job, though, like the Mustang."

She frowned. "North Carolina?"

"Hatteras Island is gorgeous this time of year."

"Damn. Canada?"

He arched a brow. "You don't own a house in Canada."

She smiled. "You're right. I don't. But I don't own one in Colorado Springs either. The owners use this place for vacations two or three times a year. The rest of the time I'm free to stay here if I want."

"That's generous of them. Old family friends?"

Her smile faded. "I don't have a family. And they're more Hawke's friends than mine."

He limped toward her and gently brushed her hair back from her face. "I'm so sorry for your loss, Bailey. I wish . . . I wish it could have been different."

She searched his eyes. "Do you?"

"Of course. I didn't want Hawke hurt any more than I want you hurt."

"You could have called Simmons, made him abort the mission earlier, when I first asked. If you had . . ." She curled her nails into her palms.

"If I had, maybe he'd still be alive?"

She nodded.

"It's possible. It's also possible that the call would have distracted Simmons while he was after your friend, and then your friend could have killed him. There's no way to know for sure, and no do-overs in life. We have to make the best decisions we can, based on the facts we have at the time."

"The facts? You sound so . . . clinical. What if one of the people involved was someone you loved? Hawke was the closest thing to a brother that I've ever known. I loved him. If he was someone *you* loved, would you have chosen to save his life, over Simmons's? Would you have at least *tried* to save his life?"

"Bailey, I don't think we should—"

"Have you ever loved someone?"

Something dark passed in his eyes, but he nodded.

"Pretend Hawke was your loved one. Now would you have called Simmons?"

He slowly shook his head. "It wouldn't be right. I couldn't trade one life for another like that, no matter how much I wanted to."

"Then you, Kade Quinn, have never really loved someone." She started to turn away, but he stopped her with a hand on her arm.

"Who was he?" he asked. "Who did you love and lose? And don't tell me it was Hawke. There's something else going on here, someone else you're remembering that has you so angry with me."

"Not he. They."

"They?"

"My mom and dad. We'd been on vacation and just flew back home to Bozeman—"

"Montana?"

She nodded. "We were in the airport parking garage, walking to our car with our luggage. I was thirsty, asked Daddy if I could get a drink from the water fountain back by the elevator. He said I could, but to hurry. So I ran to the fountain, just thirty feet away. I remember the water wasn't even cold, had a metallic, rusty taste. I spit it out and turned around to complain just as a man wearing a ski mask stepped out from between two cars and pointed a gun at my parents."

Her nails were biting into her skin now, but she barely felt the pain. She could see the parking garage as clearly as if she was standing there today. It was her curse, that time blurred the happy memories of her parents but did nothing to fade the horror of that night.

"Bailey—"

"My dad glanced at me, over the gunman's shoulder. I started toward him, and he shook his head, just a tiny little shake. I stopped. I didn't do anything, nothing at all, to help them. And then they were on the ground, the shooter running away with my father's wallet and my mother's purse. I didn't. Do. Anything. And they died. I should have done something."

He stepped closer but she moved back, out of his reach. "I don't want your sympathy, Kade. I want your understanding. I loved my mom and dad desperately. And if I could go back in time, I would do anything, anything, to save them. The law be damned. Even if it meant killing their killer *before* he murdered them. That's the difference between you and me, Enforcer and FBI agent. You wait until the crime occurs and then clean up the mess. I prevent the crime from happening in the first place by taking out the bad guys. And, for the record, I think your way sucks."

She stalked into the house, stopping in the kitchen and bracing her hands on the countertop. But her anger didn't last long. Maybe because she was too tired to be mad anymore. Or maybe because she was so hungry that being in a kitchen had her practically drooling at the thought of food. Heck, she'd eat a paper towel right now if that would stop the empty ache in her belly.

All she was sure of was that she couldn't stomach how self-righteous Kade had been acting, talking about rules and laws. It was as if he was judging her, and the choices she'd made. Had she done things she wasn't proud of? Of course. Hadn't everyone? But overall she lived her life the best that she knew how, making the best decisions she could.

Her shoulders slumped.

Wasn't that what Kade had just said? That he made the best decisions he could? How could she be mad at him for judging her when that's exactly what she'd been doing—judging him? Maybe they weren't so different after all. And maybe, just maybe, she owed him an apology.

He chose that moment to walk in from the garage. His movements were bordering on sluggish. Had he been up all night, too, without a chance to catch up on his sleep? She hadn't thought to ask earlier.

"How old were you, Bailey?" he asked, his voice quiet, his expression somber. "When you lost your parents?"

She stiffened, already regretting telling him anything about her past. That was private, her burden to bear, not something to drag out like a couple of drunks comparing scars at a party. "It doesn't matter."

"Yes. It does. How old?"

She gritted her teeth. "Ten."

He closed his eyes, swallowed. When he looked at her again, the sympathy in his eyes made her want to punch him. "You can't blame yourself. There was nothing you could do."

"I know that, Kade," she snapped. "I came to terms with that night a long time ago. Really. I shouldn't have even brought it up."

"I'm glad you did. I'm honored that you shared your story with me. And I'm sorry that I let you down, with Hawke. I really do wish it could have been different. I know it hurts to lose a good friend. Mine didn't die, but he might as well have. Other than anything work-related between our two agencies, we haven't *really* spoken in about five years."

"Five years? He couldn't have been that good a friend then."

"We grew up together, more or less. Middle school, high school, college. Even joined the bureau together."

"What was his name?"

"Robert Gannon. I always thought we'd be friends forever. But I suppose we were just too competitive. We ended up working for the same boss, Faegan. Whenever I'd get a promotion, instead of congratulating me, Gannon wouldn't speak to me for days, or at least until his own promotion got approved.

"I suppose because we were both on the same career track and he just figured he deserved it more than I did. Same thing as far as assignments. Seems like every time he'd get an assignment he was proud of, I'd end up with something better—at least in his mind. Things just sort of, soured, between us over the years. I guess the last straw was a few years ago. We were both dating the same woman."

She stared at him. "You two-timed your best friend?"

"Hell no, not intentionally. Neither of us knew she was dating both of us. She was a co-worker. I guess she was having fun at both of our expenses until she decided which of us she wanted to keep. Her game ended at a charity event that I took her to. Gannon—"

"You always call your best friend by his last name?"

"Always have, and he calls me Quinn. Started so long ago I don't even remember why we do it."

"Go on," she urged.

"Gannon was supposed to be out of the country on assignment, training law-enforcement officers on investigative techniques. But the assignment ended earlier than expected and he popped into the same event. When he saw the two of us there, together, he just . . . exploded. Sucker punched me when I wasn't expecting it. Called me a bastard and stormed out. A month later, when our boss's boss, Kendall, left for a job at Homeland Security, Gannon asked to go with him. I guess it was a great move for him. He and Kendall both racked up the promotions once they got there. Gannon's a hotshot now."

He shrugged. "Not that I know about it firsthand. That's what I've heard through the grapevine. Other than a grudging recommendation to my immediate boss—Faegan—to help me get my current assignment after the . . . accident, that was about the last time Gannon and I have spoken. There are the occasional work-related events we can't avoid when our two agencies get together. But he's pretty much written me out of his life. We're definitely not friends anymore."

"What a jerk."

"Me or him?"

She smiled. "I might have to think about that. What happened to the woman?"

"She was mortified over the whole thing. Ended up transferring to the Atlanta field office. Haven't heard from or seen her since." He shifted his stance and winced.

Whatever she'd been about to say was forgotten as she studied his drawn features. "You don't look so good. In fact, you look terrible. You're as white as virgin snow. Is it your leg?"

Without waiting for his reply, she grabbed a bottle of over-the-counter pain medicine from a cabinet and set it on the counter. She opened the refrigerator and took out a cold bottle of water for him. When she turned around, he was already tossing back four pills.

"Whoa, easy on your liver. Or kidneys. Or whatever body part you're abusing right now."

"This is nothing. I used to eat Vicodin like candy." He thanked her and chased the pills down with some water.

"What exactly's wrong with your leg? How did you hurt it in the first place?"

"I need to splash some water on my face, wash my hands. Does this place have a bathroom?"

He'd neatly avoided her question. Normally she'd call him on it. But he seemed even paler than he had a minute ago and she was really starting to worry.

She shouldn't care. He was still her enemy, after all. But they'd been through so much together in such a short time that he didn't seem like the enemy.

And it was hard not to care, at least a little bit, about a man who'd risked his life for her at every turn.

"Kade, maybe we should go back to the hospital. Have a doctor take a look at your leg."

"After what we went through to get away? Not a chance. I'll be fine, really. The pain pills are already making me feel better."

His grimace said otherwise but she was tired of arguing. She waved toward the hall visible through an opening on the other side of the family room–kitchen combo. "The bathroom is the middle door. I'll whip us up some grilled cheese sandwiches to inhale when you get back. Then we can both pass out for a few hours, or a week. Not sure about you, but I am one tired puppy."

She rooted in the refrigerator, grabbed a stick of butter, searched for the cheese. There were only four slices. Was that enough?

"Hey, Kade. How much cheese do you like on your sandwiches?"

She glanced over her shoulder, but he was already gone.

KADE JUST MANAGED to take care of nature's call and wash his hands before collapsing to the bathroom floor. His leg hurt so much that now his back hurt right along with it. Every muscle along his left side was screaming at him to stop running around and get some rest. He hated that his injury had brought him to this point. Would he ever be the man he'd been before the accident?

Abby.

No. He couldn't go there, couldn't let those memories batter him right now, not here, not with Bailey to protect. If he could just hang on long enough for the pain pills to kick in, he'd be okay. He could pretend all was well as he sat across from Bailey and ate the promised grilled cheese sandwich. Then, he could collapse in one of the two bedrooms and sleep through the worst of the pain. He was due a good-leg day. He just had to survive until tomorrow.

He popped the brace off his thigh and tossed it aside so he could massage the aching muscles. He'd make himself get up in a minute. Just as soon as he gathered his strength. He leaned his head against the side of the tub and closed his eyes.

BAILEY PICKED UP one of the grilled cheese sandwiches and stared longingly at it. The monster in her stomach poked against her ribs, demanding that she take a bite. Man oh man did she want that sandwich.

She turned sideways on her bar stool, looking toward the hall. The bathroom door was still closed, with Kade still inside. She groaned and dropped her sandwich to the plate, fully intact. When life returned to normal again, whatever post-EXIT normal was, she should see a therapist about her inability to eat before everyone else had their food.

She debated knocking on the bathroom door. But if he had an upset stomach or something, she didn't want to embarrass him—or her. She decided she might as well grab their bags from the trunk.

With her own bag secured with a shoulder strap, she picked up Kade's duffel and slammed the trunk.

That's when she saw the bullet hole.

She bent down and ran a finger across it. One of

the agents at the hospital must have hit the car as she peeled out of the parking lot. She frowned. The damage was just above the bumper. If the bullet had kept going straight . . . She jerked her head up. She ran around to the passenger side of the car and yanked open the door.

There was a bullet hole in the seat. And it was soaked with blood.

She shoved the door closed and took off in a dead run. She raced into the kitchen, her shoes sliding on the tile floor as she rounded the corner. More drops of blood formed a trail all the way to the bathroom. How had she not noticed that he was bleeding?

"Kade, open up." She rapped her knuckles on the door. "Kade?"

No answer. She tried the knob. Locked. A sense of déjà vu hit her, making her stomach churn. Her mind swirled with images of Hawke lying on the floor in the safe-room he'd built behind his kitchen cabinets.

Except that the room had been anything but safe.

"Kade, if there are any parts you don't want me to see, you'd better cover them up. I'm coming in."

She jumped up and slammed both of her feet against the doorknob. The cheap interior door splintered and flew open, banging against the wall.

"Oh, no," she whispered. She ran into the bathroom and dropped onto her knees to lift Kade's face out of the puddle of blood.

Chapter Thirteen

Monday, 1:17 p.m.

Kade blinked at the ceiling above him. He was lying on a bed, presumably in one of the bedrooms that Bailey had mentioned earlier. But for the life of him he couldn't remember how he'd gotten here.

"You're awake."

He turned his head on the pillow. Bailey stood in the doorway, her deep green eyes studying him intently, tempered with a wariness that immediately set him on alert.

"What happened? Have they found us?" He flipped up the sheet to slide out of bed. The rush of cool air against his skin had him looking down in surprise. "And why am I naked?"

He hurriedly covered himself as Bailey approached the bed, her face lined with worry.

"Don't try to get up. We're safe. No one knows we're here." She gently pushed him down on the pillows and pressed the back of her hand against his forehead. In spite of her reassuring words, she seemed tense, unsure.

He gently pulled her hand away from his face. "Bailey, what's going on? Are you okay?"

"Of course I'm okay. I can take care of . . . wait, you know who I am?"

He frowned. "Unless you have an identical twin I don't know about, you're Bailey Stark. Why are you . . . *oomph*." His arms were suddenly filled with a gorgeous redhead, hugging him tight, her soft breasts crushed against his chest.

Obviously he'd died and gone to heaven.

"Whatever I did, let me know," he said. "I want to make sure that I do it again."

The laugh he'd expected didn't happen. Instead, she pushed out of his arms, her brow lined with worry again.

"How about you don't do it again?" she said. "You'll make me prematurely gray."

He was about to ask what she was talking about, when he noticed two half-empty glasses of water and a stack of dirty dishes on the bedside table. Beside that on the floor was a pile of discarded towels. And next to that was a smaller pile of clothes, including a dark T-shirt and . . . bloody jeans.

His gaze shot to hers. "I remember I was in the bathroom. My leg was killing me and my back . . ." He reached around his left side, frowning when he felt a patch of gauze taped to his skin.

Bailey gently pulled his hand down. "You're not naked just so I could have my wicked way with you while you were delirious with fever. You're naked because I had to cut your clothes off in order to sew up the bullet hole in your side."

He really, really wanted to explore that whole

"wicked way" and "naked" thing with her, but the word *bullet* more or less canceled that out.

"The hospital parking lot?"

She nodded. "Apparently one of the agents fired through the trunk when we were driving away. It was just a flesh wound, thankfully. But you lost so much blood—" She shook her head. "Obviously I couldn't risk taking you back to the hospital. I had to do the best I could. And being the badass Enforcer that I am, I saved the day. So settle down before you ruin my handiwork. I have better things to do than stitch you up again."

Her brusque manner didn't fool him. He could tell that she'd been worried, and had obviously worked hard to save his life. Her actions amazed him considering the fact that they'd been bitter enemies such a short time ago. What were they now? Temporary allies? Whatever they were, he was certain he owed her more than he could ever repay.

"You have better things to do, huh?" he teased.

"Tons."

"Like what?"

"Lots of things." She absently toyed with the edge of the sheet, making his breath catch. "Maybe a Netflix marathon. I'm ridiculously behind on *The Walking Dead*. I need to find out if Darryl's still in the land of the living."

"Want me to tell you?"

Her eyes widened. "Don't you dare."

He laughed at her outraged expression. Then, ever so slowly, he slid his hand through her silky hair to the back of her neck.

"Kade? What are you doing?"

"I could say that I'm thanking you for saving my life." He rubbed his fingers against her skin, reveling in the shudder of awareness that swept through her. "But really, I just can't resist having you in my bed without finally seeing how you taste."

Before she could think too hard or put up a wall between them, he pulled her down and pressed his lips to hers. She was just as sweet as he knew she would be, and smelled so damn good that he wanted to keep her there forever, trapped in his embrace. But they barely knew each other, and there were a million reasons why this was an incredibly bad idea. So he kept the kiss achingly short.

She stared wide-eyed at him when he let her go. Her hands had fallen to his shoulders and were still clutching him, as if she didn't know whether to pull him close, or shove him away.

"Thank you," he said.

She looked a little dazed, which had him wanting to smile. But he didn't dare.

She cleared her throat. "For what, exactly?"

"For saving my life, of course." This time he did smile. "And for not punching me when I kissed you."

"Oh. Well. Okay then." Her fingers flexed against his shoulders. "Sounds like you're thanking me for *two* things, though." Her gaze dropped to his lips. "But you only gave me one kiss."

He couldn't have resisted that invitation if a whole army of mercenaries was breaking down their door. He speared his hands through her glorious hair again and pulled her close, until their lips were just inches apart.

"Thank you," he whispered. And then he kissed

her the way he'd wanted to from the moment he'd first looked into those incredible green eyes, and had felt her curvy little body beneath his.

The kiss was hot and wet and went from zero to sixty in the space of a breath. The mattress dipped as Bailey climbed up beside him, pressing her body tightly against his. Their tongues tangled together in a wild, wicked dance that sent his pulse rushing in his ears and had him hard and aching and wanting more, so much more. By the time they broke apart, they were both gasping for breath and his head was spinning.

Actually, the room was spinning.

He groaned and fell back against the pillows, squeezing his eyes shut to fight back a wave of nausea.

"Seriously?" She demanded, swatting his shoulder. "I kiss you and it makes you sick? Un-freaking-believable." The mattress dipped again as she climbed off the bed.

He risked opening one eye and grabbed her wrist before she could get away.

She jerked her arm. "Let me go."

"Wait, please, don't leave." His stomach clenched. He closed both eyes, drew a deep breath, then another. "I'm sorry, Bailey. That kiss was incredible. You're incredible. I just . . . need a minute. The room moves every time I open my eyes. Just . . . wait, okay?"

She bent his finger backward.

"Ouch." He swore and let her go.

Her footsteps echoed on the floor as she strode out of the room. Damn, he'd sure screwed that up. He tried to sit up, to go after her. His stomach lurched and he fell back against the pillows, groaning.

Footsteps sounded from the other room. She'd

probably grabbed her gun, to pay him back for insulting her.

A heavy sigh sounded from beside the bed. "Come on, G-man. Drink." A straw was pressed against his lips. "You're probably dehydrated. That's why you're nauseated. I tried to get you to sip fluids earlier but I gave up after half drowning you a couple of times."

He greedily drank the entire glass.

"Better?" she asked.

"Getting there. Thanks."

A thump told him she'd set the glass down on the bedside table. "If you keep thanking me all the time you'll ruin my badass reputation."

"I'll be extremely careful not to thank you in public."

"Damn straight." She adjusted the sheet, pulling it up higher on his chest.

He thought she'd leave then. But she didn't. She sat with him until the nausea settled down, until he'd taken the pain pills she brought him. And until he'd assured her half a dozen times that he was fine.

After extracting his promise to eat if she made some soup, she finally left. A few minutes later, after some wobbly first attempts, he'd wrapped a sheet around his hips and headed into the bathroom to take a shower.

Once he was clean and had downed an entire bowl of tomato soup, he felt human again. He sat propped up with some pillows against the headboard while Bailey sat cross-legged beside him.

"How *did* you manage to get me from the bathroom floor onto the bed after I'd passed out?" he asked. "You're probably a hundred pounds soaking wet. I'm twice that."

She rolled her eyes and flexed her impressive biceps. "I'm not a hundred pounds. And don't you dare ask me what I really weigh."

"Wouldn't dream of it."

She smiled. "It wasn't as hard as you think. Once I got the bleeding under control, I rolled you onto a sheet and dragged you into the hallway. I figured I'd sew you up there where I had more room to work. But you woke up just enough that I was able to badger you into getting to your feet and climbing into bed, with some help of course. After that—" she shrugged "—it was a matter of cutting off your clothes and sewing you up."

She arched a perfectly shaped brow. "And bathing you of course. Didn't want to risk infection. It was a chore, but someone had to do it."

He coughed and cleared his throat. The thought of her sliding a wet washcloth over his skin had all kinds of erotic thoughts flashing through his mind.

"Your leg hurts again?" she asked.

He frowned, then realized he was massaging his bad leg. He forced his hand to his side. "Habit. I'm fine." At her disbelieving look, he said, "Really. It doesn't hurt. Much." He cocked his head, studying her. "If you're not careful, Bailey, I'll think you're starting to like me."

"Don't get your hopes up. I could never like a Fed. It's just lust, pure and simple. If you didn't have a hole in your side, I'd be all over you."

He grinned. "Now you're just being cruel."

The teasing look on her face disappeared as she leaned forward. For a moment, he thought she might kiss him. But then her hand pressed on top of his, which was once again massaging his thigh. He hadn't even realized he was doing it.

"Will you tell me what happened?" she asked, her voice a gentle whisper in the quiet room.

He didn't have to ask what she meant. She wanted to know what had happened to his leg. His first instinct was to tell her no. It sure as hell wasn't something he wanted to talk about. But this was Bailey. The two of them had been through crisis after crisis together, cramming a lifetime of death-defying experiences into a few short days. He probably knew her better than he knew anyone, and yet, he didn't feel that he knew her at all. Still, she'd shared part of her past with him, shared her painful memories about the tragic loss of her parents. How could he refuse to do the same?

His words fell haltingly at first, as he tried to describe that horrible night.

The dark, twisting road. Tires squealing around a curve, headlights flashing in his side mirror. The other driver's soulless eyes—taunting, mocking Kade's desperate attempt to outdrive him, to escape.

Gunshots, a hail of broken glass, the poker-hot burn of a bullet ripping through the driver's door, shattering Kade's hip, burying itself in the muscles of his thigh.

Abby's screams of terror from the passenger seat, turning into shouts of warning. The century-old oak tree rushing to meet them. Kade, desperately turning the wheel. Too late. Too late. Metal crunching, popping, crushing.

Dear God. How could she even still be alive?

Laughter from the other man as he drove away, leaving Kade trapped and unable to help his new bride as she died a horrible, brutal death.

"Oh, Kade." Bailey clasped his hand in both of hers. "I'm so sorry. I had no idea. I shouldn't have asked you to share something so painful, so personal."

He entwined his fingers with hers. "That's just it. It's painful, yes, but personal?" He scrubbed the stubble on his jaw with his free hand. "It should be. Abby . . . she was my *wife*. And it tears me apart that she died such a horrible death, that I couldn't protect her. And yet, it almost feels like it happened to someone else. It's as if I'm watching a movie in my head, and the script has all these holes in it. I have so many questions and so many gaps in my memory that none of it feels real."

He squeezed her hand. "This, this feels real. More real than any of my memories of Abby. How is that possible? What kind of man marries someone and watches her die right in front of him and can barely remember what she looked like? And how the hell can I want *you* so damn much when it hasn't even been a year since Abby died? I'm a sick bastard, that's all there is to it."

He tugged his hand but she held on, refusing to let go.

"Stop it. Stop blaming yourself for what you feel, or what you can or can't remember. As badly as you were hurt, you probably suffered a concussion at the least, maybe something far worse. You can't be expected to have a clear memory after something like that."

He didn't bother telling her that he'd been in a coma, or that he'd had a severe concussion that had him seeing double for weeks. Or that it had taken months of therapy just so he could walk again. And that he didn't know, even now, if he'd ever be able to walk without pain. He told her none of those things, because he didn't want her sympathy. He wanted *her*. And as she continued to berate him for feeling guilty about his late wife, his desire for her deepened even more.

This beautiful, courageous woman with her flashing green eyes and fiery temper was everything he wanted, but exactly what he couldn't have. She was an assassin, a murderer. He'd spent his entire adult life fighting to put people like her in prison. What he felt for her was wrong on so many levels. It made absolutely no sense.

And he didn't have a clue what he was going to do about it.

She gave him a sad smile, as if she understood the battle he was waging in his mind.

Maybe she did.

He checked his watch, before remembering he wasn't wearing it. "How long have we been here? Four hours? Five? We should probably get going, before someone figures out where we are."

Her eyes widened. "Try closer to forty-eight, give or take a couple of hours. It's about one in the afternoon. On Monday."

He stared at her in shock, then swore and flipped back the sheet. He'd put boxers on after his shower, so at least he wasn't completely naked this time.

"What are you doing?" She jumped off the bed and ran to the other side just as he'd gained his feet. "You should save your strength, try to sleep."

"We have to leave." He turned, saw their go bags on a dresser and started toward them. His leg wobbled and he had to catch himself against the foot of the bed.

She grabbed his arm, steadying him. "See. Told you. You shouldn't be walking."

"Where's my brace?"

"In the bag, but—"

She let out a muffled curse when he rushed to the bag and yanked out the brace.

"Damn it, Kade. You're going to rip out my stitches. I wasn't kidding when I said I didn't want to sew you up again. Lie back down."

"We're leaving." He snapped the brace on his thigh, hating the necessity of wearing it but grateful for the stability it gave him. He reached for his shirt and she was immediately helping him pull it over his head, and swearing at him the whole time.

He reached for a clean pair of jeans but she yanked them out of his reach.

"You're not getting these until you tell me what's going on."

He turned to face her. "We have to get out of here. I had no idea I'd been out for as long as I was."

"Have you forgotten this isn't my house? Your men won't know to look for us here."

He grabbed the jeans and yanked them out of her hand.

"Kade, damn it." She put her hands on her hips and glared at him. "You're really starting to piss me off."

He sighed, his shoes dangling from his fingers.

"I've gone off the grid, Bailey. By now, even if Porter hasn't told anyone about what happened at the hospital, I'm officially missing in action. The last Simmons knew of my whereabouts, I was on my way to find Hawke, with some woman. Remember you spoke to him? How long do you think it will take for him to piece things together and figure out that it's you that I was with?"

She bit her lip, looking less sure of herself now.

"My men will either think I've turned traitor and am working with the Enforcers," he continued, "or they'll think I've been taken prisoner. Either way, by now they've got several teams scouring the city looking for me, and you. Whether Simmons is involved or he just screwed up with Hawke, I don't know. But he'll share all the intel he has on Hawke and they'll dig farther, see if there are any connections to you since you were in the same town and—"

"Sooner or later they'll find something to lead them to this place. Hawke was over here often enough. He may have the address in an appointment book or a calendar, with my name beside it. Which means, this place isn't safe anymore."

"Agreed."

She snatched his shoes and shoved him out of the way while she rummaged in his go bag.

"What are you—"

"Looking for your socks," she snapped.

He reached in and pulled out a pair.

She grabbed them and pointed to the bed. "Sit. Hurry up."

He plopped onto the bed and Bailey knelt in front of him, making quick work of putting his socks and shoes on him.

Less than a minute later, they were both dressed and ready, with pistols holstered at their waists.

She started to grab both the go bags but he yanked them out of her reach and strapped them over his shoulder.

"Don't even try to argue," he warned.

She rolled her eyes and headed into the hall, stopping only to grab some towels from the linen closet. When they got to the car, he understood why. She arranged them over the passenger seat to cover the blood.

Kade would have preferred to drive, but didn't bother arguing. He could totally see her accusing him of being a chauvinist because he thought the man should drive. In that respect, she'd be right. But even though he felt surprisingly well for having been shot just a few days ago, he wasn't a hundred percent and didn't force the issue.

Ten minutes down the road, she pulled to the shoulder. "Okay, I haven't noticed anyone following us. I think we got out of the house before they figured out where we were. What do we do now? I'm fresh out of hiding places."

"There's only one place I can think of that they wouldn't expect either of us to go."

"Where?"

"Boulder. We're going to EXIT Inc.'s headquarters."

Chapter Fourteen

Monday, 3:53 p.m.

Bailey parked in front of the building in the slot marked CEO because, why not? There *was* no CEO of EXIT Incorporated anymore. Cyprian Cardenas had died many months ago in an altercation with the so-called Equalizers. And judging by the abandoned look of the place, no one else had been here in quite some time.

Last fall's leaves were scattered around in dried clumps. Weeds choked what had once been elaborate landscaping near the building and in medians spaced between the parking lot aisles. Cardenas had been a hard taskmaster, with meticulous high standards. Seeing the place this run-down was shocking, and final proof that EXIT's reign was well and truly over.

"Kind of reminds me of that abandoned hotel in *The Shining.*" She looked through the Mustang's windshield at the imposing structure. "I half expect some evil twins to wave at me from one of the windows." She shook her head. "They've really let the place go."

"Nobody works here anymore," Kade said. "And there's no point in keeping up the landscaping when the building's going to be razed. There are just a few more loose ends to tie up and then the construction crews will be out here."

"Razed? Seems like a huge waste to just tear the place down. But then, it's probably hard to find another business who'd want to locate so far out of town. It's quite the drive out here."

"I think it's more a case of the government wanting to eradicate any sign that EXIT ever existed." He popped his door open and grabbed their bags of supplies from the backseat.

"Hey, at least let me carry one of those. Your leg—"

"Is fine and I'm not letting you carry these when I'm perfectly capable."

She shook her head and they both got out of the car. While he secured the duffel bag straps over his shoulders, she said, "You're stubborn and ridiculous, you know. I can carry my own go bag."

"Is that the worst you've got? That badass reputation isn't looking so badass right now," he teased, as they headed toward the building.

She let loose with a string of curses.

He grinned. "There's my girl."

"You wish."

He laughed and stopped at the glass front doors, which had a thick chain across them and a heavy padlock. Plywood protected the glass, as it did all of the windows on the first floor. The upper-floor windows were left uncovered. Bailey didn't know why anyone had bothered to board the place up, unless there really was something inside to still protect. Maybe it wasn't as abandoned as it seemed. She couldn't help a quick look over her shoulder. But the parking lot was just as forlorn and empty as it had been when they'd arrived.

"I guess we should get the crowbar out of the trunk to break the—" She stopped when Kade slid a key out of the lining of his wallet and fit it into the padlock.

The lock clicked open and a feeling of unease snaked up her spine. "Why do you have a key?"

He pulled the door open and stepped back for her to enter. "Because I'm the one who had the place emptied and locked up in the first place. This is where I worked when I first took on this mission."

When she didn't move, he said, "Having second thoughts about me now?"

"I'm having second thoughts about coming here, period. The place reminds me of the prison in *The Walking Dead*."

He chuckled and waved for her to precede him into the immense, two-story lobby. "After you."

Lights came on as soon as they stepped inside. She whipped her gun out and whirled around, sweeping it in a circle.

"Relax. It's just the motion sensors." Kade moved past her toward a door on the far wall.

Feeling silly for being so skittish, she holstered her gun and followed him—which, because of his limp, wasn't very difficult even though his legs were so much longer than hers. Even with some over-the-counter pain meds in his system, both his leg and the fresh injury in his side had to be bothering him far more than he showed. But her offer of some prescription painkillers left over from one of her old injuries was emphatically turned down, without explanation.

His magical key unlocked yet another door, and he led them down a long hallway, past a door labeled Cafeteria. At the end of the long hall, they stopped in front of a set of elevators and he pushed the Up button. She kept her hand close to her holster, in spite of his reassurances that the place was empty. Maybe there were zombies hiding in some of the abandoned offices.

"If no one comes here anymore, why are the utilities still on?" The steel doors slid open and a bell dinged. "And why is the elevator still operating?"

"Emptying the place out and preparing it for destruction takes time. I've been more focused on capturing Enforcers than finishing up here, which is a good thing for us." They stepped inside and he pressed the button for the third floor. "The executive offices are still furnished and Cyprian has a couple of cushy couches we can crash on tonight. In the meantime, even though most of the computer muscle is gone, there are still a few desktops we can use. And a satellite dish on the roof. We should have Internet access. Maybe we can log into Netflix and catch up on some *Walking Dead* episodes."

She grinned. "Now you're speaking my language."

Halfway down the long plushly carpeted hallway, he entered the administrative assistant's office, which was basically the reception area for Cardenas. What had been the older lady's name who'd once worked here? Jolene? Yes, that was it. Bailey wondered what had happened to the woman. Hopefully she'd been given a generous retirement package. Hopefully all of the people who'd worked for EXIT—the ones who'd worked for the legitimate tour part of the company—had been generously taken care of. It wasn't fair that Jolene and so many others lost their livelihoods when the clandestine side of EXIT went belly-up.

"Bailey?"

He was waiting for her inside the next office, the one marked Cyprian Cardenas, CEO EXIT Incorporated. She stepped into the room and her mouth fell open in awe.

"Son of a . . . wow, just . . . wow." She turned in a full circle, trying to take everything in. It was the fanciest office she'd ever seen, with expensive cherry and mahogany wood furniture, a full bar, and what appeared to be a private bathroom. Even the ceiling was coffered, much like an old English library might be.

Kade had moved to the massive desk and plopped their go bags on top. He looked up from his examination of the old-fashioned desk phone, which was the only thing on the desk when they'd arrived. "You've never been here before?"

"I've been in the building. Cyprian's admin, Jolene, met me in Human Resources on the first floor so I could fill out paperwork and get a badge. I've been to the cafeteria, too, when meeting other Enforcers. But I've never been up here. This place is like the Taj Mahal."

"EXIT was a lucrative business, both the legitimate side and the clandestine side. Cardenas could afford the best."

"I'm surprised that his daughter, Melissa, agreed to close the tour side down. She could have kept it going even after the government shut down the Enforcer program." Although she was pretty sure the Equalizers would argue that *they'd* shut the program down, by shutting down Cyprian.

"From what I hear, she wanted nothing to do with the company after she learned the full extent of what her father had done."

Bailey's gaze shot to his. "She didn't know about the true EXIT until her father's death?"

"Not from what I was told."

"Then how is she even alive? I'd have thought the government wouldn't trust her to keep their precious secrets once she found out what was going on. They're certainly eliminating everyone else who knows anything."

Kade stiffened.

She stepped toward him. "I didn't mean that *you* would hurt her, or have her hurt. I realize you weren't aware of the government's plans to eliminate everyone associated with the program."

"We still haven't established that my boss, or anyone above him, is trying to kill everyone who used to be part of the Enforcer program."

She frowned. "Hawke's death, the bullet hole in your side, aren't proof enough?"

"Your friend's death was tragic, but could very well have been an accident. Simmons and his team could have made a mistake, then realized what they'd done and didn't want to own up to it. As for my injury, yes, Porter is a bad apple. But that doesn't mean everyone on this mission is corrupt."

"The agents helping Porter try to kill us, what, helped on accident?"

"Of course not. But you have to understand how

the bureau works. We follow orders, often without knowing all the reasons behind them. If Porter gave those agents reason to believe that you and I were a danger to others, they would have helped him—as fellow agents helping another in need—without question."

She shook her head and put her hands on her hips. "And my other friends? Did you forget about Sebastian and Amber? Let me guess. Those were unfortunate mistakes as well?"

"I don't know yet," he said, his voice clipped and short. "But I would have hoped by now that you'd realized I'm not turning a blind eye to anything. But neither am I prepared to condemn everyone I work with without proof."

She shoved her hair back from her face, not sure whether to rail at him or to apologize. How could he need more proof after what they'd been through? And yet, how could she be upset at him for wanting to treat people fairly and not turn his back on them without proof of their guilt? He was noble, with his own code of honor. And she couldn't help admiring him for it, even though it drove her crazy.

She'd decided on an apology when he suddenly pressed a series of buttons on the desk phone. Movement to her right had her whipping her gun out of the holster and whirling around. But the only "threat" was a cherrywood door sliding back into the wall and lights switching on, revealing a previously hidden office.

"Sorry," he said. "Should have warned you first."

She holstered her gun and joined him at the opening. "What is this?"

"The heart of Cyprian's operation, where he conducted the clandestine side of the business. There's a desktop computer in there. It's as good a place as any to start ferreting out whether my boss and others know what Porter is up to. Come on." He headed into the other room.

She let out a deep breath and stepped inside, jumping when the panel slid closed behind her.

"Open that back up," she said. "I don't like feeling trapped."

He moved to the desk that was a twin of the one in the outer office, and pressed a sequence of buttons on the matching phone. The panel immediately slid open.

"Better?" he asked.

She nodded. "Thanks."

"Claustrophobia or something else?"

"Something else." At his questioning look, she conceded, "I don't like having my exits blocked off. Especially at EXIT headquarters." She waved toward the computer monitor. "You really think we can get any useful information out of that?"

"We may not have the resources of the FBI behind us at the moment. But I'm pretty good at old-fashioned Internet searches. Let's see what we can find on Porter and Simmons. And I should check my email to see if Gannon came through with the background report I requested on two of my agents. If they're not really agents, which is what I suspect, knowing more information on them might give us some leads to follow, too."

"Gannon? I thought you two weren't talking these days?"

"I called him from the house in Boulder and appealed to his sense of honor. Basically, the idea of mercenaries potentially impersonating federal officers was more abhorrent than speaking to me."

"I really don't like this former friend of yours."

He smiled.

"I'm thinking we should search for info on your boss, too," she said. "What did you say his name was?"

"Faegan." He powered up the computer. "The mainframe is still here, on the first floor. But it's been wiped clean aside from the operating system and the programs that control things like the lights and air-conditioning. It will be destroyed along with the building."

"Destroyed? Mainframes are crazy expensive. Why not sell it?"

"Because even though some of the top geeks in the industry were paid a hell of a lot of money to ensure that none of the data that was ever stored on the hard drives is capable of being recovered, we can't take that chance. While there's no way to guarantee that someone won't try to start up something similar to EXIT again sometime in the future, we can at least do everything in our power to ensure they don't have a head start. Cyprian's massive databases are gone. Destroyed. The backups included. See for yourself."

He motioned her to take a seat behind the desk and she did. The familiar logon screen she'd been using her entire career as an Enforcer was displayed. The same screen she and others still used to communicate through an encrypted network. It was the same network where they'd been given their mission plans, and sometimes, EXIT orders—which contained the details about some criminal or terrorist they were supposed to target.

She keyed her login and password and pressed Enter.

An error message popped up on the screen saying that the login was invalid.

"Only administrator IDs work from this system." He leaned over her shoulder and entered an ID and password.

The screen popped up a menu unlike anything she'd ever seen. None of the options looked familiar. At the top, it read, ISPF Primary Option Menu. Tabs under that had labels like Utilities and Compilers. And down the left side of the screen were even more choices, starting at 0 for Settings, then 1 for View, 3 was another Utilities option, and there were many more.

"I don't understand," she said. "What is this?"

"Essentially, it's a user interface to the operating system. Choose option three dot four."

"Three dot four?"

He leaned over her and keyed 3.4 and pressed Enter. "There, it gives you a place to look at all of the files on the system. Press Enter again, without filling out anything else on the screen."

She did, and it came up with a message saying no files were found. "Does that mean the computer is empty? The mainframe doesn't have anything on it?"

"Pretty much. Technically it means nothing exists on the system that starts with my ID as the prefix, since we're logged onto my account. But if you type a tick mark, then A, followed by a wildcard it will show you all of the files starting with the letter A. You can do that for any letter and—"

She held her hands up in surrender. "Okay, okay.

So I'm not as good with computers as I thought I was 'cause you're speaking a language I don't understand. But I was on the old Enforcer network just last week. Are you saying that's been disabled since then?"

"Not exactly. I can access that system from here, but the data that drives most of it is static. And if you were to try to maneuver around the whole system the way you used to, you'd find a lot of the links no longer work. That's because we only kept a shell running, just enough to allow communications, really. There isn't anything you or the others can access now about old missions or any sensitive data. All of that was destroyed. Basically, the front end remains to fool the Enforcers who still haven't been caught."

"And that front end is run from this building?"

He shook his head. "It's run from an FBI lab outside the city. I can log onto it from here, but most of the remaining administrative functions have to be accessed from a terminal hardwired in the lab, not remotely. If you were hoping to find all of the FBI's secrets and an org chart showing who's calling the shots on the Enforcer retraining mission, then I have to disappoint you. That kind of information just isn't here."

She sat back. "Earlier you mentioned your research on the Enforcers. Like finding all of my properties."

"Except the one in Canada?" he teased.

"Right. Except that one. Where is all that research?"

He straightened and stepped back from the desk. "You're a task driver and a half."

"Sorry, can't help it. I'm curious."

He smiled. "I don't mind. But I can't show you any of that research. Everything I worked on for this mission is maintained on the bureau's mainframes now, not EXIT's mainframe. I had access to a limited part of the files through my PC back at the house where I was staying, the one you found. And I had some stacks of property reports on the bookshelf to work through. But anything really incriminating that could be tied back to EXIT, what little of that type of data remains, has to be pulled up onsite."

"In that lab you mentioned."

"Yep. I go there once or twice a week. It's more like a warehouse than a lab, although it used to be a bustling technology center. These days a few lonely souls like myself wander in and out a few times a week to run reports."

"Where is it?" she asked again.

He frowned. "Why are you asking so many questions about the lab? I'm not going to take you there. Data on other missions that have nothing to do with EXIT are stored in that facility. And I'm not turning traitor on the FBI and revealing the lab's location."

"Then maybe you'll tell us instead," a voice said from the doorway.

Kade grabbed his pistol and whirled around, then froze. The other man was already pointing his pistol at him.

"Drop it."

Kade hesitated.

Two other men stepped from the shadows to flank the first. They were both holding guns, too.

Kade swore and tossed his gun to the floor.

Bailey sat frozen, her right hand on the butt of

her gun. But she didn't pull it out of the holster. For the first time since becoming an Enforcer, she wasn't sure what she should do, what she *wanted* to do.

"Who are you?" Kade demanded. "What do you want?"

"Our official 'team' name is the Equalizers," the first man said. "But you can call me Jace."

BAILEY SLOWLY ROSE from her seat as Jace Atwell and the two other men entered the office. One of them appeared to be about six foot four and towered over everyone else. She didn't need an introduction to know who he was. His reputation preceded him in the world of EXIT. He was *The* Enforcer, Devlin Buchanan. And he was even more intimidating in person than on paper.

She shot a worried glance at Kade, before looking back at Jace, who appeared to be the leader of this little welcoming party.

"What are you doing here, Jace? And don't tell me it's a coincidence that you just happened to come here when we were here."

Kade's eyes widened and he stared at her. "Friends of yours?"

"I'm, ah, not sure yet. Jace is the one who helped me escape your house that first night. And that man—" she pointed "—is Devlin Buchanan. A former Enforcer. I don't know the other guy."

"That's Mason," a fourth man said as he rolled into the office in a wheelchair. "He's a serious son of a bitch and has absolutely no sense of humor. I don't know why we keep him."

Mason ignored him, keeping his gaze locked on Kade, his gun trained on his chest.

"Back up," Buchanan ordered, motioning for Kade to move into the middle of the room. Mason immediately followed, like a bloodhound following a scent trail. Or maybe a Rottweiler. He was laser-focused, ignoring the others. He only had eyes for Kade.

Kade did as ordered, but his body was tense, his hands fisted at his sides. His gaze was constantly moving, scanning the room and everyone in it. Until he looked at Bailey. His jaw tightened, and he looked away.

Her shoulders sagged. He obviously thought she'd planned this, that somehow she'd colluded with these . . . Equalizers . . . to capture him. And she couldn't even be angry at him for making that assumption. She hadn't done a single thing to stop them. As soon as she'd seen Jace standing there, her loyalties had ripped clean in two. Both men had saved her life. How was she supposed to choose sides?

She pushed out of the chair just as the young man in the wheelchair zipped over beside her.

"Out of my way, lady." He made a shooing motion with his hand.

She gave him a look that should have made him burst into flames. "I don't think so."

A slow grin spread across his face. "You're spunky. I like that. But I don't have time to spar with you right now." He grabbed her hips and tried to shove her out of the way.

She karate chopped his hands down and grabbed the butt of her gun. Suddenly the cold muzzle of another pistol pressed against the side of her neck.

"Austin might be an ass," the man said, his voice

deadly calm as he towered over her. "But he's *my* ass. I'm not about to let you shoot my brother."

Devlin Buchanan.

She very slowly lifted her hand off her gun. He plucked the pistol from her holster and then he was gone, like a wraith, rejoining the others watching over Kade. She let out a shaky breath and wondered if her heart would ever be the same.

The creep in the wheelchair, Austin, winked as if this were all some amusing game. He shoved the chair out of the way and wheeled behind the desk. His fingers practically flew across the keyboard as he studied the screen in front of him.

"Austin," Jace called out. "One of these days I'm going to teach you some manners."

"That day may come, but it is not *this* day." He winked at Bailey again.

She narrowed her eyes.

He grinned.

"Did you just quote *Lord of the Rings* at me?" Jace called out again from the other side of the room.

"If you have to ask, you're not worthy of an answer." Austin hit Enter, frowned, typed some more commands.

Bailey turned around. She'd been avoiding looking at Kade, afraid she'd see the hurt and anger in his eyes again. But he wasn't looking at her. He was glaring at Buchanan, who had his gun trained on him, while Jace and Mason were . . .

"What the hell are you doing?" she demanded, crossing the room. "Let him go."

The click-click of metal sounded as Jace and Mason fastened the handcuffs into place.

"Stop it! Take those off." Bailey's divided loyalties

were no longer divided. She was Team Kade all the way. These Equalizers could suck it. She was about to take them down.

Starting with Jace Atwell.

She stalked toward him. His back was turned to her as he spoke to the others.

"Bailey." Kade's low, urgent whisper stopped her in her tracks. He shook his head. "Don't."

He was worried about her. He was also angry, bordering on furious. She could see it in every line of his body. But above everything else, he was concerned about her.

"Kade."

Jace stepped past her on his way to the desk, seemingly oblivious that she'd been about to pummel him.

"Finding anything?" he asked.

"The Ghost wasn't lying," Austin announced. "The mainframe's been wiped clean. I figured if we had a valid ID we'd be able to pull whatever files they're using to go after Enforcers. But there's nothing here."

Bailey took a step closer to Kade, her gaze locked on his. "I'm sorry," she whispered.

"Did you know?" he asked quietly.

She glanced at Buchanan and Mason standing on either side of him, before answering. "No. I didn't. I swear."

"Could they be hiding files in the system?" Jace asked from behind her at the desk.

"This isn't a homegrown interface," Austin answered, sounding like he was lecturing a child. "This is a vanilla operating system interface. Trust me. Nothing's hidden. Wherever EXIT's files are, they're not here."

Devlin pressed his hand against what Bailey now realized was an earpiece, like the ones the secret service wore. "Terrance says the Feds are ten minutes out. They must have some kind of monitoring system still active out here. We need to go."

Kade stiffened.

"You didn't know they were monitoring this building, did you?" Jace called out, apparently more aware of the scene playing out in the middle of the room than he'd seemed.

Kade shrugged. "I knew it was a possibility. But I thought it was a remote one. Did you tap into the security system? Is that how you knew we were here?"

"Nope," Jace said. "I gave Bailey a GPS locator. We've been tracking you two for days, finally decided it was time to make our move."

Bailey whirled around. "You're lying."

"Did you really think I'd carry a pathetic little Derringer Cobra as my backup gun?"

She sucked in a breath. "You bastard. You tricked me."

"Eight minutes out," Devlin announced. "This is your mission, Jace. You're the boss on this one. Make the call."

"Do it."

Bailey whirled toward Kade just as Mason jammed a hypodermic needle into the side of his neck.

Chapter Fifteen

Tuesday, 7:45 a.m.

Kade forced his bleary eyes open, blinking against the sunlight streaming through a window high above him. Once again he was lying on a bed, his mind a jumble of foggy, confusing images.

He raised his hands to rub his eyes but stopped when the chains connected to the handcuffs on his wrists pulled him up short. Another chain ran down his chest and connected to cuffs at his ankles. All that was missing was an orange jumpsuit and he'd be ready for transport to a maximum-security prison.

"Morning."

He sat up and whirled around in one swift motion, ready to attack, then stopped. A sense of déjà vu swept over him. Once again he was in an unfamiliar bedroom, with Bailey watching him from the doorway. Only, this time, he was trussed up like an animal. And he didn't know whether her being here was a good thing or a bad thing. Was she friend, or foe? Regardless of which side she fell on, he couldn't help the rush of relief that swept through him seeing that she was okay.

She was wearing a short leather skirt and some kind of leather vest top with a zipper up the front. And damned if his heart didn't skip a beat at the sight of her. He glanced down at his own sorry self, wishing he could shower and change clothes. And shave. The stubble on his face was driving him crazy.

He shook his head. Obviously whatever Mason had injected him with at EXIT was making him loopy. He didn't give a damn what he was wearing. What mattered was figuring out how to get out of here. Whether that was with or without Bailey, remained to be seen.

"I'm so sorry." She motioned toward the cuffs and chains. "That's Mason's doing. He and Devlin co-lead this group. Surprisingly, Devlin seems more reasonable than Mason and didn't want you restrained. But Mason disagreed. Jace didn't weigh in at all on the subject. And yet, Devlin and Mason have made it clear that this assignment, or mission, is Jace's to lead. I think they take turns maybe? But then when it comes to a really important decision, Devlin and Mason step in. I don't know. I can't figure these people out."

She raked her hands through her hair. "I'm out of my element here, Kade. I'm not sure what to do. I've tried to reason with them, but I'm outnumbered. They grilled me about you. At first I didn't tell them anything. But when I realized they thought you were the one behind the murders, I had to defend you. I told them what you told me, and how you tried to save Hawke. But I don't know if it made a difference. And, Kade, I promise you I didn't know about the tracker in the gun that Jace gave me. It never even occurred to me that he might do something like that. They act like they're my friends and yet they've taken my weapons. It's all a crazy mess and I'm trying to—"

He drew a deep breath and let her ramble on. Listening to her nervous chatter was just what he'd needed. A sense of calm settled over him and the fog of confusion lifted from his mind. Bailey was okay, and she hadn't gone to the dark side. Knowing *that* gave him the peace he'd needed in order to focus.

When she finally paused for breath, he said, "Bailey. Relax. I know that none of this is your fault."

She blinked. "You do?"

He tugged on the chains, wincing when the strain made a muscle twinge in his bad leg.

She rushed forward, worry lines creasing her brow. "It's your leg, isn't it? Do you need some pain pills? This hiding place of theirs seems to have every kind of supply imaginable. I'm sure I can get you something to help—"

He kissed her. He wanted nothing more than to pull her onto the bed and deepen the kiss, explore that maddening zipper between her breasts, slide his hand beneath that sexy little skirt. But this wasn't the time or the place. It nearly killed him, but he pulled back and let her go.

"I'm okay, Bailey," he assured her, smiling at the slightly dazed look in her eyes. He loved that this beautiful, intelligent, ball-buster of a woman could fluster so easily whenever he touched her.

"What about you?" he asked. "You seem okay.

They haven't hurt you, have they?" Just the idea that they might have mistreated her had his fists tightening at his sides.

"No, no one has done anything to me. Are you sure your leg—"

"I'm sure. I don't suppose you have an extra key lying around somewhere to take these chains off?"

"Not yet. But I'll get you free somehow. I'm still working on the 'how' part. There are only five of them here right now, but there were a lot more earlier. The men you saw last night—Mason, Devlin, Jace, and Austin—plus a new guy, Terrance. You remember they call themselves the Equalizers?"

He nodded. "I'm not sure what that means, though."

She frowned. "From what I understand, most of them are former Enforcers. Their goal seems to be the same goal that you have—to bring EXIT down and ensure the program isn't reinstated." She fingered the chains between his wrists, her jaw tightening. "But obviously we have a difference of opinion about how to make that happen. We've got to make sure they realize that you're not behind the killings."

"Bailey, we don't know that anyone has been killed—not on purpose at least."

Her brows drew down and a tiny spark of temper sizzled in her green eyes. "You still don't believe me about Sebastian and Amber?"

"I believe that *you* believe they've been killed. But until I have proof, I prefer to give my peers the benefit of the doubt." He glanced at his watch. "It's Tuesday."

She gave him a funny look. "Every week, right after Monday. Why?"

"I never did get a chance to check my email. I should have that report from Gannon by now."

"At this point, why do we care?"

"It's part of that proof we want."

"*You* want. I already know the truth. My friends were murdered."

"Fine," he said. "It's part of the proof that *I'm* looking for, a thread I can follow to help our investigation into what's going on here. I suspect that two members of the team that I sent after you are impersonating federal officers. They might be mercenaries. If that's the case, and I can find out who hired them, I'll be in a much better position to figure this out."

She reached for her phone, then stopped. "Damn. They took my phone along with my weapons. But there are computers all over this place. We'll just have to convince stubborn Mason to let you log on and check your email. Then we can—"

"We're ready," a man's voice called from the doorway.

She narrowed her eyes, keeping her back to him. "His name's Terrance," she whispered. "I figure I'll kill him first because he's been ordering me around all morning. Then I'll take out the smart-ass in the wheelchair. I'm saving Jace for last. His death will be slow. And painful."

Kade chuckled. He knew she wasn't serious. Or at least, he didn't *think* she was.

He leaned to the side to see around her. Terrance was impressively muscled, with dreads that hung to his shoulders. And, lest Kade get the idea that he could escape with six feet of chains woven around his limbs, another man stood in the shadows. The one Bailey was saving for last—Jace.

"We'll get through this," he assured her in a whisper. "We'll figure it out. But I would very much appreciate it if you'd refrain from killing anyone for now. I prefer to get out of these sticky situations with all lives intact if at all possible. Okay?"

"You're spoiling my fun."

"I know."

"Fine. I'll wait. For now."

He smiled. In spite of the craziness that was going on, his failed mission, the near-death experiences of the past few days, he'd smiled more with Bailey than he had, well, for as long as he could remember. Now, all he had to do was figure out how to get both of them out of here without a bloodbath.

A minute later their little entourage filed into a large room dominated by a long rectangular table. The rest of the men who'd been at EXIT last night were sitting there, waiting, with piles of folders and papers on top of the table. The one in the wheelchair, Austin, had a laptop computer in front of him. They looked like the Spanish Inquisition, ready to throw baseless accusations at him and then burn him alive.

Jace waved him to a chair at the far end. Bailey sat beside him. She scooted her chair slightly closer to his and crossed her arms. Message clear. If it came to choosing sides, she chose Kade.

"Where's the retraining facility?" Jace hit him with the heavy artillery right from the start.

Kade kept his face carefully blank. Bailey had said she'd told the Equalizers things about him. Was this one of those things? What else had she shared?

"What retraining facility?" he asked, not planning on making any of this easy on them. As far as he was concerned, they were no better than thugs.

Jace clasped his hands together on top of the table. "Let's clear a few points up from the start so we don't waste time talking around each other. Most of us used to work for EXIT. We know all about the clandestine program that was supposed to prevent future tragedies like 9/11. The main difference between EXIT and other agencies is the level of proof, and timing. The evidence used to justify an EXIT mission wasn't the type that would necessarily hold up in court."

"Like illegal searches," Kade accused.

"That's one example, yes. Since EXIT's goal was to save lives, not prosecute, the tactics were a bit . . . different. The other big difference of course is that Enforcers were often tasked with taking out the bad guys *before* they killed more innocent people. They wanted to prevent national tragedies, not wait until after they happened, when it was too late. And that's the whole problem right there. A program like that was bound to be abused. Once some Enforcers were tricked into killing innocent people by leaders intent on eliminating their own personal enemies, or worse, lining their pockets, the dangers of the program were deemed to outweigh the good. It had to be shut down. Can we at least agree on all of that? Make that the baseline for our discussion?"

Kade considered, then nodded. "Agreed."

"Excellent." Jace leaned back in his chair. "Now here's where it gets murky. EXIT as an entity was supposedly taken off-line months ago after the CEO was killed. But then someone sent messages through the Enforcers' online communication network trying to trick them into meeting up with representatives from EXIT, allegedly to discuss compensation for past services. Anyone who went to one of those meetings has never been seen again. From what we've gleaned, that's where you come in. You and some fellow FBI agents are tasked with bringing in anyone who didn't voluntarily come in. The question is what's happening to those Enforcers after you capture them?"

He waited, and when Kade didn't respond, Jace said, "You're supposedly turning them over to a retraining facility. And from there they should eventually re-enter society as fully productive individuals who aren't a threat to anyone. But that's not really the concern, is it? The concern is whether they can ever talk about EXIT and destroy the careers and lives of whoever else in the government was ever associated with the program. That's why you're capturing and *killing* the Enforcers, isn't it?"

Again, Kade remained silent.

"Why are you using mercenaries, if not to kill Enforcers?"

Kade stiffened. Had Gannon sent the promised report and confirmed that Jack and Dom were fake agents? Had these Equalizers cracked the lock code on his phone and gotten into his personal files? What else had they found?

Bailey was staring at Jace, her teeth biting her bottom lip. She seemed as if she, too, was trying to figure out where he'd gotten his information.

"What are you talking about?" Kade asked.

"Two of the members on the team that went after Bailey aren't federal agents. Dominic Wales and Jack Martinelli. But, then, you knew that, didn't you? How can you work with mercenaries and not expect that they'd be killing your mission targets?"

"I had my suspicions about Jack and Dom." He saw no reason to deny it. "Regardless, no one on any of my teams is out to kill anyone. That's not our goal."

"Hawke doesn't count? What about Sebastian, and Amber? And countless others who haven't been seen since your team ambushed them?"

"Hawke's death was tragic. I still don't know exactly what happened there. As for the rest, if anyone else has died, I intend to find out and take the necessary steps to prevent further deaths. Something I could be working on right this minute if you weren't wasting my time."

"So, you claim that you don't know anything about the deaths of Amber Braithwaite and Sebastian Lachlan?"

Kade frowned, wondering what he was leading up to. "I know nothing about them other than that they were taken before I began my mission."

Jace pulled one of the stacks of papers toward him.

Kade eyed it warily, wondering what it was.

"This is a stack of reports I took from your house the night that Bailey was there," Jace said. "They list the property owned by various Enforcers. The funny thing is, your name is listed as the person who requested these reports." He picked up two stapled stacks from the rest and slid them across the table.

To Bailey.

She frowned and thumbed through the pages. Her face went pale.

"I see you've come to the interesting part," Jace said. "Care to tell Special Agent Quinn what you just read?"

She glanced up at Kade. "These list Sebastian's and Amber's property holdings. And they're signed by you."

"Pass them to him," Jace said.

"That's not necessary." Kade didn't take his eyes off Bailey. "I didn't know Sebastian or Amber. I didn't lie about that. But part of my job on this mission is to make sure that every home, business, warehouse, boat, whatever that is owned by any Enforcers is thoroughly searched to ensure that they didn't keep any papers or recordings or anything sensitive in nature relating to EXIT. Sebastian and Amber, as I told you, were taken before I came on the job. I requested property reports on *everyone* to double-check behind my predecessor to make sure he didn't miss anything. That's it. A global request for information on all of the Enforcers who were captured before I took the job, as well as those still remaining to be taken. I didn't lie to you, Bailey."

One of the reports crinkled in her hand. She set it down and absently smoothed it.

"Bailey?"

"I believe you," she said, but her voice didn't sound nearly as confident as it had a few minutes earlier.

"Let's see," Jace said. "You work with mercenaries, but not to hurt anyone of course. And you have reports on people you claimed you didn't know. Have I got it right so far?"

"Bite me," Kade said.

Jace chuckled. "Oh, by the way. How's the leg, Kade? Doin' okay?"

"What do you want?"

"The truth would be nice. Bailey, I'm curious. Did

Kade tell you how he got injured? I'd love to hear the story."

She frowned.

"Go ahead," Kade told her. "I've got nothing to hide."

She gave a sanitized version of what he'd told her in Colorado Springs.

Jace made a show of looking through the documents in front of him. Around the table, the other Equalizers sat quietly, letting him run his little show.

Kade wanted to punch every single one of them.

"Ah, here we are. A police report for the night you were involved in that horrendous accident." Again, he tossed the report to Bailey. "If you don't mind, would you skim that and give us a summary?"

"Wait," Kade said. "I already know what—"

Jace held up his hand. "You'll get a turn. Bailey, please?"

Kade cursed beneath his breath. He'd figured out at least part of their game. They were trying to drive a wedge between him and Bailey, to prove he was the villain they believed him to be. And from the stricken look on her face, they were succeeding.

"It wasn't even a car accident," she said, her voice tight, barely above a whisper. "You were injured in your garage, working on your boat."

"I know that's what it says, but—"

"No gunshot," she continued, her voice getting louder. "No *wife*. Why would you make up something like that?"

He gritted his teeth and tried again. "The report was falsified. My boss told me about it after I woke up from the coma."

"You never mentioned a coma," she accused.

"I also didn't tell you that I was in the hospital for four months, that I was in rehab after that. There wasn't a reason to share any of that with you."

As soon as the words left his mouth he wished he could take them back. Because there *was* a reason that he should have shared. He and Bailey had formed some kind of bond, a tenuous one that was difficult to define. But it relied on honesty and openness between them. He should have told her those details. He realized it now. Caring about someone meant sharing exactly those kinds of details. And he definitely cared about her—as impossible as that seemed since they'd known each other for such a short period of time. But he was so used to keeping it all inside that he hadn't stopped to consider the damage he might do by not telling her.

"The original police report was replaced in order to keep people from asking questions," he told her. "Making my injury seem like a common household accident meant no one would look any deeper. The FBI wanted to investigate on their own because they . . ." His voice trailed off when he saw the next trap. He glared at Jace.

"Go on," Jace said. "No reason to stop now."

"Why did the FBI want to cover it up?" This time it was Bailey asking the question.

"Because," Kade said, trying to keep his temper under wraps, "the man who shot through my car door, injuring me and killing my wife, was an Enforcer. It was a mistake. He went after the wrong person. But you can imagine that the FBI wouldn't want anyone seeing the bullet hole in the door and investigating who the shooter might be."

Her eyes widened. "You have a vendetta against Enforcers. That's why you took on this mission."

If Kade had a gun right now, he very much feared he would use it on Jace for stirring all of this up. Jace should thank God for small favors.

"I wouldn't call it a vendetta. The Enforcer who killed Abby was taken to the retraining facility long before I got out of the hospital. I don't even know who he was."

"Then why did you agree to take the mission?" she asked.

He closed his eyes for a moment, trying to see a way out of the quicksand forming beneath him. But all he seemed to be doing was sinking faster.

"The bullet that went through my hip and thigh did extensive nerve and muscle damage. I was addicted to prescription painkillers and pretty much made a disaster of my life. The FBI was going to cut me loose. An old friend of mine who'd heard about the accident contacted my boss, Faegan. Then Gannon—"

"Your friend?" Jace asked. "His name was Gannon?"

"Robert Gannon, yes. He's with Homeland Security now but he used to be in the FBI. We were peers. We both worked for Faegan and Faegan worked for Kendall. Gannon called Faegan and pressured him to give me another chance. He knew my career was everything to me and that it would have killed me to lose it. That's why I took the mission. It was the first thing available once I was out of rehab. The fact that my accident was caused by an Enforcer had nothing to do with it."

"You sure about that?" This time it was Mason

who spoke. He sat a couple of chairs down from Bailey on the same side of the table. "Did you know it was an Enforcer who'd caused the accident, assuming there really was an accident?"

"I didn't even know what an Enforcer was until after Faegan agreed to put me back on active duty and gave me this assignment. What's the point of all these questions? What's the point of any of this?"

"What happened to your wife's body?" Jace asked.

Kade slowly turned toward him. "Excuse me?"

"She's not listed on the police report. Oh, wait, you said it's a fake report. Okay, so in the real report, which we don't have, what would it have told me about your wife?" He waited, arched a brow. "If I Googled her, what would I find? Where is she buried?"

He looked down the table at Austin.

"Already on it," Austin said. "Nothing's coming up for Abby Quinn."

"Abigail," Kade snapped. "We were only married a couple of months. Try Abigail Winters. That was her maiden name."

Austin started tapping on the keyboard.

"While we wait for that," Jace said, "I'm still puzzled. I should find a marriage license, or even a death certificate since that would be issued under her married name. Guess what? I got nothing."

"Then you're obviously looking in the wrong places."

"Naturally. I figured that was the problem," Jace mocked. "What's the name of the cemetery where she's buried."

"She was cremated. Her urn is on my mantel at home."

"I don't recall a fireplace when I was there."

"The house in Boulder was rented for this mission by the FBI," Kade said. "My home is in Jacksonville, Florida. And, no, I'm not taking you there to show you my wife's ashes. What the hell is all of this about?"

"Austin," Jace said. "Any luck with that Google search?"

"Nope. Can't find a driver's license, tax return, utility records, nothing for Abby Abigail Winters Quinn. It's like someone made her up out of thin air or something."

Kade shook his head. He didn't know whether to scream or laugh at this bizarre conversation. "None of this makes sense. And it has nothing to do with my work to bring in the Enforcers." He looked at Bailey, but she was staring off into space.

"You mentioned that Hawke's death was an accident." Mason's deep voice cut through the room. "Who did you say was the lead agent you ordered to capture him?"

"I'm not sure that I did. His name is Simmons."

"There was another Enforcer killed while you and Bailey were in Colorado Springs."

Kade hesitated. "Yes. There was. Henry Sanchez. Why are you—"

"Who was the lead in that case?"

"That 'case' wasn't a capture situation. I assigned an agent to perform surveillance. He ended up trying to kill Bailey and me. He's one of the men I'm investigating, if I can ever get back to the investigation. There's a strong possibility that he might be the one behind all of this, assuming the missing Enforcers really are being killed."

Mason didn't look impressed with his assessment. "His name?"

"The bad agent? Lamar Porter. Again, why are you asking?"

Mason motioned to Jace. "Show him."

For once, Jace didn't preface his search through the pile of papers with sarcasm. Instead, he was quiet, almost somber. He flipped open a folder that was beneath the papers and pulled out two photographs, which he set down in front of Kade.

Kade stared at the pictures, the blood rushing from his face, leaving him cold. Simmons had been shot twice, a double-tap to the head. Porter's death had been less precise. Whoever had killed him shot him three times, none of them probably fatal by themselves. But he'd obviously bled out from the combination.

He shoved the pictures back toward Jace. "Your work, I presume? After all, you did follow Bailey to Colorado Springs."

Jace gave him a droll look. "Nice try. The pictures are from police reports. One of our contacts in Colorado Springs brought the deaths to our attention. What did you do, sneak out of that house where you and Bailey were staying so you could tie up some loose ends? Pay the men back that you think double-crossed you?"

Bailey frowned and stared at Jace. Was she actually believing Jace's theory? Or was there another reason altogether?

"I have no idea who killed those men," Kade said. "I didn't even know they were dead. If this little interrogation of yours was legit, this is where I'd be asking for my lawyer. Since it's not, I'm putting an end to it. Nothing we've discussed is helping my investigation. You're only muddying the waters." He looked at Bailey, who was again staring off into space. "And making trouble," he said softly.

"We're almost done." Jace reached beneath the table. He straightened and placed Kade's leg brace in front of him. "Look familiar?"

Kade didn't bother answering. His stomach was already sinking. Based on how Jace was twisting and turning everything else around, he already knew what was going to happen.

"Bailey, look at me. Please."

She wasn't looking off into space anymore. But she wasn't looking at Kade either. She was staring at the GPS tracker disc that Jace had just pulled out of the lining of the brace.

"It's a backup," Kade said. "Remember, Bailey? I pulled one out of the brace in the hospital parking lot, because I didn't want anyone finding us. Everyone has a backup. Right? But I didn't use it. We're on the same side. Jace, these men, they're trying to trick you into thinking that I've been lying about everything all along. They want you to think that I'm using you—"

"Are you?" She was staring at him now, her arms crossed. Her face impassive. But it was her eyes that told him he'd already lost the war. They were cold, brittle chips of emerald ice without a hint of warmth.

"The disc isn't activated. I'm not trying to lead anyone to you or anyone else. If I wanted that, I could have done it in Colorado Springs. Think about it. My own men were turning on me. I'm not conspiring with anyone against you. I want the truth, just like you. We're a team, working to find out if the retraining facility is what Faegan says it is or if Enforcers really are being killed. Nothing has changed."

He waited, hoping she would say something. When she didn't, he tried again. "Before I met you in person, I wouldn't have thought twice about tricking you so I could capture you. Because I believed in my mission. We're way past that now. I'm not lying. And I wouldn't lie, not to you, because I *know* you."

Her eyes narrowed. "You don't know me, Kade. You don't know me at all." And with that, she shoved back from the table and stalked out of the room.

Kade didn't move, barely breathed, as the disaster of the last few minutes replayed itself in his mind. All the trust and respect that had been building between him and Bailey had been destroyed in, what, fifteen, twenty minutes? By a master manipulator.

He didn't dare look at Jace, or the others yet. He was too angry. So angry that he knew the chains wouldn't protect the men sitting around the table. In the hands of a desperate man, those chains would become nooses around their throats.

Instead, he sat very still, thinking about everything Jace had said. The reports. The Google searches. All the questions that had been raised. And Kade did what he always did with information. He began piecing it together in his mind, looking at every angle, searching for the simplest, most logical explanation. And asking the questions that Jace hadn't asked.

Like why his boss had really hired him for this mission.

And whether there was another reason Faegan was so intent on keeping the retraining facility's location a secret from Kade.

Then he wondered about one of the questions that Mason had asked, because it bore thinking about. Was it really a coincidence that an Enforcer had caused his accident, and then Kade was later assigned to run the program to supposedly *save* Enforcers?

While he knew the conclusions that Jace had drawn were wrong, there was only one conclusion he could put together after looking at all the facts.

Someone was setting him up for a very big fall.

He shoved back from the table and stood. As one, the others jumped to their feet, guns drawn, aimed at Kade. Even Austin held a gun pointed at him.

Kade ignored them all, all except Jace.

He shuffled around the table, metal jangling against metal until he stood beside Jace. He held out his hands, wrists up.

"Take off the chains. I'm taking you to the FBI lab."

Chapter Sixteen

Tuesday, 11:12 a.m.

Bailey wasn't sure what she'd expected of the FBI lab, but the lone whitewashed building visible through the panel van's windshield wasn't it. She braced herself against the wall to keep from falling as Austin pulled to a jarring stop behind the building.

"All right," Jace said. "Kade, you first. Everyone follow his lead and stay alert." He slammed the side door back on its rails and motioned for Kade to precede him.

Kade glanced at her, but she looked away, pretending to be busy rechecking the loading of her Sig Sauer. She heard his sigh, and knew he'd assumed the worst—that she didn't trust him or believe in him anymore. But that wasn't it at all. She was ashamed. She owed him an apology the size of Colorado for stalking out of the interrogation like she had. But she needed more than a quick glance, or a stolen chat in a hallway to tell him how truly sorry she was.

"Bailey, get a move on. Even Austin's faster than

you." Jace stood outside the van, motioning for her to get out.

She was startled to see that she was the last one to leave. And true to Jace's word, Austin was in his wheelchair with the others, waiting for her. Which meant she needed to get her head on straight, focus. Whatever this . . . thing was between her and Kade had to take the back burner for now. She had a mission again. The Equalizers had misread her anger during their questioning of Kade, just as he had, and now believed she was fully one of them.

The hell with that. She was still Team Kade, even if she'd been stupid enough to falter for a few seconds before her common sense kicked back in. And once she had a decent chance to talk to him, she'd make sure he knew.

Kade led them around to the front, which was apparently the only entrance and exit. Everyone was dressed in black with bullet-resistant vests—except for Kade. At his own insistence, he'd showered and changed into his usual jeans and a T-shirt before they'd left the Equalizers' hideout. If anyone else showed up at the lab while they were here, he wanted to be able to run interference and pretend he was just here for his usual—to run some reports. Of course that only worked if the Equalizers, and Bailey, weren't seen. Explaining their presence would be pretty much impossible.

In spite of the lack of fencing around the building, the security wasn't completely lax. For one thing, it was in the mountains, surrounded by woods and little else. But as far as technology went, Kade had to enter security codes and slide his badge through a reader to get them into the building. Then he had to repeat the process through countless other doors to reach the room he wanted to show them.

As Bailey waited at the back of the group for Kade to get this next door open, she felt a tingle of nerves shoot up her spine. Swiping a security badge across a scanner seemed like they'd be announcing Kade's presence to the world. If anyone was actively looking for him, wouldn't they know the moment his badge was used?

But Kade had explained the security in this facility didn't work that way. No one would know they were ever there unless they knew to specifically look in the lab's databases to see who'd come and gone. And since this particular lab wasn't used much anymore, that was unlikely. Most of the people who used to work here had long ago moved on to a more modern facility on the other side of Boulder, closer to town. Kade could only count a half-dozen other people he'd ever seen here. Which was why his boss had chosen this building to house the EXIT information. It was the last place anyone would expect something like that to be.

Kade hesitated before pulling the last door open. "The rest of this place may seem like a slum. But prepare to be impressed with this room."

He opened the door and they all followed him inside.

The door clicked shut behind them and the electronic lock engaged. Lights flickered on overhead, and all of them froze except for Kade, who pulled up a seat at one of the banks of computers. He massaged his aching thigh for a moment, then straightened and went to work keying in something on the computer keyboard.

Jace sat beside him, keeping a close eye on what he was doing. Devlin and Mason took their guns out and swept the room, looking in every doorway. But Bailey hung back with Terrance, taking it all in.

"What the hell is this place used for?" Terrance asked, his voice low.

"Supposedly for Kade's research to find Enforcers. Seems like a waste doesn't it?" Bailey counted at least forty computers in several rows of long, semi-circular white tables that faced an enormous screen at the front of the room. The tables were auditorium style, but instead of individual seats on each row, there were tables, sort of like a NASA control room. An aisle ran down the middle and both sides, with a much wider aisle along the back wall where she and Terrance stood.

Mason and Devlin met at the front of the room. Apparently having decided they were truly alone and things were secure, they holstered their guns and headed up the center aisle to where Kade was typing at a keyboard.

Terrance moved to the door to stand watch, looking through the glass with his gun drawn.

Bailey debated where to sit and finally decided to sit beside Kade. She was just too curious not to be a part of the action.

"What kind of a portal is this?" Bailey asked, looking at the reports that had automatically opened on his desktop after he keyed his ID and password. "Wait, isn't that the Sarin gas investigation that was on the news last week? The FBI shut down a sleeper cell in the warehouse district, right? They had stockpiles of Sarin and some freaky lab where they were testing it. But thankfully never got a chance to deploy it. Why do you have that report?"

Devlin and Mason crowded closer, leaning over Kade's and Bailey's shoulders to see the screen.

Kade's jaw tightened at her question, and Bailey realized how suspicious her question had probably sounded, given the way things stood between them right now.

"Kade, I didn't mean to imply that—"

"Since my EXIT missions have to be kept secret from any other agents running missions in the area, I have to keep up with who is where and what they're working on. Traffic cop stuff, really. To make sure we don't run into each other. The Sarin gas incident was even more important to me, though, given that it's exactly the kind of thing that an Enforcer might feel compelled to get involved with. They might want to go after the terrorists themselves rather than rely on the FBI to put them in prison. So I've kept tabs on what's going on and where the terrorists were taken."

Bailey could well understand his concerns. She'd been tempted herself to follow up on where the terrorists had been taken, to ensure they couldn't harm anyone else in the future. But she'd been too busy running for her life and trying to find the Ghost, all at the same time.

"I know all about Sarin gas," Mason said. "Wicked, deadly stuff. Had to take down a terrorist cell overseas during one of my missions so I had to learn everything there was to know about it. What happened with this cell?"

"Shut down, like the report says."

From the look on Kade's face, Bailey suspected that he knew a whole lot more than that. But he wasn't volunteering any extra information. Plus, that wasn't why he'd brought them here. He'd brought them here to prove that he wasn't part of the battle against Enforcers, among other things.

Kade punched a button and a document flashed up on the monitor.

Bailey leaned forward to read it. "It's your life insurance policy."

He nodded and scrolled through. "Since Jace painted me as a liar about being married, I figured I'd show him where I made Abby the beneficiary in my benefit plan." He stopped scrolling, and blinked at the screen.

The beneficiary line was in the middle of the page. It was filled out. And it didn't say Abby Quinn.

"Who is Nicholas Quinn?" Bailey asked. "Brother?" She swallowed. "Son?"

His gaze flashed to hers. "I don't have any children or siblings." He looked back at the screen. "This doesn't make sense. Nicholas is my father. But I changed the beneficiary after I got married. I can see it in my head, me sitting here filling out the forms. I know I changed that."

His words hung in the air but no one said anything.

He punched up another document from the directory that he'd navigated to earlier. This one was his W-4 form, the one he'd obviously filed with his employer to set up tax withholding. On the box for marital status, the one labeled "married" was blank. There was only one box with an X in it. The one marked "single."

He punched up more forms, checking each one for the beneficiary line, or marital status, depending on the form. Everything he brought up, from his 401K savings plan to his long-term disability, all revealed the same thing.

Kade Quinn wasn't married. There was nothing here to prove that Abby Quinn had ever existed.

"It doesn't make sense," he whispered, as if to himself.

Bailey reached for his hand, instinctively wanting to comfort him. But he pulled it back as if she'd stung him.

"I'm not lying about her," he said. "And I'm not crazy. I didn't just . . . imagine that I had a wife. I can see us in front of the judge when we got married. I can picture her next to me as we walked into a movie theater. At a restaurant across from me, laughing when she spilled spaghetti sauce down her dress." He pressed a hand to his temples, as if recalling the memories made his head hurt. "And I see her beside me in the car, begging me to save her."

"I believe him," Bailey said.

Kade lowered his hands and stared at her in surprise.

"I do," she said. "I believe everything you've said. I can see the truth in your eyes, hear it in your voice. Something isn't adding up, and we need to figure out what it is."

"He made up Abby to get your sympathy," Jace said from behind her. "That's what's going on. We never expected him to be able to prove otherwise. Which is why we brought Austin. Move out of the way, Kade. Let the whiz kid see what he can find out about who's calling the shots with your mission and how high it goes."

Bailey frowned as Kade got up and moved back, with Mason keeping pace with him, his gun out and down by his side at the ready.

"Wait," Bailey said. "What's going on?"

"What's going on," Kade said, his voice sounded tired, resigned, "is that your friends only wanted to get into the lab so they could comb through the EXIT databases." He crossed his arms. "I could have told you it would be a waste of time. The truly damning stuff about EXIT has already been destroyed. The only thing left here are the files that I use to research where to find the remaining Enforcers. Mission critical info is all gone."

"All we want are names," Jace said, as he bent over Austin's shoulder, watching him power through screen after screen of information.

Bailey backed up beside Kade. With Mason behind them, standing guard, she couldn't really have the conversation that she wanted. So, instead, she tried to show Kade what she wished she'd been able to tell him back at the hideout—that she believed in him and had been an idiot to doubt him for even one second. She'd known that as soon as she'd stormed out of the interrogation room. Jace had twisted everything around, specifically trying to influence her. And it had worked, but not for long.

She moved sideways until her shoulder touched his biceps. When he didn't adjust his stance or move away to break the contact, she took that as a good sign. She reached out with her right hand and feathered her fingers over his. He hesitated, then turned his wrist, and they were suddenly holding hands.

She let out a deep breath in relief. "I'm sorry," she whispered, for his ears alone.

He didn't answer with words. Instead, he squeezed her hand, and then his thumb brushed lightly across the backs of her knuckles. It was a simple caress, butterfly-soft. But she felt it all the way to her soul.

"What the hell?" Austin said.

Everyone drew closer to the monitor. Bailey half expected Mason to stop Kade, but he didn't. He simply followed the two of them as they crowded around the screen.

Instead of word-processor types of documents like the ones that Kade had brought up a few minutes ago, Austin's screen was full of video files.

"Do you know what these are?" he asked, looking over his shoulder at Kade.

"No idea. I don't have any video files."

"Who else has files on this system?" Bailey asked.

He shrugged. "My boss, for sure. But I can't access them. They're password protected. They don't even come up on my menus."

"Amateurs," Austin said. "No one hides files from me. Let's see what we have, ladies and gentlemen."

He punched some buttons. The first video opened on the enormous movie-type screen at the front of the room and began to play.

Bailey's eyes widened in shock.

Mason swore behind them.

The others simply stared, riveted to the movie playing out in front of them.

Kade's gaze was glued to the screen and his face had gone alarmingly pale. Bailey forced her own gaze from him back to the screen.

It was an elaborate video, obviously shot as if

from Kade's point of view, showing the inside of a car driving at a high rate of speed, trying to out-maneuver another car. The second car pulled up alongside and the man had a gun. *Bam! Bam!* Bullets ripped through the door. The car careened to the side, then slammed into a tree.

And there, screaming, crying, begging Kade to save her, was the woman he'd told them about. The same woman in the picture that Bailey had taken from Kade's wall. There wasn't anyone else in the film, just the woman. As if someone else was in the car beside her but watching her through their eyes. Bailey recognized the video for what it was—staged. And the only reason it would have been filmed this way was for Kade to think this was something he was seeing, experiencing, when it never really happened.

Austin punched up another video, then another, and another—fake Abby again, saying wedding vows in front of a judge, walking into a movie theater, sitting in a restaurant eating spaghetti, laughing when she spilled it onto her dress. There were even videos of insurance forms, 401K forms, and others, showing a single name on the beneficiary line—Abby Quinn.

And then Austin punched the last video up on the screen. This one was an interview with a psychologist, explaining his techniques and how a combination of drugs—including Vicodin—could induce a fugue state. Showing the semiconscious patient a specific type of video over and over again, if done correctly, could trick the brain into thinking the videos were actual memories. It was the latest advance in the area of mind-control, more commonly known as brainwashing.

The screen went blank. The room went deathly silent. As one, everyone turned to look at Kade.

He was still staring at the blank screen, his posture rigid, and somewhere along the way he'd let go of Bailey's hand.

"Fake," he said, his voice hoarse. "Everything I thought was real is fake. She doesn't exist. She never did."

"Well," Austin said. "Technically the woman in those videos does exist. I imagine she's an actress that was hired to—*ouch*." He rubbed the top of his head and glared at Jace who'd just smacked him.

"Shut up, Austin," Jace said. "For once. Just shut up."

Austin's face reddened but he didn't say anything else.

Kade's face, which had been so pale before, was now a mottled purple. His blue eyes had turned nearly black and his entire body seemed to shake with rage. He suddenly turned around, grabbed the nearest chair, and slammed it against the wall.

Bailey jumped and pressed her hand against her throat, not sure what to do.

"Give him space," Mason said beside her, his voice low. "Let him work through it."

Kade ignored all of them, cursing beneath his breath as he stalked across the room, pacing like a caged tiger. His limp was less pronounced than usual, as if the adrenaline pumping through his system dulled the pain. He looked every bit the dangerous predator Bailey had thought him to be the night they'd first met. The softer side, the quiet side, the polite side he'd shown her since then had disappeared. In its place was a man on the edge, brimming with fury, his fists curled at his sides.

He finally stopped pacing in front of Jace, who stood beside his chair, watching Kade with a wary stillness.

"All right, Atwell," Kade said. "You win. You were right. Everything I believed in was a lie. Which means I'm probably wrong about the Enforcers and have been a tool in their deaths without even knowing it. I'm in this with you and your team now, all the way whether you want my help or not. You really want to look through the computer banks? You think your little computer geek found everything?" He laughed without humor. "Not even close."

He waved his hand toward the rows of computer monitors. "Consider yourself in. I'll show you everything I've got. And I'll give you names—the names of everyone I've ever met or even read on a report since this whole thing started. Alan Faegan is my boss's full name. His boss is John Majors. I can give you an org chart all the way to the freaking President of the United States. We're going to stop this so-called mission right now, right here."

Jace stepped forward, standing toe-to-toe with Kade. Bailey reached for her gun, not about to idly stand by while Jace acted like a jerk to him yet again, especially after these earth-shattering blows that probably still had Kade's mind reeling.

"Don't." A hand clamped around her wrist.

She looked up to see Mason staring down at her. For the first time since meeting him, she actually saw him smile.

"Give him a minute," Mason said, keeping his

voice low. "This is Jace's first turn as sole leader on one of our missions and he's been a bit over the top with it. He just needs to settle into the role."

"I'm not standing by again while he treats Kade like crap."

"Just wait. Give Jace a chance to do the right thing here."

She tugged her hand and he let her go. But he remained by her side, watching her.

She turned back to Jace and Kade, and raised her brows in surprise. Jace had his hand on Kade's shoulder and was shaking his other hand. It looked like he might actually be . . . apologizing.

Cursing sounded from the door. Bailey realized she'd completely forgotten about Terrance. He'd been posted as lookout, watching through the glass.

"We've got company," he said. "There's a whole team of men in FBI flak jackets marching down the hall." He peeked out the corner of the window, then flattened himself against the wall. "Damn it. I count at least twenty, heavily armed."

"How did they know we were here?" Jace demanded.

Kade shook his head. "Since my boss has been playing me all along, I'm guessing he has more eyes on this place than I knew about. I reviewed the security for this facility and even beefed it up when I started my mission. Obviously that was all fake. He's probably been monitoring every move I make. As soon as I swiped a badge or logged into a computer, he knew about it."

"Fifteen feet away," Terrance announced. He yanked his gun out and backed up, aiming at the door.

Kade ran to where Austin was perched in front of the computer and grabbed the keyboard.

"Hey," Austin complained.

Bailey rushed over beside Terrance and drew her gun, flanking him as they waited for the expected breach. Devlin crouched down, aiming his weapon at the door as well. Mason had followed Kade to the computer and looked far too calm for the situation.

"They're right outside the door," Terrance whispered.

A buzzing noise sounded, like an electronic lock being released. Bailey tensed, her finger on the trigger. But the door didn't open. The buzzing noise sounded again. The door rattled, as if someone was shoving it, but stayed closed.

"I've disabled the badge system and the security panels," Kade announced. "But it won't keep them out for long." He typed something else, then punched Enter. He looked toward the door, and shook his head. "Terrance, you don't have to keep ducking under the window. It's one-way bulletproof glass. We can see them. They can't see us. This place is soundproofed, too. So they don't actually know you're all in here. As far as they are aware, based on the badge swipes and security codes I used, I'm the only one in here. Which means, you all have to disappear."

Bailey moved past Devlin and the others and stopped in front of Kade. "I don't think I like how this is starting to sound."

"Sounds like you're talking about a safe-room," Mason asked, joining them.

"Behind the screen. If they even think anyone else might be in here with me, they'll tear this place apart—including the safe-room. This is only going to work if you're out of here when they bust down that door."

A pounding noise sounded behind them, emphasizing his words. They were already trying to break in.

Kade swore. "Go. I already unlocked the door from the terminal. Once you're inside and the door is closed, it blends in with the paneling."

"You're not staying here to face them by yourself," Bailey said, glaring up at him. "I'm not about to let you do that."

"I assume once someone is inside, the controls automatically switch to whoever is in the room? No overrides?" Mason asked.

"Exactly. Wait half an hour or longer before coming out. That should give me enough time."

"Enough time for what?" Bailey demanded. But Kade didn't even look at her.

The pounding sounded again behind them, then again. The lights blinked off and on.

"Hurry," Kade said.

Mason motioned toward the others. But Devlin was already pushing Austin's wheelchair down the aisle at a run. Terrance and the others jogged after him, leaving only Kade, Mason, and Bailey by the computer screen.

Kade finally looked at her. "You need to go."

"Not a chance. I'm not leaving you." She yanked out her Sig Sauer. "Those cowardly Equalizers can run and hide but I'm staying here. With you."

Kade smiled. "I doubt your new friends would appreciate being called cowards." He glanced at Mason over the top of her head. "And I have a feeling they'd stay and fight if I asked them to. But I'm not asking. Most of the agents on the other side of that door are being manipulated and used. They're good men and they don't deserve to die just because they have the bad luck of working for a corrupt boss. I can end this without a single drop of blood being spilled and that's exactly what I intend to do. Don't worry about me, Bailey. I'll be okay."

"No. You won't. Those 'good men' out there have guns and will shoot just as readily as anyone else. You're being foolish with your life."

The door shuddered.

"Kade," Mason said, from behind Bailey. "We need to hurry this up."

"Just go," Bailey told him over her shoulder. "I'm staying with Kade."

"No," Kade said. "Trust me. Faegan has put too much effort into painting me as his scapegoat. He's obviously planning on using me as the fall guy if this mission goes south or other people find out what's going on. And from what I've seen, it's heading in that direction. He can't afford to kill me. He needs me alive until everything implodes and I'm blamed. For now, I'm completely safe."

"That's the biggest load of crap I've ever heard," she told him.

He shook his head in exasperation. *"Now,* Mason."

Bailey frowned, then, suddenly realizing what he meant, she started to whirl around. Mason grabbed her in an iron-hold and threw her on his shoulder.

"No," she yelled. "Put me down, damn it."

He sprinted down the aisle toward the screen.

"Kade," she yelled, as she pummeled Mason's back. "Don't do this. Kade!"

Mason ran with her around the screen and into the safe-room with the others.

"Close the door," Mason yelled.

"No!" Bailey struggled to get out of his arms. "Let me go!"

The door slammed shut.

SILENCE REIGNED IN the lab. But not for long. Kade knew Faegan's men would be coming through the door any second. He needed them to believe that he was here alone. He needed a diversion, something to keep them from even thinking about the safe-room.

He punched up the video of the car crash. The memories he'd seen over and over in his mind, torturing him for months, now played out, larger than life. The gunman was just pulling up beside the car when the door to the lab slammed open, crashing against the wall.

"Kade, what the hell are you . . ." The familiar voice behind him trailed off as the heavily armed team crowded around him and stared at the movie.

Gunshots. The squeal of tires. The crunch of metal. Fake Abby screaming. Hell, had there even been a car wreck? He didn't even know what had happened to his leg at this point. Had he been shot? Or was that fake, too?

"Stop the movie," Faegan ordered.

Kade punched a button on the keyboard. Abby's terrified face was frozen on the screen. He had to hand it to her, whoever she was. She was one hell of an actress. At least now he knew why his memories had always seemed muted, foggy, never completely in focus. Because they'd never been real. The guilt he'd felt for so long was for nothing. The guilt he'd felt for caring for Bailey, for wanting her so desperately when he should have been grieving for his wife had been a waste of emotion.

He slowly turned in his chair and faced the man who'd put him through hell over the past year and had sentenced him to a life of pain, assuming he survived this. The man who was probably responsible for murdering dozens of Enforcers and using Kade as his tool to kill them.

"You set me up, you bastard," Kade said.

Faegan blew out a deep breath. "It's not that simple."

"It never is when you betray someone." Kade rose from his chair. "So what's it going to be? Are you going to shoot me, like you did Porter and Simmons? Like you probably did to all of the Enforcers?"

Faegan cocked an arrogant brow. "Of course not. We're the FBI. We don't murder people." He leaned toward Kade. "That's the type of behavior a man does when he fries his brain with meds and convinces himself that he was married to a woman who doesn't actually exist."

Kade lunged toward him but several sets of hands grabbed him from behind and yanked him back.

Faegan motioned toward someone out of Kade's line of vision. "Cuff him."

BAILEY PUT HER hands on her hips and glared up at Jace. Mason had been wise enough to keep well away from her and was currently standing on the other side of the safe-room.

"We've been in here for thirty minutes," Bailey snapped. "We've waited long enough. Either you move or I'll move you."

Jace blinked and his lips quirked in an indulgent half smile. "Now, Bailey. No need to act so—*ooof*!"

She slammed her fist into his belly and followed through with an uppercut to his jaw. The shocked look on his face as he fell to the side was a reward all its own. She punched the red button beside the door and it popped open with a swishing sound.

Laughter from the other Equalizers, and cursing from Jace, sounded behind her. She ran into the now-empty computer room and sprinted up the main aisle. She'd been wanting to punch someone for a while now. It was Jace's bad fortune to be blocking the exit door when her temper had boiled over.

"Bailey, wait, damn it," one of the men called out behind her. "They might be outside, waiting for us."

"Kade might be outside, too, needing our help," she called back as she ran from the room.

It took a frustrating full minute to figure out the maze of hallways but she finally burst out the front door onto the circular drive in front of the building. Empty, just like the computer room. And the road leading up the hill to the lab was deserted, too. She was too late. Kade was gone, and she didn't know how she was going to find him again.

Chapter Seventeen

Wednesday, 12:42 p.m.

Twenty-four hours later, Bailey sat at the table in the Equalizers' hideout, listening to the others comparing notes on what they'd each done since leaving the FBI lab.

Bailey had spent the past day bouncing between the FBI lab, the house in Boulder where Kade had been staying that first night when she'd stowed away in the trunk of his car, even EXIT headquarters in case he showed up there. She'd been searching for signs of him, but had found nothing—while the other Equalizers had been focusing more on searching for Faegan.

None of them had been successful either.

"Another Enforcer was taken last night," Mason announced from his seat to Bailey's right. "That makes two since Kade disappeared. Which means that either he's back calling the shots again, or his boss is doing it without him. Either way, we've got to close the net. I vote that we shadow some of the remaining Enforcers in the area to try to catch Faegan in action."

"You mean, use Enforcers as bait?" Devlin asked. "I don't like the sound of that."

That started a whole new round of discussions. Bailey tapped her foot impatiently beneath the table and wondered what had happened to make her more worried about finding one man than about stopping the attack on her fellow Enforcers. No, that wasn't fair. It wasn't that she was choosing Kade over anyone else. It was that no one else was choosing him, so it was left to her to do so.

She shoved back from the table and stood. Conversation stopped and all eyes focused on her.

"I'm going back to EXIT headquarters," she announced.

"Again? Why? We've been there half a dozen times searching for Kade. If Faegan was still watching the place, he'd have shown up one of those times. Face it. EXIT headquarters is a dead end."

"Well, I can't sit here and do nothing. I have to keep looking for him."

Jace sat back in his chair, studying her. An expression of sympathy crossed his face, and she wanted to pummel him all over again. He and probably most of the others believed it was too late to help Kade, that he was . . . gone . . . like all of the missing Enforcers and would never be seen again. But that wasn't something she could even begin to accept.

Aside from her friendship with Hawke and *his* friends—Sebastian and Amber—she could still count on one hand the number of people she'd allowed to get close to her in the past dozen or so years. Losing Kade now, before she was even sure what he meant to her, what he *could* mean to her, would utterly wreck her. She had to keep holding on. She couldn't lose hope.

"All right," Jace finally said. "If you need us, call. You have my cell number."

She blinked in surprise. "I kind of thought you all would throw me out of your little club for doing my own thing."

He grinned. "Well, that's not how this *club* operates. You're one of us now. We may not think that looking for Kade is the best use of our resources at this point. But we're still a team. And that includes you. We have your back. If you need us, we'll be there."

She looked around the table. To a man, every one of them nodded their agreement with Jace. They considered her a team member. They weren't kicking her out.

"Thank you," she said, her voice tight. She hadn't realized how much she'd wanted their approval, their support, until she knew she had it. "I, ah, I'll call with updates."

She whirled around and headed out. The Mustang, with its bullet hole and bloody passenger seat, had been left in a junkyard to eventually be reunited with the rental company who owned it. Now she was driving one of her favorites, an old deep blue Charger with an engine that fairly purred.

She again went everywhere that she'd seen Kade before, even the little house where she'd been hiding out that first night when Hawke had warned her and she'd fled to the woods ahead of his men. But he wasn't there, and it didn't look like anyone had been there since she'd left. When she checked on EXIT headquarters, she boldly drove right up to the building and sat for a good long time, as if daring

Faegan's men—if they were the ones who'd been watching the building the first time—to come after her. At least if they did, they'd take her where they took Kade. Or so she hoped.

But no one suddenly appeared and tried to capture her. Maybe because they knew they had something she wanted, and didn't want to risk her going after them.

Frustration had her punching the gas and spinning donuts around the parking lot. Finally she stopped, her foot on the brake as she breathed in heavily, trying to calm her racing pulse.

"Damn it, Kade. Where are you?"

She tried to reason it through.

If Faegan knew Kade was helping them yesterday, then it made sense that he would have taken Kade into custody. But if he had, it wasn't through any official channels. One of Devlin's brothers, Pierce, was an FBI agent. One of the good ones, not one working to exterminate Enforcers. And he hadn't found evidence of anyone bringing Kade in for questioning. He was looking into information on Faegan, and from what she'd heard, had done a great job of getting details on his homes and official capacity, even what office he normally worked out of—again, officially. But Faegan was also currently on some secret assignment. The file that might have given them what they needed to find him was sealed so tight that no one was getting into it.

Just another way that EXIT's hierarchy protected itself.

She considered all of the possibilities. If Kade was with Faegan, then the Equalizers would eventually— or so she hoped—catch up to both of them. They were focusing on the head of the snake, and right now that seemed to be Kade's immediate boss. But if Kade had somehow managed to escape, what would he do? Where would he go?

Bailey put herself in his shoes. He'd sacrificed himself at the lab to ensure that no one else got hurt—on both sides of the conflict. Which only proved how deeply honorable he was. His choices always put the safety of others first. So if he'd escaped, and knew that Faegan's men were searching for him, he wouldn't want to do anything that could jeopardize Bailey. She was certain of it. Which meant that he wouldn't want to draw any attention to the Equalizers either. He might be on shaky ground with them right now, not really sure if they were his allies or not. But he knew they were Bailey's allies— the friends of his . . . friend, or whatever she was.

She tapped her hands on the steering wheel as another possibility occurred to her. Kade had to know she cared about him. They'd never discussed the attraction between them. But it wasn't exactly a secret either. He had to know she'd be worried. He had to know that she'd want to hear from him that he was okay. But it wasn't like they'd exchanged numbers or given each other business cards. Which meant, the only way he'd feel safe about contacting her was if she came to him. He could be hiding somewhere waiting for her to find him.

The more she thought about it, the more that made sense to her. Now all she had to do was figure out where he would hide, knowing that it was a place they both knew about. The locations that she and Kade had been to together made a very short list.

And of that list, there was only one place that she

hadn't searched—the house in Colorado Springs where she'd nursed him back to health.

WHEN BAILEY FINALLY pulled onto the familiar street in Colorado Springs, she slowly passed the house, keeping an eye out for anything unusual that might indicate that its location had been compromised. She parked a few houses down, watching the occasional car go by, studying any casual passerby. It was well past the evening rush hour now. The sun had set and traffic was light. Everything seemed normal. No suspicious cars or people wandering around. If she was going to do this, now was the time.

A few minutes later she'd parked her car inside the garage and was ready to go into the house. The excitement and hope that she'd clung to the whole drive here had plummeted the moment she'd seen that the garage was empty. If Kade was here, he'd have stolen—no, rented—a car somewhere along the way. Otherwise, how would he have gotten here? Clearly, he wasn't here. But she hadn't driven this far to turn around without being absolutely sure.

Still, she wasn't going to foolishly barge inside without clearing each room first. When she and Kade had left they'd been worried about someone finding the house. She had to assume that was still a possibility, and that someone else could be hiding inside—even without a car in the garage.

With her pistol out, she headed inside. The house was closed up like a tomb, the heavy drapes covering every window, making it dark inside even though it was only late afternoon. There was just enough light to let her navigate around furniture but not enough to see much detail.

She quickly cleared the kitchen, family room, the first bedroom and the bathroom. So far, nothing. No signs that anyone had been here recently. Her shoulders slumped with disappointment. One room left. She threw the door open to the second bedroom.

"Bailey?"

She jerked her gun hand down at the sound of the familiar voice. It was too dark to clearly see his face. But she'd know that silhouette anywhere. Good thing he probably couldn't see the goofy grin that had to be on her face right now.

"Kade. I can't believe you're really here. I was right."

"Bailey, what are you—"

She threw her arms around his waist and pressed her head tightly against his chest. "I'm hugging you. Now hug me back, damn it. I thought Faegan was torturing you or might have already killed you."

He hesitated, then wrapped his arms around her and rested his cheek against the top of her head. "Everyone made it out of the lab safely? No one got hurt?"

"We didn't get to shoot one single agent. You ruined our fun," she teased. "What about you? How did you get away? And why did you come back here?" She pulled back and flipped the hall light on. Her eyes widened as she stared up at him. "Oh, Kade. What did they do to you?"

"Nothing that hasn't been done before." He pulled the bedroom door shut behind him and took her hand in his, leading her into the family room. "I was just about to make some soup. Want some?"

"I . . . guess I could eat."

She followed him to the kitchen. Was his limp worse than before? Was he favoring his side? She climbed onto one of the bar stools so she could watch him. He turned on the stove and grabbed two cans of tomato soup from the pantry.

"Kade, what happened after we went into the safe-room?"

He set out two bowls and stirred the soup as it heated in a pot. Was it her imagination or did he seem distracted? Tense?

"I played one of the videos to throw Faegan off. He bought it. As soon as I started accusing him of using me as a scapegoat, he had me handcuffed and brought me to some compound."

He turned off the stove and began ladling the soup into the two bowls. "Crackers?" He held up a box of saltines.

Why was he acting so weird? He was acting like a . . . stranger. "No crackers. Thanks."

After placing a bowl in front of each of them, he took the stool beside her. She could see how stiff and sore he was as he sat down. And in the light from the kitchen, the bruises she'd seen by the light of the bedroom looked even worse. They were just starting to show up, evidence of a recent beating for sure. Maybe that's why he was acting so off. He was in pain and didn't want to worry her.

The eyelid on his right eye was swollen, but not too bad. The worst part seemed to be the cuts and welts, like someone had taken a whip to his neck and shoulders, and run a knife down his right cheek from temple to chin, not to mention several equally long cuts on both arms. The cuts were angry and raw, but didn't appear to be deep or in need of stitches. A couple of Band-Aids were apparently covering the worst of the cuts.

They ate in silence. But she'd only eaten half her soup before her curiosity couldn't be contained any longer. She put her hand on his left thigh as he raised his spoon to his lips.

He glanced at her in question.

"I'm so sorry," she said. "They tortured you, didn't they?"

He drank the spoonful of soup. "Eat. You look pale, and tired. When's the last time you had any food?"

"I ate plenty. I'm not hungry anymore. Kade, how did you get away?"

He took two more spoonfuls of soup, then gathered up the dishes and headed around the bar into the kitchen.

"Kade. Please answer me."

He sighed and set the dishes in the sink. "Faegan and most of his men left to take care of something. I guess he underestimated me. Maybe he figured I couldn't do much with a bum leg. The lone guard he left to keep me in line wasn't a challenge. I took the guard's car into town and ditched it. Then I used a car service to get here. Don't worry. I paid cash. No electronic trail."

She nodded slowly, wishing he'd volunteer more information. But he seemed even more quiet than he had before. And angry. She sensed it simmering just below the surface. Whatever Faegan had done had made Kade furious.

"We've been looking for you." She joined him at the double sink and helped him wash and stack the few dishes into the drain rack. "Jace, Mason, all of us searched for you. They gave up, but I kept looking. I went to the cottage, your house in Boulder, EXIT headquarters."

His head shot up. "You went to EXIT? Did anyone go after you?"

"No. Whoever was watching the place before isn't watching it anymore. Or, if they are, they didn't make themselves known. Are you worried that I brought them here? I know how to spot a tail. Trust me. No one followed me here."

"I trust you. Of course I trust you. I was just concerned, worried that you were in danger." He dried his hands on a dish towel and folded it before leaving it on the counter. "Well, it looks like you found me."

"Yeah. Looks like."

They stared at each other a long moment. He was the one who finally looked away.

She curled her fingers into her palms in frustration. "I assumed you might have come here if you wanted to hide but not draw Faegan's men to us. That *is* why you came here, right? To hide, but hoping I'd think about this place and would come here looking for you?"

As if he couldn't help himself, he slowly lifted his hand and absently stroked his finger down the side of her face. "So beautiful." His voice sounded wistful, as if he was a million miles away.

She wanted to lean into him, to soak up his touch, to slide her hands up his chest. But he seemed more of a stranger at this minute than when they'd first met. She wasn't even sure that he wanted her to touch him.

He dropped his hand, shook his head as if just realizing what he'd done. "I'm glad you came," he said, giving her his first smile since she'd arrived. "I just didn't . . . expect you quite so soon." He waved his hands at his shirt and jeans. "I haven't even showered. I pretty much passed out on top of the bed when I arrived. I'd just woken up a few minutes before you walked in."

She waved toward her yellow top and jeans. "I'm not exactly ready for a runway myself. I usually dress way sexier than this but this was easy and I was in a hurry." She smiled, but when he didn't smile back, she sighed and said, "You left the lab with Faegan and his men, and they took you, where?"

"To a house on the outskirts of town. Not far from the lab. But it obviously was a temporary location. Definitely not a headquarters. After I escaped, I went back a few hours later, hoping to follow them to the retraining center, or their main base of operations. The place was deserted."

"But you know the address? We can call Jace and have them check it out."

He immediately shook his head. "There's no point. Like I said, it's not their home base. And I guarantee that since I escaped, and they didn't recapture me, they won't be back."

She wasn't sure she agreed, but she let it drop. "Kade? What aren't you telling me?"

"What do you mean?"

"You seem, I don't know, like you're holding something back."

"There's not much to tell. I got away, but didn't manage to do anything that would help us find them again, or the retraining facility. I failed. Again. Is that what you wanted to hear?"

She blinked at the anger in his voice. "You can't possibly call that a failure. You were unarmed, outnumbered. Most men I know in your situation wouldn't have managed to escape."

His gaze slid away from hers again. "Yeah, well. There is that. I'm going to shower."

"Sure. Of course. It's late. We can stay here tonight, then hook up with the others in the morning." She pulled out her cell. "I'll go ahead and call them, let them know what's going on. Where do you want to meet up tomorrow?"

"I . . . have an idea about that. We need a location where our enemies wouldn't expect us to go. Remember how you saw that story about the Sarin gas investigation?"

She frowned, not sure where he was going with this. "Yes. Why?"

"The FBI facility that handled the Sarin gas is in the warehouse district. To anyone else, it's just a warehouse. Very few people know of its existence, including Faegan. He wasn't part of the investigation, didn't insert himself into it as I did. But I'm sure he heard about it on the news. He wouldn't want to risk going anywhere near the place."

"Doesn't sound like anywhere I'd want to go either," she said.

He gave her his full attention for perhaps the first time since she'd arrived. "There's another reason we should go there, besides it being convenient and off Faegan's radar. The facility has a computer room that's far more *connected*, for lack of a better way to describe it. Any investigations into terrorism being operated out of that facility have to have the highest access possible to as much information as possible."

"Okay. And we care because?"

"Any land, building, facilities, equipment used by the FBI within hundreds of miles from there will be accessible as information in those computers. Faegan has to be using a facility owned by the government. I sure don't see him having the resources to do what he's doing otherwise. If we can get Austin in there, maybe he can find a smoking gun to help us narrow down places Faegan has access to that might meet the qualifications of the type of place he needs for his operations."

"Like being remote, large, no neighbors nearby, good roads but still out of the way."

"Right."

"What's the address?"

He told her and she frowned.

"That old part of the city is dead. No one goes there except to illegally dump trash."

"That's what makes it ideal. No one else will be around."

She shrugged. "All I can do is ask the others. I can't guarantee they'll agree to go there."

He stepped closer to her, his limp barely noticeable, as if he were making an effort to hide his pain now that she was there. He gently feathered her hair back from her brow.

"Trust me, Bailey. This place is where we need to meet. It could be the key to ending this thing. Convince them, convince the Equalizers to meet us there. We can drive up in the morning and be there by ten. Can you do that?"

She drew in a sharp breath as he pressed closer, her pulse automatically slamming in her veins as the hard planes of his chest pressed against her softer curves.

"I missed you," he whispered, both of his hands sliding deeper into her hair.

Her gaze dropped to his lips and he made a choked sound in his throat. Then his lips were on hers. She didn't remember backing up, but suddenly she was pressed against the wall of the family room and he was doing sinful, crazy, wonderful things to her mouth.

He cradled the back of her head with one hand, while the other slid down her back, stopping just short of the curve of her ass. She whimpered and pushed closer against him, tangling her tongue with his, drowning in the heady pleasure that always seemed to consume her when she was with him. She wanted more, needed more.

She slid her fingers down the sides of his shirt and she gathered the fabric in her hands, pulling on it, trying to free it from his pants.

He shuddered against her, and then he was gripping her wrists, stopping her. He broke the kiss and stepped back, his blue eyes stormy with passion and something else. Regret?

She tried to tug her hands free and move closer to him. But he let go and hurried back several feet, almost falling when his bad leg didn't cooperate with the sudden movement.

He frowned and rubbed his left thigh.

"Your leg hurts," she said. "I can get you something—"

"No." He winced as if realizing how sharp his voice had come out. "Sorry. I'm a bit . . . banged up. I think a hot shower will help. Make that call, Bailey. Get things set for tomorrow, okay?"

She frowned. "But I—"

"Thanks, Bailey." He limped into the hall and disappeared into the bathroom.

KADE LOCKED THE bathroom door behind him and turned the shower on. After listening to make sure he didn't hear Bailey in the hall, he pulled the cell phone out of his pocket. The caller was still on the line.

He glanced again at the bathroom door, then put the phone to his ear. "I assume you caught all of that, Faegan? It's set for ten in the morning."

"You did good, Kade. This will all be over soon."

"She doesn't get hurt. Promise me, you bastard. You can do anything to the others, but Bailey doesn't get hurt."

"You're not in a position to make demands."

He tightened his hand around the phone. "We made a deal."

"Oh, settle down. I know the terms. You give me the Equalizers and I tell my men to stand down and stop following her. They'll leave her alone, unmolested, alive. Free to go on her merry way and never worry about me again. *After* I get what I want."

"You'll get it. And you'd better stick to your promise."

"Just keep the line open. Hang up the call before the meeting tomorrow and I'll sic my guys on Bailey so fast she'll never see them coming. By the way, she looks lovely in that yellow shirt today."

"Shut up." Kade tossed the phone onto the counter. But he did as he'd been told. He left the line open.

Tomorrow he and Bailey would go to the warehouse. And then he'd betray them all.

Chapter Eighteen

Thursday, 9:50 a.m.

Kade drove this time. Bailey was pretty sure she'd put them in a ditch if she got behind the wheel right now. Probably on purpose, just out of spite. So she sat in the passenger seat the whole way there, intent on giving him the silent treatment. Unfortunately, he would actually have to try to talk to her to realize he was getting the silent treatment. And Kade hadn't said a single word since they'd left Colorado Springs.

Bailey's pride—and her temper—couldn't take much more of this. After Kade had left her standing in the family room last night, she'd done everything she could to avoid him. Which was pretty easy. After his shower he'd gone into his bedroom and hadn't come out again all night. She would know. She'd barely slept a wink and would have heard him if he'd so much as opened his door.

She didn't have any regrets, though. For once, she'd put herself out there, risked her heart by going after what she wanted—Kade. He was the one who should feel guilty. They had something going, something special, and for some reason he refused to let her in. He was pushing her away before they'd really had a chance. He didn't trust her enough to share what was really bothering him, why he was shutting her out.

As soon as they met with the others at the warehouse and brought Faegan down, she was going to take off. Being on her own had always worked in the past. It would damn well work again just fine.

Maybe she'd go back home to Montana. It had been a wonderful place to spend her early childhood years, especially for a nature girl like her who preferred mucking around in the outdoors over going to a shopping mall any day of the week. Of course she'd have to live on the opposite side of the state from her hometown of Bozeman. Running into anyone she used to know could result in some extremely uncomfortable situations for everyone involved. On second thought, maybe she should head to North Dakota. It was close enough to Montana to feel like home, but not close enough to get her into trouble again.

She just wished the idea of never seeing Kade again didn't hurt so much.

It was exactly ten in the morning when they arrived at the warehouse. No other cars were in the parking lot and the street out front seemed deserted. He'd been right about it being an ideal location. No one would think to look for them here.

He strode across the parking lot, his limp barely noticeable this morning. Bailey kept pace with him, keeping an eye on their surroundings. After stopping at a side door, Kade pulled out a set of keys hanging from a lanyard around his neck.

Bailey stared at the lanyard. "Where did you get that? I don't remember seeing it before."

"It was in my go bag." He arched a brow. "This is an FBI warehouse and I've been here before. I work in the area and have a key. Is there a reason you're staring at me so suspiciously?"

"Is there a reason you're acting so suspiciously?"

He frowned and shoved the key into the lock, then pressed a code into a keypad much like the ones at the technology lab. The hairs stood up on the back of Bailey's neck.

"After you." He held the door open.

She pointed at the keypad. "Didn't using one of those things get us in trouble before?"

"The code I used on this one is the same code everyone uses. It's generic. Are you coming in or not?"

"You first."

He hesitated. "I thought your friends would be here by now."

"I'm sure they'll be here soon. You and I can check the place out first."

"Was that the plan you made last night without telling me?"

"This morning, actually."

What she didn't say hung in the air between them—that she'd altered the plans since their . . . argument? Fight? Nothing had felt right since their awkward reunion. He was holding something back, hiding something. And as soon as she'd mentioned that to Jace over the phone, they'd mutually decided to modify the plan. She would be the scout, get the lay of the land, before the Equalizers made an appearance.

"Let me guess," he said. "You're going to signal

them once I prove that I wasn't lying about the computers?"

"Something like that. Are we going to do this or not?"

"Gentlemen first."

He stepped through the door, but not before she saw something flash in his eyes. It wasn't anger, as she'd expected. It looked more like . . . worry. Why would Kade be worried?

She followed him inside, blinking to acclimate her eyes to the dimly lit interior after being outside in the sun.

Kade hadn't stopped. In spite of his limp, he was halfway across the warehouse by the time she caught up with him. Other than a few boxes stacked here and there, it was empty and boasted an expanse of extremely clean concrete floors.

There were two doors in the opposite wall. Kade stopped at the one on the left. After punching in another code, and using one of the keys on his lanyard, he pulled open the door.

As soon as he stepped inside, lights popped on overhead. She blinked in surprise at the enormous, almost blindingly white room. The middle was clear, with floors of concrete again like in the rest of the warehouse. But, true to his word, there was a bank of computers along the back wall. And on the right wall was a large rectangular glass cutout. But she couldn't see through it to tell what was on the other side.

The place was so eerily similar to the technology lab that it made her hesitate. Things hadn't worked out so well for them the last time they were in a place like this. "They" being accurate now, because her phone had just vibrated on her hip, letting her know the Equalizers were outside. They would wait for her text before coming in.

She'd wanted to cancel the whole thing, feeling more and more uneasy after her long, awkward night avoiding Kade. Surprisingly, it was Jace who'd disagreed. He'd completely flip-flopped in his attitude toward Kade after the safe-room incident. He was more inclined to trust Kade than she was.

"This looks a lot like the safe-room at the technology lab," she said, hesitating in the doorway.

"If you're worried about it then stay there." He sat in front of one of the monitors and flipped it on.

"What's behind that glass window? What's behind the other door?" She motioned toward the door to her right.

Kade lowered his hands from the keyboard and turned around.

"A control room." He motioned toward the glass. "You can see out from the other room into here, but not the other way around. There's an intercom that allows the people in the control room to communicate with anyone in this part of the warehouse."

"Show me."

He let out a heavy sigh and got up. Using the ring of keys on the lanyard again, he left the lab and unlocked the only other door in the building, then pulled it open. Again, he didn't hesitate. He stepped inside. But this time he held the door and waited for her.

"You wanted to see the control room," he reminded her.

Why was she so nervous? This was Kade. Just because they weren't pursuing a relationship didn't mean that he'd changed loyalties. From the start, he'd risked everything to save her life. He'd done nothing to earn her doubt now. She needed to just get over herself and stop treating him like an enemy.

"I'm sorry," she said. "I'm just a bit on edge. I know I can trust you and I don't mean to imply otherwise."

He stared at her a moment, then gave her a curt nod.

The guy sure knew how to make a girl regret her apology.

She straightened her shoulders and moved past him. The room was just as deep as the lab but much more narrow. And it looked just like she imagined a control room would look, with an electronic panel of buttons and dials facing the rectangular window. A row of eight desk chairs were pulled up to the panel.

"You said they used this place to investigate the recent Sarin gas scare?"

He nodded. "Everything in that other room is mobile and can be taken out in a matter of minutes. When it's not being used as a computer room, it can be used as a bio-lab. They do simulations and test detection equipment, all kinds of experiments as part of investigations, and to prepare for the worst kinds of things criminals can dish out."

Just to be thorough, as she'd promised she would be, she took a long look around. After assuring herself that there weren't any other doors or places where someone could be hiding, she headed to the other room.

Once again he sat at one of the computers and began typing on the keyboard. She followed him in this time and watched what he was keying. Although she didn't know the system he was using, it seemed fairly straightforward. Nothing he did set off any alarm bells. She continued to watch him pull up various files, skim them, then close them.

Finally he pulled up a file that, once opened, revealed a set of topography maps and land surveys.

He pointed at the screen. "See these red dots? Those are all pieces of land the FBI owns in and around Boulder. Is Austin coming or not?"

"Maybe. Why?"

He shrugged, as if he didn't particularly care whether Austin or the rest of the Equalizers showed. "I got the impression that he's the Equalizers' computer guy. He'd probably figure out a lot faster way to cull through this stuff than me. But if they're not meeting us here, fine. We just might need a few extra hours to open all of these red dots and come up with a list of possible locations that could be the retraining facility."

He clicked on one of the red dots and started skimming through the survey and associated specifications that popped up on the screen.

Bailey's phone vibrated in her pocket. She tapped a message on the screen, giving Jace the details. Thirty seconds later, he stood in the doorway, with Devlin, Mason, and Terrance crowding behind him.

A squeak heralded Austin's approach. Everyone moved aside so he could wheel into the room. He immediately shoved a chair aside and pulled into place beside Kade.

"I didn't think you guys were coming," he said.

Jace shot a look at Bailey before answering. "I wasn't sure if we were either. Good to see you're okay."

Kade nodded. "You, too."

Austin leaned toward him, staring at the screen. "What have you got?"

Soon, Kade was relinquishing his position in front of the terminal so Austin could take his place. The rest of the Equalizers formed a semicircle behind him, looking just as eager as Austin to see what kinds of information he could discover. Kade limped over to where Bailey stood by the door.

"This looks really promising," Jace said, turning around and nodding at Bailey. "We just might get Faegan yet."

Kade leaned back against the wall.

"It looks like coming here was a great idea," Bailey said. "Thanks. I mean it."

He nodded without looking at her.

She sighed. "Kade. I'm trying to apologize for acting suspicious earlier. Will you at least—"

A hand suddenly covered her mouth from behind and she was jerked backward through the doorway.

She struggled to wrench free, kicking and clawing at whoever was holding her.

Kade rushed through the doorway just as Jace and the others whirled around, alarmed at the commotion. They shouted and clawed for their guns just as Kade slammed the door shut.

And locked it.

Bailey stood in shock, blinking at the five heavily armed men surrounding her and Kade. Her hands were cuffed behind her and her weapon had been taken away before she'd even been able to register what was happening. Even the Bersa .380 had been taken out of her ankle holster. But Kade, who stood a few feet away from her, wasn't cuffed. And no one was holding on to his arm, like they were hers, to make sure he couldn't get away.

She looked toward the door. There was no window to let her see her friends who were trapped behind it. And the complete lack of noise told her the room was soundproofed, sealed, like a tomb.

"You bastard," she said to Kade. "You betrayed them, betrayed us all."

"I didn't have a choice." He pulled out his phone and handed it to one of the gunmen. "Bailey, meet Dominic Wales and Jack Martinelli, partners in crime and leaders of this sorry group of assholes."

"They're not the only assholes around here." She glared at Kade, more hurt by his betrayal than she could have possibly imagined.

His jaw clenched and he looked away.

"Where now?" Dominic asked.

Kade motioned toward the second door. "The control room."

Dominic and three of his men went in ahead of them. Kade motioned for Bailey to precede him, and Jack took up the rear. He closed the door behind them and she heard the steel bar lock jam home. She looked over her shoulder. Jack was guarding the door, a Glock 17 9mm in his hand as he calmly watched her in return. This definitely wasn't his first criminal act. He looked completely comfortable with the entire situation. He wasn't the weak link.

She stepped a few feet away, stopping beside Kade. The others moved to the viewing window. Dominic said something in a language Bailey didn't recognize to one of the other men and they laughed.

She risked a glance through the window and her heart constricted in her chest. Jace and the others were running around the lab, trying the door, feeling along the walls. Jace looked up at the glass and said something to Mason. They lined up, shoulder to shoulder, and aimed their guns at the window.

Dominic swore and motioned to his men to duck.

Kade didn't move, so Bailey didn't either.

Nothing happened.

No sounds, no exploding glass, not even a vibration.

But based on Jace's and Mason's shocked expressions, they'd definitely fired their guns.

"Bulletproof and soundproof," Dominic said as he slowly straightened. "You did good, *Lone Wolf.*" He laughed as if at some inside joke and motioned to the other men. They gathered in close and whispered in low tones to each other.

Kade looked like he wanted to tear Dominic apart with his bare hands.

Bailey raked Kade with a scornful glance. "What did you do, make some kind of deal to save your own skin?" she whispered so the others wouldn't hear. "You traded the Equalizers' and my life for yours? I never pegged you as a coward."

He seemed to drag his gaze from the others to her. "They were going to kill me, which would have been fine. But then they showed me a video—of you—going to my old house, your old house, EXIT headquarters. They were following you. And you didn't even know it. They were going to kill you unless I cooperated."

She drew in a sharp breath. She hadn't realized anyone was following her, and that scared the crap out of her.

"Did they follow me to the Equalizers' base, too?"

He frowned. "Not that I know of. I don't remember Faegan mentioning another location."

She pressed her hand against her throat in relief. She must have picked up her tail at EXIT the second time she retraced her steps and performed a second round of searches. And since she'd gone straight to Colorado Springs after that, without returning to EXIT headquarters, then she hadn't compromised any other Equalizers or their families.

Assuming that Kade was right.

"So you made a deal," she said, her voice rising. "But then you got away. You could have warned me, told me what was going on. And I could have warned them." She waved toward the window. "We could have fought them, instead of being offered like sacrificial lambs to slaughter."

He slowly shook his head. "The deal was that I had to lead them to the Equalizers, specifically to the leaders—Devlin and Mason. Those two are the ones who brought Cyprian Cardenas down. I think Faegan resents that and wants some payback. I didn't know where they were, or any way to get in contact with them. Showing up at EXIT, or my old house, or even yours, would have been too obvious. I knew you and the others would be suspicious. You might expect I was being forced to set a trap. So, instead, I told them about the only other place where you might show up."

"The house in Colorado Springs."

He nodded again. "They had the whole place rigged with cameras and microphones. If I'd even tried to pass you a note, they'd have known. And the phone they gave me was an open line to them at all times, not to mention, it had a GPS tracker. They were going to kill you, Bailey. There was no other way. I had to give them the Equalizers."

She pressed a hand to her throat again, thinking about last night in a whole new light. At least she understood now why Kade had been so remote. He didn't want the others to see or hear them. Apparently he still had some honor left after all. Her stomach lurched. But that wasn't the horrible thing here. What was horrible was that he'd made a deal with the devil, her life for the lives of her friends.

"No," she whispered harshly. "I can't let you do this. I won't let you trade my safety for their lives." She waved toward the window. "Put me in there with them. Whatever's going to happen should happen to me, too. I couldn't live with myself knowing they died because of me."

"That can be arranged." Dominic turned from his conversation with the others. He waved them to fan out farther down the control panel, leaving him standing there alone.

"That's not our deal," Kade insisted. "She goes free. As soon as it's done, you let her go. That's the agreement I made with Faegan."

"No," Bailey insisted. "Let them all go. What is it you want? You're mercenaries, right? You do jobs for money. Well, I've got money, plenty. You wouldn't believe how lucrative being an Enforcer is. There are, what, five of you? How does a quarter of a million dollars sound? For *each* of you?"

"Bailey—" Kade warned.

Dominic waved him to silence and stepped toward her. "It's clear you don't understand how mercenaries operate. Yes, money is the objective, in most cases. But our entire careers, our lives, depend on us keeping the deals that we've made. Our loyalty lies with our current employer, until we've fulfilled the agreements we've made with him. If we took bribes every time we captured someone, we'd never be employed again. And someone else would take us out for breaking our agreements. So, trust me when I tell you this. No amount of money you offer us will save your friends." He motioned toward one of the others. "Tie her to a chair where she can enjoy the show, without interfering."

"No." Kade moved in front of her. "No one ties her up. In fact, you need to take those handcuffs off her. Right now."

A wall of guns pointed at Kade.

He held his hands up and stepped back.

Bailey cursed at the man who grabbed her and shoved her into a chair. But apparently he hadn't come prepared to tie someone up. Since her hands were cuffed behind her, and she was sitting back against them, he used two more sets of handcuffs to cuff her ankles to the legs of the chair. Not ideally secure. She figured she could rock the chair back to free her legs. But in a roomful of gunmen, she had no plans of trying it anytime soon. He glared at her in warning before joining the others at the control panel.

"Okay," the leader said, motioning toward Kade. "We haven't found any traps or tricks."

"I haven't been out of your sight. How could I have tricked you?" Scorn seemed to drip from Kade's words, as if he thought these men were idiots to doubt him.

Dominic's eyes narrowed. "Careful, *boss*. You're not the one paying my fee. And you don't know what kind of deal he made with me."

Kade's face turned pale. "What did Faegan tell you to do?"

"Kill the Equalizers. That's happening no matter what. But he didn't seem to care what happened to Miss Stark here. As a matter of fact, I think he said something along the lines of 'let her go with Kade if she isn't any trouble, otherwise, do whatever you want.' I'm thinking she's been a bit of trouble. What do you think, boys?"

Laughter went up around them.

Bailey tensed in the chair.

"I'll offer you another deal," Kade said. "For Miss Stark's life."

Dominic laughed. "Unless you can bring all the remaining Enforcers to me in one fell swoop so I can finish the Enforcer Extermination and move on to the next job, there's nothing else you have to barter."

Bailey sucked in a breath. Extermination? She'd been right all along. There never was a retraining facility.

As if realizing what she was thinking, Kade asked, "Are you saying there isn't a retraining facility?"

"Oh, there is, all right. Faegan has to interrogate every one of EXIT's so-called assassins to make sure he knows the extent of any information they might have. It's part of the cleanup. But once he's satisfied that he's found all the documentation, the extermination phase goes into full swing." He sighed as if greatly put upon. "So far we've only been allowed to kill a few of them. Makes for some boring days."

He'd only killed a few of them. Could Sebastian and Amber be alive, as Kade had claimed? Bailey looked around the room, searching for anything she could use as a weapon. Somehow she had to get out of here, save her friends, and find that damned retraining facility.

"I can give you the rest of the Enforcers," Kade said.

The room went silent. Bailey stared at Kade in horror.

"How?" Dominic asked.

"Once we leave here, once Bailey is free, I can log into the Equalizers' network and warn the remaining Enforcers. I can tell them they all have to go to a specific location—of your choosing—for an emergency meeting about the leaders at EXIT who are trying to kill them."

"You bastard," Bailey hissed.

Dominic had been staring at Kade with suspicion. But after Bailey spoke, he grinned. "Very well. You have another deal, this time with me. We'll let your woman go after the Equalizers are dead. And then you'll go with us and lure the rest of them into a trap."

A sob escaped Bailey before she could stop it. "I hate you, Kade."

His back stiffened but he didn't look at her.

"Do it," Dominic said, waving toward the panel. "I'm looking forward to witnessing my very first Sarin gas attack. This is going to be fun. Go on. Kill them."

Sarin gas. *Oh, God.* That was the deal that Kade had made? That was why he'd tricked her into getting the Equalizers to this location?

Forgive me, Jace. Forgive me, Austin, Mason, Devlin, Terrance. I'm so, so sorry.

Kade opened one of the cabinets below the panel and pulled out a small canister with a big red skull and crossbones on it. He opened another cabinet above it to reveal a round hole with a red metal cover. He carefully slid the canister into the hole, then sealed the red cover over it.

"It's ready," he said.

"Kade," Bailey pleaded. But she didn't know what else to say. His mind was obviously made up. She didn't know why he'd bargained for her life. But he was committed to going through with this.

"Which button do I push?" Dominic asked.

"I'll tell you after I speak to the Equalizers."

"Speak to them? I'm not opening the door to that lab. They all have guns."

"Afraid of a fair fight?" Bailey sneered.

"I want to warn them what's going to happen," Kade said. "I owe it to them. They're . . . they *were* . . . my friends. Or at least, Bailey's friends. It's the only thing left that I can do for them."

Dominic shrugged. "Go ahead. Warn them. It'll be even more fun that way, to see the fear in their eyes before the gas strikes them down."

Bailey's stomach clenched. Bile rose in her throat.

Kade flipped a switch on the control panel and immediately the sound of the men in the other room was broadcast into the control booth. They stood in a huddle by the computers, guns drawn, apparently discussing whatever plans they were trying to make. But their exact words couldn't be heard, just a low mumble.

Kade flipped another switch, and the sounds from the other room were silenced once again.

"What are you doing?" Dominic asked.

"It's one-way communication. Now they can hear us. But we can't hear them."

"All right. Continue."

The Equalizers were all staring at the window now. Jace stepped forward and the other men joined him, except for Austin, who sat in his wheelchair a short distance away looking sullen. Jace was obviously saying something, and from the fury on his face, it wasn't nice.

"I'm sorry it's ending like this," Kade said, his voice heavy with regret.

Austin made a rude gesture at the window.

The gunmen laughed.

Bailey bit her lip to keep from crying out.

"I had no choice," Kade continued. "They were going to kill you all. I could only save Bailey. Your deaths will be quick, but painful, I'm afraid. I'm going to press a button to release Sarin gas into the chamber. You'll see a thick, white cloud, and then your lungs will begin to seize."

Mason frowned and shot a look at Jace.

"Even if you try to hold your breath, it won't matter," Kade said, sounding so matter-of-fact that it shocked Bailey. She never would have expected this of him. Never.

"The gas will affect your nerves. It will make you fall to the floor, unable to move. You'll be dead in a matter of seconds." He glanced back at Bailey before continuing. "I really am sorry." He flipped the control switch again, then moved his finger toward the red button.

Bailey jerked her head toward the window. The Equalizers stood together again, huddled like football players, including Austin. They still thought they could figure a way out of this.

"Please," Bailey pleaded again. "I'm begging you."

Kade hesitated, his finger poised over the button.

Dominic shoved him out of the way and slammed his own palm down.

A cloud of white shot out into the lab.

"No!" Bailey cried, desperately trying to free herself from the chair. She wrenched it backward and jerked her legs free, then jumped to her feet.

The gunman who'd been standing by the door stepped forward, pointing his pistol at her.

She stopped, torn about what to do next.

The sounds of cursing and coughing filled the room. The lead gunman had flipped the intercom, broadcasting the sounds from the lab into the booth.

Austin tumbled out of his wheelchair and sprawled on the floor.

Devlin shouted something and knelt beside him, then started coughing.

"How can you just stand there and let this happen?" Bailey yelled at Kade. "Do something."

"It's too late," he said, infuriatingly calm. "There's nothing anyone can do for them now."

Ignoring the man with the gun pointing at her, Bailey charged at Kade, slamming her body against him and shoving him back against the wall.

"I hate you," she yelled, kicking him. "I hate you, I hate you, I hate you."

He grabbed her in a bear hug, squeezing her against him. "I'm so sorry."

She collapsed against his chest, sobbing.

"Go," Kade said quietly over the top of her head. He leaned over the control panel and flipped something. The sounds from the other room went silent. He must have turned off the intercom. "You have what you want. Go."

"You forget, you're coming with us. That's the bargain," the leader said.

"I know. But only after all of you step out. I want Bailey to lock herself in the control booth until we're gone."

The man clucked his tongue. "I have a feeling you don't trust us."

Kade laughed harshly. "Trust you? If there was any way for me to unlock the door to the lab and let my friends kill all five of you, I'd have done it. Instead, I've killed them."

Dominic laughed. "Very well. You've honored your word. I shall honor mine." He motioned toward Jack, the one who'd been guarding the door. Footsteps sounded as Jack and the others filed out of the control room and into the warehouse. Only Dominic remained in the control booth with Kade and Bailey.

"Time to go," he said, motioning for Kade to step outside.

Kade nodded and gently pushed Bailey back. He reached his hand up as if to touch her face but she jerked away from him. He gave her a sad smile.

"Lock the door after we leave," he said.

"Yeah, no problem with my hands bound behind me," she sneered.

"Just kick the bar. It will fall down across the latch. Kick it up once you know it's safe to come out."

She turned her head, refusing to look at him.

"All right," Kade said. "We're leaving the control room now."

Bailey frowned at his odd choice of words. As

soon as the door closed, she hurried forward and kicked the bar. As Kade had said, it dropped down into place, locking her inside.

She plopped down on the ground and contorted her arms and body until she worked her handcuffed arms under her legs and in front of her. Breathing hard from the exertion, she looked around the room for something to break the cuffs. But there was nothing she could use.

No time, no time. She had get to a computer and warn the other Enforcers before Kade tricked them into heading toward their deaths. She jumped to her feet, swiping at the tears flowing down her cheeks. Damn it. She wasn't a crier, didn't want to cry. But Kade had broken her heart. Not only broken it, but smashed it into a million jagged pieces. He'd used her to kill her friends. How was she supposed to live with that kind of guilt?

She looked at the control panel. Was it wired to a security system? Were there camera views she could see so she'd know whether Kade and the gunmen were gone yet? Even though she'd tried to keep her gaze averted from the horror in the other room, she couldn't resist one quick look. She blinked. What the hell? She leaned closer to the glass, looking right and left. The lab was empty! She looked toward the lab door. It was wide open. What was going on?

Thump, thump, thump. Someone was pounding on the control room door.

"Bailey! It's Jace. Open up."

Jace? It couldn't be. And yet, that was his voice. And the lab was empty.

"Bailey!"

She ran toward the door and jammed her cuffed hands beneath the bar, lifting it up and out of the way.

The door flew open and Jace ran inside, sweeping his pistol around the room.

"It's empty," Bailey whispered, her throat so tight she could barely speak. "They're all gone."

"All clear," he yelled to the warehouse behind him. Then he holstered his pistol and grabbed her in a hug. "You okay?"

She froze in shock for a moment, then pulled back and said, "I don't . . . I don't understand. You . . . you died."

Mason and Terrance filed into the control room, with Austin wheeling in behind them. She stared at them in wonder.

"I thought you were all dead."

"So did we," Jace said, giving a nervous laugh. "Kade had us all fooled, until he mentioned the white cloud of gas. Then we knew."

She frowned. "Knew what?"

Mason cocked a brow. "Sarin gas is colorless. Kade was warning us that he was trying to trick the gunmen. So we played along, played dead."

"There wasn't any Sarin gas?" She knew it was true, or none of them would be alive. But she couldn't quite wrap her mind around it.

Mason shook his head. "Remember he kept up with the investigation. He told us all about it. He must have known they had some kind of test canisters in this place and he could use them to fool Faegan's men. The FBI sure as hell wouldn't leave deadly Sarin gas in a warehouse, even if it was part of an investigation. Those mercenaries were too stupid to know that, and thank God they didn't know that Sarin gas didn't have a color. I knew of course, and so did Jace since he used to be a Navy SEAL."

"And Kade knew that you knew," Bailey finished for him. "Because you told him the other day, that you'd been on a mission involving Sarin gas."

Mason nodded.

Bailey looked from Austin, to Jace, to Mason, and finally Terrance. "Then, it was all a ruse. But . . . how did you get out of the lab?"

"We heard a click at the door, figured Kade had remotely unlocked it. And we heard him say something about the door over the intercom. Sure enough, it was unlocked."

"He must have done that when he leaned over the control panel that last time. I didn't notice. Thank God the gunmen didn't either." She looked at each of them again. "But I thought he'd bargained your lives for mine." She started to press a hand to her temple, which was starting to throb, but the handcuffs jangled on her wrists, reminding her she was still tied up.

"Here, I'll get those." Jace stepped forward with a handcuff key, freeing her, just as he had that first night.

"Thank you." She rubbed her wrists gratefully. Then she frowned. "Where's Devlin? What happened to the gunmen? Where is Kade?"

"Come on," Jace said.

He led her and the others out of the control booth back into the warehouse. Four bodies lay against the far wall. Jace and the others must have taken them out as they'd left the lab, warned by Kade as he'd announced that they were leaving the control room. It was all starting to make sense to her now. But there had been five gunmen.

Jace waved behind her and she turned around. The fifth man, Dominic, stood against the wall, his hands bound behind him, a length of phone cord—probably taken from the lab—tying both his ankles together. And standing in front of him, pointing a gun and saying something in a low menacing tone, was Devlin. And beside *him*?

Kade.

They all joined Devlin and Kade, who were grilling the mercenary. From what Bailey caught of the conversation as she approached, he was squealing like a pig, telling them everything they wanted to know. So much for those loyalties he'd been so proud of back in the control room.

Bailey stopped several feet from Kade. Jace stopped with her.

"What happened after Kade and the others left the room?" she whispered.

"We waited until the gunmen went outside to surprise them," he said, keeping his voice low to mirror hers. "They'd handcuffed Kade by the time we got out there and he was sitting in the leader's Humvee. We heard them arguing. Kade was taunting the leader."

"Taunting him?"

Jace stared at her. "Apparently the leader had a computer in his car and expected Kade to access the Enforcer network to trick more Enforcers into coming in. But Kade had lied about being able to access the network. He was taunting the leader about how gullible he was to believe his lies. Saying as long as you were safe, that was all that mattered."

Bailey stared up at him. "He had to know the leader would kill him for that."

"Yeah. I imagine he did. I'm pretty sure he didn't expect us to make it out of there in time to save him. The leader was raising his gun to shoot Kade when Devlin leaned in and wrenched the gun out of his hand. It was close. Another second and Kade would have been dead."

"Then he . . . he did all of this, expecting to die. He didn't bargain his own life for mine. He was willing to die to make all of us safe."

"Yep. That's pretty much what we concluded, too." He put his hand on her shoulder. "He's a good man, Bailey. He was in an impossible situation and he came up with a plan that was risky as hell. But he did it to lure out the bad guys. And now that we managed to get the leader, we can get Faegan. He saved all of us." He left her to join the others.

Bailey couldn't seem to make her feet move. Everything that had happened in the past few hours kept running through her mind. And it all boiled down to one thing. They were all safe, because of Kade.

Devlin grabbed Dominic's arm and hauled him toward the exit. The rest of the Equalizers followed.

Kade gave Bailey an uncertain look, then limped after the others.

"Oh, hell no." Bailey ran after him and blocked his way.

He stopped and watched her with a wary look.

"Jace," she yelled over her shoulder. "Give us a minute."

"You got it," he yelled back.

She didn't say anything until she heard the door close.

"This was all a trick," she finally said. "You knew that you would probably die either way. And still, you bargained, to save me. Why?"

His brows lowered as if in confusion. "Why? I couldn't let them kill you, not if I could do something to stop them."

"Why?"

He glanced impatiently toward the door. "We need to go. We have a lead on Faegan and where he might be holding the captured Enforcers."

"The retraining center. You know where it is?"

He nodded. "Dominic blubbered the details. If he's telling the truth, and I think he is, then this is our best chance to finally end this."

"Why?" she repeated. "Why would you risk your life, and the lives of my friends, to save me?" When he didn't answer, she swore at him. "Is this some chauvinistic thing, protect the woman? Well that's bullshit. I can take care of myself. Do you think I would want anyone else to die for me? How could you bargain someone else's life for mine?"

His jaw tightened. "I couldn't let you die."

"So you'd let my friends die instead?"

He swore. "I had a plan. I knew they'd be okay."

"Plans don't always work out. And from where I stand, your plan was shaky at best. You had no right to—"

"I *had* to," he said, his voice raw. "Don't you get it, Bailey?" He placed his fist over his heart. "I didn't have a choice. I couldn't bear to let you die. I couldn't . . ." He shook his head and swallowed hard, his Adam's apple bobbing in his throat.

"For months, I saw shadowy pictures in my head of a woman I supposedly loved, had married. And then I watched her die while I sat there doing nothing. I couldn't save her, and I've been dying a slow death ever since. Because nothing felt right. The memories weren't real. I know that now. And I think I knew it then, somehow, in my subconscious. And I still felt guilty as hell that I couldn't save her."

He pounded his chest. "It tore me up. But nothing like the thought of something happening to you. Don't you get it, Bailey? Everything I believe in—the law, justice, that all lives are valuable no matter what—goes out the flipping window when I think about you. Nothing else matters but saving you. That's why I did what I did. That's why I risked others' lives, even though it was wrong. I couldn't let you die. Even if you hate me for it."

He stalked around her and out of the warehouse, slamming the door behind him.

Bailey blinked, stunned at the anger and hurt that had rolled off Kade. And stunned to hear him say that the one driving force behind all of the decisions that he'd made today was that he couldn't let her die.

What did that mean? Did he . . . love her? Was that even possible after knowing someone for, what, a week? Or did he just feel responsible for her for some crazy reason, because of Hawke? And her other friends? She didn't know and wasn't sure she was even prepared to handle the answer if she did know. Wanting someone was one thing. Loving? Well, that was something else entirely. The only people she'd ever loved had died. She was bad luck, bad mojo. And like Kade, she couldn't bear the thought of something happening to him.

She raked a hand through her hair. This was all so screwed up.

The warehouse door popped open and Jace leaned inside.

"Bailey, we've already got some other Equalizers performing surveillance based on Dominic's information. They've spotted Faegan. We know where the retraining facility is located. The Equalizers are going to war."

Chapter Nineteen

K ade stood beside Jace high on a heavily wooded ridge, looking down into a canyon about an hour west of Boulder. To their left and right, Mason's small army of Equalizers formed a line, ready to launch their attack as soon as Mason gave the signal.

Bailey stood about three people away, to Kade's left, discussing strategy with Mason. With everything going on, he'd barely been able to say more than a few words to her since the disaster at the warehouse. And he'd just managed to make her mad at him all over again.

He sighed and looked down into the canyon. The retraining facility was only a few hundred yards away. It was carved out of a network of caves in the side of the mountain—definitely not something the FBI higher-ups knew about or had authorized. This was all on Faegan and his mercenaries. Whoever had assigned him to clean up the EXIT debacle had entrusted exactly the wrong man with the job. And they were probably pumping millions of dollars into his program, without even realizing what he was doing with the money.

Kade was restless to start the assault, to get into those tunnels and hopefully free the men and women who'd been taken by his very own teams. It was already late afternoon. Hours had passed since they'd gotten the location of the facility. But the delay in going after Faegan had been a deliberate one. The time had been used to send all of the known Enforcers' and Equalizers' families into hiding.

Faegan wasn't governed by the old EXIT code of not going after Enforcers' families, no matter what. If the Equalizers didn't manage to capture Faegan during the raid, he might decide to have his revenge by going after their loved ones. Kade sure wouldn't put it past him. He just wished he knew for sure who was working with Faegan and who wasn't. It was hard to trust anyone these days.

He'd finally checked his email after leaving the warehouse and had a brief reply from Gannon. He hadn't gotten a chance yet to redirect any resources into checking on Kade's two agents. But from his own scans and searches, he agreed with Kade. There was something suspicious about the two men. He promised he'd do whatever it took to get something official back by the end of the week.

"I hope you know," Kade told Jace, "that the FBI isn't what you're seeing here. Faegan is a traitor to everything we stand for. The few people in the bureau aware of EXIT's clandestine side were supposed to clean things up and make sure the documentation was gone. Killing people was never supposed to be a part of the equation. I guarantee that they don't know what Faegan's up to."

"I know that," Jace said. "Devlin's brother, Pierce, is in the FBI. He's one of the most decent men I've ever met. I know the FBI itself, as a whole, isn't a part of any of this. And that most of the agents involved have no idea they're being directed to do anything wrong. I imagine most of the men working for Faegan aren't agents at all. They're mercenaries using FBI equipment. So why are you telling me all that?"

"I'm just so disgusted. I wanted to make sure you guys don't think that these . . . scum . . . are representative of most of the people who wear the badge."

"So noted." He cocked his head, studying Kade. "Why are you so fired up about defending the FBI anyway? Was it a lifelong dream to be an agent or something?"

"Sort of." He stared down into the valley. "My dad was a lifer in the Navy, thirty-one years before he retired. My days consisted of lectures on love of country, justice, and honor above all else. I guess most of it stuck."

"You were military before the FBI?"

"No. I would have been, probably. But my best friend, Gannon, was determined to be an agent. Same high school, same college. I guess his enthusiasm rubbed off on me. When he signed up, I did, too. It was more about the structure, and serving my country in some way. Where or how I served wasn't all that important."

"Huh." Jace turned and stared down into the valley, too.

"What?" Kade asked.

Jace shrugged. "It's just that, well, I guess I'm surprised that you'd put your life on the line to save

Bailey since her work as an Enforcer is the exact opposite of what you ascribe to."

"It's funny how some things seem less important once you get to know someone." Kade glanced down the line, looking for Bailey. She was standing beside Austin's wheelchair now, pointing to something on the computer tablet in his lap. Austin was apparently brilliant at logistics, as well as computers. He'd helped arrange the equipment they needed for the raid.

Kade straightened and looked away.

"Have you told her how you feel about her?"

Kade stiffened, then waved toward the other side of the canyon. "Devlin's been down there scouting the place for quite a while. Maybe someone should check on him."

"He's fine." Jace didn't sound worried at all about his friend. "He'll give us the signal as soon as he's finished the recon and taken out enough guards. So have you told her? Bailey?"

"Told her what?"

"That you're in love with her?"

Kade rolled his eyes. "I'm not in love with her."

"You sure about that?"

Kade turned to face Jace. "Is there a point to this?"

Jace shrugged. "Just that when a man is about to go into battle, it's customary to let the woman he cares about know how he feels. Just in case the worst happens."

"Battle, huh. Good to know. I hope you took care of that little detail for yourself. I heard you're married."

His whole face seemed to light up as he grinned. "To the smartest, sassiest, most beautiful woman you'll ever meet. Melissa even knows how to fire a gun. Couldn't ask for better. And, yes, I called her before we came up on the ridge. She's not happy that I'm about to face off with Faegan and his thugs. But there's nothing left unsaid between us. If something happens to me today, she won't be left wondering whether I loved her, or regretting the last words we said to each other."

"Yeah, well, it's not like that with Bailey and me."

"Oh. I see. You'd basically trade your life for any woman, like you planned on doing this morning for her."

"Shut up, Jace."

When Jace didn't say anything else for several minutes, Kade glanced at him. Jace had grown serious and was studying him, like he was trying to figure him out.

Kade let out a long breath. "What now?"

"Just keep it together down there." He gestured toward the cave openings on the opposite wall of the canyon, where they'd seen Faegan's men when they'd first arrived. "We all need to be totally on for this. If your head isn't straight, you could be a danger to any one of us. I for one don't want to not go home to the woman I love because one of the men I'm fighting with has too much going on and can't focus. Are you focused, Kade?"

"I'm here to do my job," he gritted out. "I'm focused."

Jace studied him another long moment, then gave him a curt nod. "I hope so."

"That's the signal," Mason called out from a few yards away. "Go, go, go."

They all drew their weapons and took off, racing

down the hill toward the main cave entrance. In spite of the brace on his thigh, and the handful of Ibuprofen that he'd popped earlier, Kade still couldn't quite keep up with the others. Jace noticeably slowed, keeping pace with him, which had Kade grinding his teeth. He didn't want anyone coddling him because of his handicap. But he also couldn't search for Bailey in the crowd of men and women running with them without Jace noticing. It nearly killed him not to look for her.

Jace's words kept going through his head, and he understood the man's concern. Whether Kade wanted to admit it or not, Bailey was important to him. But he was no good to anyone if he was preoccupied worrying about her.

He'd suggested that she stay back with Austin, keeping an eye on things and radioing them if there was any trouble. But that suggestion was the reason she'd kept her distance from him, after aiming a particularly lethal glare his way. She wasn't the kind of woman who wanted a man to protect her. But damned if Kade could help that he wanted to do exactly that. She knew what she was doing, and how to protect herself. He just had to keep reminding himself of that.

The first Equalizer reached the entrance and took a sharp right. The next one headed to the left. They were basing their approach on the recon reports Devlin had radioed back. No shots had been fired so far, a good sign.

More of them reached the entrance, and each one went either left or right, depending on which direction the person in front of them had gone. Too bad Devlin couldn't have scouted out the entire network of caves and radioed that back instead of just the main ones. But they were worried that if they took the time they needed to map out every single branch and fork, the Enforcers being held captive would be killed by then.

Kade and Jace were the last to the entrance.

"See you on the other side." Jace saluted him and disappeared to the right.

Kade went left, following the path deeper into the side of the hill. A string of lights in the ceiling lit the way, though not very well. But the rock floor was smooth and clear, as if many feet had passed through here. Which made sense since everything they'd seen indicated this was where Faegan and his men were operating from.

Pounding down the tunnel sent a sharp jolt of pain through his thigh every time he set his foot down. He gritted his teeth, belatedly wishing he'd taken even more pills. But he couldn't slow down. He was already the slowest man out here and he'd be damned if he missed the whole show because of his damned leg.

The light was better up ahead. He remembered Devlin's directions, that the left and right tunnels from the entrance opened into a large chamber. He slowed, raising his pistol. But when he rounded the corner, the chamber was empty, except for stacks of wooden boxes in neat rows, with labels on each one—guns, body armor, bottles of water, food. Faegan was nothing if not organized.

He stopped when he saw a trail of blood near one of the boxes. He followed it into the aisle of food and bottled water, and realized it was one of Faegan's men, most likely one of the guards that Devlin had taken out. Kade hated the loss of life, but knew that the mercenaries Faegan had hired wouldn't hesitate to kill him and the others.

He jogged to the next set of tunnels at the far end. There were three to choose from. They'd each been assigned to go down one of the tunnels, splitting them into three groups. He was assigned to the tunnel on the far left. He'd just started down it when the sound of gunshots echoed from behind him. He whirled around and ran back into the chamber, scanning his pistol back and forth, looking for the threat. Empty. There was no one there. Another shot sounded, followed by a shout. Kade whirled around again. The sounds had come from the tunnel on the right.

BAILEY GASPED FOR breath as she crouched behind a boulder. She'd barely made it behind the rock to avoid being shot and her pulse was buzzing in her ears. On the other side of the cavern, two Equalizers she'd only met a few hours ago motioned to her to stay down. No kidding. If her quick glimpse of the situation before diving for cover could be relied on, she and her two companions were pinned down by at least six gunmen.

"Put down your weapons," she yelled. "You're outnumbered four to one."

One of the men across from her raised a brow, obviously doubting her math skills.

She shrugged.

"Toss your guns down and no one will get hurt," she added, just for fun. Because, really, if you couldn't joke in a situation like this, what was the point?

A volley of shots rang out in answer to her jibe.

She cursed and covered her ears, mildly surprised when her hands didn't come away bloody. The cave amplified sounds, and those gunshots were at about the decibel level of a jet airplane.

Well, if nothing else, the shots had probably alerted more Equalizers, and someone would be here soon to even the odds. Assuming, of course, that they weren't pinned down in a similar situation in another tunnel. One could always hope.

She counted down from five, four, three, two . . . she leaned around the boulder and fired off two quick shots. Score! One of the men flew backward, obviously dead before he even hit the ground. The others let loose with another barrage of gunfire in her direction. She dove back to cover and held her hands over her ears. Across from her, the two men were glaring at her like *they* wanted to shoot her. As soon as the bullets quit whining through the cave, she answered their glares with two middle fingers.

Damn, she'd missed this kind of excitement.

If her two supposed allies would just do something . . . anything . . . to help, then maybe they could all walk out of here in one piece. As it was, she was going to have to keep picking off the enemies one by one. But her odds weren't good, not when they knew she was behind this boulder. And the next boulder was a good ten feet away, with no cover.

"With dozens of people on the team you'd think I'd end up with at least one who was willing to do more than hide behind a damn rock," she grumbled, hopefully loud enough for the two Equalizers to hear but not loud enough for her enemies.

Another volley of shots rang out. She jerked around. No, the two men across from her hadn't shot their weapons. So what were the bad guys shooting at?

A blur of movement off to her right had her whirling toward the motion, gun raised.

"It's me," a deep voice yelled, as he dove toward her. Kade.

She swung her pistol up toward the ceiling just as he slammed into her, crushing her against the rock.

Gunshots echoed for a full minute as the bad guys took aim at the newcomer. But thankfully the rock was solid. When the echoes died down, she shoved at Kade.

"Move," she hissed. "I can't breathe and I think you broke two of my ribs."

His eyes widened and he lifted himself off her just enough to run his hands up her shirt.

"What the . . . stop it." She slapped at his hands. "What are you doing?" she whispered.

"Checking your ribs. You said—"

"It's called exaggeration. Like when a guy tells you he has a big . . . foot. I'm fine."

He grinned. "I wear size thirteen shoes, in case you're curious."

"Not going there." She shoved his hands down, flushing hot because he'd turned her on like a light switch the second his hands had touched her skin. And being turned on right now was more than awkward when, (a) she had an audience one rock over and (b) she was supposed to be mad at Kade. He'd had the gall to suggest that she sit on the hill while everyone else had fun in the tunnels.

"What are you doing here?" she demanded, struggling to keep her voice low instead of shouting like she wanted to.

"Rescuing you." He finally lifted himself off her and moved to the side. He looked at the other two who were eying them curiously. "Who are Bert and Ernie over there?"

"Bert and Ernie?"

"You know. *Sesame Street.* The eyebrows?"

"Oh, yeah. I see what you mean. The blond guy does kind of remind me of Bert."

Blond guy in question was now glaring daggers at them.

"So who are they?" Kade asked again.

"No one. Pretend they don't exist. In the good-guy bad-guy column it's five against two, counting you and me. Those guys are in the decoration column."

"Decoration?"

"Here for looks only. They haven't contributed a single thing to helping us get out of here."

He raked them with a scornful glance, which had Bailey smiling. Then she remembered she was mad at him and stopped smiling.

"It's six, not five," he corrected.

"No way. I shot one of them."

"I saw. But I still counted six alive and kicking when I came down the side tunnel."

"Damn." She looked past him, in the direction he'd come from. "Side tunnel? I don't remember one over there."

"It's there, just past that boulder."

She nodded. "I thought that was where a light was burned out. It's small, not like the other tunnels." She raised her pistol. "If you made it to me, then we can both make it to the tunnel."

"What about those two?"

"Screw 'em."

He cocked a brow.

"Okay, okay," she grumbled. "We'll save their asses, too."

"Hey, we can save our own asses," one of them whispered, sounding none too happy with her.

"It speaks." She rolled her eyes.

Kade leaned down and kissed her. It was hard, and wild, and far too short. When he pulled back she blinked up at him.

"What . . . what was that for?"

His expression went from smiling to serious in the space of a heartbeat. "Someone told me to never go into battle with anger between you and someone you care about. You never know what's going to happen."

She stared at him, then looked away. "I think anger is putting it mildly. Kade, what you did at the warehouse . . . what I did, the things we both said . . . we need to—"

He pressed his fingers against her lips. "I know. We need to talk. There are a lot of things we need to discuss. But that's a conversation I want to have without an audience. And you and I both need to focus right now so neither of us gets killed. How about a truce?"

She pulled his fingers down from her lips. "A truce. Okay, I can do that. As long as we have that talk, soon."

"Promise."

"Did you come in here with a plan?" she asked. "This rock isn't wide enough for you, me, and the two Muppets over there."

"Hey, lady," the blond guy whispered. "Would you stop—"

"Talk to the hand." She held up her hand and didn't bother looking at him.

He swore. Loudly.

Gunshots rang out again, echoing around the cavern as the bad guys shot at them again.

When the shooting stopped, Bailey gave blondie an incredulous look. "Seriously?" she whispered.

He glared at her and clamped his lips together.

Kade hefted his pistol. "The plan is to even the odds a bit more."

She grinned. "I like how you think. In three?"

"Two, one . . ."

He leaned right. She leaned left. They popped off a good eight shots each before they were forced to duck back for cover again. Screams of pain erupted from some of Faegan's men.

"I winged two," she said. "They won't be able to shoot at us. I think you took out the one on the right."

"That leaves three. The odds are ever in our favor now."

"Hunger Games. Love it." She gave him a fist bump.

Gunshots rang out right beside them. Kade instinctively threw himself on top of Bailey. They both turned their heads to the side, realizing at the same time that the two Equalizers had finally joined the fight. Blondie and his partner finished firing a dozen or more rounds before ducking back down.

Cursing and shouting sounded from the bad guys.

The man on the other side of blondie held up one finger, not the middle one.

"Hey, looks like he got one." She gave him a thumbs-up.

He grinned like a kid in a candy store.

"About time you grew a pair," she whispered loudly.

His smile disappeared. "Bitch," he whispered back.

"Takes one to know one," she answered.

"Bailey," Kade said. "Are you always like this when people are shooting at you?"

She thought for a moment. "Yeah, probably. Why?"

He kissed her again, taking his time, in spite of their audience. Bailey didn't even try to stop him. It felt way too good. By the time he lifted his head, she was breathing heavy.

"Wow," she said.

He laughed. "What's it going to be? Run for the tunnel and lay cover fire for our two friends when it's their turn? Or try to improve the odds one more time?"

"Improve the odds," they both said together.

This time, when she and Kade jumped up and began shooting, the two Equalizers did the same. There was no diving back behind the boulder for cover. Bailey's aim was true and there weren't any more bad guys to shoot.

"Good aim," Kade said, truly impressed.

"Thank you." She popped out the magazine and slammed another one home. Then she shoved her now reloaded pistol into her holster. "Ready to look for more bad guys?"

"Just a minute."

He stepped over to the other two men.

The one closest to him held his hand out to shake Kade's hand.

Kade slammed his fist into the man's jaw, knocking him to the ground. His eyes fluttered closed and he slumped against the dirt, lights out.

Blondie blinked at Kade in shock. "What the hell was that for?"

"He called her a bitch."

Bailey stared at Kade in shock as he walked back to her. Then she started laughing.

He grinned. "Now I'm ready. Let's go."

THE FIGHT SEEMED as if it was over before it had really begun. Kade stood beside Bailey with the rest of the Equalizers outside the main cave entrance. She was quieter than usual, having just finished talking to the Enforcers that they'd rescued. None of them knew anything about Sebastian or Amber.

"We'll find them, or find out what happened to them," he whispered to her. "Promise."

"Don't make promises you may not be able to keep," she said. Then she sighed and squeezed his hand. "I didn't mean that in, well, a mean way. I'm just saying, we might not ever find out what happened."

He squeezed her hand in return, then let it go.

"Twelve dead mercenaries," Jace announced, as they all gathered in front of him. "Only one wounded Equalizer, and that was a flesh wound." He motioned toward the man a short distance away whose arm was being bandaged by another Equalizer. "We rescued half a dozen Enforcers. I'm afraid we must have been too late to save the others. We didn't see anyone else."

He waved toward the large band of handcuffed mercenaries being led toward the trucks they'd brought for just such a purpose. "Twenty-three prisoners to figure out what to do with."

Bailey patted her pistol at her side. "I have an idea about that."

Kade gave her an admonishing look. "Judging by the hardened look of most of them, there are probably outstanding warrants or parole violations we can use to turn them over to law enforcement. Austin can help with the research."

"On it," Austin called out from a few feet away, his fingers flying over his computer tablet.

"And the rest?" Bailey asked.

"I know a place in the warehouse district with a great locking mechanism that can hold them until we figure that out."

Jace nodded. "Good idea. As long as we cut Internet access from the computers and take away their cell phones, that'll work great. Devlin? Mason?"

"Agreed."

"Ladies and gentlemen," Jace announced. "I pronounce this retraining facility officially closed."

A loud cheer went up from the crowd, and they began to disperse, moving toward the vehicles that had been pulled up to the cave now that the fight was over. Austin drove his van. The large truck carrying the prisoners followed behind, with a contingent of Equalizers to guard it until they could secure the mercenaries at the warehouse. Before long, only the core group remained—Devlin, Mason, Jace, Kade, and Bailey.

As one, they turned from the cave and headed toward the Humvee they'd appropriated after the fight at the warehouse. They all piled in, with Jace behind the wheel and Devlin sitting beside him. Kade and Bailey sat in the second row of seats, with Mason in the back.

"What about Faegan?" Bailey asked. "Was he one of the prisoners or one of the dead?"

Everyone looked to Kade, and he suddenly realized that he was the only one who knew what Faegan looked like. He slowly shook his head. "He wasn't one of the dead. I assumed he was one of the prisoners."

"I'm sure he was captured, but I'll double-check," Devlin said. A couple of minutes later, he passed his phone back to Kade. "Austin sent an email. He took all of the prisoners' pictures as they were loaded into the truck. He plans on running the pictures through facial recognition software to search for outstanding warrants. The program will take a while to run. In the meantime, do you see Faegan?"

Kade was already flipping through the photos and finished just as Devlin finished his explanation. "He's not here. He must have left the cave before we got there."

Devlin swore. "We need some pictures of Faegan. Finding him is imperative to make sure this thing is really over."

"I'm sure I can locate some." Kade reached for his phone, then stopped. "All I have is the burner phone I got this afternoon. Faegan took my FBI-issued phone when he picked me up at the computer lab. He switched it with the GPS tracked one that Dominic took back from me at the warehouse. I don't have any of my photos."

"What about the cloud?" Bailey asked. "Do you upload your pictures to a backup server?"

He nodded. "I do."

She handed him her phone.

He tapped through the menus and logged onto

his cloud server, finding several pictures of Faegan from company functions, pictures taken long before he'd turned against the honor for which the FBI stood. He handed the phone back to Bailey.

She looked at the screen. "I'm going to need everyone's email addresses so I can send these pictures to you."

Soon they were all studying the pictures on their phones.

"Did you send one to the email address I gave you for Austin?" Devlin asked from the front seat.

"Yeah. He should have it by now."

Devlin punched some numbers on his phone. "Austin, yeah. Bailey just sent you some pictures of Faegan. We realized he wasn't at the cave. If he saw us coming, he may have tucked tail and ran, didn't even bother to warn his people. Can you . . . oh, you're already doing it? Great. Thanks. Call me with any updates."

He ended the call. "As soon as his phone buzzed with your email, he pulled over and went to work on the pictures you sent. He tapped into the facial recognition programs at Homeland Security." He shot a look at Kade. "You never heard that."

"Don't have a clue what you're talking about," Kade said drolly.

Devlin smiled. "Anyway, if Faegan is on the run and tries to hop a bus, a train, or a plane anywhere, we'll be notified."

The Humvee fell silent, and soon everyone was glancing around at each other.

Kade was the one who broke the silence. "That was too easy, wasn't it? At the cave?"

"That's what I was thinking," Bailey said.

"Me, too," Jace added, glancing at them in the rearview mirror. "If they were taking in dozens of Enforcers to interrogate, the place should have looked like a maximum-security prison where we found that handful of Enforcers. But there were only two cells for holding prisoners. Kade, do you have a list of all of the Enforcers from when you began your mission, and who's left to capture?"

Kade cleared his throat, fighting down bile as he thought about the numbers. "A lot of Enforcers went off-grid after Cyprian Cardenas was killed. Since they haven't been seen or heard from again, Faegan agreed that searching their properties to destroy any leftover EXIT documentation was sufficient for that group. What remained was a list of . . . sixty-two names."

Devlin cursed.

Bailey sadly shook her head, probably thinking about Hawke and her other friends in addition to the overwhelming number.

Kade swallowed hard and continued. "We freed six here today. There are two confirmed dead—Hawke and Sanchez. Subtracting the ones my team hasn't captured yet, that leaves twenty-seven that Faegan needs to account for when we find him."

Devlin nodded. "Okay, best case, all twenty-seven are being held in another location. Faegan can't simply kill them outright without knowing whether they have safety-deposit boxes or other kinds of safeguards out there that could bite the government. Enforcers are trained to withstand torture. So even if Faegan is brutal with them, it will still take time to break them down. We've still got a chance to save some lives, if we move quickly. But to do that, we have to figure out where he's holding them."

Kade nodded his agreement. "The security at the cave wasn't anywhere near what I'd expected. The security where he's got them would have to be much better. With electronic systems in addition to armed guards."

"It would have to have cells, too," Bailey said. "To house the Enforcers. Say, four or five prisoners per cell, he needs at least six cells, five in a pinch."

"A cafeteria to feed them," Kade added. "Guards to watch over them. Not to mention offices, computers, phones, whatever Faegan needs to run his operation. Obviously this place here was more for supplies, and a decoy if he needed one. Like he did today. The real headquarters for his operation needs to be out of the way, so all the vehicles coming and going won't be noticed. And it needs to be far enough away from a city or any other facilities so that no one will hear any gunshots and call the police. It's probably secluded, with woods all around it. And yet, it will be close enough to major highways to allow easy access." He looked at all of them. "I'd think the EXIT building would be perfect, except that I've been through every inch of the place. It's basically been gutted."

Devlin stiffened. "I think you're onto something. EXIT headquarters would be perfect for Faegan's needs. But not the facility in Boulder. He must have his operation running out of the other building, and he's been using these caves when he needed to be here in Boulder."

Kade frowned. "Other one? Are you talking about the EXIT building in Asheville, North Carolina?"

Mason nodded. "Right in my hometown."

"That can't be Faegan's base of operations," Kade said. "The building was emptied and sold before I took on this mission. Another company is operating out of it now."

"It really is perfect," Mason said, seemingly ignoring Kade's statement. "Plus it has the last remaining requirement that the Boulder facility doesn't have."

"Tunnels," he and Devlin both said at the same time.

"With cells," Mason further elaborated. "There are half a dozen of them hidden in the tunnels beneath the building."

"Wait, hold it," Kade said. "Did you not hear the part where I said another company is operating out of that facility now?"

"What kind of company?" Mason asked.

"It's . . . ah, hell."

"What?" Bailey asked.

"It's a personal security corporation. Which of course is the perfect ruse to cover the kinds of comings and goings that Faegan's men would be doing there. We need to get to Asheville. Fast."

Devlin grabbed his phone. "I'll arrange a plane at a private airfield so we can get around security and bring our weapons. We can be in the air in thirty or forty minutes."

Mason pulled his phone out, too. "I've got a few tricks of my own. And plenty of friends in Asheville."

Chapter Twenty

Thursday, 6:15 p.m.

Bailey curled her fingers around the plane's armrests as it taxied toward the runway.

"If you close your eyes during takeoff, that helps," Kade whispered from his window seat beside her.

She frowned at him before turning to see whether the others had heard him. It was a small plane, but not so small that everyone had to sit close together. Still, she could see Mason, alone as seemed to be his preference, two rows up. Devlin and Austin sat quietly talking a few rows behind her across the aisle. The rest of their little party was somewhere behind them.

"They can't hear us if we keep our voices low," he said. "You can hold my hand if you want."

She ignored his hand and blew out a frustrated breath. "This is stupid. It makes no sense. I should be terrified of parking garages, not airplanes."

"Want to talk about it?" he asked.

"Want me to punch you?"

He sighed and looked out the window.

She tamped down the twinge of guilt that shot through her. He was only trying to be nice. But she didn't want him or anyone else fussing over her, especially when she was desperately trying to will away nausea. The plane made its final turn, ready for takeoff. She dug her nails into the armrest and drew deep breaths. She could feel Kade's eyes on her again but she no longer cared about trying to hide her weaknesses. She was too busy swallowing, hard, and then closing her eyes as the engines revved. Around her, the muted conversations faded away. Her brain felt like it was floating around in her skull. Oh, God. Was she going to faint?

The plane started forward again.

No. Just one more minute. I need one more minute to figure out how to survive this without freaking out.

"Hold my hand."

Kade's harsh whisper close to her ear took her mind off her stomach just long enough for her to look at him. Then she saw the trees rushing past the windows.

"Oh, God," she repeated, then flushed when she realized she'd said it out loud this time.

Kade put his hand beneath her chin, forcing her to look at him as he leaned over. The rushing trees had her gasping for air and she tightly squeezed her eyes shut. Then, suddenly, his lips were on hers. She was so surprised she didn't think to pull away. Then it felt so good she didn't want to.

She opened her mouth for his tongue and he swept it inside. Heat flooded through her as she answered his wild kiss with enthusiasm. She wanted this, wanted him. She just wanted . . . more. He groaned low in his throat, or that might have been her. She reached for him, trying to pull him closer, but their awkward angles and the seat belts made it impossible.

Someone cleared their throat.

Someone else laughed.

Kade broke the kiss and told them to knock it off.

"There, that wasn't so bad, was it?" he asked. "You barely noticed when the plane took off, am I right?"

Her eyes fluttered open and she looked past him, shocked to see that they were indeed in the air, flying, not dying. Barely noticed? She hadn't noticed at all.

"You kissed me to distract me," she accused.

"Yep."

She should have been mad. Instead, she smiled. "It worked. Want to distract me again?"

He gave her a pained look and adjusted his position in his seat. "More than you could possibly imagine."

She grinned again. Maybe she'd finally discovered the way to get through her fear of flying. No, make that just the landings. Really, that's what killed— landing. The takeoff was just the precursor that got her nervous for the next part. Kade just might have to pull her onto his lap and do some heavy petting to get her through that next phase. Thinking about that made her laugh.

"What's so funny?" he asked.

"Nothing."

"Was it a rough flight, that last one, with your parents when you flew home to Montana after your vacation? Do you think that's why you associate their deaths with planes?"

"Why are you asking me that?"

"Because I *care*. People who care about each other share personal details about their lives. I forgot that before. I won't forget again."

The truth was in his eyes, in the intensity of his gaze locked onto hers. He cared. About *her*. How long had it been since anyone had *really* cared? Too long. That had to be why she was so susceptible to him. He was too sweet, too good-looking, too charming, too smart, too . . . everything.

After years of keeping people at a distance, she'd grown used to them not even trying to get past the wall she'd put up. Even Hawke had never asked her about her past, offered to hold her hand during takeoff. If he had, she probably would have punched him, or ended the friendship. And that's exactly what it had been with Hawke, friendship. But Kade . . . Kade was . . . something else.

He settled against the back of his chair, eyes closing. He didn't push her to answer him. He just accepted that she couldn't, or wouldn't, and didn't get mad about it. Didn't press. He accepted her. Like no one else ever had. They still hadn't talked about the warehouse. There'd been no apology from her—and she sure as hell owed him one now that she'd calmed down enough to put everything into perspective. And yet, she had a feeling he'd never expect one. And wouldn't hold it against her either. She'd never met anyone like him. And wasn't quite sure what to do.

"Why?" she whispered.

His eyes cracked open like a sleepy cat. "Why what?"

"Why do you care? About me? I don't understand it."

She had his full attention now.

"I know I'm pretty," she said.

"And modest," he added.

"Whatever." She waved her hand in the air. "I've got the hair, the boobs, a smokin' ass."

"I'm not arguing with you there." He grinned.

"I'm just saying, is it . . . physical? Is that all there is? Is that why you flirt with me and treat me so nice even though I don't deserve it?"

He started to say something, but she pressed a finger against his lips to stop him. "I'm serious, Kade. I'm not a froufrou girl. I don't wear frilly dresses or put on a lot of makeup. I don't go to church on Sunday, even though my parents would probably roll over in their graves if they knew that. I'm not easy to get along with. Sometimes, most of the times, I'm rude or downright mean. I'm prickly, and ornery, and selfish, and—"

He drew her finger into his mouth, making her breath catch. He lightly sucked, before kissing her finger and pulling her hand down from his face.

"You about done?" he asked.

She swallowed. Nodded. He was doing something sinfully delicious with his thumb on the fleshy part of her palm, sending shudders straight down her spine.

"It's definitely physical." His deep voice tingled across her nerve endings. "I can't deny that I want to slide my hands up your shirt right now, cup them inside your bra, squeeze your—"

"*Kade.*" She glanced around, cleared her throat and scooted lower in the seat. "Stop it."

"I haven't even gotten started." He grinned, then sobered. "But even if you weren't mouthwateringly gorgeous, I'd still want you, in every way that a man can want a woman. Because it's *not* just physical. If you were froufrou and loved to shop, I wouldn't mind. But I'd probably be bored out of my skull. Trust me, sweetheart, you're anything but boring. I find you utterly fascinating. I love your sarcasm, your intelligence, the way you can handle a gun better than most men I know—when it's loaded, that is."

She smacked his shoulder. "I hadn't slept in two days. I get a pass for that."

He smiled. "Yeah, you do." He pressed a whisper-soft kiss against her lips. "You're not mean. You're clever, and funny, and maybe a little impatient with people who aren't as quick and bright as you. But, hey, no one's perfect. And I wouldn't want you to be. I love that you're unpredictable, and impatient, and—"

"Gee, I'm really feeling the love."

"Okay, maybe I'm not eloquent. But my point is that you're a good person. And if you ever call yourself selfish again, I might have to spank you."

"I have a leather whip and feathers at home." She waggled her eyebrows.

He smiled. "Bailey, if you were selfish, you'd have disappeared at the first hint that someone was tracking down Enforcers. I know you have plenty of money. I've seen the land you've bought, the houses you own, the cars parked in those garages. If you were concerned just for yourself, you'd have gone to Fiji or New Zealand or somewhere else and started a new life like a lot of Enforcers have. But you didn't do that. Why? Because you knew that what was happening to your friends was wrong. And you cared about them, cared enough to risk your own life to fight for them, even to fight for Enforcers you've never met. That's why I care about you. Because you care, sometimes too much. I love that about you. I love everything about you."

He traced a finger down the side of her neck to the upper swells of her breasts. "Sometime, soon, I'd like to show you just how much I care."

Her seat belt clicked. The armrest between them lifted. And suddenly she was lying on top of him, sprawled across both seats as he scooted down low in his own seat so that no one could see them. And then he was kissing her, devouring her, consuming her with a heat that fairly crackled around them. His hands were everywhere, stroking down her arms, around to her back, sliding up beneath her shirt to trace across her ribs. Everywhere he touched left a trail of fire. Her body softened and readied itself for him, and that's when she knew she had to stop this madness. Because if she didn't, she would tear off his clothes right here and make love to him—in a plane full of men on their way to stop a madman.

She broke the kiss and pulled his wicked hands down. "We have to stop," she whispered.

His eyes were heavy-lidded, so dark they reminded her of the ocean right before a storm. He tugged one of his hands free from hers and lightly feathered her hair back from her face. Then he was lifting her, settling her back into her seat, securing her seat belt. He pressed a soft kiss against her lips then entwined his left hand with her right one.

"I'm sorry," he whispered. "I'm sorry that I hurt you at the warehouse. I'm sorry that I risked your friends' lives to save you. But, Bailey, I'd do it again."

"I know," she said. "And I still may not really understand why you seem to care so much about me. But I do understand why you did what you did. And I'm sorry, too. I should have trusted you more. I should have known you would never become one of the bad guys. I'm sorry that I didn't have enough faith in you. You deserve better than that, Kade. You deserve better than me."

He slowly shook his head. "Sweetheart, no one's better than you."

Her heart clutched in her chest. Such beautiful words. And yet, they only proved that the woman he cared about was really a fantasy. He seemed to think she was a good person. But she wasn't. Not even close.

"Bailey?"

She ignored him.

"Bailey, what's wrong? Did I say something to upset you?"

She squeezed her eyes shut, drew a shaky breath. "If you think I'm a good person, then you don't know me at all. You've convinced yourself that I'm in this because I care about people, that I'm not a monster deep inside. But you've never really asked me the one question you should have asked in the beginning. Ask me, Kade. Ask me the one thing you want to know, need to know about me. And then we'll see whether you think there's anyone better than me."

She rolled her head on the seat back to look at him. A tear traced down her cheek, and she angrily wiped it away. He was watching her intently again, his jaw tight, his lips drawn into a firm line.

"Ask me," she whispered.

He drew a shuddering breath, then said, "Why did you become an Enforcer?"

"There it is," she said, wiping another tear from her cheek. "It all boils down to that one question, doesn't it? You can only care about a woman like me if you whitewash the truth and ignore the person that I really am. I don't regret my decision, Kade. If I had to do it all over again, I would still have said yes the day that one of Cyprian's men approached me about working for EXIT. Not because I have a driving need to prevent another 9/11. Not because I'm altruistic and searching for justice in a world where very few people really get justice. No, my reason, my one and only reason for becoming an Enforcer is far more gritty, more simple, and yes, far more selfish—I didn't want to go to prison."

Chapter Twenty-one

Thursday, 10:47 p.m.

Bailey ran her hands across the cool, smooth Carrara marble island in Mason Hunt's kitchen. She didn't think she'd ever seen a more beautiful home. His Asheville house was probably large by most people's standards, a mansion by hers. She'd been so busy traveling and working for EXIT that she'd never chosen a place to settle down. Even the houses she'd bought, scattered around the country, looked pretty much the way they did when she'd purchased them. They were investments, nothing to decorate or to put the time in to make them, well, a home. Seeing this place had her dreaming dreams she'd never dared before, like falling in love, starting a family.

"Can't sleep either?"

She clutched the edge of the counter at the sound of the deep, familiar voice behind her. Then she slowly turned around. Kade lounged in the doorway about five feet away, his broad shoulders taking up most of the space. His hair was slightly damp and he was wearing a different shirt since the planning session for tomorrow's assault on EXIT had broken up. Had he gone for a swim in the pool? Or taken a shower?

"You've been avoiding me since the plane. We really need to talk." He straightened and walked toward her.

"You aren't limping," she said, surprised.

"All that exercise in the caves might have hurt like hell but it loosened up the muscles. After a few minutes in the hot tub I'm feeling better than I have in ages."

"Maybe you should buy a hot tub then, after all of this is over."

"Maybe."

He stopped in front of her, forcing her to lean her head back to meet his gaze.

"Where do you live anyway?" she asked. "I mean, *really* live. When you're not in an FBI rental."

"Jacksonville, just south of the Georgia border on the Atlantic Ocean. I grew up there, have pretty much spent my whole life there, except for when I'm traveling on assignment. That's where my dad is, so I imagine I'll go back there once Faegan is captured. Unless someone gives me a reason not to."

She clutched the countertop harder. "I've never cared much for the beach. I'm more of a mountain and snow girl myself. Montana."

He nodded, not looking surprised. Her heart stuttered. Did he already know about her past?

He edged a little closer. "The tide is turning. Mason and Devlin's reconnaissance tonight proved what we thought, that the EXIT building is being used by Faegan's men. Security is tight, but we'll figure out a way in tomorrow. We're optimistic that we'll find the prisoners there."

She should have been happy, thinking about possibly finding her missing friends. Instead, all she could think about was this incredible man standing in front of her.

His right hand lifted toward her face, as if he wanted to touch her. But then he lowered it to his side. His deep blue eyes were so intent, as if searching for . . . something. He seemed . . . different, somehow. Something elemental had . . . changed between them since that plane trip.

It was as if she was seeing the real Kade for the first time, the man he'd been before Faegan's horrible manipulations, and the accident, and the fake-Abby guilt he'd borne for so long. This Kade was confident, strong, willing to put himself in danger to save her, but not recklessly as he'd done before. This Kade was tender touches, wild kisses, and impossible dreams. He was the reason she was admiring marble countertops, and thinking about the future.

And it terrified her.

She was terrified that, if he knew the truth, he would reject her, turn away in disgust, and never want to see her again. She was even more terrified that he wouldn't.

"Bailey, about what you said on the plane. I need you to know that I—"

"I'm surprised Mason isn't worried that someone from EXIT will look for us here." She waved at the opulent kitchen surrounding them. "And even more surprised that he didn't send his wife into hiding like everyone else has done."

He glanced around the kitchen as if noticing it for the first time, then shrugged. "I imagine it's listed under an alias or he wouldn't have risked bringing us here. Faegan isn't as good at ferreting out property records as I am." He smiled. "And from the argument I heard out by the pool earlier, the fact that Sabrina was here when we arrived was just as much a surprise to Mason as it was to anyone else. I gather he'd told her to go off the grid and she'd refused."

"By the pool?"

"I was in the hot tub and they didn't notice. I was about to announce my presence when they, well, ended the argument. Let's just say, don't go near the pool for a while. I think they're still out there."

A burst of laughter escaped her and she covered her mouth, looking around, worried she might wake someone. She wasn't exactly sure where everyone else was bunking for the night. Someone might even be out in the family room on a couch.

"I love when you smile. It makes your eyes light up." This time when he lifted his hand, he didn't stop. He gently traced her jaw. "Bailey, I've made some poor choices over the past few months. Hell, the past year. But the ones that I regret most are the ones that hurt you."

His hands shook as he caressed her face. "It kills me to think that if you hadn't gotten away that first night, I would have turned you over to Faegan." He shuddered and pulled her against him, wrapping his arms around her, with his cheek against the top of her head. "I'm so, so sorry, sweetheart," he whispered.

She blinked at the endearment that was fast becoming a habit of his, and tried not to melt against him. He held her, gently swaying as if to music only he could hear. Except that she could swear that she heard it, too—in the feel of his strong arms around her, in the whisper of his breath against her hair, in the thud of his heartbeat beneath her ear.

Danger. Her mind screamed the word. *This* Kade could destroy her. He couldn't know what he was doing, looking and smelling so wonderful, calling her sweetheart, holding her like he never wanted to let her go. It was cruel, to both of them.

She pushed against him, forcing him to drop his arms and step back.

"I can't do this," she whispered. "You're making me want things I can never have."

"Sweetheart—"

"Stop calling me that. I'm not who you think I am."

"I *know* you, Bailey. You don't have to be afraid. Let's go somewhere and talk—"

"I have to get some sleep," she said. "It's a big day tomorrow." She headed toward the kitchen side door that led outside.

Kade was suddenly there, moving faster, and more gracefully, than she'd ever seen him move. He opened the door for her, and waited.

"Thank you. Good night." She stepped outside, and started down the brick path toward the guest-house at the back of the property that she'd been given for the night. Parts of the path curved right beside the pool, with gaps in the foliage to open up the view. She glanced through one of the gaps and was relieved to see the pool area was empty. Mason and his wife must have gone back inside the house.

The sound of humming had her turning around.

Kade was just a few steps behind her, humming

some kind of upbeat tune. He stopped when she stopped, and arched a brow in question.

"I'm going to my guesthouse," she said. "Where are you going?"

"To my guesthouse."

She narrowed her eyes suspiciously. "I thought there was only one."

He blinked. "Surely Mason wouldn't have assigned us to the same sleeping quarters." He opened his right hand to reveal a small key. "I guess we'll just have to find out." He took her hand in his and tugged her along with him.

She was too surprised by this flirtatious—and far-too-charming—side of him to pull back. Besides, his hand holding hers felt too good to stop just yet. They headed down the long, curvy path until it stopped at a little one-story cottage. White railings boxed in a quaint front porch, with a trellis of thick, green leaves climbing up both sides to provide privacy. She imagined the vines would be thick with some kind of blooms every spring.

He slid his key into the lock and watched her as he turned it. The lock clicked.

"Looks like this cottage is mine," he announced, as he pushed the door open.

Bailey leaned past him, looking for another cottage. But she didn't see any. "Mason must have made a mistake."

He leaned inside the cottage, looking around, then straightened. "I don't think so. The main house is big, but there are only so many guest rooms. This one looks to have a bedroom and a very comfy couch. He probably assumed we could share." He arched a brow. "Or are you afraid of being in the same house with me?"

She narrowed her eyes. "I'm not afraid of you."

He braced his arm on the railing beside her and leaned in close. "Then what *are* you afraid of?"

Teasing Kade was gone, and in his place was a man determined to get the truth.

"I don't want to talk to you right now."

"Tough."

She blinked. "Excuse me?"

"You heard me." He shifted, bracing both hands on the railing on either side of her, boxing her in. "Ask me."

"Ask you what?"

"Ask me. Ask me what you most want to know. Ask me the one question you should have asked on the plane, but were too much of a coward to ask. You can't just throw a comment out like you did and shut me down afterward. You never even gave me a chance to talk it out. People who care about each other—"

"Share," she whispered.

He nodded. "Let's try it again. Why did you become an Enforcer, Bailey?"

She swallowed, licked her lips. "Because I didn't want to go to prison."

"And what does going to prison have to do with deciding to become an Enforcer?"

She pushed against his chest. He grabbed her hands, threaded his fingers through hers. "Bailey, you have to know that I already know everything about you, everything that can be read on paper at least. It was part of my research to decide the best way to capture you."

Her eyes widened. "No. You can't know."

"Why not? Because I'd feel differently about you if I did? Because I wouldn't want you if I knew what happened after your parents died and you were placed in foster care? That you made friends with another foster girl in the same home. And that you found out she was being abused."

"Wendy," she whispered, her voice cracking. "I told them, anyone who would listen. And the state came and investigated." She fisted her hands at her sides. "She was so scared, too scared to tell the truth. So when they asked her about what I'd said, she lied and told them I was making up stories. They left her in the home and moved me to another home. I didn't help her. I wasn't strong enough to make them see what was really happening."

He smoothed her hair out of her eyes. "You were eleven. You didn't fail her. The adults in that home, her social worker, they were the ones who failed."

She shook her head.

"Then there was Samuel," he whispered, stroking her cheek. "He was bullied at school. You stuck up for him, ended up in the hospital."

"I failed again. Interfering only made it worse. And I was declared too violent to return to that school. The government put me in a school for troubled kids." She laughed bitterly. "I had to defend myself. They picked on me, called me names, put bugs in my food. I had to defend myself."

"I know, sweetheart. You were strong. You did what you had to do."

She ducked away from his hand. "Stop acting like I'm normal, like I'm not defective and violent and . . . just stop. I beat up a kid at that school, broke his arm, his nose, gave him a concussion. I could have killed him."

"But you didn't."

She raked a hand through her hair, shoving it back off her shoulders. "I was an idiot. I ran away and did what a normal kid would never do. I joined the freaking militia. Is that in your reports, too, Kade? I was a gun-toting, radical, crazy person trying to stick it to 'the man.'"

"You were trying to survive," he said, still with absolutely no judgment in his voice, in his eyes. "Your parents were killed and the government never found the killer. They threw you into the system. But instead of putting you in a loving foster home, they stuck you in a bad one. When you told them about the abuse, they punished you instead of the abuser. And when you stood up to bullying, once again the government stepped in, placing you in a facility for juvenile delinquents where you had to fight out of self-defense. Bailey, good grief. You're a poster child for the kind of background that makes a person desperate and easy prey for groups like the militia. Hell, I might have done the same thing in your circumstances. No, scratch that. I probably wouldn't have even survived."

He grasped her shoulders, making her look at him. "You got mixed up with some lunatics and did what you had to do to survive. And when the government came down on the militia, that's when someone else preyed upon you again. Someone from EXIT offered to get you out of a possible prison sentence if you joined their organization. You were eighteen. Almost half your life you were used, abused, trod on, and forced to fight for your very life. Is it any wonder that when EXIT offered you a chance to break the government's own rules, to give the finger to traditional law enforcement and fight for justice for the common man, that you jumped at it?"

"You don't get it, Kade. I've killed people."

"So have I. As part of my job, when I had to."

"That's just it. I didn't have to. I wasn't upholding any laws. I got an EXIT order and I enforced it, took people out. That's not something you can just look at and say it's okay. I'm not the good person you want me to be."

"Are Mason, Devlin, and the others bad people?"

"No."

"They were Enforcers, too."

"I know, but—"

"But nothing," he said. "People are complicated, Bailey. They make choices for a variety of reasons. But when you boil it all down, you and the others killed people who needed killing. There. I said it. Does that shock you? Mr. Law and Order agrees that the people you've killed weren't the types of people who should be walking around on this planet, breathing the same air as you and me. I bet if you asked any cop out there, any decent, law-abiding citizen in this country that if they knew what they knew now, and could take out those terrorists before they took out the twin towers, they'd do it. Hell, I'd stand in line for the privilege."

His hands shook as he cupped her face. "I want the EXIT program permanently shut down because of the potential for abuse. Because it scares me that someone can be judge, jury, and executioner without oversight, without their peers reviewing the evidence first. I don't want to risk innocent people being killed because a maniac twists the program to their own purposes. But, sweetheart, if Faegan, or anyone else, threatened you in any way, I wouldn't hesitate to take them out. I would be judge, jury, and executioner if I knew that was the only way to ensure your safety. Call me a hypocrite, but that's what I would do."

He traced her bottom lip with one of his thumbs, making her shiver.

"Ask me, Bailey."

She swallowed.

He kissed her, a light brush of his lips against hers. "Ask me."

"I can't."

He lifted her onto the railing and stepped between her thighs, his heat causing a delicious shiver to run up her spine. He pressed a kiss against one cheek, the other, her forehead. "Ask me."

His hands speared into her hair. His body pressed intimately against hers, letting her know how much he desired her. His voice was thick, almost a growl when he said again, "Ask me."

She shuddered against him, gripped his shoulders, and looked deep into his beautiful blue eyes. "Does my past matter?" she whispered. "Can you forgive me for the choices I made? In spite of everything that I've done, can you . . . can you . . . love me?"

"Oh, Bailey. There's nothing to forgive. I want you, all of you. I want the little girl that no one believed in. I want the courageous warrior who tried to save a young boy from a bully. I want the young woman, fighting for a cause. I even want the assassin, whose actions saved dozens, hundreds of innocent lives. I want all of you, Bailey. The girl you were, the woman you've become. Can I love you? Sweetheart, I already do."

He scooped her off the railing and carried her into the cottage, kicking the door shut behind them. She thought he'd take her to the enormous king-sized bed that dominated the room. Instead, he let her legs slide slowly down his until she was standing. And then, while he stared down into her eyes, his fingers began to work the buttons of her blouse.

"Someday," he whispered, "I want you to wear that short leather skirt, and the leather vest for me."

That he would say there might even be a "someday" had her damn tear ducts acting up again. She wiped her eyes.

He raised a brow.

"Allergies," she said. "And don't you dare say otherwise."

He grinned, then sobered and began to slide her shirt off her shoulders, his gaze dropping to her chest. As each inch of her skin was slowly revealed to him, his face got more tense, his eyes darker, the pupils dilating. Bailey couldn't imagine anything more erotic or sexy than watching him drink in the sight of her. It was heady, knowing she could affect him this way.

The blouse dropped to the floor. And then he went to work on her bra. It would have taken her less than a second to unclasp it. But he seemed intent on taking his time. His fingers traced the delicate lacy band beneath her breasts, slowly, ever so gently, following the material from the front, around her ribs, to her back. He stared, seemingly fascinated by the swells of her breasts above the lace, as his fingers cleverly worked the clasp behind her back. One hook, two, and the bra loosened. But he didn't let it go. A second ticked by, two. His Adam's apple bobbed in his throat as if he was savoring the tension.

The tension was killing her.

"If you need some help, I can pull the damn thing off for you." She reached up to the straps, but he stopped her, laughing.

He kissed her, with her bra loose and barely hanging on, but still on nonetheless. When he pulled back, he was serious again, like a predator ready to devour her.

"I've been fantasizing about undressing you since the day I saw your picture in a stupid database." His voice was husky, deep. "Let me take my time. Okay?"

She couldn't have told him no if her life depended on it. She shivered, but she wasn't cold. Her lower belly was already almost painfully tight, her body readying itself for him. And she wasn't even naked yet.

Since he seemed to be waiting for her permission, she nodded, and let out a shuddering breath as he finally, finally began to slide the straps down her shoulders. He stepped close, his chest holding up the bra when it would have fallen away. And then he bent and kissed the skin where the straps had been, his hot tongue dipping into the hollows at the base of her throat.

When he finally stepped back, the shock of his warm hands replacing the cups of her bra almost sent her into a climax. She had to put her hands on his shoulders to hold herself up. And then his fingers began a slow, maddening path up the undersides of her breasts, gently squeezing, molding. His head dipped down again, and the feel of his mouth closing around her nipple had her crying out at the sheer pleasure of it. The heat of his breath, the brush of his tongue, the gentle suckle of his mouth, drinking her in nearly drove her over the edge. She curled her nails into his shoulders, whimpering against him. Then he finally released her nipple and blew across it.

She moaned his name.

By the time he finished lavishing her other breast with the same meticulous attention, she was sobbing and begging him to just do it. But he was bent on torturing her. He hooked a finger into her waistband. The sound of the snap popping open made her jerk against him. She bit her lip as he traced both hands inside the top few inches of her waistband, from front to back, his fingers dipping down, down, but stopping just short of where she most wanted them to be.

"Kade, you're driving me crazy," she panted. Once again she tried to speed him up, by grabbing her zipper to get out of her damn jeans.

His hands closed around hers, and instead of unzipping her pants, he raised her fingers to his mouth, and sucked.

She almost exploded, her hips jerking against his. She arched against him, reveling in the feel of him through his jeans.

He stepped back, just enough to break contact. One last suck, and then he pulled her hands up to his shoulders. Then he swooped down and kissed her, pressing her body tightly against his, doing sinful little circles with his hips in rhythm to the even more sinful things his tongue was doing to her mouth. When he finally broke the kiss, she was relieved to see that he was breathing just as hard as her. A fine sheen of sweat had broken out on his forehead.

"Okay. This has been great." She gave a nervous laugh. "Really, reeeallyy great. You get a big fat check in the box for fantastic foreplay." A shiver ran down her body just at the memory of his lips on her breasts and she shifted her legs restlessly. "Extraordinary foreplay, actually. Now let's see about checking that other box, the one where we actually do it, okay?"

She grabbed his hand and tugged him to the bed. Then she turned around, hoping to quickly undress him.

He dropped to his knees and grasped the pull of her zipper with his teeth. Her belly clenched so tight she cried out again.

"Kade, please, I can't . . . oh my. . . . ooooohhhh." She curled her hands against his shoulders and threw her head back. Her jeans sagged down to her ankles. She didn't know where her thong was. And she didn't care. He played her body like a finely tuned instrument, his fingers and tongue finding nerve endings she'd never known she had, tugging and kissing and building the pressure inside her until she was weeping at the pleasure-pain of it. One last wicked stroke of his tongue and she exploded around him, her knees buckling as she cried out his name.

He caught her against him, and slowly lowered her down to the floor. Onto him. She stared in amazement at his naked shoulders, his naked chest, his naked . . . everything. How he'd managed to get undressed and put a condom on, all while driving her wild, was beyond her. And she was so glad that they were both finally, finally going to do this that she wanted to sob.

But once again, he stopped, the biceps bulging in his gorgeous arms as he held her poised over him, barely touching, her back against the bed.

"Kade, if you stop now, I will kill you," she gasped.

He grinned and slowly, slowly, lowered her. He was so exquisitely gentle she wanted to pound his shoulders in frustration. And then he pushed more fully into her, and her eyes flew open. He was watching her as he slowly rocked against her, inching in just a little more. The pressure was intense, uncomfortable even, until her body began to soften more around him.

"Are you okay?" he whispered, his voice so hoarse she almost didn't recognize it.

"Getting there." She grasped his shoulders, balancing her calves against his thighs, and lowered herself more fully onto him. "You weren't kidding about the shoe size, were you?"

He groaned and rested his forehead against hers. "Do you want me to stop?"

"Are you freaking kidding? Don't you dare. You're every woman's dream."

His shoulders shook with laughter until she gyrated her hips, pulling him deeper inside. He sucked in a breath, then pushed deeper. Her body had finally adjusted, the discomfort replaced with a pleasure so intense she spasmed against him.

And just like that, he became the wild lover she'd

craved from the moment he'd begun this delicious dance with her. He rocked against her, pulling her down onto him, pushing deeper, and deeper, filling her as she'd never been filled.

He transported her to another place, a world filled with love and passion, where there weren't any bad guys waiting to hurt anyone. He took her to a world where her friends never died. He took her to heaven.

The intensity of her climax shook her entire body, a wildfire of pleasure roaring across every nerve ending, bowing her back, thrusting her breasts forward. He greedily took what she unwittingly offered, suckling her while his hands molded her bottom and he drove in powerful thrusts that had her climaxing all over again.

He shoved deep inside her again and again until he tumbled over the edge with her. When he shouted her name, she didn't think anything could have ever sounded so sweet.

BAILEY LAY ON her side in the bed, her legs tangled with Kade's as she watched him sleep. The moonlight shined through the tops of the plantation shutters just enough to let her see his face, so handsome, relaxed, with no worry frowns marring his brow. His long lashes formed dark crescents on his cheeks. And for once, there were no winces, no intakes of breath that she was so used to whenever the muscles cramped in his hurt leg. He was resting peacefully, and so beautiful her heart melted.

Awake, Kade was incredible.

Asleep, he was devastating.

It was five in the morning. They'd made love twice more since that explosive, surreal first time that she would always treasure and never, ever forget. Then they'd sunk into an exhausted sleep. But Bailey had been restless, waking up just a few hours later.

Because she was afraid.

Never before had she dreaded an assignment, a mission, or a task given to her. She was confident in her abilities, at peace with whatever plans she'd made. But she was realistic, too. No one was perfect. Everyone made mistakes. And she'd accepted long ago that she might make a mistake one day during a mission that would cost her her life. The thought of dying had never bothered her. And it still didn't. But the thought of Kade dying tore her up inside. For the first time in her life, she was terrified about an upcoming mission. Because for the first time in her life, she had something—some*one*—to lose.

Chapter Twenty-two

Friday, 6:15 p.m.

What Bailey and the others hoped would be the final assault on EXIT Inc. was about to begin. She tugged at the harness strapped to her body and looked past Kade to the others, standing in small groups on the field putting on their harnesses.

Austin stood with Devlin, deep in conversation. He'd surprised them all this morning by *walking* into Mason's dining room instead of using his wheelchair. Apparently he'd been working with his therapist on the side and was finally ready to try out his brand-new prosthetics.

Of course, his hope had been to accompany everyone on the raid. But after a heated argument with his brother, he'd finally conceded that he could become a liability if there were any issues with the prosthetics. So he would stay behind and do what he did best, logistics. Anything the team needed, from weapons to far larger equipment, he would wheel and deal with the devil if necessary to ensure they had it. Which apparently included today's mode of transportation.

Bailey tugged at the harness again.

"You're going to wear that out if you keep pulling on it," Kade teased.

She blinked. "Really? Maybe I need a new one then."

"Bad joke. Forget I said that. Trust me, you'll be fine. I won't let anything happen to you."

"You know I've been taking care of myself for years now, right?"

He pressed a whisper-soft kiss against her lips. "Humor me. I like to pretend that you need me."

She shivered and pulled him down for a much more thorough kiss.

"I do need you," she whispered.

His eyes darkened at her words, much as they had darkened last night each time they'd made love. She immediately regretted her teasing and looked down at her harness, pretending to check it one more time.

Somehow she had to stop getting caught up in the moment with him, stop making him think they were a couple. Because lying on the bed for hours this morning worrying and thinking, had finally revealed the truth to her—that she was kidding herself if she believed that she and Kade could ever be anything more . . . permanent.

No matter how she looked at the future after EXIT—assuming they even survived—she couldn't picture herself as the wife, or even girlfriend, of an FBI agent. For one thing, how could Kade continue to do his job post-Faegan and pass the scrutiny of security clearance investigations when the woman he was with had a fake past? Would it stand up to the kind of scrutiny the FBI would put on it? If even a hint of her past work for EXIT surfaced, it would ruin everything.

She didn't have anyone in the "real" world who could vouch for her. Even trying to pass a background check would be asking for trouble. Being with her would surely mean giving up everything he'd worked for his whole life. Could she really ask him to make that kind of sacrifice? Could she live with herself if he did?

"You can do this," he said, apparently taking her silence as worry about the upcoming assault. "I'll be there with you the whole time."

She forced a smile. "I know you will. I'll be okay. I thought you were going to wear your leg brace?"

He rapped his knuckles on his left thigh, making an echoing noise. "Under the jeans this time. I borrowed a pair of Devlin's since he's a size larger than me, and trimmed off some of the extra length. I don't want to broadcast to our enemies that I have a bum leg. It would be like painting a target on my thigh."

"Clever."

"Yeah. Too bad I didn't think of it when you and I first met." He winked and leaned in for a kiss.

"You two ready?" Jace's voice intruded from behind Kade.

Kade straightened and moved to stand beside her. "We're ready."

"ETA is five minutes out."

Kade nodded as Austin joined them. His gait was a bit awkward on the prosthetics. But he was doing an incredible job just standing upright since the field they were in wasn't completely level. It was only about a quarter mile from EXIT headquarters, with thick woods separating the two. Which made it perfect for their approach.

"Excited?" Austin asked, his eyes twinkling with mischief.

"No," Bailey said.

"Yes." Kade put his arm around Bailey's shoulders and pulled her against him.

She sighed heavily. "Yes," she said, changing her earlier statement. "Can't. Wait."

"No worries," Austin said. "I'm in charge of logistics. And I don't make mistakes."

Jace rolled his eyes.

Austin elbowed him in the ribs.

Jace glared at him and rubbed his side. "I'll get you back for that when this is over."

"You don't scare me," Austin retorted. "A day may come when the courage of men fails . . . but it is not THIS day."

"Maybe you need to watch the *Lord of the Rings* movies again. You've used that line already."

"Certainty of death, small chance of success— what are we waiting for?" Austin said.

Jace rolled his eyes. "He's twelve. Ignore him. Don't laugh or he won't stop."

"What we're doing today is very much like the last *Lord of the Rings* movie," Austin continued, as if Jace hadn't spoken. "You know, where the hobbits are trudging those last few steps to toss the evil ring into the fires of Mordor?"

"EXIT is Mordor?" Bailey asked.

"Bailey," Jace warned. "Don't. Encourage him."

Austin nodded sagely as if Jace hadn't spoken.

Bailey gave Jace an apologetic look, before asking,

"And we're . . . hobbits?" She looked down at her feet, just to make sure they hadn't sprouted tufts of hobbit-hair.

He nodded again, as if he were an oracle instructing a student about the meaning of life. "We're improving on the original, though. There were plot holes all over that trilogy. Ever ask yourself, if Gandalf had access to those giant eagles all along, why didn't he just have them fly the hobbits up to Mordor and toss the ring into the lava to begin with?"

Jace shook his head. "Why are we having this ridiculous conversation?"

"Because I'm the logistics wizard. I improve upon the original. Gandalf may have had giant eagles. But I have something far better."

Bailey glanced at Kade but he seemed just as confused as she was.

"Okay, I give," she said. "What do you have that's better?"

He motioned toward the sky. "A helicopter."

Sure enough, the enormous chopper they'd been waiting for was coming in for a landing. It was surprisingly quiet, which Austin had already told them to expect because it had a stealth mode. How he had access to a multimillion-dollar military-grade helicopter she'd prefer not to know.

"Remember," Bailey yelled to be heard over the sound of the wind generated by the rotors. "Whoever reaches the hostages first, find out whether Sebastian and Amber are with them or if anyone knows where they are."

They all nodded.

"Good luck," Austin yelled to the group.

Jace clapped Austin on the back in a "bro" hug,

surprising Bailey. The two argued, a lot, and traded insults all the time. Who knew they were actually friends?

"Come on," Jace said, waving them forward as he headed toward the chopper.

"In a minute," Bailey said, grabbing Kade's hand to hold him back.

She waited until all the others had hopped onboard. Finally, when there were no more excuses to wait any longer, she blew out a shaky breath. "If I fall to my death, don't cremate me," she yelled to be heard. "I'm afraid of fire."

"You're not going to fall to your death."

"Promise me. No cremation."

He gave her a quick, hard kiss. "I promise. Come on. Let's go before someone sees or hears the chopper and we lose the element of surprise."

She ran with him and he lifted her inside, then climbed in behind her. As soon as he cleared the doorway, the chopper lifted off.

Bailey fell back toward the opening but Kade grabbed her, steadying her.

She swallowed hard, looking down at the ground rushing past them, and at Austin who was rapidly becoming a speck on the horizon.

"I think I'm going to be sick," she said.

"Can you wait until we're on the roof?" Kade teased, as he clipped some kind of lead to her harness.

The other end was suspended from a bar on the helicopter. He quickly attached the belts and pulleys to her harness, just like the others were doing, except that none of them appeared to need help like she did.

"Has everyone done this before except me?" she called out.

As one, they all nodded.

She cursed beneath her breath.

Kade gave one last tug on her gear and then went to work on his own.

"Put your gloves on," he reminded her.

She dug them out of her pockets and pulled them on.

Kade put his own gloves on, then performed one last inspection of her equipment, nodding his approval.

"It's a go," Mason called out from his position in the open doorway. And then, he was gone, leaping out into thin air.

Bailey clutched Kade as Devlin moved to the opening.

"We're there already?" she squeaked.

"We're there. Come on. This will be no different than what we practiced on the balcony at Mason's house today."

Devlin leaped from the opening and was gone.

"Oh my God," Bailey said.

"Are you afraid of heights?" Kade demanded.

"I'm afraid of landing!"

His eyes filled with pity. "The plane. I should have thought of that. Do you want to stay here?"

"Yes!"

"Okay. The pilot will take you back to—"

"No! I *want* to stay. But I'm not going to. I'll do it. I just don't want to."

Another Enforcer, one of many that they'd gathered together this morning to help them with the assault, jumped out of the chopper.

All too soon, the only ones left were Kade and her.

He tugged her toward the opening.

"Wait," she said. "I'm not sure I can do this. Rappelling from a balcony is one thing. There was a pool to fall in if I screwed up. If I screw *this* up, I fall off the top of a building."

Click. Click.

She looked down to see what had made the noise. A short length of cable with two carabiners connected Kade's harness to hers. She was snugged up against him, chest to chest.

"What are you doing?" she demanded.

He leaned down and whispered in her ear. "Taking care of you."

And then he leaped out of the helicopter, pulling her with him.

She would have screamed, but the terrifying fall stole her breath. And then, they were landing on the roof of EXIT Inc., as gently as if they'd bounced on a trampoline, because Kade had taken the brunt of the landing, lifting her up so that she didn't feel the full force of rappelling onto the roof. How he did it with his bad leg, she didn't know. Now it was probably hurting again, because of her.

With practiced ease, he disconnected their equipment and waved to the pilot. Soon the chopper was a dark dot against the sky as the pilot returned to whatever airfield Austin had bribed him to come from.

Kade dropped the harnesses and ropes on the roof and pulled his gun out. "Ready?"

She pulled her Sig Sauer out. "Ready."

Jace passed her and Kade, leaving Bailey to close the door. She gently pulled it shut so that it wouldn't echo through the stairwell. Their little army might be small, but if things worked out as planned and they disabled the security systems from the inside, Mason had lined up a score more men and women to breach the building from the outside. It was a good plan, as plans went. But there were a host of unknowns that elevated the risk to extraordinary levels. The riskiest part being that Mason and Devlin only had one full day to perform reconnaissance.

Normally a mission like this required weeks of surveillance, so they could be sure how many enemy combatants they had to deal with and what weapons were at their disposal. But with potential hostages down in the tunnels who could be killed at any moment, they were taking more risks than usual. And Mason believed the manpower losses at the caves meant that Faegan was operating with a skeleton crew.

The Asheville building was smaller than the one in Boulder. There were only three floors, and the executive offices were on the first level. Security was too tight to approach the building from the ground, thus Austin's genius suggestion to rappel from the helicopter onto the roof. Sure enough, they'd encountered no alarms and no security forces so far.

They'd decided the best approach would be to sneak into the security offices on the first floor to disable the alarm and hopefully take out a few guards while they were there. So the team split at the first landing, with Devlin, Mason, and two of the other Enforcers heading down the stairwell to the ground floor.

The remaining six of them stood ready to clear the third floor, believing that it would be empty since the sun was going down soon and the parking lot only had a handful of cars left. Even Faegan and his men had to keep some kind of work hours. And since they wouldn't expect an assault here, hundreds of miles from the caves in Colorado, the only people left in the building should be Faegan and whoever he considered to be his most critical support staff. Kade was betting that Faegan would keep the same habits he'd always kept in the past, of working well past sunset every night. The man was committed to his cause.

Jace held up a hand to ensure silence, then slowly pulled the door open and peeked through the slit. He gave them a thumbs-up, then yanked the door all the way open and motioned for them to hurry through. As if they'd been a team for years, they worked perfectly in tandem, clearing one room at a time before moving to the next. In little time at all, they'd confirmed the entire floor was empty.

Two more floors to go. Then they could hit the tunnels.

They raced to the bank of elevators to secure them. They flanked them on either side while Kade pressed the button. A few seconds later, a small chime announced the elevator's arrival.

Bailey's finger tensed on the frame of her gun as she waited for the doors to open. *Swoosh.* She crouched down and aimed her pistol into the opening. Empty. Jumping back out of the way, she waited while Kade used a special fireman's key to lock the elevator and prevent it from returning to one of the lower floors.

He pressed the button to call the second elevator and they repeated the same procedure. Second elevator empty, locked. So far, everything was going exactly as planned.

Jace pressed a button on the earpiece that he was wearing. "Sitrep," he whispered.

Bailey stood beside Kade, waiting for the update. Jace nodded and gave them a thumbs-up sign.

"Alarm's disabled," he whispered. "After we clear the second floor, we'll signal them and they'll open the doors for the rest of the team to begin the assault on the primary target." He signaled the rest of the team, and the Enforcers with them led the way, running toward the stairwell. Jace, Kade, and Bailey took up the rear and soon they were all at the landing, ready to begin clearing the next floor.

Guns at the ready, they plastered themselves against the wall while, once again, Jace gently pulled the door open a crack to peer inside.

Bam! Bam!

Bullets blasted through the wall, slamming one of the Enforcers into the railing. Bailey lunged for him but he toppled over and was gone, his body thudding sickeningly on the concrete below.

Bam! Bam! Bam!

Jace and the others returned fire through the open door. Kade grabbed Bailey and yanked her out of the line of fire.

Jace made a winding motion with his hand. They ducked down while he laid cover fire, then Kade was out the door, leading the charge. Bailey and the others took up the rear.

Two bodies littered the carpet about twenty feet in, blood pooling beneath them. Bailey knelt down and checked both for a pulse, then shook her head.

"Mercenaries," she told Kade, pointing to the tattoos on their arms.

He nodded, then yanked her back and laid fire toward a door that had just opened across from them. The gunman in the opening fell soundlessly to the floor without ever firing his weapon.

More gunfire sounded from farther down the hall where Jace and the two other men with him were engaging more of Faegan's guys. One group was in a set of offices to the left, the other to the right. Even more gunfire sounded from downstairs. Lots of gunfire. Which meant their team outside the building had now joined the battle and was trying to break their way into the ground floor.

"Jace is pinned down," Kade said. "We need to find a way to get behind the gunmen."

Bailey looked around, getting her bearings, picturing the blueprints that she'd studied earlier today as part of the prep at Mason's home. With three floors of layouts to remember, it was hard to separate them and get a clear idea of where they were.

"The conference rooms." Kade pointed to the door directly across from them. "Didn't Mason say there was a parallel hall across the back wall that connects all the meeting areas to the offices?"

She studied the door he'd pointed to, noted the room number hanging on the wall. The pictures in her head snapped together and she knew exactly where they were. She counted the doors down to where the gunmen had Jace and the others pinned.

"Through there," she agreed.

They both looked up and down the hall, then ran for the other side. One of the gunmen spotted them and leaned out into the hallway. Kade jumped in front of Bailey and fired.

The gunman's arm exploded in a hail of gunfire from both Kade's and Jace's directions. The man screamed in pain. Another shot rang out and he dropped to the floor, dead.

Kade threw the door open and Bailey ran inside with him. They rushed to the end of the conference room to the only other door. Kade held up his fingers, counting down . . . three, two, one. He pulled open the door and Bailey squatted down, then lunged into the opening, sweeping her Sig Sauer back and forth.

"Clear," she whispered.

They headed into the back hallway, which was brightly lit from the rows of windows across the front of the building. The sound of gunfire continued to ring out both from down the hall and below stairs. But they didn't risk running past any of the rooms without clearing them first. At the next office door to their left, Bailey was the one to count down. On one, she threw the door open and Kade swept his gun inside.

"Hold it," he yelled. "Drop your weapon. Drop it!" He cursed and squeezed the trigger, the explosion of sound nearly deafening in the confined space.

He straightened and ran into the room, with Bailey following.

Kneeling down, he checked the gunman for a pulse, then shook his head.

"Damned idiot," he said. "He didn't have to die."

Bailey put her hand on his shoulder. "You're a good man. He obviously didn't think twice about trying to kill you."

The look on his face told her she wasn't making him feel any better. And it highlighted one of the major differences between the two of them. Killing mercenaries who had no loyalties other than to the almighty dollar didn't even cause a blip on her guilt-o-meter. And yet, every time Kade was forced to shoot one of Faegan's men she could see him die a little inside. She'd tried not to think about what that said about her. Maybe she really had been doing this job far too long.

"Two more rooms to clear and we'll be there," he told her. Then he headed out into the back hallway.

No one else tried to stop them, and they were soon poised at the door where they knew the gunmen were holed up who were trying to kill Jace and his men.

"I wish we knew how many were in there," Kade whispered. "I'll go in high, you go in low. Ready?"

She moved her finger from the frame of her gun to the trigger. "Ready."

Kade slowly and quietly turned the knob. He held up the usual three fingers, then two, then—

The door yanked open before he could push it open.

"Hold it, hold it!" someone yelled.

Kade grabbed Bailey's gun, shoving her hand up just as she let off a shot. It went wild into the ceiling above them. Then she realized who was in the room.

"Oh my God," she whispered, horrified. "I almost killed you."

Jace had gone pale, and wiped a shaky hand across his forehead. "Maybe not, if you'd hit the vest. Still, that was close."

She squeezed Kade's hand in thanks, still shaky from her near-miss. Working in teams was definitely not her forte.

Kade and Bailey stepped into the room with Jace. Four gunmen lay dead on the floor. One of the Equalizers who'd been with Jace was currently handcuffing two more gunmen back to back. But both appeared to be unconscious.

The door to the outer hallway was open, and in the hall could be seen another body.

"Oh, no," Bailey whispered. It was a member of their team who'd been pinned down with Jace.

Jace's tortured gaze met hers. "He put up a damn good fight. We wouldn't have been able to charge the room without him, and without you shooting in that back hallway. That distracted them, gave us the window we needed to rush them." He checked the loading on his gun and popped in a new magazine. "Let's finish clearing this floor. Sounds to me like most of the action is going on downstairs without us. I haven't been able to get in touch with Mason or Devlin." He tapped the earpiece he was wearing. "Hopefully their equipment's just messing up."

She exchanged an uneasy glance with Kade.

Jace's jaw tightened. "Let's go. We'll start with the next door down on the other side of the hall."

He peered out into the hall, then ducked around the corner.

Kade reloaded, then looked at Bailey. "Ready for round two?"

She glanced at the dead Enforcer, picturing Hawke's face there, and swallowed, hard. "Ready."

They peered down the hall, left and right, then ran for the next door. The rest of the floor was cleared in just a few minutes. The four of them raced back toward the stairwell, slamming the door open without even pausing.

A gunman was in the stairwell and whirled around toward them.

Kade slammed his body against the gunman, sending him careening over the railing. Kade winced but pounded down the stairs after Jace and his teammate, with Bailey following behind.

They took up positions on either side of the door, pistols out, backs to the wall. Kade did the countdown, then pulled open the door.

Boom!

Chapter Twenty-three

Friday, 7:13 p.m.

Kade blinked up at the sky above him. A red sky. Solid red everywhere he looked. Wait, that didn't make sense. His ears were ringing. But other than that, everything was quiet. Jumbled images bumped through his mind. What was the last thing he remembered? The field, leaving Austin there, standing on his new prosthetics. The helicopter. Bailey, looking terrified but doing her best to hide it. She was so damn proud, and competent in so many skills. But deathly afraid of flying, or "landing" as she'd informed him. And of being cremated. Odd things to learn right before they went into battle.

Bailey.

The stairwell, opening the door.

An explosion.

A shout sounded off to his left, tinny, but clear. Another shout sounded from his other side, louder now. His hearing was coming back. Gunshots, footsteps, people running both away from him and toward him.

The door, it had exploded as he'd pulled it open. Everything snapped into place. The red sky was the red metal door. It had taken the brunt of the force, blew him backward, protected him from the blast.

He shoved it to the side, tossing it toward the wall, or where the wall should have been. Lights from the parking lot, dulled by dark smoke, shined through the exterior wall, in a hole large enough to accommodate several men. Which was what it was doing right now. Men were running past him, coughing as the smoke got thicker, carrying guns, shouting, directing others through the debris and out the hole in the wall. Not Faegan's men, *his* men, Equalizers. And men he didn't recognize but that were being helped by the Equalizers. The hostages—they must have found them and were evacuating them from the building.

But where the hell was Bailey?

He shook his head again, trying to clear the buzzing noise, and shoved himself to his feet. Everything ached, like he'd been pulverized with a giant meat tenderizer. His bad leg pounded in rhythm with his pulse.

"Bailey? Bailey?" He turned in a circle, a sick feeling starting in his chest when he didn't see her.

"Kade, over here." Jace's voice echoed from a corner on the opposite side of the stairwell.

Kade ran to him, climbing up mountains of debris as someone else he didn't know but recognized as an Equalizer joined him.

"Name's Brady, sir," the man said.

"I'm Kade. And that's Jace under there. Grab the other end of that desk. The damn thing must have blown through the wall and landed on him."

Between the two of them, they pulled the desk off Jace's body. There was a hole where the wall to the first floor should have been. The hallway was filling with smoke, eerily lit by emergency lights. And flames, at the far end. They needed to get out of here. Now.

While Brady helped Jace to his feet, Kade turned in a circle again, looking at the piles of debris, half-expecting to see Bailey sitting there, perhaps shaking her head. Stunned, shaken, but alive and well. The scene was utter chaos, with people still running past. But the gunshots had stopped. And Bailey wasn't anywhere to be seen.

He looked back at Jace who was standing now, checking the loading on his pistol. He had a bloody gash on the side of his head but appeared to be okay, otherwise.

"Where's Bailey?" Kade asked, unable to keep the desperation from his voice.

Jace looked around as if just noticing that she wasn't with them. "She was right beside me when the explosion went off."

The three of them called her name, frantically digging through the piles of debris.

Kade shoved chairs and large pieces of wood aside, yelling for Bailey. He found the bodies of the two men who'd fallen to their deaths earlier and tossed them out of the way in his attempts to find her.

"I don't think she's . . . here." Jace looked just as confused as Kade felt.

Brady shook his head, letting them know that he hadn't seen her either.

"She has to be here," Kade yelled. "Keep looking."

After sifting through every inch of the stairwell,

twice, the three of them stood in the middle of the debris.

Kade's heart was pounding so hard he could hear the blood rushing in his ears. "She couldn't just . . . vanish. Where the hell is she?" He coughed and wiped at the tears that had started streaming from his eyes from the smoke that was beginning to fill the stairwell.

Another man stumbled through the destroyed doorway, soot on his face and arms, his shirt in tatters. He headed toward the parking lot lights shining through the far wall, but stopped when he saw them.

"Kade," he yelled. "Jace."

"Mason?" Jace said. He hurried forward. "Good grief, you look like the walking dead."

"I'm sure I look worse than I am. I had to pull a few guys out from the other explosions."

"Other explosions?" Jace asked.

"Two, one at the end of the building on the other side, another closer to the middle. Not as powerful as they could have been. We were lucky. We got the hostages out of the tunnels in spite of everything else. The teams that breached from the outside are picking them up in trucks and taking them back to the field for medical attention." He shook his head. "Bailey's friends didn't make it."

Damn. Kade looked around again, trying to fight down his alarm. Where the hell was Bailey?

"I caught a glimpse of Faegan at one point, cowering in an office doorway," Mason continued. "But I couldn't get to him and he disappeared. I'm hoping one of our guys found him and has him in cuffs somewhere outside. I'm about to go check." He jabbed his thumb over his shoulder toward the hole in the wall. "The building's lighting up. You need to get out of here." He frowned. "Where's Bailey?"

"She was with us right before the explosion. We haven't found her yet," Kade said, his panic growing.

"Hang on a sec. This headset's been spotty the whole time but I'll give it a try." Mason tapped his earpiece while they all moved closer to the opening in the wall, where the air was better. "Austin, this is Mason. You copy?"

A crackling noise sounded and Mason winced, then adjusted the volume. "Austin, Bailey is unaccounted for. Have you . . ." His eyes widened and he looked at Kade. "Got it. Right. Hang tight. We've got your back. On the way."

"What's going on?" Kade demanded. "Austin knows where she is?"

Mason waved them toward the opening. "This whole place is going up. We need to get out of here."

"Mason." Kade grabbed his arm. "What did Austin tell you?"

Mason glanced at Kade's hand. "You're gonna want to let me go."

"Not until you tell me what the hell is going on. Does Austin know anything about Bailey?"

They stared at each other until Mason finally swore and shook his head. He looked at Jace when he answered.

"Faegan's men are making a stand in the woods near the field. It's hand-to-hand combat out there, guerrilla warfare. Austin and the rest of the team are in the thick of it. We need to get out there."

Jace immediately took off through the opening,

racing across the parking lot toward the trees. Brady sprinted after him.

"Mason," Kade gritted out, waiting.

Mason let out an impatient breath. "I don't have anything solid. But Austin says Devlin reached him a minute ago. He'd followed Faegan through the tunnels but never caught up to him. He lost his trail outside because it was too dark. But another man told Austin that he thought he saw Bailey in the woods at the western edge of the field." His gaze slid away from Kade's. "And that the man she was with might have been Faegan."

Kade swore and shoved past Mason. He took off across the parking lot in the same direction where Jace had just disappeared.

BAILEY STUMBLED AGAINST a tree, this time on purpose and not just because it was difficult running through unfamiliar woods by moonlight. She was trying to slow Faegan down in the hopes that someone would see them and help her escape. Or, even better, that she could make *him* fall and wrench the pistol out of his hand. Then it would be her turn to make him squirm.

He jerked her arm and jammed the muzzle of his pistol against her right ear. She heard the cartilage crunch a split second before agonizing pain shot through her ear and jaw. She bit her lip until it bled to avoid giving him the satisfaction of her crying out.

"You'd better find your balance, Miss Stark, or I'll decide you're more trouble than you're worth and grab another hostage."

Fighting through the pain, she focused on not

stumbling again. He wasn't bluffing about killing her if she caused him any trouble. She'd seen the proof in that when he'd shot one of his own men who got in his way as he was trying to escape with her. The explosion had somehow knocked her into the hallway instead of back into the stairwell, and Faegan had been right there to shove her into one of the executive offices. Devlin must have seen Faegan because Bailey heard him shout from the other end of the hallway as he was following her into the office.

But Faegan didn't slow down. He led her through that office and opened a panel in the far wall, then rushed her through a hidden office much like the one she'd seen in Boulder. Then they were running down a tunnel, lit only by emergency lights. They'd passed the cells she'd heard about, and she was relieved to see the doors were open and the cells were empty. The hostages must have already been freed.

After they'd emerged from the tunnels, Faegan hadn't even slowed down. Even in near darkness, he'd known exactly where he was going. He forced her to run and soon they were in the woods.

He'd picked off three Enforcers who probably never saw him coming.

The occasional sound of gunfire erupted far behind them. More often they heard shouts. She would have been tempted to shout herself if she thought there was some way to avoid having Faegan immediately shoot her. For now, she would have to do whatever he told her. At least until she figured out a way to get the upper hand.

"Where are we going?" she asked.

"Where no one will think to look for me." He

shoved her forward, following behind her now. "Keep moving, straight ahead."

They topped the ridge and she stopped, surprised to see they were right back at EXIT, standing at the end of the parking lot. The entire right side of the building was engulfed in flames.

"Why are we back here? You can't want to go into the building. It's a death trap in there."

The bore of his pistol filled her vision. It was only three inches away. "I had to leave faster than I'd intended so some big giant of a man didn't catch me. Everything I've accumulated during this mission is inside the safe in my office. I'm not losing it all to some curious firefighter once they make it all the way out here, or some police officer intent on ensuring the so-called rightful owner gets his valuables back. It was hard work getting all those Enforcers to give up the information on their bank accounts and safety-deposit boxes when we were interrogating them. There are millions of dollars' worth of Swiss bank account numbers in that safe. So, I think you can see, Miss Stark, why we're not going anywhere until I open it."

"You were interrogating Enforcers so you could get their money? Let me guess. You figured out that Henry Sanchez didn't have any money, so you didn't even bother capturing him. That's why you killed him."

"It's called being efficient, Miss Stark. I may have enormous resources at my disposal for this little operation. But I still have to use them judiciously. Sanchez was a wastrel. Once I realized there was no point in expending the time to bring him in, I had him eliminated."

"I guess I was too much trouble too since your men have been trying to kill me instead of going after my money like they did with other Enforcers."

"Can you blame me? You've escaped one too many times. Definitely not worth the trouble. Now, if you please. Get moving."

"But the building is on fire."

"Then we should hurry before it spreads, don't you think? Move."

THE FIELD WHERE they'd taken off in the helicopter was dark now, illuminated only by moonlight. But thankfully it was almost a full moon, so Kade could see much better than on another night. Still, even though he'd been looking everywhere for Bailey, he'd yet to find any trace of her.

He spotted a glint of metal not too far away, just inside the tree line. Friend or foe, he couldn't tell, so he was as quiet as possible while he made his way toward where he'd seen that flash. He was about fifteen feet away when he realized that what he'd seen was moonlight shining off a piece of metal on Austin's prosthetics. He stood with Devlin, Mason, and Jace and was apparently unaware that he presented an easy target.

"Austin," Kade whispered loudly as he hurried toward them. "Get back, your legs—"

The sound of a gunshot rang out.

Austin flew backward, landing on a bush.

Devlin returned fire from where the muzzle flash had come. A scream from the other side of the field told of his success. Then they were all crouching over Austin, who was cursing nonstop as he pulled himself up to sitting. He bent over his right prosthetic, which now had a hole right through the middle.

"Damn it," he said. "Do you know how much these things cost?"

"I'll buy you another one," Devlin said. "Are you hit anywhere else?"

"Only in my pride," he grumbled. He looked up at Kade. "I'm guessing you were trying to warn me. Maybe next time you could do it more quickly."

"Have any of you seen Bailey? I still can't find her."

Austin shook his head, for once looking serious. "Not me." He lifted what appeared to be binoculars hanging from a strap around his neck. "These are night-vision goggles. I've been radioing in directions to our guys so they can take out the bad dudes. We've got most of them on the run. But I haven't seen Bailey." He pointed behind him back toward EXIT. "I've been watching the field and the rings of trees around it. But I haven't been watching back behind us. That's probably the only place she could be for me not to have seen her out here."

Kade whirled back toward the direction of EXIT. The sky was lit with a flickering shade of orange that had nothing to do with the moonlight. The entire building was on fire. If Faegan had taken Bailey there, she was in worse trouble than he'd feared.

He tore off across the field, trying to ignore the throbbing in his thigh that had started right after the blast. If he hadn't worn his brace, he wouldn't be able to stand, let alone run. The pounding of footsteps sounded behind him as either Mason or Jace or both ran after him.

He headed toward the left side of the building, the same side they'd all escaped earlier. Black smoke belched from the rips in the outer wall. But the flames didn't appear to have reached this part yet.

Jace grabbed Kade's hand before he would have disappeared into the building. Mason was beside him, gasping for breath after their sprint.

"Wait, Kade. Let's think this through," Jace said. "We'll only get one shot at finding her and getting out of this inferno in time, if we even have that."

"Assuming she's even in there," Mason added.

"Someone should tell Devlin—" Kade started.

"He'll watch out for her. He stayed back with Austin," Mason answered.

Kade nodded. It killed him to wait to go into the building. But what Jace said made sense. "All right. What's the plan?"

A scream shattered the night, a scream that sounded like it had come from inside the building.

"We improvise," Kade snarled. He ran through the opening.

Smoke blasted him, making his eyes stream with tears. He had to duck down to try to find breathable air. Behind him, Mason and Jace coughed and cursed but kept pace with him down the hallway. The smoke was like a curtain, reaching out to them, sucking away the oxygen.

Kade ripped his shirt off and tied it over his nose and mouth, like a bandana, to filter out the smoke. The others did the same.

Flames lit up the far side of the hallway and crept closer to them. Kade figured the only reason the fire hadn't already consumed the building was that Cyprian Cardenas had probably spared no expense buying fire-retardant carpets and paint. It was probably the only good thing the man had ever done.

The roaring sound of the fire was so loud they had to make hand motions to communicate. They headed into the nearest offices, clearing them like they'd done earlier.

Another scream sounded.

Kade raced back into the hallway where Jace and Mason met him. He pointed toward the next office down, which had probably once borne the name of Cyprian Cardenas, from the posh look of the entryway. He took the lead, rushing toward the doorway. He flattened his back against the wall and the others did the same. With pistol in hand, he ducked down and leaned around the open doorway. His heart dropped to his stomach when he saw what was inside the office.

Bailey was on her back on the floor, her hands wrapped around Faegan's wrists. He was on top of her, a pistol in his right hand, struggling to point it at her.

"You bitch," he yelled. "Spit it out. Spit it out or I'll blow your brains out!"

Kade aimed his gun at Faegan. But Faegan saw him and rolled to the side, yanking Bailey on top of him, and in the way. Kade swore and jerked his gun to the side. Faegan jumped to his feet, pulling Bailey with him as a human shield.

Mason and Jace flanked Kade, pistols pointed at Faegan, but their fingers on the frames of their guns so they wouldn't accidentally shoot Bailey.

"Spit it out," Faegan yelled in Bailey's ear.

She shook her head, and it was then that Kade saw the flash of white in her mouth.

"Let me go before the ink dissolves," she yelled around what Kade now realized was a wadded-up piece of paper.

"I'll shoot you," Faegan yelled, sounding desperate as he ducked behind her to keep from presenting the others with a target.

"My blood will destroy the numbers on the paper," she yelled back in a muffled voice.

Jace nudged Kade and pointed to their left. A wall safe sat open. Whatever had been inside it must now be in Bailey's mouth. The woman was both brilliant and crazy. She'd probably bought herself some time by shoving whatever the paper was into her mouth. But Faegan would no doubt shoot her the second he realized that the paper was now worthless, if the ink did dissolve as she'd warned.

The dull roar of flames from down the hall suddenly whooshed loudly, shooting past the open doorway. Mason slammed the door shut, but fire was already licking at the carpet beneath the door.

Faegan dragged Bailey backward, his gun pressed against the base of her skull. The open doorway to another office, probably Cardenas's hidden office like the one in Boulder, was just a few feet away.

"We can't let him into that office," Mason said.

Jace stepped to the right, cutting off Faegan's path.

"Move or I swear I'll kill her," Faegan yelled.

Kade motioned to Bailey, trying to silently communicate what he needed her to do.

She slowly nodded.

Faegan dragged her back another step.

Jace moved forward.

Faegan suddenly shifted his gun toward Jace.

"Now, Bailey," Kade yelled.

She lifted her feet off the floor and fell right out of Faegan's arms.

Caught off-balance, he lurched toward Jace, his gun going off. It hit Jace and he spun around, back against the wall. Mason brought his gun up and squeezed off a shot just as Faegan leaped through the doorway into the other office.

"The tunnels," Jace said. "He's going into the tunnels."

Kade ran to Bailey, who was making odd noises in her throat. "Bailey, sweetheart. Bailey?"

Mason started to kneel down to check on Jace, but Jace waved him back. "Body armor. I'm fine. Let's get the bastard."

They both ran into the other office.

"Bailey?" Panic had Kade's own throat closing and he had to force the word out. He suddenly realized what was wrong. She was choking on the ball of paper she'd had in her mouth. He grabbed her up in his arms just as the door exploded in a rain of glass and flames behind him. He ducked down and ran into the other office, then pulled the panel shut, cutting off the flames.

He sank to the floor with his precious burden and rolled her onto her stomach. Then he squeezed his fists together beneath her diaphragm and jerked them back against her—once, twice. The wadded-up paper flew across the room. Bailey gagged and threw up on the carpet.

Kade pulled her hair out of her face, holding her until she stopped retching.

"I thought I was going to lose you," he said, when she finally looked up at him. "I thought I was going to lose you."

She grabbed him and buried her face in his neck.

He rocked her in his arms. "What was on that piece of paper that Faegan was so worried about?"

"Swiss bank account numbers," she said, her throat sounding raw. "He stole money from all the Enforcers he murdered. I couldn't let him get away with that. I couldn't let him profit from their deaths."

He shuddered at how close she'd come to dying and clasped her more tightly against him.

"Kade, the Enforcers who were captured, we have to find them. Sebastian and Amber—"

He pulled her back, looking into her eyes, hating what he had to say next. "The Enforcers who were in the tunnels have already been rescued. Bailey, I'm so sorry. Your friends didn't make it."

She squeezed her eyes shut and shook her head. "That bastard. Faegan is going to pay for this."

Another loud roar sounded from outside the doorway. Black smoke belched underneath it and the first finger of flames clawed its way under the threshold.

Kade grabbed her hand and pulled her up. "We have to get out of here. Let's go."

She nodded, and he was so damn proud of how courageous she was. He could see she was hurting over the deaths of her friends. But she was strong, a survivor. She tamped down her grief and focused on what had to be done.

They raced through the opening on the other side of the office, down into the tunnels. They never saw Mason or Jace as they ran toward the exit that would take them into the woods. Sirens sounded overhead. Fire trucks were finally arriving. They were careful not to draw any attention to themselves when they rushed from the little landscaper's hut at the end of the parking lot that was really the tunnel exit.

Ten minutes later, Bailey and Kade were back with Devlin and Austin in the woods near the field. Kade couldn't seem to let Bailey go after coming so close to losing her. He had his arms around her shoulders and kept her tucked up against him. She seemed to be struck with the same affliction as him, because both of her arms were around his waist and she was holding on tight.

"Have you heard from Mason and Jace?" Kade asked. "We lost them in the tunnels when they were chasing Faegan."

Devlin nodded. "They caught him and cuffed him, said they'll be here in a few minutes."

Kade exchanged a relieved look with Bailey.

Austin was on his cell phone, trying to arrange some alternate transportation for them. With the fire trucks and, soon, police all over the EXIT parking lot, they wouldn't be able to use their cars, parked just inside the woods. Thankfully the rest of their crew had already left, just ahead of the fire trucks' arrival.

He hung up the phone. "We're gonna have to hike through the forest about a mile and a half to get to a second rendezvous point. I'll have some vehicles waiting for us there." He frowned down at the hole in his prosthetic leg. "I hope this thing lasts that long."

Bailey looked down at Kade's leg.

"Don't even say it," he said. "If Austin can make it, so can I." He kissed her to soften his rebuke. It felt so good, he kissed her again.

"Here they come," Devlin said.

Kade turned to see Mason and Jace striding toward them. "Give me a minute," he told Bailey. He gave her another quick kiss, then strode over to intercept the two before they reached the group.

"Devlin said you caught Faegan. Where is he?"

Mason and Jace exchanged a glance, then shrugged.

Kade stared at them. "Did you kill him?"

"Not yet," Mason said, sounding defensive. "We figured we'd interrogate him when we get a chance. Just to be sure there aren't any more loose ends we need to tie up. I'm sick to death of EXIT Inc. and don't ever want to go through something like this again. I'm getting too old for this crap."

Jace nodded and stood shoulder to shoulder with Mason.

"Do you really think that's going to stop me? Where is he?"

"What are you going to do? Arrest him?" Jace scoffed.

"He deserves justice," Kade said. "None of this vigilante crap you're so used to dishing out. It's vigilantism that got us all in this mess to begin with. I can't think of a better night to end that kind of thinking than tonight. Can you?"

Mason frowned. "It's not like he can get his say in a court of law. He'd tell them everything about us. We'd all end up in prison for all the laws we've broken, even though most of them were broken in service to our country."

The bitterness in Mason's tone wasn't lost on Kade. He knew what this war against EXIT had cost Mason, and what it had cost Jace. They shared a lot of war stories in the past few days, planning this assault. Both of them had nearly lost the women they loved because of EXIT. But so had Kade. He'd almost lost Bailey. And he had a right to see it through to the end—to its rightful end—just as much as they did.

He glanced back at Bailey, then said, "Take me to him."

Mason cursed, but turned around and led the way deeper into the woods, with Jace and Kade following. They'd gone a good quarter mile from EXIT by the time they stopped. Faegan sat at the base of an oak tree, his arms and legs bound to the lower branches. With shoe strings.

Kade looked down at Mason's and Jace's shoes, which were missing their laces. Faegan's shoes were missing the laces, too.

"Seriously? Shoe laces?"

"It was all we had," Jace said.

Kade turned back to face Faegan, the man who'd ruined his life in every way it could be ruined. He'd never wanted to kill a man in his life. But this man, who'd nearly killed Bailey, tempted him.

"Faegan, you're under arrest," he said.

Mason and Jace swore beside him.

"Go to hell," Faegan said.

"I vote we leave him out here tonight, like Jace and I had planned." Mason looked at Jace and Kade. "Give him some time to think about his sins while the possums and rodents chew on his flesh."

"Works for me," Kade said, knowing full well he wouldn't do that. But he wouldn't mind giving Faegan a few tense moments thinking that he would.

The three of them turned around and headed up the hill.

"I don't care where they lock me up," Faegan yelled after them. "I'll get out one day. And when I do, the first thing I'll do is track down your women and kill them."

Kade stiffened, then stopped, his back still to Faegan.

Mason and Jace stopped with him, exchanged glances.

"That's right," Faegan yelled. "Sabrina, Melissa, and Bailey. I know all about them, where to find them."

Kade closed his eyes, tuning out Faegan's tirade as he thought back to another time, not so long ago, when he and Bailey had been talking about Hawke.

"What if one of the people involved was someone you loved? Hawke was the closest thing to a brother that I've ever known. I loved him. If he was someone you loved, would you have chosen to save his life, over Simmons's? Would you have at least tried to save his life?"

He'd said something self-righteous and condescending, he was sure. Because he'd thought himself to be so honorable at the time, his faith in the law, in justice, unshakeable.

More of Bailey's words came back to him. *"Have you ever loved someone? Pretend Hawke was your loved one. Now would you have called Simmons?"*

He'd replied, *"It wouldn't be right. I couldn't trade one life for another like that, no matter how much I wanted to."*

And Bailey had said, *"Then you, Kade Quinn, have never really loved someone."*

He opened his eyes. She was right that day. He had never really loved someone. But he did now.

"Keep looking over your shoulders, boys," Faegan

taunted. "Because one day, I'll be there to do my worst. I'll gut all three of them. And I'll save Bailey for last. I've got millions of reasons for her to suffer most of all."

Kade looked at Jace, then Mason. Then they slowly turned around and pulled out their pistols.

Chapter Twenty-four

A week later, Friday, 9:30 p.m.

Jace Atwell and his wife, Melissa Cardenas, had excellent taste. Kade could say that for them. He leaned against the chunky marble banister on their twelfth-floor condo's balcony, looking out over Boulder's twinkling night lights while he sipped a particularly exquisite glass of twenty-year-old bourbon.

The floor-to-ceiling glass doors behind him had been pushed back into the walls on either side, opening the expansive balcony to the family room and turning it into one enormous entertaining indoor-outdoor space.

But Kade didn't much care for entertaining at the moment. He'd only come to the "post-EXIT" celebration out of respect for the men and women he'd fought alongside during the harrowing battles a week ago, both here in Boulder and in Asheville. He much preferred the quiet, and something on a far less grand scale. Which was why he was on the far end of the balcony, alone.

He took another sip of bourbon, enjoying the

burn, and wondering just how much longer he had to endure the party before he could leave without offending anyone.

The moment that Bailey stepped out of the condo, he sensed her presence. He didn't smell her perfume—she wasn't the type to wear any. And he didn't hear her laugh, or her smoky, sexy voice—she wasn't saying anything. But he still knew she was there. Something about her always sent a jolt of recognition, of sweet, painful yearning through every cell in his body.

He turned around, noting the surprise on her face as she stopped in front of him.

"I didn't think I made any noise," she said.

"You didn't."

"Then how did you know I was here?"

He shrugged, since he couldn't explain it without sounding like a love-sick puppy. He'd made the mistake, apparently, of hinting around about marriage right after Asheville. She'd looked terrified enough to bolt, so he'd backed off, not sure what to do. He didn't need months of dating to tell him what he already knew. He loved her, God how he loved her. And he wanted her so much he ached. Not for one night, or even a week, he wanted her in his life forever. But talk of forever for some reason petrified her. So now he was stuck in limbo, wondering if he'd pushed too hard, too fast, and the price would be that he might lose her forever.

The very thought nearly killed him.

She took a sip from his glass, then wrinkled her nose and handed it back. "Yuck."

"Yuck? That's twenty-year-old bourbon."

She held up the bottle in her hand. "Three-week-old beer." She took a deep sip then set the bottle on the railing. "Yum."

He laughed and set his glass down.

"EXIT really is no more," she said. "Hard to believe."

"Yeah. Hard to believe."

"Why are you alone?"

He shrugged.

She gestured toward Mason and his wife, Sabrina, on the other end of the balcony, laughing and talking with Austin, who must have replaced his damaged prosthetic because he wasn't in his wheelchair. "Have you met Austin's twin? Matt?"

"Twin? *Another* Buchanan? How many are there?"

"Six, seven, eighteen? Who knows? I'm thinking their mom was a good, devout, procreating Catholic."

"That's not a politically correct thing to say."

"I was raised Catholic. I'm allowed."

He laughed. She always made him laugh. He wanted to tell her he loved her again, like he had the night they'd made love in the cottage. He wanted to get down on one knee, beg her to spend the rest of her life with him. Why was she pushing him away?

He was losing her.

And he didn't understand why.

"What's next for you?" he asked.

Say you love me. Tell me you want to be with me. Say it, Bailey.

She shrugged. "Vacation, I suppose. I need some time to decompress after all of this. You?"

He stared at her a long moment, then turned back to the baluster. "Now there's a question." He watched the slow-blinking light of a plane flying in the distance. "Going back to the bureau doesn't seem possible. How would I explain everything that happened? For all I know, the net Faegan wrapped around me is still there, ready to pin everything on me if I go back. No, I suppose the safest thing to do is move on. Maybe I'll go on vacation, too, before making any big decisions." He looked at her. "We could vacation *together*, if you want to."

He was an idiot. He didn't want a vacation with her. He wanted forever. Where the hell had that question even come from?

"You're . . . not going to be an FBI agent anymore?"

He grew still, watching the shadows flicker in her gorgeous green eyes—the doubts, the worry. Was that it? Was it that simple? Could his beautiful, smart, confident Bailey be thinking she couldn't fit into his life and that's why she'd been so afraid of him proposing?

He slowly shook his head. "I don't see the point. I don't think that men like me, after the things I've done, should be the ones upholding the law. It's time to move on, let someone else take a turn."

She swallowed, cleared her throat. "Then . . . you'll do . . . what? Have you thought about how you're going to spend the rest of your life? I mean, I thought being a special agent was all you ever wanted. Do you think you could be happy if you aren't in the bureau anymore?"

Unable to resist the urge to touch her for even one more second, he gently stroked his thumb across her jaw. He loved the way she shivered every time he touched her.

"Do you think you could be happy hanging out with a washed-up, former FBI agent?"

Her smile could have powered all the lights of

Boulder, and then some. "As it turns out, I'm looking for a new career, too. Maybe we can both retrain together." She smoothed her hand up the front of his shirt. "I've no doubt that I can figure out something appropriate to your . . . skills."

He cocked his head, his heart feeling lighter than it had in days. "Are you flirting with me, Bailey Stark?"

"If you have to ask, I'm losing my touch."

He grinned.

"Ask me about that vacation thing again," she said.

"Would you like to go somewhere on vacation with me? Preferably somewhere hot, where you feel inclined to shed as much clothing as possible."

She laughed, and the sound had his soul wanting to shout for joy. Maybe there was hope for them after all.

She took his hands in hers and kissed his knuckles. "I'd love to go away with you, Kade. I've got a bikini I've been wanting to try out."

He was pretty sure he just swallowed his tongue.

She clasped her hands around the back of his neck. "I also have this little leather skirt, and a leather top with a zipper I sometimes need help with."

He swallowed. Hard. "I'm good with zippers."

Her gaze fell to his mouth. "Yes. You most definitely are."

He smiled and glanced down the balcony at Mason, then just inside at Jace, and the others. And then, as often happened these days, his thoughts drifted back to everything they'd all been through. And he wondered.

"Something's bothering you, isn't it?"

He blew out a long, slow breath. "Yeah. I guess it is."

She took a sip of her beer and waited.

"It's Faegan," he finally said.

She ran her hand up and down his arm as if to comfort him. "Are you having regrets?"

"No." His tone was sharp. He grimaced and lowered his voice. "That was the easiest decision I've ever made in my life. You're safe. That's what matters. It's just . . ." He shook his head. "I know he was in on everything, and he sure acted like it was all his idea toward the end when cornered. But I just can't picture him being the ultimate mastermind of all of this."

"Because he didn't seem smart enough?"

"No, he was smart. Brilliant actually. It's more that, well, I guess I never thought that he'd be able to pull everything together like he did—the teams, the facilities, the computer resources. He wasn't high enough in the organization to have the kind of clout I'd have expected to be necessary to get all of that without someone questioning him."

"You think, what, that he was working with someone else?"

"Yes. No. Hell, I don't know. I just wish I had some hard evidence in front of me."

"What about the mercenaries we captured in the caves? Were they interrogated? Did they reveal anything new?"

He shook his head. "Devlin took charge of all the prisoners, said he had contacts who'd ensure they did some hard time and couldn't hurt anyone else. But I didn't even think to ask whether they'd been interviewed."

"Maybe you should."

"Maybe."

He sipped his bourbon, then set it back down. The smoky flavor didn't give him the pleasure that it had earlier. Those little doubts that had started up the moment the fight had ended were getting stronger now. He shook his head. "I just don't buy it. There's something more to all of this. There has to be."

"Work through it then. You say Faegan wasn't high enough up in the FBI. Who's higher than him? Who would have the clout you think was necessary? Ignoring all the agents at the same level as him, just looking at the ones above him, that's probably a pretty small number, right?"

He slowly nodded, thinking about the men and women in positions above him, above Faegan. Kendall was the first name that came to mind. But, no, Kendall had left the bureau when Gannon had. They'd both gone to Homeland Security together. So who did that leave? He counted them up. "Not that many, less than ten."

"And you know them?"

"Every single one." He picked up the glass again and turned it around and around as he thought through the list. "None of them fit. I just can't picture them being a part of hiring mercenaries and becoming cold-blooded murderers. Which means Faegan must have been at the top of the food chain as far as EXIT goes. He did what he did to protect himself, to keep anyone else from finding out."

She studied him, her head cocked to the side. Then she slowly shook her head. "Nope. You don't believe that. You still think he was taking orders from someone else."

He was about to deny it, but then he said, "Yeah. I guess I do."

"But it's not anyone you know of in the FBI?"

"Not that I can think of."

"How about other agencies?"

"What do you mean?"

"You know, like the CIA or Homeland Security. I was talking to Jace earlier and he mentioned that there used to be a Council that worked with Cyprian Cardenas, to oversee his activities."

"Well, that didn't work out so well, did it?"

She smiled. "No, it didn't. At the time, though, it consisted of people from several different alphabet agencies. Which means, it's possible someone in those other areas still has some knowledge of EXIT and what it used to be. Maybe one of them was working across organizations with Faegan. I don't see why not. It's not like everything was on the up-and-up, going through official channels. If they met at some social function where several agencies were in attendance, they could strike up a conversation, realize they both had the same goals, and start up a partnership."

He stared at her, her words triggering some kind of memory that he couldn't quite bring into focus.

"If you follow that theory," she continued, "Faegan would have worked with someone he trusted, and they each would have used their positions at their respective agencies to help cover their tracks. Going with that theory, is there anyone you know at another agency who hates you and would want to ruin your life? We're not talking someone who wants you dead. If that were the case, you'd be dead already. No, whoever did this wanted to make you crazy, to ruin your reputation, to make it impossible for you to ever work at the FBI again."

"Go on," he said. "What you're saying makes sense."

"Okay, well, the person who wants to ruin you wouldn't want you to go to prison either. Because they would never let someone with inside information on EXIT go to prison for fear that they'd talk, right?"

"Right."

"So this enemy of yours, hypothetically speaking—if your worries are right—wanted you to live with the guilt over not being able to save your supposed wife. He or she wanted you to go down the path of self-destruction. Whoever it is, they wanted you to lose everything, to hit rock bottom. Had you ever done anything to Faegan that he might hold against you enough to want to destroy you?"

He slowly shook his head. "I've been thinking about that myself, ever since I realized I was being set up. And it's baffled me from the get-go. There's nothing that I can think of that would have made Faegan want to destroy me."

"Well, there you go. That's why this isn't sitting right with you. It may be that all Faegan needed as incentive was the money, and you were just convenient. It wasn't personal at all. But if it was personal, then you need to think about anyone you might have slighted, even unintentionally, who might hold a grudge they could never let go. Things that start out small can eat at a person and sour them from the inside out. What seemed like nothing can become a mountain of rage after years of letting it fester."

The last piece of the puzzle fit neatly into place.

And he suddenly knew exactly who hated him that much, who blamed him for missed promotions, missed opportunities. The same person who'd once been his best friend, but who was always second best when they went up for a raise, a promotion, a coveted assignment. The man who blamed Kade for stealing his girlfriend. A man who'd refused to forgive Kade, even years later. They'd both worked in the FBI for the same bosses—Faegan, and *his* boss, Kendall—for years. Then his friend had left with Kendall for an opportunity in Homeland Security. As for Faegan, he could have kept in touch through the many social gatherings between FBI and Homeland Security agents, just as Bailey had predicted. It had been right in front of Kade this whole time and he'd never even realized it. The man who'd set him up was Robert Gannon. Had to be. A few quick calls and he could have Robert's home address.

"You've thought of someone, haven't you?" she asked, watching him.

He shook his head, carefully schooling his features to not give anything away. "I'm still thinking it through." He drained the last of his bourbon, then held the glass up. "Looks like you're ready for another beer. Can I convince you to get me another bourbon while I'm lazy out here?"

"We're not finished with this conversation," she warned. "I'll be right back." She headed into the condo, then disappeared into the kitchen.

BAILEY SMILED AT the two women standing by the kitchen sink. One of them had red hair, like her, that hung almost to her waist. Tessa maybe? The wife of one of the Buchanan brothers that she'd met earlier.

The other woman was a very short brunette that she couldn't remember at all.

"Hi, Bailey," the brunette called out, offering her a warm smile.

Damn. "Hi." Bailey drained the beer bottle, then put it in the recycle bin in the pantry before setting Kade's glass on the granite kitchen island. She grabbed one of the bottles of whiskey sitting in the middle and was about to pour some when the woman who'd spoken put her hand on Bailey's arm, stopping her.

"If that's for your guy, Kade," she said, "this is the one he got earlier." She picked up a different bottle and set it in front of Bailey.

"Um, thanks. And he's not my guy." *Was he?*

She laughed. "Yeah, I'll be sure and remind you that you said that at your wedding. I'm Madison by the way, in case you forgot. My husband is the good-looking Buchanan." She braced her elbows on the island, and didn't even have to lean over to do so. "I've never met a female assassin before. What made you want to do that? Did you just wake up one day and say, hey, I'd like to kill some bad guys?"

The redhead groaned and grabbed Madison's elbow. "Sorry, Bailey. I'd tell you that Madison has had a little too much to drink tonight. But, honestly, she just doesn't have a tactful bone in her body. Come on, Trouble. Let's leave Bailey alone. She's obviously preoccupied."

Madison grumbled something to Tessa but obviously wasn't really upset at her since she smiled at Bailey over her shoulder.

"We'll talk later," Madison promised, before she was practically dragged out of the room.

Thoughts of the two women faded as she poured the bourbon into Kade's glass. She had something more important to do before taking Kade his drink.

Surf the net.

Kade had thought of someone when they'd been brainstorming earlier. She was sure of it.

And so had she.

There were only two names she knew of in relation to people he'd worked with who were now at another agency—Robert Gannon, and Kendall. Unfortunately, she didn't know Kendall's first name. But she was still curious what she might find in a search. Maybe it would be enough to pressure Kade to tell her the whole truth.

The search on Kendall was a bust. But the search for Robert Gannon yielded one extremely interesting fact—he lived in Boulder, not far from this condo. That would make it pretty easy to check him out and see whether he had anything to do with Faegan's machinations.

With a fresh bottle of beer in one hand and Kade's drink in the other, she headed out to the balcony. Her heart sank when she found it empty. After a quick search of the condo, she couldn't deny the obvious.

Kade was gone.

Chapter Twenty-five

Friday, 10:02 p.m.

Kade ducked down behind the air-conditioner unit outside Gannon's house as a car drove past and headed down the street. When the car turned at the stop sign, he straightened and continued around to the back. The house was a brick two-story—maybe three thousand square feet—but nothing overly outlandish or fancy for this neighborhood. Gannon was a smart guy. He wanted to fit in, not stand out. He was a master at staying below the radar, which was part of the reason that Kade had never even suspected his involvement in everything that had happened until the evidence was right in front of his face.

There was no fence around the backyard and Gannon didn't have any plants up close to the house, either. Kade was completely exposed as he went to work on the security system that was hooked into a utility box bolted to the brick wall. All he could do was hope that none of the neighbors looked out their windows until he made it inside. But even if they did, he wasn't all that worried. He didn't need more than a few minutes to accomplish his goal. Even if someone called the police, it was unlikely they'd arrive in time to stop him.

The alarm took longer than he'd hoped to disable and bypass. Gannon had installed a state-of-the-art system that would foil most burglars.

But Kade wasn't a burglar. And he had more incentive than most.

He eased through one of the back French doors into a mudroom and took his time, carefully "clearing" the kitchen, then the ornate dining room with its fancy place settings that Kade would never have expected of a bachelor like Gannon. The agent must have hired a decorator, because nothing here reminded him of the man he'd once known. Gannon was a minimalist, fond of straight, clean lines, and very little clutter. This house looked like something out of a magazine.

Kade hated everything about it.

The next room over, toward the center of the house, was what should have been a family room, meant for watching football games with friends in front of a sixty-inch monstrosity on the back wall. Instead, there wasn't a TV in sight, just more elegant, stuffy-looking antiques. He shook his head. Gannon had changed, really changed.

A massive winding staircase led to the second floor, but it was the open doorway near the front of the house that had Kade freezing in his tracks and bringing up his pistol. From his vantage point, ten feet away, he could see a wall of bookshelves on the left-hand side of the doorway, but little else. A light was on, its soft-yellow glow flooding out into the two-story hallway. And he could hear a one-sided conversation, as if someone was talking on the phone. The side he could hear was a voice he recognized.

Gannon.

"No, sir. I haven't worked with Special Agent Faegan in some time, not since I switched agencies. I don't know why you think I might know something about some operation in Colorado Springs or another one in Asheville."

A pause, then, "Of course, Special Agent Kendall. Yes, I heard that. It is a tragedy that our brothers at the FBI lost Special Agent Simmons . . . No, I never met him . . .

"Understood. Faegan was a loose cannon back when he was my boss. And so was Quinn . . . I'm not surprised at all to hear you say that Quinn could potentially be involved. He's been spiraling out of control for months . . . What's that? Well, of course sir. I'd be happy to contact the FBI and act as a liaison until this is all properly investigated. It would be an honor. Yes, sir . . ."

He mumbled something else into the phone that Kade couldn't make out, then said, "Thank you, sir. Good night."

Footsteps sounded from inside the room.

Kade aimed his Walther PPK at chest level, just as Gannon appeared in the doorway. The other man froze, his eyes widening as his gaze met Kade's.

"Quinn, what the hell are you doing here?" His dark gaze dropped to the gun before looking up again. "Put that away." He slowly raised his hands, his suit jacket tightening across his shoulders. "There's no need for a gun. I'm unarmed."

"Yeah, well. Forgive me if I don't believe a single

word coming out of your mouth." He waved his hand in the air, gesturing toward the paintings on the walls, the coffered ceiling twenty feet above them. "Nice place, if you don't mind living in a museum. Seems to me I remember you more as a beer and nuts kind of guy. Where's the big-screen TV? The carpet? You've changed, Gannon." He moved his finger from the frame of the gun to the trigger, and enjoyed the flash of fear that crossed Gannon's face as he followed the movement. "And not in a good way. Lose the jacket. I want to see for myself whether you're wearing a gun."

"Why are you here?" Gannon asked, as he slowly pulled off his jacket, then tossed it aside to land on the floor near the bookshelves.

"I'm one of the people who's going to make sure that everyone knows you colluded with Faegan to kill innocent people and line your pockets. Did you really think you two would get away with trying to set me up as your fall guy while you both garnered millions of dollars and killed the Enforcers and anyone else who could bring down your scheme?"

He took a step closer, then another, but was careful to stay out of range so Gannon couldn't lunge at him.

"I don't know what you're talking about. Let's sit down and figure this out together."

Kade laughed harshly. "Still lying, even up to the end, huh Gannon?"

"I'm not lying. I don't know anything about . . . what did you call them?"

"If I didn't know you better, I might actually be convinced. You're a good liar, I'll give you that. But the problem is, conspiracies have a way of getting out, don't they? How did it happen? Did you meet up with Faegan at one of those dinner parties they make us go to? And he told you about EXIT and that he'd been ordered to shut down the remnants of the Enforcer program? You must have realized right away that you both had a gold mine at your fingertips. Most Enforcers made hundreds of thousands of dollars per hit or protective detail. And you thought that money was yours for the taking. But you knew you'd need a fall guy just in case things went wrong. Clever, really, to choose two. Me, as the first fall guy. Faegan as the second. Too bad you didn't plan a way out of this if both of your scapegoats didn't work out. Turn around."

"You're talking crazy, Kade."

"Am I? Tell me, are you still working on that background report I asked for? Sure is taking a long time."

"I told you in my email that stuff like that takes time. I had to keep it under the radar so I wouldn't tip off Faegan if he was doing something wrong. If I'm guilty of anything it's that I didn't follow up."

"Oh, I'm sure you followed up—with Faegan, to let him know I suspected something was going on. Now turn around."

Gannon slowly turned. He wasn't wearing a holster, and Kade didn't see the telltale bulge of a gun anywhere.

"Lose the pants."

He swore and looked over his shoulder. "What the hell for?"

"Don't look at me like that, asshole. Lose the pants so I can be sure you aren't concealing a backup gun anywhere."

Gannon mumbled beneath his breath and took

off his shoes, then shucked off the pants, tossing them onto the jacket. He held his hands out, looking ridiculous in his dress shirt and tie, black socks and red-silk boxers peeking out from beneath the bottom of his shirt.

"There. Satisfied? I just got home from work a few minutes ago. I locked my gun in the safe and was about to go upstairs to change. I'm not armed."

"Excellent. That makes us even." Kade held up his gun, popped out the magazine, then ejected the bullet from the chamber. He set them aside on a skinny, decorative table by the stairs, vaguely surprised the thing didn't collapse beneath the gun's weight. He clenched his hands into fists. "Now you can't say that I didn't give you a fair chance."

The surprise on Gannon's face quickly changed into a sneer. He took up a boxing stance, fists raised and stepped toward Kade.

"Leave it to you to let your ego get in the way. You should have kept the gun, Quinn."

He took a swing at Kade's jaw, but Kade had anticipated the move and ducked down, swinging his own fist in a vicious uppercut.

Gannon stumbled back, wiping at his bottom lip, his hand coming away smeared with blood.

"You bastard. I should have had you killed instead of setting you up as a fall guy. You've been nothing but problems from day one."

He charged forward, managing to get a punch in this time, slamming Kade's left shoulder hard enough to make him stagger against the wall. But Kade used the momentum to swing around, slamming his foot into Gannon's knee before the other man could jump back.

Gannon swore and fell back against another decorative table, which collapsed beneath his weight. But he managed to remain upright, standing at an awkward angle as he tried to keep most of his weight off his injured knee.

They both faced off, slowly circling each other. Kade couldn't help but laugh.

"Looks like we both match now." He indicated the leg Gannon was favoring.

The man's eyes narrowed. "Too bad that gunman only managed to hit your thigh the night your wife was killed."

Kade narrowed his eyes. "I know everything. I broke into the lab, saw the films, figured out that you used hypnosis and mind-control techniques to make me think I'd been married when I never had. All so you could, what, drive me crazy? Make me vulnerable, at rock bottom, so I'd buy anything you were selling? So I'd think Faegan was doing me a favor by giving me this one last mission, a chance to redeem myself?"

Gannon shrugged. "So you finally know. Good for you. It was an easy setup. Car accidents are easy to arrange. Of course, the bullet hole in the door was a problem, so I had to get creative afterward—make the car disappear. Bribe a police contact into filing a false report."

Kade shook his head in disgust. "I know that you're behind the murders of the men and women who once worked as Enforcers at EXIT Inc., doing the government's dirty work. I know that you set up Faegan as your go-between to murder the Enforcers, and that you set me up as your main fall guy, making me think I was saving people while you and Faegan were actually murdering them."

Gannon wiped his bleeding lip again. "Why are you wasting my time talking about all that crap? You're like a dog who's been kicked one too many times, begging for table scraps or a pat on the head. Fine. You need me to say it? I guess you've earned it. Everything you said is true. I'm behind everything, and set you up to take the fall. Feel better?" He gestured toward Kade's left leg. "You know about the lab, and the mind-control experiments we ran on you. But you don't know the full story, do you?" He laughed harshly. "You don't know the best part. Who do you think put that bullet in your damn leg in the first place?"

Gannon's laughter turned to a hiss when Kade slammed into him. They both fell to the floor, punching and kicking at each other. Having learned from his earlier fights with Bailey, Kade focused on keeping his bad leg out of Gannon's range. One good kick or punch to his thigh and he'd be out of commission. But trying to fight while protecting his leg was nearly impossible. And Gannon, as if sensing his struggle, began punching and kicking even harder—everything aimed toward Kade's bad thigh.

Kade managed to slam his own fist against Gannon's hurt knee. Gannon's answering shout of pain was music to Kade's ears. He shoved free of Gannon's arms and rolled away, then used the stairs to pull himself up. Grabbing one of the ruined decorative table's legs like a baseball bat, he hefted it and raised it to slam down on top of Gannon's shoulders.

"Do it and I'll drop you where you stand."

It was the voice, more than the words, that made Kade freeze. His gaze flew to the doorway between the main room and the kitchen, and he slowly lowered his arms. A woman stood there, pointing a pistol at him—the same woman who'd haunted his nightmares for months.

"Abby?" The word barely made it through his tight throat, and he felt foolish as soon as he said it. But even though his mind knew she wasn't his wife, had never been his wife, he'd lived with the falsehood for so long that he was having difficulty getting past the shock of seeing her again. Part of him wanted to drag her to him, to protect her, even though she was the one with the gun.

"Abby, huh? Is that what you told him my name was, darling?" She spoke to Gannon but kept her gaze firmly fixed on Kade.

"I thought it had a nice ring to it." Gannon brushed bits of wood from his legs and stood with his back to the wall beside the doorway. "Just shoot him already. I'll tell Kendall that Quinn was behind everything just like I'd originally planned. And I'll tell the cops there was an intruder, which there was."

The woman let out a sharp cry of pain and fell to the floor, the gun wrenched from her hand. Gannon whirled around, but froze when he came face-to-face with both Abby's gun, and the Sig Sauer nine-millimeter the other woman—the one who'd snuck up behind her and slammed her to the floor—had always favored.

"Give me a reason," Bailey snarled. "Trust me, it won't take much."

Gannon slowly raised his hands in the air and backed away from her.

"Bailey, what are you doing here?" Kade demanded.

"Saving your ass. You can thank me later."

He shook his head. "Damn it, woman. I didn't need saving. And all you've done is make this more complicated." He unbuttoned the top button of his shirt.

Bailey blinked. "Kade, what are you doing?"

He looked down at the fake Abby, lying in a fetal position on the floor, not looking nearly so tough without her gun. Then he looked at Gannon, who was still backing up, keeping both Bailey and Kade in sight. After unbuttoning two more buttons, he decided to hell with the shirt and ripped it open. Buttons went flying and pinged off the wall.

Bailey started laughing when she saw the wires taped to his chest.

Gannon's eyes widened with horror.

"Did you get all of that, Kendall?" Kade spoke into the wire that some Homeland Security agents had strapped on him right before he'd driven to Gannon's house.

A man in a business suit stepped into the room, having come in through the same door that Kade had used a few minutes ago. Several others converged into the room holding assault rifles and wearing flak jackets with the words POLICE, DHS on the front and, POLICE, HOMELAND SECURITY printed across the backs.

Gannon went as white as a sheet.

"Every word, Special Agent Quinn." The agent stared at Gannon in disgust, then motioned toward some of his men. Two of them cuffed fake Abby and hauled her out of the room, while two others cuffed Gannon.

"You're making a mistake," Gannon yelled. "You misunderstood. I was just agreeing with Quinn to get him not to kill me." He struggled against the hold the agents had on him, but they easily managed him. "For God's sake, Kendall, at least let me get my pants on." His curses followed him outside as the agents dragged him from the room.

In his boxer shorts.

Kendall waved another agent over to take the listening device off Kade. When that was done, Bailey practically knocked the agent over in her zeal to reach Kade's side.

"I can't believe you partnered with the Feds to get Gannon," she said, as she pulled the edges of his shirt together. But she gave up trying to make it stay closed without any buttons.

"I'm a Fed, too," he reminded her. "Or, I was."

"Yeah, well. Everyone has to have a flaw. I suppose that's yours."

He laughed and kissed her.

"Special Agent Quinn?" Kendall said.

He tucked Bailey against his side, before answering. "Yes?"

Kendall nodded at Bailey, and shook Kade's hand. "Thank you for contacting me tonight and clueing me in on what was going on. I'll need a full statement, probably several days' worth to figure out all the details and wrap this thing up nice and tight. But, personally, I'd like to get some sleep tonight. So how about you call me up in the morning and start then?"

"You got it. Thank you, sir."

He smiled. "It's good to see you again. Sorry it wasn't under better circumstances."

"No problem, sir."

Kendall gestured toward a nearby agent. "Has that call come through yet?"

"Just did, sir." The agent handed the phone to Kendall, who handed it to Kade.

"You might want to step into the kitchen to take that," Kendall advised. "You'll want to be able to hear everything without all this noise out here." He waved toward the increasingly chaotic scene as the agents began searching every drawer, every cabinet in Gannon's office and the main room. Some of them were even heading up the stairs.

Kade took the cell phone and stepped back out of the way, pulling Bailey with him. He didn't think he'd ever be able to let her go again. It had practically killed him when she was in danger during the fight with the mercenaries. And then, seeing her standing in the doorway earlier, worried she might get hurt, that had nearly killed him all over again. He pressed a quick kiss to the top of her head, and then held the phone up to his ear.

"This is Special Agent Quinn."

When the caller announced who they were, Kade straightened and stared at Bailey. "Yes, Mr. President. It's an honor to speak to you."

Bailey's eyes widened and her mouth fell open.

It was a short call, and very much to the point. "Thank you, sir. Understood." He stepped into the other room and returned the phone to Kendall.

"I don't know how to thank you," Kade said.

"Just doing my job. I didn't see any cars out front when I got here. I take it you both took cabs?"

They nodded.

"I figured. I took the liberty of ordering a car

brought around for you. I'll send someone over to pick it back up after you call me tomorrow." Kendall handed Kade his card. "Let me know if you need anything else, anything at all."

He held Bailey's gun out to her as if he were handing her her purse. "Ma'am."

"Um, thanks." She shoved it into the holster at her waist.

He handed Kade his pistol, too, then gave them both a jaunty salute before joining some of the other agents in Gannon's office, which seemed to be the main focus of the search.

"Let's get out of here," Kade said, taking pity on Bailey, who looked like she was waffling between asking him about the phone call and jumping out of her skin every time one of the agents looked at her. She definitely didn't like being around Feds, not that he could blame her. Her sole experience with them hadn't given her any reason to trust them as a whole. He was still amazed that she trusted him.

"Thought you'd never ask." She led the way through the front door.

Kade followed her to the car that Kendall had waiting for them, which turned out to be a black Mustang GT. He grinned as the agent guarding the car handed him the keys.

"Thanks."

"Yes, sir." The agent hurried across the lawn toward the house, to be part of the action. Thankfully, the real action was over.

Or so Kade hoped.

Chapter Twenty-six

Friday, 10:45 p.m.

"**Y**ou're frowning," Bailey said, as they got into the Mustang and buckled up. "Gannon's been arrested. Kendall seems like an up-and-up guy and is going to ensure none of this comes back on you. You apparently got a call from the President, which has to be a good thing or we wouldn't have been allowed to leave. So, why exactly are you upset? That *was* who the call was from, right? The President, you know, of our country?"

He gave her a lopsided grin as he revved the engine and pulled away from the curb. "One and the same. Hopefully he doesn't know that I didn't vote for him."

She laughed, and the sound was like a balm to his soul.

"What did he say? How did you get Homeland Security to believe you and set up a wire so fast? What happened? Spill." She lightly punched his shoulder. "And don't ever lie to me again and take off the way you did. You scared me."

He kissed her hand and began answering her

questions. He drove through the neighborhood and down a two-lane road out of the city. On autopilot, not really thinking about where he was driving, he explained how he'd left Jace's party after realizing Gannon had to be behind everything. And that he knew the only way to stop this once and for all was to call someone he'd admired in the past, who was high enough up in the food chain to help. Thankfully, Kendall was just as trustworthy, and quick to action, as Kade had remembered. He'd pulled agents off a nearby task force, already geared up and ready to go, and arranged to have them back Kade up at Gannon's house. The wire had been put on Kade several blocks from the house. Kade had also arranged for Kendall to call Gannon to rile him up and make sure he was awake. The timing was perfect, with Gannon stepping out of his office right after Kade had gotten inside.

"How did the President get involved?" Bailey asked.

"I assume Kendall went up the chain after I called, all the way to the top. As soon as Gannon was in custody, the agent who helped us at the house reported in, and the President was notified. He didn't say much, other than to tell me he'd been briefed on the Enforcer situation and he personally guaranteed that EXIT Inc.'s legacy was destroyed, once and for all. He said he's launching an internal investigation to ensure that the Enforcers and their families are compensated for the losses that they've suffered. And he's going to ensure that anyone else who helped Cyprian, Faegan, or Gannon is held accountable."

"Held accountable. It's not like they'll want this in the courts or in the press."

Kade shrugged. "I didn't ask for details. I don't want any. I just want to know that this is all over. I'm going to have to put my faith in the President that he'll keep his word. He certainly could have silenced us if he had any intention of playing the bad guy."

A bright orange light lit up the sky over the ridge ahead of them, and suddenly he realized where he'd driven. The EXIT Inc. Boulder headquarters was just over the top of the next hill.

Bailey had noticed the glow, too. And both of them heard the approaching sirens not far behind them. She peered intently through the windshield as he topped the rise.

"No way," she said.

He pulled the car off the road to allow the emergency vehicles to pass, and drove through a gap in the trees a good fifty yards off the road before stopping the car behind some bushes. They both sat in stunned silence as they watched the hungry flames consuming every floor of the EXIT Inc. office building below them. There wasn't a single window that wasn't either blown out from the heat or that didn't have thick black smoke roiling out of it. In the parking lot, three fire trucks raced toward the building, stopping a good distance away beside some enormous fire hydrants that Cyprian had no doubt insisted upon to protect his precious headquarters. But no amount of water was going to save his legacy now. The best the firemen could hope for was to contain the fire so it didn't spread to the woods. And judging by their lack of urgency as they surveyed the situation, they knew the building was beyond hope as well.

"I guess someone decided to move forward with my original plan to raze the building," Kade said.

"The timing sure seems suspect, doesn't it?"

"Sure does. If I had to guess, I think the President is keeping his word. He's destroying EXIT Inc., once and for all."

She ran her hands up and down her arms as she watched the flames. If he didn't know better, he'd think she was . . . afraid.

"It's over, Bailey. You're free to do whatever you want to do now. You don't have to look over your shoulder ever again."

"I know that."

"Then what are you afraid of?"

"Who says that I'm afraid of anything?"

The outrage in her voice had him smiling. "Maybe 'afraid' is too strong. But something is worrying you."

"Why didn't you kill Gannon?"

Her question surprised him. "Are you worried he won't be held accountable?"

"I worry that he didn't get what he deserved . . . after what he did to you, and to others. He shouldn't be alive when so many others are dead. Kade, if I'd known that he was behind all of this, that he was the man who'd ultimately pulled the strings to kill my friends, to kill Hawke." She closed her eyes briefly. "To kill Sebastian and Amber as we confirmed just a few days ago. He hurt so many people, including you. I'd have killed him. Once I realized that you had no intention of killing Gannon, I was prepared to take care of it. If that agent hadn't come through the door when he had, Gannon would be dead right now."

He gently pushed her hair out of her eyes. "I know."

She shoved his hand away from her. "And?"

"And what?"

"You can't just say you know, and act like everything's okay." She thumped her chest with the flat of her hand. "I'm a killer, don't you get it?"

"Bailey, I've killed, too. Even before the fight with the mercenaries, I've killed. And you're one of the few people who really knows what happened to Faegan."

"That's different." She turned back toward the fire just as the roof of EXIT Inc. imploded, consumed by the flames from the top floor.

"It isn't." When she ignored him, he put his hand beneath her chin and gently forced her to turn her head. "You can stop this martyrdom mentality. I'm not going to let you get away with it. We've both done things we're not proud of, but we did them with the best of intentions. Neither of us is some evil bad guy wanting to run around hurting people. Everything we've done was to save and protect others. We've got nothing to be ashamed of."

Her jaw tightened and she didn't look at him.

"Did you enjoy killing people?"

Her brows drew down. "Of course not."

"Did you ever kill someone for fun, when you didn't have an order to go after them?"

"That's just sick."

"Then I pronounce you a normal person. You're not some psychopath intent on killing innocent people. And Gannon was far from innocent. I can understand you wanting to take him out. It's part of your training, to take out the bad guys. But you didn't."

"I couldn't. The Homeland Security guys—"

"Came into the room after you trained your guns on Abby and Gannon, but not that exact second. If you really wanted to kill him, you had time. And you didn't do it."

Confusion clouded her eyes, as if she were considering what he'd said.

"You're a good person, Bailey Stark."

She shook her head no.

"You're a good person," he repeated.

A single tear traced down her cheek. "Not good enough," she whispered.

"Good enough for what?"

"You."

That one word, sounding so desolate, nearly broke his heart. But it also gave him hope. He smiled, and the fact that she frowned in response had him smiling even more.

"What's so funny?" she demanded.

"Are you always going to be prickly?" he asked.

"It's worked for me so far."

He chuckled and pulled her close. Then he kissed her. She stiffened, so he pulled her closer and worshipped her mouth with his until she groaned and sagged against him. The kiss turned hotter, and by the time they broke apart they were both out of breath.

"Ask me," he said.

She stared at him a long moment, and then whispered, "Do you love me?"

"More than life itself. Now it's your turn. I've waited an eternity to hear the words from you. Do you love me?"

Tears glistened on her lashes.

He kissed them away.

"Sweetheart, do you love me?"

She squeezed her eyes shut as if in pain. "I can't love you. I'm not made for white picket fences and baking cookies."

"I never asked you to bake me cookies, although I wouldn't mind. But I can buy those just as easily, or make them myself. As for picket fences, I'm more partial to iron, with a great security system. And maybe a Doberman."

She rolled her eyes.

"Bailey, I love you. To hell with vacations together. I want a real future with you, something far more permanent. But if you're not sure yet about me, we can slow it down. Enjoy each other. Do the vacation thing. And then you'll see that we *can* be a couple, that if there's a question of someone not being good enough for someone, it's me who's not good enough for you."

He framed her face in his hands. "But I'm too selfish to let that matter. Because I can't imagine my life without you. All I ask is that you try hard to look past my faults, and accept the imperfect man that I am. Give me a chance. Give *us* a chance."

She sniffled. "I've never had a job except with EXIT. I don't even know what to do for a living now."

"I'll get a job. I'll take care of you."

Her eyes flashed with anger. "I don't need to be taken care of."

"Maybe you can let me think I'm taking care of you now and then, just to boost my ego." He smiled. "I'll let you stay at my house until you get a job and get back on your feet. We can keep a tab. You can pay me back later."

She rolled her eyes again. "I have plenty of money. Probably more than you. I'm a good investor."

"You haven't seen the size of my 401K." He winked.

"I may want to go back to college."

"Sounds like a great idea."

She moved her hands to the top of his shoulders. "I suppose I could maybe stay at your place while I'm in school. Wait, you don't live in the suburbs, do you?"

The look of horror on her face had him laughing again and he put his arms around her waist, ignoring how the gearshift dug into his abdomen.

"My house isn't in the mountains," he said. "But maybe you can get used to the beach. At least, until we figure something else out."

"Don't expect me to clean it. I don't do housework."

He shrugged. "I know how to run a vacuum." He pressed a kiss against her cheek.

"I don't cook either."

"You make a mean bowl of soup."

She seemed to consider that a moment, then nodded. "True."

"I don't judge prospective mates based on their cooking and cleaning abilities," he teased. The way she stiffened had him immediately regretting his word choice. "Not that I'm asking you to marry me. I'm just asking you to—"

"Move in together?"

He studied her face, looking for signs of flight or fear. "Yes?" he said, hoping he was giving the right answer.

She relaxed in his arms.

Right answer then.

"Okay, move in together. I can handle that. No sense in dating when we've already rounded all the bases."

He coughed to keep from laughing again. "Um, yeah. Exactly."

"And once I graduate, then we'll talk about next steps. Maybe."

"Once you graduate?" He hated the note of panic that seeped into his voice. But having to wait to make Bailey his for four years? That might very well kill him. He already knew that he wanted her, now and forever. He just needed a little time to convince her, but not four years' worth.

"Are we talking an AA degree?"

She shook her head. "Oh, please. Anyone can get a two-year degree. I want the whole enchilada."

"A bachelor's?" *Maybe* he could survive four years of waiting. Maybe.

She shook her head again. "Nah, I'm talking going all the way." She slid her arms around his neck. Her breasts pressed against his chest, making sweat pop out on his forehead as he tried to ignore the pleasure-pain of his body's immediate response and focus on the conversation that would decide his fate.

"What does all the way mean?"

"A master's degree. Or maybe, hey maybe I could go for a doctorate. That would pretty much guarantee me a career anywhere."

"What would that take? Ten years?" he choked. "And we . . . wait . . . that whole time . . . to move forward with our relationship?"

"I think you can take your master's and doctorate

programs simultaneously. It might not be quite that long."

His mouth had gone dry. He didn't even know what to say. One thing was for sure, the part of his body that had been straining for release a few minutes ago was no longer at attention. He was too damn depressed to be excited anymore.

She framed his face in her hands this time. "Can you wait for me that long, Kade? Can you wait ten years?"

"Yes. It would kill me, but I would wait. I will wait. However long you need me to. I love you, Bailey. Nothing is ever going to change that."

Her eyes widened, and then the tears started up again, spilling down her cheeks.

Ah hell.

"What did I do wrong this time?" he asked.

"Nothing. You did everything right. You really do love me, don't you? With all my faults."

She didn't wait for his answer. She plastered her body against him, and kissed him like she'd never kissed him before. By the time she stopped, his body was standing at attention again, so hard it brought tears to *his* eyes.

She was laughing when she pulled back, her hands moving to his shoulders. "Is that a gearshift or are you happy to see me?"

"Both."

She laughed again, then tugged on his earlobe with her teeth, her warm breath making him shudder, both with longing and misery in thinking about how long he'd have to wait for her.

"Kade?" she whispered, before moving her lips to his neck, and sucking.

He shuddered, *really* wishing he. where else when she did that. His?s were some-around her. "Yes?" Had he just whim's tightened as hell hoped not. ?He sure

"Did I ever tell you how much I h growing up? And that just the thought o college makes me want to curl up and die? ol

It took a few seconds for her words to sink

"Wait, then you were—"

"Teasing you?" She grinned, then grew seri. "Yes and no. I honestly couldn't believe that y could really care about me with all my faults, my past, the horrible things that I've done."

"Bailey—"

"No, wait. Let me say it. Everything has happened so fast—in my career, my life, and now, with us. I didn't trust it. Couldn't let myself trust it. Because I've lost so much that I was afraid that if I really let myself go, if I let myself believe that whatever this is, this thing that's happening between us, is real, that I'd lose that, too. But if the only way to protect my heart is to never let myself share it, then that's not really living. I want to live, to love. I want to love you, Kade. I love you. Now. Forever. No matter what happens."

His hands shook as he feathered them across her face. "I love you so much."

She smiled through her tears. "I've got you. Don't worry," she whispered. "I'll take care of you."